Some
Like it
Hot

GW00372307

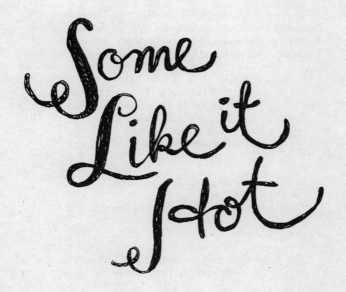

AMANDA BROBYN

POOLBEG

This novel is entirely a work of fiction. The names, characters and incidents portrayed in it are the work of the author's imagination. Any resemblance to actual persons, living or dead, events or localities is entirely coincidental.

Published 2011
by Poolbeg Press Ltd.
123 Grange Hill, Baldoyle,
Dublin 13, Ireland
Email: poolbeg@poolbeg.com

© Amanda Brobyn 2011

The moral right of the author has been asserted.

1

Copyright for typesetting, layout, design
© Poolbeg Press Ltd.

A catalogue record for this book is available from the British Library.

ISBN 978-1-84223-489-1

All rights reserved. No part of this publication may be reproduced or transmitted in any form or by any means, electronic or mechanical, including photography, recording, or any information storage or retrieval system, without permission in writing from the publisher. The book is sold subject to the condition that it shall not, by way of trade or otherwise, be lent, resold or otherwise circulated without the publisher's prior consent in any form of binding or cover other than that in which it is published and without a similar condition, including this condition, being imposed on the subsequent purchaser.

Typeset by Patricia Hope in Sabon 11/14.5

Printed and bound by CPI Group (UK) Ltd, Croydon, CR0 4YY'

www.poolbeg.com

About the Author

Liverpool-born Amanda Brobyn lives in Northern Ireland with her husband and two young children.

Amanda started out as a scriptwriter before moving on to become a successful novelist. In December 2010, she graduated with an MA in Film & Television Production, Management & Policy from the University of Ulster. *Some Like It Hot* has already been written as a television series and the pilot episode is currently being circulated to production companies in the UK and Ireland.

Amanda's debut novel, *Crystal Balls*, was also published by Poolbeg.

Acknowledgements

A huge thank-you firstly to the wonderfully talented Cathy Kelly for reading *Some Like It Hot* and for being so effortlessly virtuous. Thanks a million, Cathy.

Thanks to my first-draft readers, my European travelling companion BBC journalist Maggie Taggart, and Karen Walsh who has been my best friend for more years than I care to admit!

To the entire team at Poolbeg Press who I drive crazy with my endless requests and hare-brain ideas – thank you! To Gaye Shortland, my wonderful editor who always seems to know best, much to my annoyance!

Thank you so much to Richard Crawford who worked with me on this piece as a television series. Let's hope it makes it on to the box soon, Richard.

Thanks to my mum Annie, Barbara and Val who were the original inspiration behind the book. It was they who formed 'The Curry Club' and their regular gatherings provided the premise for the plot. Cheers, ladies!

Thanks to my own friends who have also played 'The Curry Club' game with me, providing with me with material and insight: Romilly Moore, Sue Begley, Karen Brobyn (sister-in-law), Claire Noble, Vivienne Walsh and

Agnes Fee. Thanks for the drunken nights and for giving us a spicy side order of your own private lives!

Thanks to Cyril and Doris, my in-laws, for cheering me on and for editing my website!

Thanks to my mum and dad for being so amazing that it brings a lump to my throat and to my sister Jo Valentine who I would literally walk over hot coals for. I love you so much, Jo. Thanks to my niece, Annabel Star Valentine, who lost sleep over trying to come up with a new title for what was formerly *The Curry Club* – I will remember your offer of *Princesses*, Annabel. Thank you.

Lastly, because you simply are the best, to Stephen, my husband. This year has been extremely difficult for us, but life is all about the future and I can't wait to spend mine with you, always, and our breathtakingly beautiful children, Josh and Harriet. 'Wow' is all I can say, the rest I can only feel, and sometimes it hurts because I love you all so very much.

Finally, thanks to life for bringing us into it and for giving us the skill and determination to dodge the fire-balls and to develop a layer of heat resistance. As human beings, we're a pretty amazing species, capable of so much in the face of adversity and yet incapable of allowing the full magnitude of ourselves to be released, to be freed and to simply be what we are meant to be.

For my incredible parents, Annie and Martin.
This one's for you.

1

The room looked cloned from a magazine illustration. Glossy and dense, it reeked of money. It was perfection, just like its owner.

Jude sat elegantly at the head of the table like a ship's figurehead, her delicate bone structure reminiscent of a wooden carving of a Greek goddess set for sail, head held high at the stern of a ship, watching the waves and praying deep into the ocean for the gods of the sea to make a safe passage.

At least that is how she looked until she unwrapped the tightly folded piece of paper. She looked a lot paler after she had read its contents. She read the note again and looked up nervously, her green eyes uncertain for once.

"Come on, Jude! What does it say?" Sophie's curiosity got the better of her. Patience was not a virtue of Sophie's. In fact, *virtue* was not a word in Sophie's world – period.

Jude put the paper face down on the glass table. Her hands wobbled noticeably. "It says . . ." She paused to collect herself. "Forgive me for the language but it says *'Your husband is shagging someone around this table. Take a close look at who your friends are.'*"

A loud gasp escaped from Helena's open mouth.

"No way!" Sophie cried. "Not one of us! It couldn't possibly be true." Her face contorted with repugnance. "Never mind not one of *us*, I should have said not one of *them*! I've seen your husbands and you can keep them!" She giggled lighheartedly but you could cut the air with a knife such was the tension.

Jude picked up the paper and passed it around. She could say nothing more.

As usual the question was typed in Arial and font size twelve. It could have been from any one of the women – there was nothing distinctive about it. It was the same-sized slip of paper they used every week and was folded in the way stated in the club's constitution. But it certainly wasn't the slip she had put in, which meant that if the statement were true it might well be *her* husband it was referring to.

Jude began to cast her mind over Clive's behaviour of late until she caught herself. They were happily married. He adored her and she him and they had been childhood sweethearts, well, more like teenage really as they met during university. Clive was in the final year of his Law degree and she was a fresher studying a BA in Interior Design. It was love at first sight for her and lust at first sight for him. Nothing had changed.

"But it has to be true," Roni snapped, scanning the group suspiciously. "Why put it in otherwise? Everyone knows the rules of the Curry Club – you put in a question for discussion . . ." she paused for dramatic effect, "or a statement which you *know* to be true." Her emphasis on the *know* was such that she captured everybody's attention. For once.

Kath shook her head and tried to digest the contents. She turned the slip of paper every which way possible in an attempt to find a clue as to its owner – even though that was against the rules – but the paper looked like every other that had been pulled from the Curry Club dish, a clone of all the other slips which had been drawn out since the club began.

But none before had matched the destructiveness of today's statement.

Jude sipped thoughtfully from a long-stemmed champagne flute, leaving no mark on its paper-thin curved lip as she set it back down in regal style.

In contrast Kath took a long greedy gulp of red wine, drinking it like she had stumbled across a vineyard in the middle of the desert.

"You know, ladies, this statement has been put to the Club so we must follow the rules and discuss it." Jude looked somewhat confused. "Although it does seem to be a rather paradoxical statement . . ."

"Speak English, woman!" Kath interrupted.

Kath was a fitness freak with an in-depth knowledge of human anatomy but her vocabulary was severely limited, unless of course there was any reference to alcohol where she suddenly turned into an all-round genius and general know-all regardless of word-length, language or pronunciation. And she was right every time. If there was a language of love, then there was a language of drink and Kath knew everything there was to know about it. She spoke it universally.

"Sorry, Kath, it means perplexing, a little bewildering."

Kath downed the entire contents of her glass as she took in the English-language lesson while the others watched in amazement. For a health fanatic she certainly did appear to drink excessively but it seemed that she was the only person not to notice it.

"You mean it's absolute bollocks, Jude," she said. "Someone is talking out of their arse."

A collective nodding of heads followed. Kath had a point. Though, on the other hand, there was one person around the table who knew differently – at least she thought she did. She wouldn't have been prepared to cause such a stir if she hadn't her facts right. Would she?

"Okay, here goes." Sophie sat up bold and confident, her bronzed skin revealing a little too much breast. She caught Roni glancing down at her ampleness and out of badness crossed her arms under her breasts, hoisting them further north. "I know we're not supposed to guess . . . but, having said that, I can't help but wonder about the use of the word *shagging*."

A disgusted tut came from Roni's direction.

"*I* use the word *shagging* and perhaps one more of you at a push," Sophie went on, "but there are clearly more *ladylike* individuals around this table who wouldn't use that word if their lives depended on it." She smiled kindly at Jude, clearly offering her the compliment. "Plus, unless whoever he is and one of us were actually caught in action, then the claim is not only without evidence but it is quite possibly a knee-jerk reaction to something which may be entirely innocent."

"You're not allowed to narrow it down, Sophie. And

the use of the word *shagging* might just be to disguise the owner's identity," Helena applied logically.

Kath clasped her empty wineglass tightly. The multicoloured beads on her wrist jangled in tune to those layered around her neck as she threw her fiery red hair back from her gypsy-green eyes. Like Kath herself, her hair had a mind of its own and it too was unpredictable.

"Let's stop guessing, it goes against everything we want this club to be about. Anonymity. Pure and simple." Kath refilled her glass, oblivious to the other empty glasses surrounding her.

An affronted Jude leapt from her seat, taking up her role as perfect hostess by topping up the ladies' glasses. Her cheeks flushed with embarrassment. "Sorry, ladies, the distraction seemed to take my manners with it."

"Well, I think the wording on the slip counts me out," Helena said, preening.

"In what sense?" said Sophie.

"Well, I don't have a husband so at least I know Nathan's not shagging any of you!" Helena chuckled in apparent relief.

"Perhaps not but is he shagging *you*?" Sophie was quick off the mark. "I've only ever seen him ruffle your hair like some sort of family pet."

Helena cast Sophie an unforgiving dagger but she knew the words rang true. Nathan was so immersed in his work that he had no time for passion. His passion was wrapped up with self-absorbed paper and secured tightly with a bow of rope. A rope which Sophie secretly hoped he would use to hang himself with. The bloke was nothing but a loser, and she was still convinced he was gay. She should know. She worked with enough of them.

Also, she knew Helena well. They'd been friends since their schooldays and she also knew how much better she could do than stay with that loser. Nathan was a loser with a capital *L*.

"I think we need to stay on the subject, Sophie," said Jude, "until we have reached a conclusion, although I'm not sure what more *I* can add apart from a gut feeling that someone has made a mistake on this one."

Roni glanced down at her diamond-studded Rolex. Its mother-of-pearl face glistened in the candlelit room. "Well, someone here seems to think they have sufficient evidence to bring it up," she preached to the room, excited by the tension and determined to add to it. Anything to brighten up her dull existence. "So I suggest you be vigilant, ladies, and watch your husbands like hawks."

There was a bitter tone attached to Roni's statement and both Jude and Sophie noticed it.

"That's all very well, Veronica." Sophie was enjoying herself immensely. Herself and Roni rarely saw eye to eye. "And good advice . . . but while they're watching their husbands . . . who will be watching yours?"

Sophie preened herself in the mirror opposite, partly for vanity and partly because she couldn't stand the snobbery and poker-like mannerisms of Roni and she knew only too well that her own beautiful exterior turned Roni a shade of shamrock green. She made it her business to provoke Roni at every opportunity. "You know, Roni, it might be that it's *your* Peter *shagging* one of us."

An immediate silence cocooned the room, trapping it with a fierce tension fuelled by curiosity and cynicism.

Sometimes, Sophie Kane could be such a bitch.

2

Darren stood before the wrought-iron gates of The Tudors and pressed the intercom once more. He waited patiently, watching as smoke from the exhaust of his clapped-out Fiesta danced around like a mini-typhoon, swirling in fast-moving circles before dispersing into a climax of nothingness. The engine rolled and chugged, gasping for breath. The tin machine was on its last legs but it was all he could afford, for now anyway. He had his hopes, he always did even as a child, but for him it was all about achievement and civic contribution – materialism was way down the list. This house was certainly out of his league but he didn't care. Money meant nothing to him, it was a means to an end.

"Hello?" a hoarse voice emitted through the intercom.

Darren leant forward to speak into it. He hated those damned things. What use was a stunning house if it was hidden from view? In his mind he compared it to a fine wine, too fine for opening. Pointless.

But that was how Veronica Smyth liked her life to be. Hidden from view and shared when it suited.

"Good morning, Mrs Smyth. I believe you are expecting me?"

He stood back from the speaker, observing the mansion-sized house. It was the size of his old campus block at university. His eyes scanned its Tudor-styled facade, taking in its decorative half-timbering and its distinct mediaeval flavour. He counted the number of window frames, some small and square, others tall and narrow but plenty of them and none matching the other. There was nothing symmetrical about this house. It was busy, uncoordinated and beamed to within an inch of its life.

Darren smiled as he felt an immediate attachment to its mismatched exterior with its unusual charm and its dare-to-be-different air in Cheshire's millionaires' row.

Roni peered through the bedroom curtains, catching sight of the new arrival. She pressed the remote-controlled key-fob and watched as the heavy gates opened with an incongruous action, almost feather-weight. She closed them shut once the red rusty heap had crossed the threshold. No-one else need bother her today. She was a busy woman.

She stared at the clock on the white antique bedside table: she had overslept. Damn Kath and that last cocktail, but the problem was that you simply couldn't say no to her. She was a party waiting to happen, that girl, and in a strange sort of way Roni envied that about her. She was vivacious and yet serious in equal doses, whereas Roni was just serious. Or stuck-up, some might say. She knew for sure that was exactly the opinion of Sophie Kane – then again Sophie was a blonde, tanned bimbo like all hairdressers. What the hell did she know about class?

A flustered, hungover Roni, who had dressed in the first top and leisure-pants that had come to hand, swung open the front door. At five-foot-two she was a midget compared with Darren. Her eyes met with his chest which was covered in a tight-fitting T-shirt and her head travelled north as she took in the youthfulness of his toned physique, stopping at his face which was smiling broadly. His body was more mature than his teenage face which was boyishly handsome with a post-adolescent clearing of acne, barely there yet still noticeable from close proximity.

Her anxiety and thumping head were instantaneously erased from memory and she felt herself infected by his young charm and compelling grin. She continued to stare at him, smiling uncharacteristically for this time in the morning. Smiling uncharactistically.

By now most of her housework would usually be done and the home would be under her complete control, hoovered, polished and mopped to precision. Not this morning however. Her domestic habits often bewildered Peter who could never understand why his wife refused to bring in a daily help. Money was in abundance but for some unknown reason Roni insisted that no-one could clean as well as she could. She had graduated in '*domesticology*' she told him. But the truth was that Roni was opposed to having strangers in her home. She was a prisoner in her own premises, hiding behind those electric gates and, perversely, it suited her down to the ground. She kept in what was hers and shut out the rest of the world.

The Curry Club was her only lifeline. It was her way of sharing information, secrets and problems in complete anonymity which suited her furtive and clandestine approach to anything living and breathing. 'Open yourself up to the best friends in the world!' That's what Sophie had said anyway and in a way she was right. They were her best friends – they were her *only* friends – and they had helped her with complicated dilemmas without even knowing the dilemmas were hers. It was perfect.

Darren looked at the miniature woman in front of him. He noticed the darkness of her roots as he stared down, he took in what looked like tea-stains on her top, and the remnants of last night's make-up with a dollop of smudged mascara tainting her naturally pretty face.

"Is the lady of the house in, please?" Darren's tone was neutral, neither subservient nor artificial, just polite and in keeping with his unchanging and consistent temperament. For a young man he wore his heart on his sleeve and refused to be anything he was not. Playing was for other people. He was a bona-fide young man with a gift of wisdom which extended way beyond his years.

Roni stood, openmouthed and clearly affronted. Her Bambi-eyed fixed stare dissolved as the real Roni snapped out of her short-term hypnosis and accelerated back into her conservative chassis.

"I am the lady of the house!" she declared through flared nostrils.

Darren simply stood unperturbed. It was an easy mistake to make. She did look a bit rough in fairness and she certainly didn't fall into the category of the stereotypical millionaire's wife, not from where he was standing anyway. Not that it bothered him – on the contrary he found it refreshing, endearing.

Roni noticed how undeterred Darren was. He hadn't

even flinched when she bit back at him with pointed fangs and demonic eyes. She had managed to scare people her entire adult life – even when she wasn't trying to be scary, but this young guy stood fast and this threw her.

"In that case you must be Mrs Smyth." He beamed, oblivious to any faux pas. "I'm Darren, nice to meet you." He thrust out his hand.

Roni didn't usually shake hands with people. You had no idea where people had been. She was anal about cleanliness through and through. "Come on in. You're early."

Darren ignored the fact that his hand had remained untouched as he brushed past Roni, his broadness in stark contrast to her tiny frame and narrow shoulders.

"The swimming pool is through the rear," she said. "Don't let me hold you back."

She closed the door behind him, catching sight of herself in the brass mirror set on the Sheraton sideboard. Like everything in her house it was over the top and priceless. She shrieked loudly at the dishevelled woman looking back. Any wonder he thought she was the cleaner.

She took the stairs two at a time, clutching the oak bannister rail for support, until breathlessly she reached the top. Her uncleansed face was flushed and her chest rose and fell erratically as she hyperventilated, desperate for air. She was in bad shape but it was nothing that a few sessions with Kath wouldn't sort out. It was on her 'To do' list, but she kept postponing it.

Sophie's blonde hair splayed across the pillow. Her tanned leg slipped abruptly from the confines of the bedclothes, waking her from the alcohol-induced sleep. She felt around the floor for her mobile phone, moving with a deliberate slowness so as not to wake her latest victim – whatever his name was. She was never any good with names. Never had been. Never would be. It was all part of the fun for Sophie. A name meant getting personal and that would never do.

"Shit!" she cursed with muted volume, rolling out of bed naked but for her mobile phone. Her bronzed body was lithe, toned and proportioned to perfection, if a little top-heavy. Her naturally blonde hair and stark blue eyes afforded her much attention but in truth it was attention which Sophie despised. She repelled the chat-up lines and the gazes of admiration but she took free drinks from any man offering. Her alcohol comsumption was their financial loss. If they were stupid enough to send drinks across to a total stranger then she was more than prepared to drink them – it would be rude not to. Sophie's facade was her most fierce opponent, her antagonist, but beneath that beauty lay a woman who was a serious contender and not one to be messed with.

She tiptoed around the bedroom gathering her belongings and dressed as she made her way downstairs to the front door. She cast a momentary glance behind her before closing it. It made no sound as she pulled it firmly shut, not daring to breathe until she was firmly out of sight and out of earshot.

"I need a taxi, please," she whispered, holding the phone tucked between her ear and shoulder while rummaging through her bag and pulling out a compact mirror. Her eyes were puffy and tinged with a redness, so stark against the blue backdrop. Even without make-up

12

it was plain to see that Sophie Kane was a headturner. For both sexes. Women too seemed to find her irresistible and while Sophie was completely heterosexual, she did enjoy going to first base with the odd girl. Why the hell not?

"Where am I? Shit! Good question."

With her back to the apartment block, she glanced around and spotted the road sign. "Frazer Street. As quick as you can. Thanks." Sophie snapped her phone shut, pouting seductively. "Another one bites the dust," she muttered to herself.

She was totally exhausted, but by God the sex was worth the sleep deprivation. It wasn't always like that, but this guy was a selfless lover, one of the few she had experienced over the years. She groaned aloud as she remembered his vigorous thrusting against her exploding clitoris. She couldn't recall any other time when she had come three times in one night. That was one for her diary, the secret diary stored away deep in her grey matter.

A clamminess came over Sophie and she wafted her hand in front of her face, in need of a cold shower. This guy might just be the one.

The aroma of watery bleach hung thick in the fake Mediterranean air, sticking to the pine-timber ceiling and dark-wicker furniture. Plastic palm trees stood to vertical attention in oversized Ali Baba pots and hanging baskets draped long fake evergreen which clung to the circumference of the overhead glass velux. Outside the sun shone through it as though its size was designed to perfection, letting in every available sunray without an inch to spare – the core of the sun captured in a single pane of glass.

"How does that look, Mrs Smyth?"

Roni leaned over to take a closer look. In truth, she had no idea what she was looking for. She had yet to dip her big toe into the pool.

"Fine. It will do."

Darren wrapped the vacuum hose tightly around his elbow and shoulder, repeating the circular action until the entire hose was fully wound. Holding it firmly, he gathered a ribbon of black velcro and taped the hose together, securing it firmly in place. It made it easier to carry and less of a risk in terms of tripping over it. At six-foot-four, he had a long way to fall.

"Would you not consider getting a recreation slide or something fitted, Mrs Smyth? It would certainly bring this place alive. They're great fun."

His youthfulness broke through with the words he spoke and Roni could imagine the fun *he* might have belting down the slide, not she.

Roni went to speak but hesitated, and Darren saw the change in her body language as her arms folded across her ample chest and her thin lips pursed together. Suddenly he knew. He heard her speak the words of admission with muted silence. Once again his strange insightfulness had broken through.

"You can't swim, can you, Mrs Smyth?"

Roni looked away. She was embarrassed and humiliated. Damn that kid and his big mouth, and how the hell did he know anyway?

Darren edged closer to Roni, disturbed by her down-trodden exterior, as temporary as it might be.

"You know, Mrs Smyth," he said as he picked up his

bag and made his way to the glass door, "I could teach you to swim if you like? I'm a qualified lifeguard. I had to be as part of my Sports Science Degree – it was part of the course. I work down at the leisure centre during the summer holidays."

Roni composed herself, shaking her head determinedly. "It really doesn't interest me, thank you. I'm just fine the way I am."

"But how sad to have such an amazing feature in your home and not even be able to u –"

"It's just water!" Roni snapped.

Darren knew it was time to concede. He had said more than he was invited to.

He opened the door wide enough to pass through with his equipment, trying to make eye contact with Roni but she was clearly avoiding his gaze.

He spoke boldly one last time. "You know . . . it might save your life one day."

The door closed behind him with a fluid movement that didn't disturb Roni's train of thought. She looked around her at the ostentatious dwelling. She thought about the fleet of fast cars in the garage which she drove slowly, and as she gazed at the blue-tinged water rocking away in a tide of complimentary hypnosis, the words rang in her ear: *'It might save your life one day.'* The cheek of it, she fumed. But still, how strange that this young man talked as if he could see right through her. *Her*, the woman who on the outside had it all. One only had to cast a glance at her life to see that she was a woman who was indulged, ruined. There was nothing she didn't have that she didn't want.

But Roni wondered why it was that she so often felt like she had nothing, that she was a decorative shell with a cavernous inside.

Perhaps her life did need saving.

3

It was 5.00 a.m. as Jude drove into the brightly lit schoolyard. She reluctantly parked the car across two spaces, leaving sufficient room to allow for the length of the skis. She hated being inconsiderate but there was no way they were going to get out the two pairs of Carvers without adequate space. She smiled apologetically at the owner of the silver Audi Q7 who pulled up alongside her.

Tom and Anna jumped out, Anna with uncontainable excitement and Tom as cool as ever. Tom was as laid-back and good-natured at his mother.

Anna immediately spotted her friends and took off, skipping away carefree and leaving Tom to do the lugging and heaving of both the skis and suitcases. He was too much of a gentleman to allow his mother to do it. As he lowered the first of the cases to the ground, he witnessed his mother's dejection from the corner of his eye. He knew she would miss Anna and him hugely.

Tom embraced Jude with boyish affection, throwing his arms around her neck lovingly. He didn't care if his friends saw him or teased him over it. He was a mother's boy through and through but not in an effeminate way – there was nothing effeminate about Tom – he played a superb round of golf, played rugby competitively and was a natural and gifted tennis player. He was also on the reserves of the Alderley Edge polo team. He was bright, intelligent, dashingly handsome and he adored his mother. And she him. He was practically perfect.

Jude often thought that her son would be a great catch for a lovely girl, light years ahead, providing he kept the down-to-earth attitude he had managed to retain so far, which was some achievement considering the stylishly affluent life he lived. The twins were indulged and she knew that, but whereas Clive did so much out of snobbery and for effect – a kneejerk reaction to the life he never had himself – Jude worked hard to keep Tom and Anna grounded, roping them into her charity work at every opportunity.

"It's only for a week, Mum," said Tom. "It will fly in."

"I know, darling. I'm fine honestly." Jude stroked his soft cheek as she lied unconvincingly.

"Anna!" Tom yelled across the schoolyard. "Come and say bye to Mum!"

Anna rushed over to Jude, planting a kiss on her cheek. She turned as quickly as she had come, shouting behind her. "Bye, Mum! Love you – look after Polly for me!"

Tom rolled his eyes after his sister and Jude smiled a watery smile.

As the last of the pupils embarked on the luxury coaches, the doors hissed to a definite close. It was five thirty and still dark and Jude's eyes fought against the black backdrop, trying desperately to make out her children through the vehicle's tinted windows.

She stayed put until the coaches heaved their way through the prestigious public-school gates, waving frantically until they were out of sight. Only then did she allow herself to shed tears for which she immediately felt silly – selfish in a way. These were the years that Tom and Anna would remember for the rest of their lives. The school trips, sports days, endless groups of friends which Jude hoped they would keep and take with them on their journey.

But her tears carried more emotion than simply missing the children. She missed them after just a day at school, but there was something else she missed.

Jude climbed into the car where she sat at the wheel, daydreaming away. The carpark was empty bar her and she was lost in her own thoughts once again. The same thoughts which had recurred for more years than she dared to remember, and Jude knew then that something had to change. Her life needed to be about more than just her children. It was more a feeling than a pragmatic decision. She had been there for them since the day they had been born, not working so she could immerse herself in maternal bliss, and it had worked beautifully. They had benefited from her patient attention, her dedication to their education and her massive contribution to their social skills as she chauffered them from middle-class hobby to hobby.

But with the prospect of doing something for *herself* came immediate feelings of iniquity which for some reason Jude could never seem to shake off. For fifteen years she had lived the repetitious experience of motherhood and while she had absolutely adored every moment of it, she wanted to create something new. Something for herself but, for some continued reason, it felt undeserved.

The wheels rolled down the kilometre-long gravelled driveway, assisted by a cartography of trees which mapped the route to the driver's destination. Each tree was gifted with directional branches pointing towards the house, whatever the weather. Even on a windy day with a high inconsistent breeze the trees continued their battle to protect the entrance. They were a floodgate of watchful foliage and vigilant guardians to the inhabitants of The Firs, the seven-bedroomed listed building set in acres of mature gardens. The black BMWX5 continued its trek down the bumpy lane, shining back at them with a blinding glimmer reflecting a message of thanks that their extended arms held back their tender caress from the immaculate body paintwork. The car was the guts of sixty thousand pounds and every living breathing mortal knew how much Clive Westbury adored it – although he did think it was wasted on his wife. She didn't appreciate its high-speed performance nor understand its technical specifications. Jude had pointed out, '*What is the use of high speed when the law dictates what speed you should drive at, Clive*?' Clive had answered that he was the law. Or a lawyer at least.

Jude pushed the controls into park and pulled up the handbrake. She opened up the boot, pulling out endless bags of Marks and Spencer's groceries, lugging them towards the house and dumping them on the front-door step before heading back for more.

As she set down the last of the bags, she fumbled deep in her pockets for her keys to The Firs. The door yanked open from the inside, causing her to stumble backwards with fright, and a friendly face beamed at her.

"Hello, darling!" Hattie leaned forward to embrace her daughter, her only child.

"Mum!" Jude was breathless, brought on by the shock. "I didn't expect anyone to be home. You almost gave me a heart attack."

"I knew how sad you'd be with Tom and Anna being away, darling, so I thought I might surprise you."

Hattie bent down to collect the bulging shopping bags which slouched lazily on the step, basking in the first signs of spring and allowing themselves to be teased and tickled by its light and unpredictable rays.

Jude marvelled at her mother. How thoughtful that she should remember the children being away. She never failed to support her. She never had.

As a daddy's girl Jude missed her father desperately, but her mother certainly compensated in every way imaginable. Had it not been for her maternal guidance, over the past fifteen years particularly, Jude would not have possessed such virtues as she had – they were a gift from her mother, a legacy, and her life had been enriched by the virtuous works Hattie had undertaken. The problem with Jude was that her humility denied her the right to feel deserving of even helping others more needy. *She* was never part of the equation, she never allowed herself to be, and that had always suited her and pleased her mother. That was the way it should be, she had been told time and time again. '*It should never be about you, Jude,*' her mother had told her many years ago. '*Real living is about putting everyone else before yourself.*'

"What are you doing this week, darling? Making the most of your freedom, I imagine?"

Jude ignored the hissing coffee-maker momentarily and stared at a picture of the twins set in a thick glass frame. They were so alike to look at, although chalk and cheese in character. She smiled a watery smile, turning to her mother. "I don't know what to do, Mum. I feel lost when the kids aren't here." She continued to fumble with her new beverage-machine – an expensive and complicated-looking gadget with knobs and whistles on, one that time-travelled collecting fresh coffee beans straight from the pure volcanic soil of high altitudes. Okay, maybe not, but if there were such a gadget there was no doubt that Clive Westbury would simply have to have it. And he would have to be the first. He had bought it as a gift for Jude.

A loud tinny bang startled the women. Hattie jumped, hurling a measure of discomposed coffee granules across the black granite worktops. They landed like a poorly planned missile, exploding in all the wrong places and wiping out nothing bar the cleanliness of the place.

"Make the most of it, Jude," Hattie advised as she cleared up the mess, sweeping the wasted coffee into her cupped hand. "Take time out and do something with your friends while you can, darling."

"Once upon a time I would have thought that was easy, Mum, but I'm so used to the fetch-me carry-me scenario that I'm honestly not sure who I am any more . . . I never know what to do with myself when the kids aren't here. My identity seemed to get lost somewhere in motherhood. Don't get me wrong, I love it, I adore it in fact, it's just . . ."

"Nonsense, dear," Hattie soothed. "Motherhood *is* an identity. It's rewarding, fulfulling and a far less stressful life than what these millennium-type women who try to be all things to all people have. They've got it wrong, darling." Hattie patted Jude's shoulder lovingly. Her eyes emitted a kindness but one carried with a determined conviction. "It's you who has it right."

Jude advanced through the wide hallway towards the front door where a pile of post had landed with careless attitude. She inhaled the fragrance from the tall vase of fresh trumpet lilies. Breathing deep, she immersed herself in a floral cosmos, dizzied by its antidote which was potent enough to induce an intravenous relaxant into the strange tenseness she had felt when her mother's words echoed. *'They've got it wrong, Jude . . . it's you who has it right.'*

Jude trusted her mother with her life and what she said went. After all, she always had her best interests at heart and Jude's life had turned out to be rich and fulfilled with many achievements. But few of them for herself or about herself. How on earth, Jude wondered, could something so right suddenly feel so wrong? There was something missing in her life, a void which needed filling.

Her eyes lit up as she gathered up the post. She spotted her lifeline – it was screaming out to her to be undressed – needing a release of oxygen to bring it to life.

Interior Designs was the highlight of Jude's month. She literally counted down the days for the next publication. Her heart raced and her mouth dried at the wonderment of its content as she speculated over the latest fabrics, wondered at the new spring colours. With life-dependent speed, Jude jumped into it with both feet.

The salon was state-of-the-art and cutting-edge and the people who worked in it were as glamorous as any of the Hollywood 'A' list – both males and females.

All Sophie Kane's decisions were calculated to the nth degree. She hired not only the most talented of stylists to work in her Kane'n'Able salons, but those who looked the part from physique to dental impeccability. They were the window to her business, a sample of the goods on offer and a prototype of the transformations available – all at a costly premium.

Sophie stood at the retro reception desk chatting to Karl, her right-hand man. A lustful smirk stained her flawless face.

To anyone else she simply looked like a contented woman glad to be at work, but to Karl Keating she looked like the woman she had been last night – or, more accurately, the woman who had been with a man last night.

Karl watched Sophie take the brush from Mandy, an Academy trainee. He watched as she demonstated the correct way to hold the brush, allowing it to grab the hair from the roots, blow-drying it upwards for greater height, holding the nozzle pointing down to follow the natural shafts of hair.

Sophie stood and watched Mandy for a few minutes until she was satisfied that the client would be satisfied. More than satisfied. As a general rule of thumb, most stylists wouldn't care too much about the students or freeloaders – they got a free hair-do out of it every Tuesday morning – but Sophie felt differently. Today's students were tomorrow's customers and they were treated with all the respect of those spending obscene amounts of money. Everyone that walked out of Kane'n'Able felt the *experience*. Sophie had created more than just a salon – and she was about to create another.

"Karl, can you hold the fort for me later on for you know what?" she said.

An exasperated Karl glanced at Sophie. His grey eyes delivered an incongruous message of affectionate frustration. He tutted loudly. "Miss Kane. *I* am the manager here, not you." He shook his head at her, narrowing his eyes. Behind them his true feelings oozed. Sophie needed to step back and let him manage without her continuous interference; give him some space. "What on earth do you pay me for?"

Sophie let out a belt of raucous laughter. "You know, sometimes I ask myself that very question."

Karl had to laugh. "I left myself wide open for that, didn't I?"

Sophie licked her lips lasciviously. "Talking of wide open –"

"Sophie Kane, will I ever make a lady of you?" Karl interrupted with a clipped tone which Sophie heard loud and clear. "Who was the poor bastard this time?"

She turned to look in the immaculately gleaming circular mirror which hung behind the curved reception desk, tucking her hair behind her ears, puckering her lips for deliberate effect. She knew only too well how annoyed

Karl got when she talked to him about her sexual escapades. His thwarted behaviour shone through as he made no attempts to hide his annoyance. When Sophie was feeling especially provocative she took great pleasure in watching his mounting irritation. So what? The guy was gay. What she did mattered little to him, surely?

"Clive Wesbtury. He's quite a good lay actually. Particularly for a lawyer."

"What! How could you do that to Jude, for crying out loud!" he whispered crossly.

"I'm kidding, Karl!" Sophie was taken aback that for a moment he actually believed that she was capable of sleeping with one of her best friends' husbands.

"It *sooo* wasn't funny . . . besides I wouldn't put anything past you!" Karl teased her, the relief changing his tone mid-sentence. "Floosy!"

Sophie shot him a hurt glare. "Thanks for the vote of confidence, Karl. Anyway, Miss Frigid-pants Veronica seems to think that one of us *is* shagging one of their husbands . . . I know full well everyone will think it's me."

"When did she say that?" Karl swept a piece of stray hair from the steel reception counter into his hand and straight into the bin. He hated mess of any kind.

"*She* didn't say it, the Curry Club did, but I know full well it was her comment, Karl. What I don't know is where the hell it came from . . . but if it is true, it's definitely not me that's getting it!"

Karl exhaled as the moment of worry dispersed. Sometimes Sophie was so unpredictable that he daren't think about her true capabilities. For a moment he had believed her tongue-in-cheek sarcasm and he was glad of her admission.

"Okay, who was the poor bastard then? Not Peter or James, I take it!"

"I don't know and I don't care, Karl, but by God was he a good shag!" Sophie looked serious for a moment. It didn't suit her playful blue eyes nor her dangerously bee-stung lips. "You know, he might just be the one."

"The one for what?" Karl laughed out loud. "The one where you actually bother to ask his name?"

"That I'll never do. Men are there at my disposal and to be used and abused by my good self." Her face contorted with a flash of anger. "It could quite easily be the other way around, you know, Karl. It's alright for you guys to go out getting your end away all in the name of testosterone but when we women do it we're labelled slags." She retouched her lip gloss, applying an extra dollop on her bottom lip. She put the small tube back into the pocket of her Diesel jeans. "So for all the single, independent ladies out there . . . *I'm doin' it for you*!" she sang.

Karl sniggered. As far as he could see singing was her one weakness – well, that and her loose morals – but those apart she was perfection personified.

"The one, Karl," she said, reverting to his cynical question. "The one where I actually go back for more, you eejit." She stood back waiting for him to react.

He turned his face to avoid her gaze, to bury deep his feelings. He was conscious that she was still his boss regardless of his opinions on her night's activities.

"What is it, Karl?"

Karl metamorphosed in real time from a disdained

man to a masked street performer and his expression shifted to one contrived and in full character. "Nothing, Sophie. I just think you can do so much better than picking up one-night stands, never to see them again."

"I've just said I might see this one again."

"Forgive my cynisism but that's hardly ringing wedding bells, is it!"

Sophie, for once, allowed herself to hear the subtle but watchful tone of his voice. But, as in the case of all men, Sophie didn't take him seriously.

"I'm sorry that *my* personal life offends you so much, Karl. Anyway, who else did you have in mind?" she snorted. "You?"

Karl thought for a moment that had he not known the *real* Sophie Kane he wouldn't have lasted more than two minutes working for her. Not only was the place cutting-edge, *she* was cutting-edge.

No, actually, she was just *cutting*.

4

Helena dragged on a cigarette, inhaling it with such vigour that her epitaph began to engrave itself. In her mind it did anyway. She was a loser, Nathan was an even bigger loser, and she was still in the same job she had taken on a temporary basis after graduation and was still wishing she hadn't.

How useless her psychology degree had turned out to be! Although, in fairness to her, she excelled with everyone else and their problems – but try as she might to free herself from her own, she drew the short straw every time. Psychology might well have helped her with Nathan during his numerous bouts of depression, or during the time he went stir crazy after receiving yet another batch of rejection letters, but one thing it couldn't do was pay the bills. Nothing could unless it made a 'ker-ching' sound.

Nathan Bream was the son of Herbie Bream, a failed inventor, who died trying to invent a vacuum which hoovered all by itself. Or the voice-activated television remote control. Nathan, it seemed, had inherited his father's eccentric and egotistical ways.

In their earlier courting years, Helena had supported Nathan out of love and a conviction that one day his board games would be snapped up by one of the worlds multinational corporations and be dropped down the chimney into every domestic dwelling, like *Swingball* or *Monopoly,* and he too would become a hugely recognisable brand. Only a decade later, Nathan had received only a few thousand pounds as option payments, but no-one had bitten the bullet enough to commission any orders. The response was always '*It could do with a little modification.*' or '*Two players are too few.*' They were at a juncture where life was tough, money a scarcity and Helena knew with gut-wrenching desperation that something had to change. She just didn't know what.

She stubbed the cigarette butt against the wall, dropping it through the hole into the chrome cigarette bin, squinting as the spring sun tickled her face with its mild rays. Her nose itched with the early signs of pollen. Helena loved the sun and the summertime particularly, but her hayfever was a killer.

She mounted the steps to the bank reluctantly, taking them a deliberate one at a time, sniffing on every step as though the steps themselves were wrapped in pollen of the highest levels. She prayed silently for free prescriptions, knowing well enough that she didn't have sufficient money to buy her much-needed antihistamine. She didn't have enough money to buy anything in life as it stood.

Inside the banking hall the queues were endless and Helena watched the customers jump from queue to queue in the hope that the next one would be quicker than the one before. This amused her, always had in fact, and she wondered why they lacked the ability, the control to remain still and at least accepting of their situation. It was a queue for heaven's sakes – it wasn't a life or death situation. A little waiting wouldn't harm a person.

"Can I help you, sir?" Helena approached an elderly gentleman, taking him from the queue and escorting him over to her *Personal Banking* desk which sat in the foyer of the opulent banking hall. Its position was close to the door so that she could answer on-the-spot queries or point customers in the appropriate direction. She was a meet-and-greet member of staff and a cashier too when needed.

Helena took her rightful place, plonking herself down on her chair, rolling in closer to the staid mahogony desk. The desk was equipped with an abundant supply of paper slips, compartmentalised in a black-plastic desktop sorter, all within grabbing distance of an extended arm. A black plastic pen was chained to its holder and a brass desk-lamp sat bent over and shy in the corner – angled for aesthetic effect. The lamp was on permanently, so dark was the building's interior.

Helena smiled at her customer. Those that knew her well enough would know that the smile was contrived like everything she did when she was at work. She hated it.

"Thank you for taking me out of the queue, erm . . ." he smiled at her, taking in her name badge, "Helena. I'm not sure how long my legs would have held up. It's always so busy in here."

"That's what I'm here for, sir. Now what can I do for you?"

Out of the corner of her eye, she suppressed a smirk as she saw an oversized pinstriped suit hop from queue to queue. He was only missing the relay baton, she giggled away in her mischievous mind. The exercise would do him the world of good by the looks of things.

"I'd like to withdraw some money, please, Helena."

Helena took a red passbook from the elderly gentleman. She removed its plastic cover and opened the book, stifling a gasp at its balance.

The man beamed with pride. "I'd like to withdrawn forty thousand pounds please, dear. It's my grandson's 21st birthday and I want to give him a deposit for a house."

Helena looked morose as she stared absently at the pages before her. She thought about her own student-type digs with its eclectic mix of second-hand furniture. At thirty-one she should be well on the property ladder by now, but with only one income – hers – unless something changed drastically this was never likely to happen.

Helena snapped out of her own cruel world back into the real one.

"Certainly, Mr Peters."

She leaned forward, pulling two slips of paper from the perfectly organised plastic tray to the side of her.

"If you could just sign this withdrawal slip for me, please, Mr Peters, that would be great."

Helena watched his hand as it shook uncontrollably in perfect rhythm to his leg which tremored beneath the table. She felt the effects of it banging against the hollow bottom of the desk and she wondered if this was excitement or old age. She also wondered if she would end up like him. Not old. But rich. She thought not. Ever the realist.

"Do you have identification, Mr Peters, please?" Helena hated asking this question. It was obvious he wasn't a crook. "It's simply to make sure that it really is *you* withdrawing your own money, sir. Our job is to protect your money from fraud by carrying out these protective identity checks."

Unperturbed, he handed over a wad of utility bills rolled up and held together with an elastic band. Helena listened as the elastic played a tune with each roll as she fought to remove it. It really did sound quite musical, especially the ping at the end as it almost flew out of her hand. It reminded her of the percussion triangle she played in her primary-school orchestra – its ever-familiar tinging sound.

Hiding her amusement once more, Helena checked over the documents, copying down their printed reference details on to the second slip of paper in the small box marked *Identification*. Satisfied that everything was in order she stapled the paper slips together, moving around the desk to help the elderly man from his chair.

"We will have it ready for you by 3p.m., Mr Peters. It needs to be counted twice over for accuracy and given it's such a significant sum of money, it might take a while! Is there anything you can do while you're in town . . . you know, to keep busy?"

"There's always stuff for me to do." He winked at her playfully. "I'll have one for the road while I'm waiting."

"Have one for me too while you're at it," Helena joked. She would have killed for a beer at that very moment. She wasn't sure why but she was in a giddy mood that afternoon. "Are you sure I can't persuade you to have the money transferred electronically, Mr Peters? It's a lot of money to walk around with, don't you think?"

He stood, wobbling a little, and Helena noticed that his eyes hadn't aged but his body had. They sparkled like a teenager's when she looked deep into them. The ageing process baffled her. Little changed on the inside but the outside bore the brunt of the cruel but inevitable process.

"I'm going to ring my sons once I've collected the money and wait here for them to take me home," he reassured her. "They're gym junkies the pair of them. I can't see anyone messing with me while I've got my lads by my side."

Helena took his arm and headed for the exit at a snail's pace. She pushed the silver-and-blue disability button on the left of the exit and watched as the doors opened. She helped Mr Peters through the doors and down the concrete steps until he was safely at the bottom. It felt good.

Helena watched him hobble along the busy high street until he made a sharp right turn, disappearing from sight. She breathed in the second-hand smoke from her colleagues as they took their '*fresh air*' break. It was all she could do for now. She had used up her last smoke earlier on and she had no money to buy another packet.

Helena thought bitterly about the man's grandson. Her face contorted with the injustice of it all. Having all that money handed to him on a plate. *The lucky bastard.* Maybe she should dump Nathan and date him? The grandson, not the grandfather. But she knew that was never likely to happen. Nathan had her just where he wanted her, and for all her understanding of psychology she had realised very early on in their relationship that

Nathan would always outwit her. What she couldn't quite work out was why she allowed it.

The music boomed from outside the gym studio. Its hardcore beat was a complete contrast to the pipe music which floated and danced its way into the psyches of Kath's Tai Chi class.

"Okay, ladies, this move takes a little coordination but keep practising. Here we go!"

The high-energy chant continued to boom through aggressively and Kath tutted, peering through the glass walls of the workout studio, desperately trying to catch the eye of someone on the reception desk. Its volume was disrupting her class.

The guy on reception looked up to see Kath mouthing at him through the glass. He couldn't understand what she was saying to him but he guessed that she wanted the volume lowered. It was the fingers in the ears which gave the game away.

"That's better." Kath relaxed under the hypnosis of her own pipe music as the external beat was lowered to a barely audible volume. Its hollow softness soothed her tired body. This was her fifth class of the day and she could think of nothing better than going home, plunging into a hot bath with a glass of Chardonnay, and having an early night.

She had been going through money at an accelerated pace lately and was putting in all the extra hours available to make up for the apparent hole in her purse, but the added hours were taking their toll on her energy levels.

"Jean, you really must *try* to stand on one leg. This move is called a *single weighted stance* for a reason. It won't work while you're on both feet. Surely the name gives a clue?"

Kath manhandled Jean into position, holding her while she wobbled comically. Touching was against the rules but Kath didn't care – sometimes people needed a little physical help and she for one wasn't afraid to get stuck in. It was something Marina Young, The Hamptons' manager, disapproved of, however. *'If they get injured, Kath, it's you and the club they'll sue. Don't touch the members!'*

But Kath rebelled against the protocol of the club's rules. How on earth could you teach fitness without some degree of physical interaction? *'Don't touch them?'* What on earth was the world coming to with its ridiculous health and safety regulations and its over-the-top political correctness?

"Jean, just pretend you're a flamingo or something," Kath teased her. "Worse, pretend you've had your other leg amputated!"

Kath continued to hold Jean's hand until she was suitably balanced, then let go. "Keep all your weight on the back foot, Jean. Good."

Kath walked around the heaving class, squeezing through barely there gaps, observing the techniques of the participants.

"Fingers extended, everyone, please – left palm facing the inside of the right elbow, Jude."

Kath winked at Jude. She hated telling her what to do but she understood that she had to treat everybody the same way. She had yet to talk Roni into coming to the gym, despite the exorbitant monthly payments which were debited from her bank account. Or Peter's. It was a joke. But The Tudors was already equipped with a state-of-the-art gymnasium. That too wasn't used by her. Kath often thought about what she would do if she had Roni's money. She would put the world to rights with it. She also surmised that Roni could do with a little Tai Chi in her life. Heaven knew she was so uptight that a little relaxation and chanelling would be a perfect remedy for her. But there was a lot about Veronica Smyth that Kath would change. She liked her but for some reason she just couldn't quite relate to her. They were polar opposites and not just financially but in their contrasting outlooks on life. Roni's wasn't a *life* as far as Kath was concerned. It was an *existence*.

Kath scanned the room again. She was a perfectionist and her job was not only to deliver fitness and relaxation classes to the members of the exclusive gym. In her opinion it was her job to educate, to correct, and to encourage members into looking and feeling more confident – and if they improved their sex life in the process then that too was a massive boost.

Kath made no attempt to hide the joy she felt in sex and all it stood for, and she swore that exercise was the principle element behind her religous three times weekly. Needless to say, Kath's classes were packed and booked out two weeks in advance.

But an improved sex life wasn't the members' *only* reason for attending – it was because of the contagious joie de vivre that Kath had, which was incomparable to anything they had ever encountered before. She was strangely serious and yet animated in corresponding measures, a rare breed indeed. She certainly wasn't a millionaire's wife like many of The Hamptons' members, but what Kath and James had was something that the members' combined fortunes couldn't ever buy. Their endless love.

But it hadn't always been like that. At nineteen when Kath became accidentally pregnant with James' child, there was uproar in the Hamilton household. His mother had labelled her a 'slut' and banned her from the family home with clear instructions that none of James' brothers or sisters were to have anything to do with her. Neither was James. Only things had progressed a little too far for that.

On the day of the delivery, Kath had received a surprise visit from Elizabeth, James' mother. She had rubbed her eyes disbelievingly as she saw the slightly built, dark-haired woman walking towards her with a clear purpose. She watched her wilful stride and her heart had pulsated with terror.

"How much will it take to keep you away from my son?" she had asked with all the nonchalance of someone asking a stranger the time.

Kath was speechless.

"Name your price – it's as easy as that," Elizabeth said calmly. Her eyes dared to glance over at the plastic crib covered in a white hospital blanket. "You get the money and James gets the child."

A fire welled up inside of Kath like nothing she had ever experienced before. She grabbed her son from his sterile crib, her chin trembling with a fierce protectiveness that almost winded her, shaking her head in utter disbelief.

"You witch!" she snarled with uncontrollable venom.

"Take your money and get out of here!" She gripped the baby to her chest, burying his head from sight. This horrible woman didn't deserve a look at him. "How dare you! Just stay out of our lives!"

Elizabeth stood calmly, compared to Kath who shook with violent rage.

"You're dead as far as we're concerned!" she spat at the woman who was supposed to have become her mother-in-law.

"And my son is dead as far as I'm concerned," Elizabeth retaliated with alarming calmless. "And it's all your doing."

Kath watched her walk away and her body convulsed with both shock and fear. *What had she done?* She had come between a son and his mother and left nothing but past memories and an empty future. His life would never be the same again because of her and the angry words which had spilled out.

But as Kath stared down at her precious bundle of joy it all made sense. Life made sense. At that very moment Kath had turned from a young girl into a woman – a mother who had carried and given birth to her first descendant. She had stretched her skin for him and bore the permanent evidence to prove it. She had offered her breast to nourish him and her body still ached from when she had pushed him out into the world until her skin down below was ripped apart. And Kath swore with a vengence that nothing and no-one would ever come between her and her own family. What type of mother could abandon her own son, punishing him for simply falling in love?

As Kath clutched hold of the writhing baby, kissing the soft down of his head, he gripped her finger with such intensity that she was sure he understood what had just happened. She looked down at his minute flaky hands and extraordinary long fingernails and smiled. "I love you too, son," she whispered. "Always."

5

Jude removed her leather jacket and flung it over her spare arm. Its Burberry label gazed at her sulkily – it was far too expensive to be tossed to one side – hidden from sight.

Clive had indulged her after a hefty bonus and treated her to the brown leather longline aviator coat, double-breasted with Burberry-engraved buttons. Jude liked it, she liked it a lot, but when she saw the price-tag she gasped. You could have a fed an entire developing country for a week on what it had cost. But she hadn't complained, no, that would be impolite and she accepted the gift with geniune thanks and appreciation. She would have done the same, however, had Clive presented her with last week's newspapers.

She glanced at her watch once more. It was just past midday.

Sophie had called her yesterday to arrange the meeting but Jude had no idea why and Sophie would give nothing away.

Jude knew that Sophie's silence was out of character and that she had something up her sleeve. She just didn't know what.

A thought passed through her innocent mind and she shook it off immediately. Why would Sophie have something to confess? She was thinking a load of old nonsense she was sure of it – but the last session of the Curry Club had left her shaken and suspicious like never before. Was Clive sleeping with one of her friends? He couldn't be. Could he?

Jude tutted aloud at her stupidity. Sophie was one of the most reliable people she had ever met, and yes, those who knew her well enough also knew of her animalistic capabilities, but not with her friends' husbands. And surely not Clive with Sophie either? She could trust her husband with her life.

Sophie pressed the button on the dashboard to heat up the driver's seat of her Audi TT roadster. Outside, its bold red colour made a statement to passersby as it flew past them at law-breaking speed using all six gears.

Sophie had been stopped for speeding more than once, but she had only to smile at the many male officers who, dazzled by her beauty, let her off with a warning each time. The girl had nothing on record. Anyone else would be behind bars.

She was late and she hated to keep anyone waiting. She spotted Jude waiting patiently on the busy high street. At least she won't have been bored, Sophie thought. There was so much happening on Alderley Avenue that you could spend the entire day simply people-watching.

She watched Jude resting against the old wooden

windowsill of the derelict shop. Its racing-green paint was peeling away and Jude was picking at it, desperate to see the quality of timber beneath. Sophie could see as clear as daylight that Jude would kill to get her hands on a project like that. Jude's mind never stopped when it came to anything related to design.

She smiled and flung the car across the pedestrian pavement. Its angular, anarchic parking demonstrated clearly her inability to respect the law and its simple regulations. Nobody told Sophie Kane what to do.

Jude looked on as a thick mane of blonde hair thrust its way out of the pillar-box-red vehicle. Sophie's hair was tousled to perfection, edged with a just-out-of-bed look, and Jude knew that Sophie would have spent the entire morning achieving a look which at first glance seemed effortless and understated. What Jude didn't know was that, as beautiful as Sophie was, she herself was everything that Sophie Kane was, only ten times more. But she was as natural as a rainbow following a sunshower, a vision of colourful beauty which captured the attention of many.

At five-foot-nine, Jude was very slim, with never-ending legs and sallow skin which carried an all-year-round tan. Her olive-green eyes were complemented by a backdrop of dark-blonde hair which fell like a sheet of silk halfway down her perfectly arched back and when Jude smiled her face illuminated, casting out rays of regal enchantment. The girl had it all and she was effortlessly stylish – she was also effortlessly humble.

Jude stood with concern as she saw Sophie walking away from the car. She yelled out to her friend. "Won't you get a ticket, Sophie? It's on the pavement!"

Sophie's brisk walk meant that she reached Jude in no time. "Not if the traffic warden's a bloke, I won't!"

Jude giggled.

Sophie Kane was a law unto herself and Jude had often thought that she reminded her of a female version of Clive. They had so much in common. Perhaps that was why from the moment she had met Sophie they had hit it off like lifelong friends and they took no time at all to fill the empty pages of their short history together.

Jude erased once more that feeling of apprehension when she thought of Clive and Sophie together. Damn the Curry Club with its painstaking honesty and damn the question that she had pulled from the bowl. She was usually impregnable against insecurities and she listened to mindless gossip with closed ears. Perhaps, she thought, she was feeling rather exposed and slightly rocky with the children being away?

Tom and Anna were her lifeblood and without them she felt drained and redundant.

The girls embraced, uninhibited and fuelled with genuine affection. They adored each other. Sophie glanced down at Jude's coat, still draped over her arm.

"Is that a Burberry, Jude?"

She grabbed the coat from Jude, slipping into it immediately. In length it drowned her, stopping at her ankles whereas on Jude it came to mid-calf.

Sophie admired her reflection in the empty shop window.

"I've never seen you in this before, Jude – it's amazing."

Jude looked a little embarrassed. "Thanks, Sophie, I do wear it . . . but it just feels a bit, erm, flashy sometimes." Her cheeks flushed.

Sophie just laughed, shaking her head. "Jude, there's nothing wrong with being a bit flashy, you know." Sophie kept the coat on as she removed a set of keys from her oversized Anya Hindmarch bag. "I would have thought that someone with an interior-design background would understand about taste and opulence?" she teased.

Jude grinned at Sophie. She wasn't easily wound up. In fact, she couldn't be wound up full stop. She was as chilled as the Arctic Circle on the exterior while inside her heart burned away, fuelled with a fire of magnanimity.

"That's different though, Sophie. Decorating a room is about bringing it to life or applying a thematic approach which suits the natural aura of the place." How she was lost in a temporal world. "It's about discovery and reveal and salvaging mor –"

"Okay, I get the point." Sophie clicked her fingers just inches in front of Jude's face. "When I count to three I want you to wake from your short-term hypnosis!"

Jude chuckled as she ducked from the close proximity of Sophie's clicking fingers.

"I did it again, didn't I? You know what, Sophie, I can't help myself . . . it's like I become sucked into a strange universe and nothing else exists. I'm not sure if it's a good thing or a bad thing."

"It's a good thing. A very good thing."

Sophie scanned the bunch of keys in her hand, singling out a simple silver Yale key. She shoved it into the Georgian wooden-framed glass door.

Through the glass, a pile of post lay scattered and messy on the bare concrete floor and Sophie pushed the door hard against the resisting mail, kicking it away, careful not to scuff her designer riding boots. The weather was becoming a little too warm for boots, she thought as she admired the tightly fitted Louis Vuittons, the soft calf-leather wrapped around her slender legs. She smiled, noticing how complementary the mokka-coloured boots were against Jude's Burberry jacket. She might have to make Jude an offer. And grow a foot in height.

"Sophie, what are we doing here?" Jude asked, her forehead furrowed with curiosity.

"Wait and see."

6

As Sophie beckoned her friend towards the rear of the building, her mind cast back to the day they had all met. The forge of five unlikely friendships, which somehow worked.

Jude's garden party would always be remembered as the day where keeping secrets and suffering embarrassment at discussing 'taboo' subjects was brought tumbling to the ground, aggressively decimated by the strength of five women. That was the day the Curry Club was conceived.

Sophie remembered it like it was yesterday, every minute detail of it.

A huge marquee had been erected centre-stage on the immaculately mown lawn of *The Firs* rear garden. It was clear to see that the grass had been treated with tender loving care and its shade of green was the perfect prototype for any serial grass-lover. Sophie recalled commenting on how jealous Alan Titchmarsh would be at the grandness of the garden and Jude had simply smiled away her embarrassment.

To the left of the white circus-style marquee was a pond-cum-lake thick with water lilies and obese carp and an old wooden rowing boat which bobbed merrily along backed by a mild supportive breeze. A charity auction was taking place inside the marquee with ostentatious sums of money being verbally exchanged inside its decorative, voile-curtained walls.

Jude had arranged it. Single-handed. Since her father died, she had become a supporter of The Michael Stern Parkinson's Research Foundation, and Jude had done all she could to raise awareness of the debilitating condition of Parkinson's disease while simultaneously raising huge sums of money. It made Jude feel closer to her father. There was not a day went by that she didn't long for his presence. His comfort and wise words had borne all the hallmarks of a great leader but it was his quietness that had spoken volumes to Jude, a glance here and gaze there leaving her knowing and understanding him. They had shared a father-daughter telepathy which no amount of quantum physics could explain. They just knew each other and Jude often felt his presence around her. When she did, she knew she was safe.

As Jude's hairdresser, Sophie had been invited to the prestigious 'invitation only' event along with a guest. Sophie had brought Helena, her best friend. While it was true that she and Helena had little in common in terms of how they lived, they had shared twenty-five years of secret diaries and kiss-and-tell. They had been each other's Agony Aunt as they had each announced the loss of their virginity, crying short-lived tears as each of them waited for the results of their HIV tests. Kenya was certainly not the wisest of places for them to have tried out the local talent and they had both learned a wise and valuable life-saving lesson. It could have been so very different and they knew it.

Jude had also invited Kath, her fitness instructor from The Hamptons exclusive health club and spa, and Veronica Smyth – aka Roni – the wife of self-made millionaire Peter Smyth, one of Clive's sailing companions and well-known Cheshire entrepreneur.

As the women were introduced to each other, Jude noticed how Kath and Sophie gripped each other with a firm handshake, neither showing any weakness to the other while at the same time it became immediately obvious to both of them, and to those observing, that a new friendship had been born. They had met their match in each other and a natural chemistry sparked between them.

Helena and Roni were a different breed altogether. Roni was standoffish and not in a shy way either, but in a rude, condescending way which also didn't go unnoticed. But still there was something intriguing about her. She was a closed book, but one where the front cover made you want to read on, more so with its unusual page design and captivating external graphics. That was Roni through and through – eye-catching and intriguing, just like a book synopsis. Only with Roni you carried the risk of opening the book, digesting the core of its story and feeling it was one of repugnance and self-absorbed arrogance and yet, for some reason, you simply couldn't put it down even if it were the most challenging read. Few would like her. Many would abhor her. Veronica Smyth was her own worst enemy.

Suprisingly enough, the women hit it off with their

eclectic mix of characteristics and extremely diverse backgrounds.

As usual it was Sophie Kane who threw a spanner in the works, creating a chink in the seamless platonic mechanisms which had taken all day and the guts of half a dozen bottles of wine to build.

Jude followed Sophie as she led her around the derelict and needy premises. She stayed silent as Sophie talked away, but her mind was far from that. It raced with prospects for the place and she was already seeing the finished product in her mind's eye. And still, she had absolutely no idea what Sophie was doing there. Nor what she was doing there with her.

"So what do you think?" Sophie beamed a luminous grin. If ever she had looked a vision of blonde bombshell beauty, it was that very moment.

Jude gazed adoringly at the petite goddess standing before her.

"It's got a huge amount of potential, Sophie, particularly with the size of it . . . but why are you showing it to *me*?"

"It's mine, Jude!" Sophie beamed. "My second Kane'n'Able salon. I've signed a five-year lease with the option to buy at the end of the term. I have been waiting bloody years for a place to come up here on Alderley Avenue and now it's all mine!"

Sophie threw herself at an emotional Jude, whose eyes had already started to well with pride for this young and ambitious friend of hers.

"Oh, Sophie, I am so so proud of you!" Jude embraced her with all the vigour of a gloating parent. The girl was awe-inspiring.

Jude's mind raced with thoughts of where her own career would be at that very juncture had she not given it up when the twins were born, with a little coercion from Clive and her mother. They had made a great team. But she had no idea what the answer was. She quickly erased her thoughts, scolding herself for wanting, and changed her focus away from her own selfishness.

"So what are you going to do with it, Sophie?"

This was the very moment Sophie had been waiting for. "Well . . . that's up to you, Jude."

Jude simply stared at Sophie. Her heart felt like it had stopped ticking.

"Sorry?"

"It's yours, Jude. It's all yours."

It was Sophie's turn to gush with rare emotion and she was loving every minute of it. "I'm giving *you* the contract as my new interior designer. Do what you will with the place but just keep it in budget or I'll haul you over hot coals!" She laughed. "I know how expensive your taste is, madam."

Sophie pulled out a contract from her bag and handed Jude two copies.

"I've had my lawyer draw this up. It doesn't do you any more favours than if I had got someone else in – but I have to treat you the same as anyone else." Sophie's tone was apologetic. "It's a business transaction through and through."

The hairs on Jude's arms stood on end and her spine tingled as though someone had walked over it. She felt a cold chill on the back of her neck and her legs froze, glued solid to the floor.

Sophie could not take her eyes off Jude. She had

been waiting to offer her friend a lifeline for so many years.

True, they had the Curry Club, but what Jude needed was something more. Sophie had listened to Jude's desires as she sat in the hairdressing chair talking non-stop of nothing but design, antiquities, restoration and so much more. Sophie had hung on to every word she had said because she adored her affluent friend though their relationship on paper would have been an absolute non-starter.

"Jude?"

Jude went to speak but her mouth was dry and her hands were shaking. Her heart thumped through her chest and for the first time in her life, she was unable to control herself. Something else was controlling her, an emotion so overwhelming had taken her over that she could do nothing but bite her bottom lip to prevent herself from crying.

Sophie giggled at Jude's silence and at her strange inability to communicate.

"Is that a yes?"

The night sky was dotted with glittery stars and the moon was in full decorative costume – subtle and translucent. It lit up the fourteen-acre garden of The Firs as though it was on hire for the evening and solely for their use.

As it shone down on the five women it illuminated the white slips of paper on which they wrote – all bar one. Roni simply stared out at the dark lake, glassy and frighteningly still. She stole a glance around the table at the other four women giggling away as they wrote with giddy hands and blurred vision. She was finding it more difficult than they but that didn't surprise her. Communication had always been difficult for Veronica Smyth but she did see Sophie's point that this was a way to communicate under some sort of cover – and this she liked. She liked anything covert.

The charity event had been a huge success and Dale Winton had kindly provided his services as auctioneer. In a way which only he could get away with, he had coaxed the 'Cheshire set' out of much of their surplus funds – "All going to a good cause," he had repeated with consistency throughout the day.

Jude reached up, flicking the switch on the tall, free-standing patio-heater, inching it closer to the table with a little help from Kath. The air was chilly with a slight wind, and a little warmth would mean they could stay out for longer. The sleepy breeze teased inside the marquee, puffing at its voile lining and blowing carelessly the unused napkins, leaving them dotted around and alleviating the emptiness of the place with messy attitude.

The guests had left hours ago bar the five women whose night it appeared had only just begun – as had something new in their lives – they just didn't know it yet.

"Are we done?" Sophie scanned the table and held out her hand eagerly.

"Almost." Roni applied herself to the task, scribbling down practically indecipherable words before folding the slip of paper with all the precision that Sophie had instructed earlier on.

She had written in block capitals and was pleased that the writing looked unlike her own careful script. Not that the women would recognise her writing.

Roni placed the paper slip into an empty wineglass offered to her by the hand of Sophie. She watched as it slid on top of the other slips of paper and then Sophie placed her hand over the mouth of the glass, shaking it vigorously before plunging in with a finger and thumb and removing a tightly folded slip. Her face was filled with a mixture of apprehension and excitement.

For a split second, Roni too felt a moment of exhilaration as she wondered if it were her question Sophie had pulled out. She had watched to see if her slip remained on top of the glass but as they were all folded in perfect symmetry, it was impossible to see any longer which was hers amongst the others.

Sophie unwrapped the tight folds and ironed the paper between her bronzed hands and French-polished acrylic nails.

"Here goes," Sophie said with a hint of a slur. "The question is . . . '*When does adultery* actually *become adultery?*'."

"The moment you even think about it," Roni jumped in with both feet. She was a woman of strong and determined morals and when you made your vows you meant them.

Sophie threw her head back and laughed. For the first question it was quite meaty and she was glad they had something to sink their teeth into – in her case all eleven grands' worth which had been her cosmetic bill.

"Roni, *thinking* about something isn't criminal as long as it stays in your head. It's the doing that is the dangerous bit."

"Actually, I think it's good to think about other people and to fantasise about them when you're having

sex. James and I do it all the time." Kath never minded
being outspoken. To her, sex was as natural as taking
in a breath of oxygen which you needed to survive –
you needed sex in equal measure to feel alive. They
went hand in hand. "You can't be all things to all people
so pretending or even carrying out role-plays is a
brilliant way to keep your sex life alive. I recommend
that everyone in my fitness classes should try a little
invention."

Kath's matter-of-fact words silenced Roni with a
punch. She had never encountered anybody like her
before. On the one hand she found Kath repugnant and
crude, but on the other she longed for her openness and
her ability to be so unashamed of matters which Roni
considered private and sacred.

"But isn't that kind of cheating, Kath, you know, if
you're sleeping with your husband but thinking about
someone else?" Jude asked with interest.

"No way!" Sophie interruped. "You should see some
of the guys who get their hair done. I'll never bag them
because they're my clients but if I'm with someone else
who isn't really doing it for me, I just take my pick of
their gorgeous faces and fit bods and wonder away! It
takes me no time at all once I'm in the zone!"

Jude chuckled at Sophie's honesty and Roni's tongue
lifted as she tutted aloud.

Helena sat quietly, deep in thought. She and Nathan
didn't have too much of a sex life. They lived more like
friends than lovers and Helena was desperate to be
touched. She wanted to feel wanted. She longed to feel a
hot, passionate tongue in her mouth moving down south
and staying there until she climaxed. His apparent

neglect suddenly angered her. So much about her relationship with Nathan angered her.

"You know what," she said boldly, sitting upright, "I think that people give adulterers a hard time. If you're not getting it at home and you feel like you've done everything to try keeping your sex life alive . . . then . . . then why the bloody hell should you not look outside for it?"

The women were shocked at Helena's contribution. She had been quiet and generic in her opinions throughout the day, so this outburst forced them to listen.

"If he's not giving it to you, then someone else will," Helena continued, "and I for one wouldn't feel guilty for a moment. There is only so long a person can be expected to go without sex and, personally, I blame the person that doesn't bother their arse trying . . . *not* the person who has gone out to find the very thing which they are being deprived of behind closed doors."

Sophie had never heard such an admission from Helena. She understood from that moment that Helena Wright was hurting but there was not a thing she could do about it until her friend either packed her bags and dumped the loser, or threw him and his crazy hare-brained ideas out for good.

What Sophie did understand was that this game – the Curry Club – was a healer. It was a way of allowing people to open up and to share ideas and opinions. And Sophie Kane had decided on that glittery-starred, moonlit night they had met, that in order to find any degree of commonality between the five of them and to fully trust each other, this game they had all played and enjoyed during their first encounter would need to be formalised. A hot curry followed by a spicy confession, that was her game plan.

She knew immediately that Roni would never open up of her own accord. In fact, she knew through Jude that Roni didn't have a social life much to the dismay of Peter, he himself being a social butterfly. Similarly, she recognised that Jude took her privacy and personal matters with her to bed each night and that unless provoked she would continue to fail to open up to people and Jude deserved better than that. She deserved reciprocity of the listening ears that she provided for everybody else and their problems. Kath was well up for it, Sophie thought, as she observed the thrashing colours of her bohemian-style top and listened to the many bangles on her pale arms jingle tunefully. Kath was the harmony in their group, she was the accord they needed amidst the clash of egos. Kath was up for anything and Sophie loved this about her. And Helena, well, she simply needed escapism and a new man in her life, Sophie surmised. Sophie also knew at this moment in time that she could only provide one of those, the other had to be procured by Helena herself.

And so it was that Sophie Kane with her strong and persuasive business abilities sold the concept of 'The Curry Club' to her new friends – a strange eclectic group of both ordinary and extraordinary people who barely knew each other – and surprisingly enough, they had all bought into it – the facticity of it.

Once again Sophie Kane had orchestrated something that she herself wanted to happen. Her fiery curiosity had presented her with an opportunity to be privy to the comings and goings of four people's lives and with this information, combined with the widsom and input from the rest of the women, came the opportunity to advance in maturity. To cultivate all she learned from her collective educators and to embrace and use their insight for her own judiciousness.

7

Kath jumped off the bus, throwing up her hood as the rain came thrashing down.

"Thanks, Dave," she yelled at the driver with whom she had struck a firm relationship over the years.

Kath and James had no car. Kath couldn't drive and didn't see the point in it when you could hop on public transport, plus it supported the labours of the country, and as James drove for a living he simply refused to get behind the wheel of anything unless it was a heavy-goods vehicle equipped with its own bed, microwave and with luncheon vouchers thrown in for good measure.

The weather was relentlessly wet and Kath was soaked through in no time. The fleece which usually kept her warm was no defence against the unforecast climate of the North West.

She upped her pace and accelerated past the row of 1950s semi-detached homes in the street where she lived, head down to avoid the torrent.

As she stormed past Number 11, Kath heard her

name being called out. She turned back to see her neighbour beckoning her, the front door open and inviting.

Kath hurried down the path and into the porch where she kicked off her wet trainers and removed her saturated fleece. She had no waterproofs on because she hadn't been expecting the downpour.

Kath and Norma had been friends for years. Their kids had gone to both primary and secondary school together and Norma was the closest thing that Kath had to family. True to his mother's word, her threat, James' family had continued to live in isolation from them. The entire family had bowed down to Elizabeth's wishes subserviently and James was no more in their eyes. Still, it was their loss, Kath thought regularly and she had got over it. Her family had got over it as much as they could, but the one thing she could never get over, ever, was the fact that a mother could disown her own son.

This had always remained a bitter pill to swallow.

Norma pulled Kath from the chilly porch into the narrow hallway which was made darker by the mahogany doors and deep navy carpet. She was fuelled with emotion and Kath could see she was itching to gossip to somebody.

"What is it, Norma?"

"Did you hear about poor old Gerry? What do you think about that?" she blurted. "If I ever get my hands on the bastards that did this – I'll – I'll bloody well strangle them. The po –"

"Stop. Stop a minute, Norma. What are you on about?"

Kath was clueless and Norma's eyes opened like flying saucers. Her jaw dropped down like a heavy weight was attached to it. "Kath, where have you been? Gerry's house got ransacked yesterday. They took everything they could get their scummy hands on . . . and get this . . ." Norma placed her hands on her hips in true fishwife style. "They even took his wee grandson's *DSi*. I mean, how nasty is that?"

Kath went an immediate shade of pale. "I hadn't heard," she muttered quietly. "When did that happen, Norma?"

"Yesterday afternoon, anytime between two and four they reckon."

Kath's mouth dried up and she felt a repetitive twitch in one of her eyelids. She hoped it was a twitch she could feel but not one which Norma could see.

"Are you okay, Kath? You don't look well."

With her pale face, sopping hair stuck to her head and smudges of mascara streaked down her cheeks, Kate looked anything but healthy.

"I'm fine, Norm, don't go worrying about me."

As she turned to leave, Kath gripped the bannister rail as the hallway closed in on her. Her knuckles held on tightly as she was spun around on an out-of-control carousel. At least it felt that way.

"I'm fine," she lied. "I've been working so much overtime lately I'm just a little under the weather – exhausted probably."

Norma lifted a clump of wet hair. "Literally *under* the weather," she laughed, patting her friend affectionately on the shoulder. She offered her a dry coat and Kath allowed herself to be dressed by her and ushered out of the door.

Despite the incessant rain and the urgent need to stay dry, it took her forever to make the journey to Number

15. She struggled to put one foot in front of the other as she tried to convince herself that she was perhaps coming down with something. Only her raw, maternal instincts told her that was not the case. This was not an ailment which could be fixed. Something else was wrong.

Roni sat in the security room of The Tudors watching the miniature television monitors which captured the happenings and comings and goings both inside and outside the family home. They told the simple and understated story of life at The Tudors and it reminded her of the film *Sliver* – only when Roni looked at the multiple screens nothing looked back. Nothing with any life to it anyway. Just permanent fixtures and loose fittings – they were lifeless images, just like her own lifeless life.

She picked up the smallest of the remote controls and wound back the tape. With shaking hands she pressed the 'play' button, standing to watch. Her breathing was erratic and she tapped her foot with nervous impatience until the screen flickered to life. Roni clutched at her chest as she fast became engrossed in the home movie . . . with Darren Ford as the protaganist.

She stared at the montage of the morning's events, watching as Darren's red Fiesta pulled up outside The Tudors. She smirked as she witnessed the awkwardness with which he squeezed his six-foot-four, broad frame from the tiny door-opening, and she suppressed a loud snort as he shook the gates before ringing the intercom, trying to gain access to '*the lady of the house*'.

The cheek of it.

She noticed how he took in the exterior of the house, scanning it with interest, from the slate roof down to the gravel. But mostly what Roni thought about was how nonchalant he was. Expressionless. How unmoved he appeared to be as he regarded her multimillion-pound exclusive home in Alderley Edge. And how strange it was that something so palatial and so obviously oozing practically criminal wealth could draw not a flicker of emotion from this young man.

Roni watched the tape again and again. And again.

Kath woke as the front door creaked loudly. It was in desperate need of oiling. Another job on James' list. She called out to him. "James, is that you, love?"

Prising herself from the sofa, she muted the television, waiting for a head to pop around the living-room door.

"It's just me, Mum."

Kath rushed out into the box-sized hallway and turned up the brass dimmer-switch which immediately lit up the small, square space.

"Jason, where have you been, love? We've been worried sick about you."

Jason was armed with attitude. The chip on his shoulder weighed him down firmly. "Nowhere." He stared down at the digestive-carpeted floor.

"You can't have been nowhere, love. You didn't come home last night. Where were you, son?"

Jason brushed past his mother into the kitchen. He yanked open the fridge, poking his head in deep to avoid meeting her eyes.

"Your dinner's in the oven." Kath took Jason's arm in a firm grip and he retreated from the fridge. "Jason, do you know anything about Gerry Fleming's place getting burgled?"

Jason shook off his mother's grip and scowled. "Why would *I* know anything about it?" he snapped, making no eye contact. "I bet you didn't ask our Neil the same question, did you?"

Kath took a deep breath as she took in the handsome but troubled young man standing before her, eyes lowered.

Neil had been such an easy child from the moment he was born. He still was. He was considerate, kind and loving, and both Kath and James were incredibly proud of him. Jason had been and still was a walking time-bomb on the verge of constant explosion. He needed to be treated with delicate care and Kath knew early on that her fears were truly realised – Jason, it seemed, had inherited her family's bad blood. Still, he could have inherited the *witch's* blood and that was far worse.

"In fairness, Jason, I didn't see Neil walking down the street yesterday afternoon with a black holdall across his back . . . did I?"

Jason didn't move a muscle.

"I kept shouting out to you but you obviously couldn't hear me," Kath continued, "or perhaps you had other distractions?" She was shaking although she tried hard to stay calm and authoritative.

Jason continued to stare at his feet. He said nothing.

"What was in the bag?"

He looked up at his mother with such a huffy glare that it unnerved her. "I stayed over at Scott's house. I took some CD's and my Wii. Okay?"

He sulkily removed his dinner from the oven, put it into the microwave and banged the buttons angrily. The usual pinging sound seemed altered with his heavy-handed touch. As he waited for the sixty seconds to end, Jason slouched against the formica worktop, crossing one foot over the other, and Kath watched his arrogant posture from the grimace on his face to the position of his feet and an anger welled inside of her.

"Where did you get the money for those then, Jason?" She pointed to the immaculate trainers on his feet. They were the latest Nike brand and were so immaculately clean that they bore the straight-from-the-box look. Kath knew those things didn't come cheap. She also knew that Jason had no job which meant little money.

Jason took his dinner, grabbed a fork, slamming the drawer closed with his hip and left the kitchen without a word. He tutted at the sight of his mother following him.

"Jason," Kath said softly, "I love you so so much that it takes my breath away . . . and no matter what you have done I will never disown you like that old *witch* did to your father." She touched his hand as he turned to go upstairs. "Talk to me, please – I can help you with whatever is going on in your life."

"There is nothing going on in my life, Mum. I did a bit of manual work for a mate and I bought these with the money. End of."

Kath relaxed a little and she reached out to touch his face. To her he was still a child in need of protection and even in that moment where she wasn't truly convinced that all was well, she continued to wonder how Elizabeth could have turned her back on James. He was a good son, a decent man all round and he could have provided her with the joy of two grandsons. It made Kath all the more determined that no matter what was thrown at her, she would never *ever* abandon her own child despite the challenges Jason brought to her home.

His odd behaviour had gone from bad to worse since he left school with no job in hand and a set of unimpressive GCSE results. Kath had used all the contacts she knew of to secure work for him. But for some unknown reason he couldn't hold down any of the jobs. He either didn't enjoy them or he found them too physical or they just didn't 'float his boat'.

Something was troubling him and as such it was troubling her. Kath knew that, whatever it was, it needed to be fixed sooner than later, before the boy she had watched grow up over the years turned into someone unrecognisable.

Roni didn't hear the front door close nor the sound of Peter's stomp as he took the stairs two at a time. Why would she? The thick red carpet absorbed much of his weight and the front door was so far away from her she wouldn't have been able to hear it open, hard as she might have tried. Her thoughts were far from Peter anyway.

Roni watched the monitor flicker. Darren continued to retain his close-up pose. He was paused and static and Roni could do nothing but stare at him – her lips slightly apart, a look of longing on her face.

She didn't hear Peter's deep strides as he went from room to room looking for his wife. Similary she didn't hear him calling out to her, so focused was she on the youthful vision before her.

Peter hid the oversized bag behind his back. He was

excited. He loved to please Veronica and he couldn't wait to give her the gift and break the news to her. While he already knew that her reaction would never be the one he would have liked, he knew his wife well enough to be able to capture her appreciation, deeply buried and in need of excavation. He wasn't an archaeologist but he knew it was there alright.

He pushed open the door to the security room and saw his wife, standing facing away from him, her hands on her hips. He took in her pear-shaped roundness and noted how the ends of her hair looked dry and in need of a little attention. Still, he loved her for better for worse, like she him.

"Roni, love, I've been calling you for ages."

Roni froze, averting her gaze from the screen in front of her. She flipped round to face Peter, perching on the desk in an attempt to hide the screen image behind her. Her plumped-out broadness covered the monitor sufficiently. What it could not hide was the surprised look which was painted on her face.

"I didn't hear you, Peter, sorry," she lied effortlessly. "I was cleaning away in here."

Peter tutted in frustration. "Will you let me get you a daily help, love? Even someone who can come in once a week?" He implored. "I hate to think of you stuck here when you could be out enjoying yourself."

He winced as the stiff paper of the gift bag brushed against the back of his jeans. "Look at all the friends you've got now." He beamed proudly. "You could be at the gym with Kath or out shopping with Jude."

Roni was desperate to be removed from the precarious situation. She would be terrified until she had led him firmly from the room. "I'll give it some thought," she humoured him.

Peter stood tall, puffing out his chest. He had that *look* which Roni recognised.

Pulling the bag from behind him and holding it with one hand, he used the other to prise Roni away from the desk.

"I've got you a present."

The bag was swung around and Roni took the expensive package by its handles, peering deep inside. She loved gifts and she really did appreciate them, so much so that most of her gifts remained mummified in their original tissue paper or plush packaging – they were just too good to use.

Roni delved in until her short arm was buried in the purple bag. She pulled out a swimsuit, gasping as the label stared at her, bold and bragging.

"You spend three hundred pounds on a swimsuit? Are you mad?" were the first words from her mouth.

Peter smiled. He knew she liked it and any reaction was a good one.

"There's more," he said, preening.

"What is it?" Roni smirked. "Complimentary armbands!"

Peter threw back his head and belted out impulsive laughter. If only people knew this side to his wife. The dry, witty side to her which was tidied away in its relevant compartment, coming out for special occasions – weddings, christenings and bar mitzvahs.

Peter kissed his wife hard on the lips and surprisingly she kissed him back. He was feeling amorous at the thought of seeing her in the high-legged swimsuit which he knew was a little young for her – but still. He longed to see its blackness wrapped around her curvaceous body, lifting her breasts until they spilled out, and he was desperate to see the outline of her feminity as it clung to all the right places.

Roni too was feeling strangely lustful. As a rule, daytime sex was banned, she was usually far too busy and her mind was elsewhere, but today her chemical reactions were too strong to be ignored and she longed to lubricate Pete's manhood – impressed with her ability to deliver the goods without the support of K-Y this early in the day.

Roni removed her made-up lips from her husband's abruptly.

"Where's the rest then?"

"Rest of what?" Peter muttered, pulling her back towards him.

"The rest of my present," she said.

He released his grip as he pointed past her. "It's behind you."

Roni turned to the display of monitors and technical-looking switches.

"Hey?" She could see nothing.

Peter pointed again in the direction of the CCTV screens, singling one out in particular. He shoved his finger at Darren. "Swimming lessons, love! Darren is going to teach you to swim!"

Roni was instantly chilled to the bone. Good God, this couldn't be happening.

"No. Absolutely not, Pete."

"It's okay, love, this time it will be better. That other guy was useless but Darren is young, patient and he's properly qualified plus you won't even have to leave the ho –"

"But I c –"

"I won't take no for an answer this time, Veronica. You won't come on the yacht because you're afraid of drowning, I can't get you in the sea on holiday which is just sacrilege – and you know why else, Veronica?" Peter was unusually fierce. "Because it might bloody well save your life one day."

Roni was shocked at his outburst.

The truth hurt. Twice.

Roni nodded, giving in to him. A rareness in itself but she had seldom heard him speak with such passion and conviction.

"He starts on Thursday at 10a.m. and then every consecutive Thursday, same time."

Peter's contorted expression softened as he sneaked up behind her and placed his hands one on each breast, massaging them. Frustrated with the barricade of material, he slid his hands beneath her baby-pink V-necked sweater, yanking up her bra, catching her breasts as they fell into his hands. His fingers made a beeline for her saucer-like pink nipples, big and for the moment soft in his pen-pusher hands.

Roni could do nothing else but watch Darren on the screen – Pete had her in a fixed position, facing away from him.

As he held each nipple between finger and thumb, he tugged away at them, stretching them before allowing them to contract and he felt each nipple become harder and more alert. Roni let out a loud groan which delighted him. She felt a gush of wetness soak her La Perla ivory-silk pants. Responsively she grabbed Pete's hand and thrust it amongst her bed of dark pubic hair. She had yet to experience the joy of waxing.

Peter bent his wife over the desk. He lifted her A-lined skirt, yanking at her pants and he thrust his fingers deep inside her, one first, then two, and then all bar his thumb.

As Roni gasped for breath, she lifted her head to see Darren in his fitted white T-shirt, noting how it clung to his firm pecs, outlining the perfect shape of them. His thickset muscular arms symbolised his hardworking, no-nonsense approach to life and Roni found herself wondering how his boyish but brute strength might be different to Peter's touch.

Was Darren inexperienced in that department? Would his strength be detrimental to his providing her with anything bar a heavy-handed touch? Would she feel like she were having sex with a giant or would it feel illegal like having sex with a minor?

He at six-foot-four and she at five-foot-two were hardly the perfect match. Then again, surely being horizontal would remove the height differential?

Suddenly, the strength of her emotions took over and she longed to feel his hardness against her, imagining herself riding him with wide-open legs and a tight, wet pussy. A wave of animalism clawed from within her as she roared to an orgasm so loud and so greedily taken that Pete too could wait no longer. He thrust himself inside her, desperate and on the verge himself. His wife had created an impetus which he could not compare to any other sexual occasion, and in a few short thrusts he too had come with a desperate hunger.

Unsatisfied with the short duration of his pleasure,

Peter grabbed Roni's hand and led her across the gallery landing to the bedroom where he forced her down onto the white four-poster bed, brushing off a mass of pale-blue cushions. He had never witnessed his wife orgasm like that before, nor had he felt her come with such a flood that he felt its pressure as it squirted against his fingers which were still inside her. His wife was alive on this grey Monday afternoon and he was determined to live as though it was his last day on earth.

It never occured to him to question her sincerity and the authenticity of her actions. Daytime sex? Orgasms? That was not his Veronica. But Peter didn't care who she was – this stuff was too good to turn down.

But Roni knew the truth behind her heightened sensitivity. That young man was an aphrodisiac like she had never known before. His youthful torso was the perfect antidote to his almost aloof and detached exterior and it was this that drove Veronica Smyth wild. For once, she was being treated like the girl next door and, for once, it never occured to her to challenge it.

8

Clive jumped aboard *The Trophy* which he jointly owned with William Cavanagh – aka Will – an ex-client of his law firm. The sailing season had recommenced now that the dark nights had lifted their depressed and endless winter mask, allowing him once more to indulge in his ultimate passion of yacht-racing. And winning.

Clive ducked his head as he unlocked the cabin to the eight-berth area below and flung in his sailing bag. He was, quite rightly, anal about safety on board the yacht and anything that could result in a man overboard, or a stumble, or even worse – a lost race. Plus, his insurance demanded that the surface area of the entire deck be cleared from obstruction and debris in order that the premiums be kept to a minimum.

But damage limitation didn't come cheap. Yachting didn't come cheap as a hobby. The insurance was hefty even with all the safety checks. The mooring fees were plentiful and if the boom broke or the sails tore, twenty thousand pounds would barely cover the cost of any second-hand replacement.

That was why when Will had suggested they become joint owners of *The Trophy*, Clive had nearly bitten off his right hand. So Will paid his way and the equity was shared fifty-fifty. It made sense all round. One yachtsman alone could not sail a boat – it took a skilled team of people to operate her.

Will was a property developer working in the south of England during the eighties and nineties, moving to the midlands post-millennium – his focus primarily on Birmingham, the next capital outside of London he had heard – he had won tenders for some of the world's largest hotel chains, government buildings, and more recently, his firm had been awarded the contract to rebuild the UK's most exclusive public school which dated back to 1870.

The guy was filthy rich beneath his unkempt exterior but his unbrushed dark-blonde hair and stubbled face provided the suitable financial disguise that Will desired. He hated gold-diggers – heaven knows they saw enough of them at the yacht club – plus he was paying ludicrous amounts of maintenance to his ex-wives. He could spot a money-grabber a mile off and he despised them.

What Will wanted was an equal.

Clive sprang off the boat on to the pontoon which paved the way like a child's puzzle from the marina to the boathouse. He listened to the water slosh beneath as it lapped against its timber structure which was impaled deep into the water bed, underpinned by concrete foundations. He smiled a happy, content smile from the inside out. He was home, this place was where all his troubles dispersed as quickly as the waves broke, pulling back into nothing but calm waters and open seas.

This place gave Clive the clarity to be himself and not some pompous lawyer in the courtroom delivering an Oscar-winning performance filled with lies and exaggerations. But if that's what it took to win then so be it. Winning meant everything to him.

Clive knelt down on both knees, leaning into the boat's exterior to analyse the winter damage to his baby. Beneath the water he could see the endless cockles, urchins and other marine life which had attached themselves to the keel but, bar that, she was in super condition and he couldn't wait to get his hands on her. His knees creaked as he stood up and stretched out his back which was stiff from spending the day with his head bent down, immersed in endless paperwork.

He was pleased with how she looked, delighted in fact. *The Trophy* was only two years old so it was only fair that her condition be superior to many of the older yachts moored at the marina but it didn't give his team any more of a winning edge, given the years of experience many of his fellow yachtsmen had gathered under their belts. Some of them could sail a raft with an old sheet attached to it with winning skill.

The official racing season kicked off after May Day, taking place weekly on both Tuesday and Thursday nights and Clive already had his eyes on the prize trophy for this season – the one he never got his hands on last season.

Clive always wanted *more,* regardless of what the *more* was. He wanted nothing but the best. He had to come first in everything he did and he definitely came first when it came to getting his hands on Jude. But it was still not enough for him. Nothing was ever enough for Clive Westbury even though he had already won. He'd won when he got his hands on the ultimate trophy over fifteen years ago. She was at home.

Jude pored over the contract.

Sophie was right, she had done her no favours in terms of her consistently high standards and demanding timescales, but what Sophie had done for Jude was the biggest favour of her life since the twins had been born. She had offered her the salvation she had been craving for years now. She had created an opportunity for Jude to fill the void which had eaten away at her with carcinogenic speed. But more importantly in Jude's mind, she had shown her that she had listened to her intently, and Sophie was the only person with whom Jude had dared to be truthful. She had been right to place her trust in Sophie Kane.

Sophie knew that Jude rarely opened up the way she did with her and as such when the timing was right for them both, Sophie swore that she would bring her friend back from the dead – like Jesus did to Lazarus – only Sophie knew that she held no higher biblical powers. But what she did hold was the power to resurrect her friend from the soporific life she lived. A life she had lived for everyone else but herself. It was time for her to take a little bit back.

The yacht club was heaving and Clive spotted Will at the bar surrounded by tanned, leggy women. While he was smiling and appeared to be immersed in great company, Clive knew that Will would be grimacing inside and that his act was nothing short of a disguise intended to humour the bimbos surrounding him.

Both of the men knew only too well that most of the models who hung around the place were only after one thing: money, dosh, lolly, whatever you wanted to call it and Will despised that in them. But many of the *older* members liked signing in these stunningly beautiful girls with their fake breasts and peroxide hair. It gave them kudos, took years off them – inwardly at least – and it made them instantly popular with plenty others of the male species who also owned impressive vessels just yards from where they sipped champagne, or Pimm's and lemonade. It gave them sex too. For a premium.

Clive squeezed his way to the bar, stopping to shake hands or offer a peck on the cheek to the people he liked. He was no fool and Clive held little regard for those he didn't feel an instant chemistry with. To those people, he simply nodded. It was all very civil and certainly courteous enough. He and Will played a good game.

"What are you having, mate?" Will thumped his pal on the back with genuine affection.

"I'm in no hurry tonight, Will, and I've dumped the Jag so I'll order a bottle of wine, I think." Clive beamed at Will until his mouth was wide with delight. As wide as it could go. His perfect teeth were recently bleached and he carried an all-year-round pale tan which he had worked on over the years. He wasn't blessed with Jude's olive skin but he tried to maintain a constant glow. In truth, much of it was down to windburn.

Will looked keenly at his friend, noticing that Clive's brown eyes carried something surreptitious. Will waited patiently for his friend to make an announcement. To him, it was obvious that Clive was ready to spill some sort of breaking news. He was still in the fixed grin he had broken into a minute earlier and there was no sign of it budging.

"Well then, Clive? What's the craic?"

"I'm celebrating, mate."

Will raised his eyebrows and then frowned thoughtfully. As he did so, the brows met in the middle where they fell into a deep inset decorated with a mass of tiny blonde hairs. He grinned back at Clive knowingly. "Jude's pregnant!"

"Christ, no! I hope not anyway, mate." Clive shuddered. He had life just where he wanted it. "If she is it's not mine!"

"Nor mine!" Will added as he thought for a moment before slapping his thigh. The penny dropped. His memory wasn't great but he did recall Clive mentioning it to him earlier on in the year. "You got it, didn't you?"

Clive nodded, scanning each side of him warily.

"I did!" He punched the air in an awkward, understated way, conscious that no-one could know until he broke the news to Jude.

Will had no such discretion. "A bottle of Dom Perignon, Mick!" he shouted across the bar to the silver-haired barman who had worked there ever since he could remember. "And one for yourself, mate."

Jude was more nervous than she had been in a long time – and she did know why.

The glass dining table had been washed and dried until it gleamed and Jude had decorated it with a theme of black and deep reds which complemented perfectly the high-backed Italian black-leather chairs and the single wall painted in a deep crimson colour.

The ample dining room opened out onto a huge

orangerie, the two areas separated by sliding glass doors. She stood back to examine the glass table once more. Ever the perfectionist, she ducked her head this way and that way, trying to catch out the remnants of hidden fingerprints from Tom or Anna. They might be fifteen but Anna was still a slob and she loved being waited on hand and foot and, in the name of perverse motherhood, Jude also loved to fulfil Anna's charged expectations although she knew that from now on things would have to change. Anna would need to learn to undertake more domestic chores herself.

Satisfied, Jude scanned the rest of the room taking in the other two walls, noting their opulent, warming blaze of orange. She loved to experiment with paint, applying different shades to different walls, all of which matched harmoniously of course, such was her talent.

Clive had gasped when she told him she wanted to paint the three walls in different colours, a rich blend of crimson red on the main wall, with fiery orange on each of the side walls. He had eventually caved in, allowing her to steer away from his own choice of magnolia. And of course, she had been right. With the sterility of the plain glass and the harshness of the stiff-backed black-leather chairs, the blazing walls were an explosion of colourful heat spilling out an ambience of the natural elements.

The dining room was her favourite room of the house and she was grateful that, since the Curry Club, the room was used at least once every five weeks. Sometimes more, and Jude loved the life which the women had brought to it – each in their own unique way.

She was still not sure about the words read out during

the event she had last hosted. It shouldn't have bothered her. But it did. Still.

The house was luxuriously spacious with every room large enough to host a party, but it was the kitchen and dining room which made Jude the happiest. She was happy when she was entertaining others and giving them whatever she had to give.

It was still cold for April and Jude decided to keep the orangerie doors closed this evening. She wanted intimacy and comfort tonight, and to share the news of her career resurrection with her husband. She couldn't wait to see how proud Clive would be of her.

She chilled a bottle of Muscat Grand Cru 2006, which was given to her by Roni on her last birthday. *'She's probably just pulled it from her own wine rack,'* Sophie had bitched, but Jude was touched that Roni had remembered and that was all that mattered to her.

Jude smirked as she recalled Sophie's catty tone. There was a side to Sophie which she herself thankfully had never been at the receiving end of.

Clive and Will walked along the path to where the taxi was waiting. It was gone eight o'clock and Clive knew not to be late for Jude's cooking. It was too good and with all the excitement of the day he was desperate to see her.

A silver Mercedes waited patiently as the gentlemen climbed in, a little tipsy and giddy with the cheer of good news. News which meant they could trade in *The Trophy* for something bigger and better.

Helena cursed as she panted louder with each step. She

knew she had to give up smoking but, the problem was, it was her only vice and ten times a day for five minutes a go she could switch off and remove herself from her own mundane life.

Weighed down by the load, she muttered about the *crappy* apartment block they lived in where once again the lift was out of order. *Damn it.*

As she reached the fourth floor, panting furiously, Helena kicked at the front door hoping that Nathan would hurry to answer it before the indents of heavy carrier bags in her hands became permanent. She waited patiently, listening for sounds of life, then kicked the already scuffed white paintwork again – only louder and more aggressively.

"It's going cold!" she yelled at the door.

Nathan's face appeared within seconds, carrying a put-out scowl until he saw her laden with food.

"What's this?" His eyes lit up at the sight of carry-out as the cartons of food bulged through the white plastic which was close to splitting.

"*Din-ner, dah-nah, din-ner?*" Helena laughed at her own stupidity as she sang her new song, inhaling the sweet smell which made her salivate instantaneously.

"Indian or Chinese!" Nathan guessed with insatiable excitement.

"Chinese!"

Nathan reached out to Helena and pulled her towards him. For a moment she thought he might kiss her – and he did – on the forehead.

"My Helena." He beamed at her. "This is absolutely brilliant."

He rescued her from the weight and Helena shook

out her hands with relief. She had carried it for the past fifteen minutes and she hoped it was still warm enough to eat without reheating it. Nothing ever tasted the same reheated.

She thought about how long it had been since herself and Nathan had eaten anything that wasn't marked down with an ugly yellow label and an insulting barcode and would be thrown to the dogs if people like themselves didn't buy it. But it was all they could afford and Helena was momentarily proud of how she had pleased Nathan. No matter how shortlived it might be.

Jude stood back and took a last look at her reflection in the cheval mirror which was angled to perfection in the corner of the huge sweeping bedroom. A hanging rail attached to the rear of it carried an arrangement of outfits selected for the evening and underneath it was a drawer packed with cosmetics and dozens of closed boxes. Jude was a neat freak to the point where much of her make-up was housed in compartmentalised boxes, labelled and as neat on the inside as on the outside. Jude loved boxes and anything trinket-like, but there had to be something special about them to win a place in her stylised home. The only make-up or cosmetics she allowed to sit loosely in the drawer were the things she needed to get at fast: her moisturiser, her deodorant, her naturally shaded lip-gloss, her Clinique mascara and her rose-coloured blusher which tinted her tanned cheeks whenever she felt they needed a little lifting.

Jude edged closer to the mirror, checking out her eyes – too subtle. Pulling out a silk-covered lilac box from the open drawer, Jude opened it, selecting just one eye shadow from the guts of one hundred, her hand making a direct beeline for a small round container – her MAC eyeshadow – which was by far her favourite. Its smoky grey shades set off her colouring to perfection and enhanced her stunningly green eyes and even *she* felt sexy in it.

With her olive skin and regal looks, Jude needed little make-up bar a touch of mascara and a double dose of Mother Pucker Lip Plumper which always made her giggle when she read its label. Her mother had once asked her what she was wearing because Jude's lipstick had made Hattie's lips tingle. Jude knew she could not tell her and so she lied to her. Not a big lie but a small white lie. There was absolutely no way Jude could say the words *mother-pucker* to her mother without being sent to her bedroom, even at thirty-nine years of age.

Tonight she wanted to remember what it felt like to dress up like she was actually going to work, to apply her make-up to perfection and to select her outfit with such regard that she became her own immediate business card. Jude Westbury was back and open for business and in her mind's eye she had already become the creator of 'Westbury Interior Design'.

Jude, for the first time in as long as she could remember, was excited about the rest of her life and more than excited about sharing her joyous news with Clive.

Helena opened the button of her navy work trousers. The material was bobbled and pulled from careless activities and although she possessed two identical pairs, Helena wore only the one pair for work. The other pair she kept in her wardrobe, new and pristine in case she ever needed to look smart for forthcoming interviews – preferably relative to her academic qualifications.

She heaved a sigh of relief as her stomach escaped from the pressures of the waistband. She wasn't used to the waistband touching her waist, it was usually slung around her skinny hips but she had been unable to stop eating tonight, greedily devouring the Asian feast until her stomach bulged and she felt content yet gorged at the same time.

Nathan let out a roaring, lengthy belch and Helena stared at him in disgust.

"That was revolting."

Nathan, as usual, displayed no embarrassment. "Better out than in I say."

Helena chose not to continue the conversation. She could never win and she had long given up trying.

The remnants of Chinese food sat on the chipped walnut coffee table. Its sticky sauce had spilled over the foil cartons onto the scuffed wood where it had set like gelatine.

Helena cast her eyes over the food, already sick of the sight of it, but she was determined to put on a little weight. She probably had in the past half hour, she reckoned. She was far too skinny, but hey, that was what empty pockets did for you. Her salary came in and went out on the same day every month by the time she had paid for the rent, rates, water, gas, electricity, car insurance and petrol, and what little was left went into the food jar. The fuel for their bodies was ranked bottom of the list. Second to the roof over their heads.

"Where did you get the money from, Hel, to pay for the Chinese?" Nathan asked without actually looking at her. He continued his focus on *University Challenge*.

"I got a bonus at work. We had a sales campaign where we had to sell income-protection policies and I sold the most."

Nathan looked at her for the first time since he kissed her at the front door. He slid his hand towards hers with genuine affection and the hairs on Helena's arms stood to attention. She hadn't seen that loving expression for far too long. She leaned towards him, mirroring his devoted gaze and as his hand squeezed hers, she parted her lips in preparation for a kiss.

Nathan used his free hand to ruffle her hair, oblivious to the fact that the woman who sat next to him was yearning for his attention. But that was as romantic as Nathan got these days and Helena was affronted as she snapped her mouth shut. More so, she felt humiliated.

"Oh, Helena, my Helena! If only you could get more bonuses at work you would able to buy me more time to perfect this board game. I'm nearly there, H, I'm on to something big here. This could be the next *Deal or No Deal*." He paused. "Hey, is there any money left from your bonus? We could go to the pub if there is!"

"It's going in the food jar, Nathan," she told him sternly. "For next week's food and even the week after if we manage it well enough."

"Fine," he answered sulkily.

Nathan turned back to watch the television, leaving an abashed Helena to fix her tousled hair. She had felt like a dog being patted by its owner for good behaviour and now he had the audacity to ask for more time! The pressure was becoming too much for her. She had held Nathan's career in her hands for long enough now and more time meant more money. Something neither of them had.

Helena's heart fluttered and her stomach churned, making her feel nauseous and dizzy after all the food she had gorged on. She couldn't cope with it all, there was only one of her. Why should she be the one to carry his burdens both emotionally and financially? No, she couldn't cope with it.

But the more she thought about how impossible life was about to become, the harder it appeared Nathan's grip had become on her bony hand. It was as though he could read her every thought.

Helena excused herself and hurried to the bathroom. The place was filthy, awash with Nathan's hairs which were embedded on the bottom of the bath. The toothpaste he had so obviously spat out that morning had dried into a pulp as it slid towards the plughole and his towel was left in a collapsed heap on the floor. Nathan Bream was a lazy slob.

Helena splashed her face with ice-cold water and stared at herself in the mirror. She had once felt beautiful, been beautiful in fact, but now she was dangerously thin with sunken cheekbones and her teeth had yellowed from excessive cigarettes – most of them bummed from other people – her colleagues, strangers in a night club. Anyone.

What she had done today was the only secret she had ever kept from Nathan bar her smoking. He knew everything else about her and if he could smell smoke on her, he had never said. She was surprised that he didn't spot it.

Helena tried to erase her mind of thought. Nathan need simply stare at her and she could feel him absorb the information which was stored in her brain, allowing it to transfer to his through a form of telepathy which only he could control. He had only to look at her and she spilled out the truth in unspoken words but she certainly had no idea what was going on in his head.

Well, she thought, as a fire welled inside her, he didn't know what she had done today and he wouldn't *ever* get to know. No-one would.

But one thing she was sure of: she would never do it again. Ever.

9

Jude heard the front door open and rushed down the long walkway towards the front of the house. As she did her floaty black dress swooshed around her knees and a single satin strap fell off her right shoulder.

Clive took off his jacket and loosened his silk tie, undoing his top button. He looked like a rebellious schoolboy and Jude grinned at how youthfully handsome he was.

"Something smells gorgeous. I'm starving." Clive reached out to grab the picturesque sight in front of him. He nuzzled into her neck, kissing it passionately. "It's you – *you* smell gorgeous," he told his wife with sincerity. "How come you're so dressed up, Jude?"

Smiling, she swung around and walked away, without answering. He followed her into the open-plan kitchen through the extensive hallway where the walls were covered with framed photographs, mainly of Tom and Anna, from birth upwards. The montage told a story in chronological order giving a visual history of their elite lives.

As Clive caught up on his wife's determined stride, he took in her perfect back, arched and tanned. Her waist was tiny, her hips narrow and Jude had legs which went on to infinity. Clive felt a horniness arise in him. This girl was so perfect and she was all his. His trophy wife.

"I'm cooking a romantic dinner," Jude beamed, keen to play it down until the time was right to break the news, but she had to take deep breaths to avoid blurting it out. "We've got the house to ourselves for once and we hardly ever get to talk without interruption of '*Mum, have you seen my tennis racquet?*' or '*Mum, where are my riding boots?*'!" She chuckled although the chuckle dispersed into an immediate sadness as she thought of the empty beds upstairs. She suddenly felt the quietness of the house wrap itself around her slender frame, chilling her skin until she remembered. She remembered that her life was about to begin all over again just as it had been before the twins came along and yes, her heart ached that she might not be able to indulge her children with the same devotion as before, but she knew they would understand. She had given up her life as she knew it for them and to please Clive and her mother, but now it was her turn and even though it pained her to admit it, she was taking something for herself. She was so almost back in the game and Jude had never felt so alive and so injected with euphoria that she could not only help one of her closest friends but, in doing so, that she could and would be awakened and restored.

At least she hoped that would be the case. Somewhere deep down, Jude couldn't help wondering whether she still had it. Whatever the *it* was. Had she lost her ability and capability over the past fifteen years? Better still, did she have the confidence to go out to work after years of domesticity and motherhood? But her worst fear of all was whether she had the ability to deliver.

She had never been arrogant in her work and she was her own worst critic – disregarding completely the skill it had taken to produce her own opulent home which was a designer prototype – but for her there was always something she could have done better. She had always felt that way, such was her unassuming nature.

Jude bit her lip hard as she tried to eradicate the doubts which were eating away at her. Surely it must be like riding a bike? She was only forty for heaven's sake – not even that – but fifteen years away from an ever-changing industry was a long time.

"How was sailing?"

"Great, thanks, darling. We didn't take the boat out though. She still needs a bit of work but we're lifting her out of the water this Sunday to clean her up. She's in desperate need of a good anti-foul treatment."

Clive opened the stainless-steel fridge and pulled out a wine bottle. His face lit up when he saw Jude's choice and he held it up to her. "Muscat? Do you know this is nearly thirty quid a bottle, Jude?"

Jude's heart thumped through her chest. The wine matched the occasion and she could wait no longer. She was about to deliver a single line of news which she had hoped to deliver years before.

"We're celebrating!"

"We are indeed celebrating, my little princess."

"You've heard?" Jude was puzzled.

"I have. I heard today!" Clive burst out.

"You don't mind then?"

Clive picked up his wife and swung her around the kitchen. "Mind, darling, how could I mind? I've been made partner, Jude, the youngest ever partner of Staines & Greer!" He set her firmly on the floor and threw his fist towards the ceiling. "What is there to mind about being the *youngest ever* partner of the oldest and most established law firm in Northern England?"

Clive was ecstatic. Elation seeped from his every pore but, wrapped up in his own delight, he failed to notice that a light had died in his wife's eyes right before him.

He pushed his hair back from his face before opening the wine with a Lever Model Corkscrew which was firmly attached to the edge of the granite work surface. Another celebratory *pop*. He poured the wine into the crystal glasses Jude had left so perfectly arranged next to the fridge. He took a large gulp and sloshed it around his mouth before swallowing it with obvious gratification.

"It means I'm going to have to put in a few more hours here and there but you can hold the fort here, can't you, darling?"

Clive stood still in his own wonderment for a moment before setting his glass on the speckled worktop. He moved closer to Jude, put his arms around her neat waist and kissed her hard on the lips. "Sorry, darling," he went on. "That was patronising of me. I didn't mean for it to come out like that. Of course you can hold the fort – that's what you do best, isn't it?" He took her hand and kissed it. "You know, Jude. I don't know how I would cope if I didn't have you. You're my rock. You hold this place together, you are the life and soul of our beautiful house – home, I should say – and I for one wouldn't have it any other way, my lovely."

Sophie waved her hands at the smoke wafting towards her as she stood outside the popular wine bar, trying to get a signal on her mobile phone. *Damn those smokers.* She moved away from the carcinogenic fumes as she fought to get reception. She was desperate to hear from Jude to see how Clive had taken the news. Jude often said they were alike, herself and Clive, but Sophie couldn't see it. To her it was no compliment.

She wobbled in her zebra-skin heels as she tried Jude again.

At five-foot-four she was in need of a little elevation but she had been drinking since five o'clock and was definitely a little worse for wear, and the four inches stuck to the end of each foot certainly weren't helping her balance.

Sophie gave in and sent Jude a text. She didn't want to interrupt her in case she was still celebrating – in the kitchen or the bedroom. If she wasn't answering, it meant she was otherwise occupied.

Can't wait 2 hear from u. Fone me ltr. Sofi X

Sophie shuddered in the cold air. The blackened sky had brought with it a tinge of frost and the warmer climate of the past week had fast dispersed. Still, at least the torrential downpour of the other day had passed. She regretted not bringing her jacket outside as she stood shivering.

Sophie looked on as one of the smokers flicked his cigarette-butt on the floor without a care, puffing out the last of the smoke from deep within his polluted lungs.

She hated littering but she hated smokers more. Them and their anti-social habits. It was better now that they were banned from smoking in public places but did they have to stand at the exit and entrance of every public building just to make their point? Sophie was adamant that this was a political stance, in rebellion against being outcasts.

"You know there's a cigarette bin on that wall behind you!" she snapped at the culprit in disgust as she flipped her phone shut.

No older than his early twenties, the young man bent down to retrieve his litter and threw it in the walled bin close to the entrance of the bar. He turned to Sophie, grinning.

"Anyone else and I'd have told them to fuck off." He scanned her from head to foot. "But you, you can tell me what to do any day, gorgeous."

Sophie smiled sweetly at him, a full-on flirtatious smile. "Come back when you're twenty-one, kid."

A belt of raucous laughter filled the starlit sky as his friends jeered at him. "Loser! Loser!" they yelled in unison through chilled breaths which floated away like ghostly apparitions.

Sophie felt the warmth of his scarlet face as she brushed past him and the taunting gang, fully aware that they were watching her confident swagger. She was glad she had tanned and oiled her legs. The fake-fur black-and-white animal-print skirt rode up further with each pace and Sophie made no attempt to pull it down. She knew full well that there wasn't a guy amongst them who wouldn't have bedded her there and then – if they had the chance.

She smiled a knowing smile before re-entering the affluent wine bar to join the salon employees as they celebrated Mandy's twenty-first birthday and her graduation from the Academy.

Jude sat alone in the kitchen sipping slowly on a gin and tonic. She had no school run to do in the morning and she needed a little time to gather her thoughts and to digest the full-on occurrences of the evening.

Through closed lips, a tiny sound escaped and she delivered a half laugh as she reminisced on the collision of events. It was like the buses, she thought – everything had come at once.

Jude was delighted for Clive. She knew how long he had wanted to be a partner at the firm and she knew how hard he had worked to achieve it. Of course, she was by his side every step of the way, supporting him and entertaining the senior partners with elegant cooking and faultless hostessing. She was the strong woman behind the successful man. He knew that.

Jude knew the coming months would be tough for them and that the twins would have to learn to become more independent, and this worried her in itself but it was a worry she would have to contend with because her life was about to begin – on the right side of forty.

Grabbing her iPhone, she replied to Sophie's earlier text, knowing full well that Sophie's impatience would be getting the better of her.

All gr8 here thx Sofi. Clive delighted. Loads 2 tell u 2m. Jude. PS I can nevr thnk u enuf. PPS whoever HE is stay safe won't u!

The dimly lit hallway was awash with shoes messily

placed and a pile of coats had been thrown on top of each other, hanging clumsily over the white glossed bannisters. The worn carpet was green with an eighties paisley design and it was long overdue a replacement by the looks of things. In fact, the entire place was in need of a good tidy and a damn good clean.

Sophie didn't fail to notice the basic surroundings as she continued with her tongue bath, attacking her latest victim with a soft, pink lashing.

A dog barked from behind one of the cheap wooden doors with their scratched brass handles and Sophie broke free from her oral embrace.

"I hate dogs." She looked around anxiously to see which door the sound came through.

Her victim ignored her, pulling her protectively close where he kissed her open neck with heavy and lustful kisses.

"Me too," he continued breathlessly, "but I love pussies!"

Sophie half laughed, half groaned as he yanked at the zip on the side of her black bustier. Losing patience, his hands plunged down its front and returned with her breasts which he left to sit high, spilling out of her top, but held firmly in place by the strong bones of the bustier design.

Sophie looked down to see her breasts so close to her. She tried to reach down with her mouth but couldn't, instead she flicked out her tongue with an impressive aim and it landed centrally on her hard brown nipple. She circled it around the areola before pressing the tip hard into its centre.

Her one-night stand watched in awe, yanking at the

belt of his jeans. He thrust them down past his knees, allowing his manly erection to break free and, grabbing Sophie's hand, placed it around its base with its impressive width. Sophie's hand slipped lower and felt his rock-hard balls.

She fell to her knees, her mouth wide open, and took them in her mouth, sucking at them with lascivious desire before reaching up and taking the whole of his cock deep within her oral grasp. He groaned loudly, drowing out the barking dog and all other sounds until he climaxed with a thunderous shudder which shushed the dog into silent retreat.

Sophie wiped her mouth and pulled up her skirt. She sat on the bottom stair, hitching it up further until her neatly shaven pussy was displayed and accessible – her legs slightly parted.

"My turn now, kid."

She watched the smoker's eyes light up before he plunged down on her as though it were his last supper.

10

Donna Summer belted out her song through the bedroom speakers.

"Hot stuff, talkin' 'bout hot stuff."

"Yeah!" Roni yelled out in time to the music.

She loved Donna Summer and knew every word to each and every one of her songs. It whiled away the hours as she immersed herself in the clear-out of the century.

Roni sat, singing away, amongst piles of clothing, alone and performing to an imaginary audience. She belted out the words with remarkable cheer as she flung items this way and that way forming two deep, messy piles.

"Charity shop," she muttered as she hurled a floral Laura Ashley number into the corner of the walk-in closet. The item still had its label on.

"Dry cleaning," she cursed as she spotted a red-wine stain on her cream woollen A-line skirt.

She stood up, stretching, arching her back with discomfort, and headed back towards the rails. She pulled apart the hanging clothes with conviction, ignoring the screech of the metal hangers as they scraped angrily across the steel bar. They hadn't been disturbed in years and they made no attempt to hide their dissatisfaction. She handled them roughly.

Roni continued with her quest to cleanse her soul. She yanked garments from their hangers, pulling at their necklines until they fell reluctantly – either that or by dragging them off their hangers by their hems – they didn't stand a chance against the force of her determined strength. However she did it, Roni knew exactly where each item was headed for. Charity shop, dry cleaning or recycling. Out with the old, in with the new.

That went for herself too.

Her white towelling dressing-gown gaped open, exposing her white flesh and large sagging breasts. Her full white calfs were in desperate need of shaving and Roni had yet to experience the pleasure of bikini-waxing. Veronica Smyth had always liked the French way, au naturel, and Peter had never complained.

Bored with the railed garments, Roni turned her focus towards the floor-to-ceiling solid walnut shelves where she chose a single shelf at random, sweeping its entire contents to the floor with a graceful swipe. She watched as they fell with a soft thud at her feet. Once again, she flung items every which way, whistling to the tune of 'Bad Girls'.

Sophie Kane was definitely a bad girl.

Roni stopped dead as she saw the swimsuit – the recent gift Peter had purchased for her – but this time around she ignored the exorbitant price tag. She had other things on her mind. She held its lycra against her round torso with one hand, pulling down the gusset with the other hand. It was going to be tight but it should fit. Just about. She had yet to try it on.

Roni stood back for further inspection, holding the exquisite garment by its thin diamante straps, taking in its splendour with its ruched bustier decorated in the centre with a large diamante brooch. She marvelled at the high-legged cut and held it against herself once more. The legs were so highly cut that Roni wondered why bother with the infinitesimal slice of crotch-material which appeared to be sewn in at the last minute, offering a little piece of decency, but only just.

Slowly, she dropped the bathing suit to the floor and dared to go where neither she nor Peter had been for a long time. She pulled open the tapes to her dressing-gown exposing her naked body and bent down to study the mass of hair on her pubic region.

Roni bolted upright. That would never do. One of them had to go. It was a toss-up between the mass of dark overgrown hairs which had spread right across her curved thighs, thick and untamed, or the swimsuit. There was no room for both of them in her life.

Roni laughed loudly at the ridiculousness of her thoughts. Then she laughed at herself for laughing. How uncharacteristic that she should even be considering change of any description, from clearing out her clothes to considering the possibility of hair removal. She had loved her organic look, but she knew that if she wanted that sexy black number wrapped around her body, the hair had to go.

She cast her mind back to the last encounter with Peter, groaning with lust as she relived the moment she had allowed herself to be animalistic and unleashed. She smiled to herself. She loved Peter with all her heart and she only ever wanted to be with him but there was something about that encounter she'd had with Darren Ford, something which had lifted her from the lazy state she had been in for too long now. Roni knew at that moment, when she had climaxed, it was because she was thinking about *him* when it was Peter that was inside her. She also knew that since that powerful orgasm, she walked with a spring in her step and she felt a newness towards life. Roni made a firm decision there and then that faking it was firmly in the past.

Before, she had always thought that sex was hyped-up, overrated. She felt very differently now and for a split second she envied the pleasure she knew Sophie must be experiencing with regularity.

A '*bad girl*' indeed.

Something had stirred within Roni and while she was unable to define it exactly, she knew that she liked it and that she wanted more of the same. Her problem was that she'd been an antisocial, ill-tempered prude for as long as she could remember and she wasn't sure she knew how to be anything else.

Perhaps she could confide in the Curry Club? Surely they would have all the answers?

Karl stood at the window of his bedsit and watched the orange flicker of the streetlight as it danced away defectively, ill-timed and flashing on a violent high. This normally bothered him as he tried to sleep. It illuminated his room and then darkened it, imitating the actions of an outdoor rave, forcing him awake to join in the street party and he submitted more often than not. But tonight, as he stared distractedly out at the street – empty but for the flash of orange glow – he had only one thing on his mind. Sophie Kane.

Karl checked his phone once more. Still no text from Sophie. He had rung and texted her at least half a dozen times but still no reply.

He too had drunk in abundance but, hard as he tried, he couldn't quite recall the moment Sophie had left the bar. Nor who with.

She could be lying dead somewhere.

Karl panicked at the thought of her being hurt or in some sort of trouble but he quickly overcame it with his own summation. Sophie was not soft. She was shrewd and streetwise, plus she threw a mean right hook.

He closed over the curtains to his open-plan bedsit, succumbing to tiredness.

The streetlight continued its all-night affair but he was too tired to do anything but sleep. He sank under the dark throw which was covered in a mass of yellow stars, placing his mobile phone carefully to the side of his pillow. He stared at the ceiling until his eyes began to blink, fast at first and then slowing down until he blinked no more.

He would have to stop worrying about Sophie – that was his last thought before the night carried him with it into total blackout.

Sophie turned the key to the right once and then to the left in an anti-clockwise circle before pressing the button to lift the shutter, exposing what was very soon to be the new Kane'n'Able hair salon on Alderley Avenue. She gloated as she did her sums – all of which added to a massive *ker-ching!*

Alderley Avenue was one of the most affluent streets in one of the richest areas of the entire country and even she wasn't quite sure how she'd managed it, but she had bagged an empty unit, swiped from beneath the feet of all those on the waiting list.

And she didn't have to sleep with him to get it.

As she closed the Georgian front door behind her, Sophie turned to be greeted with a cloud of dust and a thick blinding smog.

She knew that Jude had her work cut out – the place was a mess – but she also knew that a girl like her would breeze through the project, lapping up every last moment of it.

Sophie wondered how Jude had got on with Clive last night. She had received her text but it was the *finer* details she wanted, like how Clive had got on with Jude in terms of how he took the news. Much as her impatience willed her to call her friend, she knew that as soon as Jude was ready to dish the dirt, she'd be the first to know.

Sophie skitted from room to room downstairs. There were five rooms in total and each room was partitioned by a solid brick wall. Structurally, there was so much to do, in order to transform the place into an open-plan state-of-the-art salon, that Sophie took a deep breath for her friend in anticipation of the stress to come.

Sophie Kane was a businesswoman through and through, but what she wasn't was a project-planner. That's what she paid other people to do while she herself had built her business on relationships and on impeccable high fashion cuts and colours with an unrivalled level of service which she knew, with understated arrogance, was her signature.

Her feet trudged through the ground refuse, kicking dry particles in the air with each small step. She put her hand over her mouth, which was already dry as a bone from the amount of alcohol consumed the night before and, coughing violently, quickly scarpered to the green front door which she yanked open, throwing herself outside, desperate for air. She coughed relentlessly.

"Sophie!"

Sophie continued to wheeze, bent double until her eyes streamed and she retched with each inhale.

She had seen Jude racing towards her but could do nothing but gasp for breath. Next time she would wear a mouth mask.

Jude rubbed her friend's back as tenderley as rubbing a new baby with traped wind until she was sure that her recovery was complete. She grabbed a bottle of Perrier from her bag, removing the lid, wiping the top before holding it close to Sophie's lips.

"Take this."

"Uuughh . . ." Sophie laughed a gritty, congested laugh. "I think the next time I go in there, Jude, it will be on the night of the opening party." Her voice was hoarse as she handed the green glass bottle back. "Thanks a million. That's better."

Jude smiled fondly. "Where's your inhaler, Sophie? Aren't you supposed to carry it around with you?"

Sophie retrieved a packet of tissues from her Coccomatto cappuccino-coloured bag. She blew her nose, dabbing her eyes with a clean corner of the tissue before throwing it back into the bag Tardis which held everything but the kitchen sink.

"I don't want to rely on it, Jude, to be honest – and

anyway I'm not convinced it really is asthma – I'm just not very good with dust." She blew her nose. "Sure, these days you forget something and they say you've got Alzheimer's. You clean a lot and you've got OCD. Poo a lot and you've got IBS. It's pathetic!"

Jude laughed loudly. Sophie made her laugh like no-one else. She adored her frankness and her ability to make light of something serious.

Sophie pulled the door to a close, locked it and turned to Jude. "This *has* to go." She pointed at the flakes of green paint and rattled the brass handle, her face twisted with disgust. She cast her eyes up and down the rest of the avenue. "Any wonder the estate agent put a shutter on this unit. At first I wondered why on earth you'd need a security shutter on Alderley Avenue – nothing ever happens here – there's virtually no crime." She winced as she stood back, looking hard at the shop unit. "But now I know – it's to hide the ugliness of this shop compared with the retro-modernity of the other shops surrounding it."

Jude beamed at Sophie. "Well put, Ms Kane – I couldn't have put it better myself! Anyway – not for long. Let me loose in there and I'll have the place ready for the end of August – providing there's no dry rot, environmental issues or anything else which crawls out from under the woodwork, that is."

"You've just listed all my worst nightmares!"

Sophie stood on her tiptoes and reached up to hug Jude. Jude was wearing boots with a thick wedged heel and Sophie felt like a dwarf beneath her.

"Thanks, Jude. Thanks for agreeing to work with me on this. I need you to keep telling me it is possible to turn this place around because when I look at it all I see is a load of shit and no place for it to go. I wouldn't know where the bloody hell to start in there. Anyway, enough of me! Tell me, how did Clive take the news?"

Jude stared into the empty shop with longing. "He was fine about it actually. Pleased in fact." She snapped out of her creative moment and turned to Sophie. "He was made partner yesterday, Sophie, isn't that amazing?"

"Wow, it was definitely a night for celebrations in your house, wasn't it! I wish I'd been there."

"It was indeed," Jude answered. "He is officially the youngest ever partner of Staines & Greer. I'm so proud of him, Sophie."

Sophie wasn't suprised. Clive had always been a go-getter. Once he had something in his grasp he went for it, head down, horns locked and if he had to take a man down in the process, then so be it.

"Well, tell him I said congratulations, won't you? A dual celebration," Sophie said thoughtfully. "How will you guys cope with the domestic situation when the pair of you are working, Jude?"

"I've got my mum, she's brilliant, plus the kids are coming up sixteen, Sophie, and it's about time they learned to carry out a few domestic chores themselves."

Sophie scoffed. "Princess Anna will love that."

Jude broke into a smile. There were many things Anna loved to do but housework was not one of them.

Helena handed over the rest of the fare in copper. She had raided her money box to buy a packet of ten cigarettes, and even though she felt quilty for dipping into their emergency rent fund the burst of relief was worth the feelings of guilt. She needed some escape for five minutes every hour from the awful place she worked in. It kept her there for eight hours every day, plus overtime which she grabbed at every opportunity, given her work bonus hadn't lasted too long.

Helena thought about the Curry Club the following night at Sophie's waterfront apartment, which meant that she was to host it the week after that. In turn, that meant two things for Helena. Firstly, she would have to get rid of Nathan for the evening, and secondly, she would have to magic up some money to put on a good spread like the rest of them did week in week out. She knew that her culinary offerings ranked bottom compared with the capabilities of the others, but she also knew that the women didn't care about what she gave them and that they appreciated the thought which she put into the evening whenever it was her turn. And thoughtful she was. As much as she could be without money.

Back at her desk, Helena lifted the handset to her personal extension which had begun to ring out.

"Good morning. Northern Direct, Helena Wright speaking," she sang cheerily down the receiver, her eyes and her voice in paradoxical contrast.

"Helena, it's Maggie here. The queue is out the door again. Can you open your float just until it goes down, please."

"No problem!" Helena replied as cheerily as she had answered the initial call.

However much she hated the job, she needed the money so it was a no-brainer for her in terms of how she acted.

She preferred her role of Personal Banker as opposed to the role of helping out as a glorified 'cashier' which she did whenever the banking hall was busy. She had a first class honours degree in Psychology for God's sake! Counting money and handing it out really wasn't the challenge she was looking for.

Jumping from her seat, Helena stood for a moment, unable to move. Her head spun like a merry-go-round and her knees buckled. Her vision was blurred and for a moment she thought she might faint. She sat down, lowering her head towards her legs, allowing the blood to flow to her brain.

To passers-by, it looked like she was simply digging deep into the drawer to the right of her where all the bank's pre-printed application forms were neatly organised in green hanging files. But she knew the truth behind how and why she felt so weak.

Helena waited until the feelings had passed before standing up again. Slowly.

She made her way to the queue, seeking out those she thought might have difficulty standing in line for too long, regardless of how many people were in front of them or how long they had waited. Young as she was, sometimes she felt like one of those people, frail and weak and in need of a little added attention.

She would eat something soon, she promised herself.

"Where did you get to last night?"

Sophie turned to Karl haughtily. "What are you – my mother all of a sudden? What's it got to do with you?"

Karl swallowed hard. He knew Sophie hated his gentle ways, particularly how much he worried about her, but one of these days she was going find herself knee-deep in shit and this genuinely concerned him.

"You never even said goodbye, Sophie, or told anyone you were leaving. Even Mandy was scouring the place looking for you . . . we're supposed to stick together when we're out . . . you know that."

"When the horn kicks in, Karl, you just have to go with it." Sophie grabbed the black towels from the tumble-dryer. She held them against herself, stealing their heat and letting it penetrate her skin.

Karl set down his coffee and began to help Sophie fold the towels with symmetrical perfection. Everything Karl did was neat.

"Karl, you're on your break." Sophie's tone was warm and soothing. "Sit down and relax, I'll do these."

"So who was it last night? I didn't even see you talking to anyone – that's what was so suprising when we realised you'd gone awol."

He sat down, picking up his coffee mug, holding it in both hands. His grey eyes watched his boss intently.

Sophie stopped what she was doing and laughed loudly. In contrast, her sea-blue eyes carried a wicked expression and Karl knew from that look that she had dominated the poor sod whoever he was.

"You know, there's something to be said for younger men. True, they might not have all the experience of an older man, but by God they're willing to learn!" She grabbed another armful from the tumble-dryer, repeating the folding action, whipping the black towels into perfect squares. "I wouldn't fancy getting too close to that poor fella today though." She grinned. "His breath must stink."

Karl tutted with genuine revulsion and Sophie couldn't fail to notice the disgusted look on his face.

"What?" she barked at him. "Would you prefer I take it up the bum like you?"

Karl slammed down his mug and stormed out of the staff-room-cum-laundry-room. He was furious. He was not gay, damn it! But for some unknown reason Sophie Kane had decided that he was and she flung it in his face regularly.

But Karl had never actually told her he *wasn't* gay. He shouldn't have to and it had become a point of principle. He was as heterosexual as the next man and he only had eyes for one woman.

II

Kath dressed at breakneck speed. She had taken on an extra class at the last minute and now she didn't want to be late for Sophie's night.

Sophie always threw such a great party that Kath hated to miss even a minute of it.

She hurriedly got herself into a dark-brown layered skirt, lightweight and flowy, pulling it over her hips, yanking up the side zip. Standing back, looking at the clothes in her side of the wardrobe, she mulled over what else to wear. There were no more than a couple of dozen garments hanging there and those, in addition to some drawered items, were the height of Kath's materialistic worth – in terms of clothing at least. She had no need for an abudance of items like Roni nor hundreds of pairs of shoes like Sophie. She preferred life plain and simple. *'You come in with nothing and you go out with nothing.'* She used this philisophy with consistency. She believed it.

James popped his head around the door, hoping to catch his wife and her toned body on display.

"Shucks!" he teased. "You're quick tonight – you've only just got out of the shower." He edged closer to Kath, squeezing past the double bed which devoured the small bedroom, leaving little room for much else. "I was hoping to catch you without your bra on at least."

Kath shook her head. He was like a dog on heat and she knew if they were both together more, he'd inisist they did it three times a day not three times a week. They were a perfect match.

"Help me with this zip, will you, love?"

Kath pulled a brush through her wild curly hair as James carefully zipped the back of her cream fitted top which had green and red flowers and plunged at the front. It nipped in at her waist and he wondered at the firmness of her breasts even after breast-feeding his two children.

"Don't even go there! I'm late already," Kath warned him. She knew that look.

"What?" James gawped innocently, only they both knew his thoughts were far from innocent.

Kath's fitness clothes had been flung across the room where they had landed on various parts of the carpeted floor or the limited furniture. Her white sports bra had landed on the windowsill for all the neighbours to see. Her lycra fitness pants and fleece were strewn across the bed and her gym socks had been thrown and left where they landed – on the bedside table.

James set about picking up after his wife. He never minded. Housework was not her thing, but he couldn't fault her and there was nothing he would have changed about his perfect wife. She was a wonderful wife and an incredible mother.

Kath had been adopted at the age of eight by the family that had fostered her since she was two. In the end, the Smithsons just couldn't let her go, so solid were the foundations they had built during their happy six years together. The child was vibrant, full of life and full of love and she had proved that she was too much to sacrifice. They made her a permanent and legal addition to their family.

She never knew her real parents but she had been told that they were a waste of space, and that, whoever they were, they couldn't afford to keep her. Apparently it was more a pragmatic decision based on the limitations their lives offered than simply not wanting her and Kath had forgiven them for it with ease.

A loud honk sounded and James knelt on the bed, allowing himself an elevated view of the street below where he saw the blue Ford Mondeo taxi with its yellow luminous sign.

"Ready, love?"

"Almost." Kath dusted her cheeks with blusher and swiped her eyes with a simple coat of pearlescent eyeshadow. She would have to do. She turned to James, squealing as she roughly stabbed her ear with the sharp metal of the earring, missing the hole in her haste. "Ouch!" she yelled, rubbing her earlobe. "Jim, can you get me twenty quid from under the mattress, please, love?"

James lifted the corner of the light mattress. He set it down again, moving to the other corner until he had lifted all four corners.

"There's nothing there, Kath. You must have put it somewhere else, babe."

Kath grabbed her cheesecloth fairtrade bag, shoving her belongings into it. She flung it over her shoulder and lifted the bottom right-hand corner of the mattress. Her face paled and she felt a wave of bile attack the back of her throat.

"It must be there . . . I saw it only yesterday."

But they both knew that the money had gone. This had happened too many times before.

At first they had thought they were going mad, but then came the harsh reality that someone was taking what wasn't theirs to take.

"James, I can't cope with this much longer." Kath bit her bottom lip to fight the overwhelming emotion which was threatening to escape and to consume her – ruining her night. She fell into his arms, burying her head deep into his neck. She felt safe there.

He smelled of diesel.

"We're going to have to do something, Kath. He'll send us into an early grave if he carries on like this. If we doubt ourselves any more we'll be in padded cells next to each other."

Kath lifted up her head as the taxi sounded its horn in three consecutive short blasts, each appearing more impatient than the last.

"I'm scared, Jim," she whispered, clutching his hand. "Scared of losing a son and ending up in a rerun of what happened to you all those years ago . . . because I'm not sure how much longer I can cope with this."

James took his wife's hand and together they headed down the biscuit-coloured stairs and into the porch with its icy-cold tiled floor and fake pampas grasses.

"Nothing that kid does will *ever* make our family

113

relinquish him. I had it done to me and I know what it feels like." James' eyes narrowed and his lips tensed. "You never get over it and no matter what he's done, or he does, Kath, we'll get through it . . . but there's going be some tough measures put in place starting from now."

"I don't mean 'lose' as in turn our back on him – I mean lose as in watch the bond we've worked so hard to keep tight start fraying at the seams . . . it's happening already. *We're* losing the boy that he once was."

James shoved his wife out of the porch door with loving force and kissed the back of her head. "Get out of here and enjoy yourself," he told her, brave-faced, "and if you still remember my name when you come in I'll be disappointed in you."

As he closed the door behind her, his beautiful wife, his mind drifted back to the day his mother had told him he might as well be dead. He had visited her after hearing Kath's account of the hospital saga and she had told him exactly the same thing. Not that he didn't believe his wife but he simply couldn't account for the sudden loathing his mother seemed to feel towards him. It came from nowhere. *'You are dead as far as I am concerned.'* It was true. He heard it with his own ears. And for what reason? He had done nothing but fall in love with a girl, and she him.

James swore that no matter what his sons ever did to him, they'd always be welcomed as part of his family. No son of his would ever be made to feel like an outsider by their own flesh and blood, not while they carried his DNA.

James knew that the situation with Jason needed to be handled and handle it he would. But not like

114

Elizabeth did. Jason needed extra attention to get to the root of his trouble. Turning his back on him would solve absolutely nothing.

Helena leaned forward in the black taxi, watching the meter like a hawk. Each time it increased in price, so too did her blood pressure.

She had worked overtime making dozens of telesales calls to customers of the bank, trying to flog them loans with loan protection policies they simply didn't need or want. Under strict instruction she had also tried to talk them into increasing their overdraft with a '*special offer*' rate of interest. Why not?

It was this side of banking which she abhorred. The sales side. The bank had turned into nothing more than a retail outlet, a shop where you went to browse but came out a signature stuck to the end of some needless policy which you were instructed you '*absolutely needed*'. Helena was ashamed of what she had to do to make money. The word 'bank' in the current climate translated as '*hard sell*'. Still, points made prizes and those prizes made money – the stuff that made the world go around.

Helena stared at the windscreen wipers as they speeded up in time with the heavy rain which had just started to come down like a raging waterfall. She watched them sway to the left before they swished and flopped over to the right and their seamless silent movement hypnotised her. She liked the feeling of that temporary calmness; the only things she needed to move were her eyes.

As the meter clocked once more, its greedy melodic churn woke her from the anaesthetic trance she had been in and she yelled at the driver.

"*Stop!*"

The driver slammed his foot on the brake and the cab skidded to a dangerous halt. Its back end shot out as the front wheels absorbed most of the shock.

As it did so, Helena was launched from the back seat where she had been perched – her weight too inconsequential to hold her down – and she was flung violently against the plastic glass which separated the driver from his passengers. Her head butted it with brute force.

She lay on the floor for a moment, dazed and aware that her head had begun to throb. She pushed herself upright, holding on to her forehead which was already beginning to swell under her twig-like fingers, wondering what the hell had just happened.

As did the taxi driver.

"I'm sorry, love, but you yelled so loud I thought there was a problem so I did a full-on emergency stop."

The driver looked stunned and confused as he left the safety of his front end and risked the rain to assist Helena from the rear of the cab. He saw the immediate swelling on her forehead and watched as she shakily counted out every penny owed to him, noting how she handed the mixture of coins over to him with embarrassment and avoidance – two pound coins, some silver but mostly copper. A bagful of it.

Normally he wouldn't have accepted so many coins but under the circumstances the poor girl looked upset enough, he thought. Plus she could do with a good feed.

He held out his hand to help her and she gladly took it.

"You know, it's a good job there wasn't anyone

behind me when I slammed on, otherwise you'd probably have a broken neck to go with that bump on your head."

"Sorry," was all she could manage as he assisted her onto the pavement where she tried desperately to get her bearings through the relentless rain. Her eyes fought against the cruel liquid until she recognised where she was. It was okay. She could walk from here.

As she braved the weather, her chin wobbled with the pain from her forehead and her right hand also ached from where she had used it to protect the rest of her body from plunging into the foldaway seats in front of her. It felt like she had sprained her wrist.

Helena knew why she had yelled '*stop*' with such urgency. The meter had instructed her to do so.

"*Fucking bastard meter!*" she cursed as she set about taking the rest of the journey to Sophie's apartment on foot.

"*Fucking bastard money!*" she muttered out loud.

One day she'd have no money worries. She'd have a driver like Peter had to take her everywhere and a waterside apartment like Sophie's. She just needed Nathan's talent to be recognised by the powers that be, although she'd been waiting a bloody long time.

Helena chided herself for the immature thoughts. Get a grip. Life was not a fucking fairytale, she scolded herself bitterly. Hers certainly wasn't – it was a brutal prison sentence where she had shared a cell with a torturous browbeater who had managed for too long now to oppress her.

"Well, no more." Helena talked openly to herself as she ploughed through the rain with vigour and determination. "No fucking more!" she shouted up to the sky.

The bump to her head had distorted her typically negative chain of thought and from the wetness of her soaked feet to the rain which rolled down her forehead across her pronounced cheekbones, staining her cheap blusher, Helena felt a strength from within that she could only put down to concussion. Perhaps it was the shock, was it possible? But Helena had been slapped so severely around the face that she felt revived, strangely alive, and it felt good – unlike the concealed and imaginary slaps that Nathan had given her over the years – this one felt bloody good. It felt like the world was full of promise.

She could finally see a way out.

Inside Sophie's waterside apartment the atmosphere was unusually tense and Sophie could see from Jude and Kath that they had brought their problems with them. They wore them as transparently as their clothes, draped around their necks as accessories, wrapped around their waists like tight restricting belts, and so when Helena Wright stormed through the front door armed with attitude and ready to seize the evening, she stood out like an unarmed civilian in the middle of a war zone.

"What's up with you, Hel?" Sophie took in her sopping wet friend. "You look a mess – worse than a mess – but kind of – well – strangely *happy* at the same time."

"Cheers, Soph. I think there was a compliment in there somewhere!"

"Your eyes are red. Is the pollen count high today?"

Helena kicked off her wet shoes and headed straight for the bathroom, Sophie following in her wake, where she removed her cheap clothes and wrapped a pink towel around her long brown hair which was dripping against her bony shoulders.

Sophie stared at Helena's skeletal body. She knew that she herself was perfectly slim, but as she took in the sight of Helena in her mismatched bra and pants she gasped. Her hip bones jutted out alarmingly. They were as narrow as a child's and you could hang your coat over her collar bones they protruded so violently. Helena looked practically bulimic although Sophie knew this would not be the case. Helena didn't have the money to gorge in the first instance, yet alone regurgitate it.

"Oh my God, Helena, when did you get so skinny?" Sophie gasped. "I could play the ribs on your back like a xylophone!"

Helena turned to her best friend, wiping black mascara from beneath her eyes. Her face was stained a shade of pink from the thrashing rain which had stopped, ironically, just as she arrived at the communal entrance of the apartment block. The irony of life.

"Since I've got no money to eat," she replied matter of factly. "And since that loser stopped giving a fuck about the finances, leaving them all to me . . . since I work so much bloody overtime that I am too tired to eat. Does that answer your question?" She didn't wait for Sophie to respond. "But you know what, Soph, he's still a fat bastard so something, some-where, doesn't add up, does it?" Helena smirked.

Sophie couldn't help but emit a giggle.

Helena was an odd sight in her tatty mismatched undergarments, her face streaked with mascara. As Sophie watched her, all she saw was a vision of paradox

– the exterior of her body seemed frail – but her face bore the confidence of someone who had just accomplished their life's goal.

Sophie smirked at her friend's bitchiness towards her partner. True, Nathan had always had a belly and he had always been lazy but Helena knew this when she met him. In fact, Sophie had warned Helena about him, but like many women when it came to men, she didn't listen and that was why Sophie kept men at arm's length. They weren't to be trusted. She should know.

Sophie went to speak but Helena could see it coming.

"Don't even go there with the '*I told you so crap*'! I can read you like a book, Sophie Kane. Remember, we've been friends since the age of five and there's nothing I don't see coming – you're so damn predictable – eejit!"

The girls laughed and Helena flung her arms around her best friend. Sophie's arms could have wrapped themselves around her friend's torso twice over and she felt strangely fat by comparison.

Helena knew Sophie and she knew of her secrets, the real reason why Sophie reacted so harshly when it came to the opposite sex. They were inseparable as friends went, although so far apart in personality and ambition.

"I wasn't going to say '*I told you so*'." Sophie stuck out her tongue just like she used to when she and Helena fell out at primary school. "I was going to offer once *again* for you to come and live with me until you get yourself sorted out."

Helena froze, holding the damp, blackened piece of soggy toilet roll in her hand and Sophie could see her mind ticking over. She didn't want to say too much but she did want to make sure that Helena could clearly see the lifeline she was being offered. Again.

"I won't treat you as a charity case, Hel, I swear, but I do want to help you get yourself straight – you know, maybe save a deposit for a place of your own or something and so I won't take any rent from you . . . that's not up for debate," she added quickly, sensing that Helena about to raise an objection.

Sophie squeezed Helena's bony hand. "Just promise to keep the place tidy and buy your own shopping. Deal?"

Helena turned to face the mirrored bathroom cabinet above the sink where she continued to drag at the skin on her face until it was cleansed of smudged make-up. She could think better with a cleansed face – it was as though she were wiping the dirt away from her life too.

Sophie winced at Helena's beauty regime until she was forced to intervene. "Keep doing that and you'll look like a pensioner by the time you're forty!" she lectured. "You're pulling all the elasticity from your skin! What's wrong with you, girl? Do you want to age unnecessarily?"

Helena belted out a peal of hoydenish laughter. "Sophie Kane, I'm about to leave the man I have lived with and loved for the past nine years and embark on a new life and all you can think about is how I look? Do you even know how to be anything other than a superficial bitch?" Helena lifted the lid of the toilet and flung the used tissues into its mouth. A splash of water bounced back and landed on the bleached white toilet seat. "You're as shallow as ever but I can't help but love you."

"I love you too, but if you splash my toilet seat again

121

I'm going to have to ask you to move out before you've even moved in!"

Jude and Kath appeared at the door to the bathroom, drawn by the hilarity. From the living room they had heard Helena and Sophie deep in conversation and had decided to leave them to it as it sounded heavy. They had no idea what had happened while they were admiring the view from the lounge and sipping on Long Island Iced Tea. But they soon realised that Helena had finally come to her senses. She was leaving the loser at last.

12

Roni raced into the taxi which had been waiting patiently outside The Tudors for a good ten minutes, the tails of her coat flapping wildly. She was late. Late for Sophie's Curry Club and the last thing she wanted was to be chastised over it and one thing she most definitely couldn't do was be honest about the reason she was late.

The car pulled away, its wheels crunched along the gravelled driveway and Roni turned to watch the gates close behind her. She trusted no-one.

"You're running a little late tonight then?" The driver was hinting for an apology.

Roni grunted something which he couldn't quite make out and he quickly realised that she was one of them – people with big houses who thought they were better than everyone else – and one of those who had all that money but looked like their lives were about to end.

Snobby cow!

Roni sat back and focused on the view of Cheshire's finest mansions which flashed by her like a kaleidoscope as the driver – now late for his next pick-up – flew past them at a dangerous speed. Roni glanced at her Cartier watch. Jewellery was her one weakness and she took great pleasure in indulging in it. Peter had bought the watch for her last Christmas to replace another one which she had seemingly misplaced. While Roni was keen to claim off the house insurance, Peter wouldn't have it. '*What if it turns up somewhere and we've made a claim, Roni, my love? That would be fraud.*' But Roni had tutted at him and told him that was what insurance companies were for. '*To cough up,*' she had put it. Still, Peter knew everyone. Someone who could do something, who could do something for him. A phone call later and Roni's gift was fedexed from Paris to her front door.

The cab stopped in the communal carpark of Maritime Wharf. Without looking at the meter Roni threw a twenty-pound note at the driver before getting out without a word of thanks.

He turned to call her with the change but Roni had already fled the scene and he immediately felt better for receipt of such a generous tip. He never minded taking money off a rich bitch like her. And a bitch she was, he decided, as he made his exit through the security barrier where he waved to the silver-haired guard as he passed through.

"You're late, Mrs Smith," Sophie teased as Roni handed her a bottle of Châteauneuf-du-Pape even though she knew full well that Sophie drank only white wine. She did it every time and Sophie had gone past the point of annoyance.

"It's Sm-y-th," Roni corrected her and was about to continue when she saw Sophie tittering away, trying to hold it in.

"You're so uptight, Roni, relax and take a chill pill."

Sophie handed Roni a cocktail poured from the jug she had made earlier. Long Island Iced Tea was her signature cocktail and she made it as well as any renowned cocktail bar and with measures which would bankrupt them.

She put the jug back into the fridge of her open-plan luxury pad. "Or better still have some sex," Sophie whispered to Helena who spat her drink back into its glass almost choking on it.

"What was that, sorry?" Roni hadn't heard. She wasn't meant to.

"Nothing, Roni. I was just talking to myself." Sophie beamed at her with the charm of a hostess whose very life depended on the evening's success.

As Roni turned to join Kath and Jude on the balcony she let out a yelp. Her knees pushed together and she held her groin as she bent over slightly to ease the pain.

Jude came rushing to help, leaving the stunning view of the rainbow which beamed its rays of colour across the square fourth-floor balcony.

"What is it, Roni?" She held Roni's arm and tried to support her but Roni remained hunched like she had aged thirty years within a matter of seconds.

"It's nothing." Roni's face was flushed with embarassment and Sophie was keen to know why. Sophie was keen to know everything.

"Women's problems?"

Roni scowled at Sophie, lifting her head to glare at her. "No."

"Coil fallen out?" Sophie asked in earnest.

"No!"

"Prolapse?"

Kath let out a screech of laughter. "Sophie!"

"No, it's not a bloody prolapse!" Roni flared. She could take it no more. She knew Sophie Kane well enough to know that she would never tire of guessing until she discovered the truth. That was why she loved the Curry Club so much. No-one needed to know whose life they were dissecting when it came to the really personal stuff. But this she couldn't keep *completely confidential,* it seemed.

"I've had a bikini wax," Roni blurted out, scarlet with humiliation. She hadn't planned on discussing the removal of her pubic hair with anyone. It was very much a private affair between herself and what was left down below. "Happy now?"

Sophie edged closer to Roni and the corners of her mouth turned up. Her eyes were filled with a fun wickedness and Roni immediately knew what was coming.

"No!" said Roni.

"What?" Sophie feigned innocence.

"No, you can't look, Sophie!"

Jude shook her head at Sophie, suppressing the evident humour she found from the situation, but she was also warning Sophie because she knew that Sophie Kane didn't know when to stop. Sophie pretended not to see Jude's warning signs.

"Am I that transparent?"

"Yes!" The women shouted in unison.

"Whatever," said Sophie. "I just want to see what you got done, that's all, Roni. I'm a hairdresser after all. It doesn't matter to me where the hair is!"

Jude, Kath and Helena could cope no longer. The air was filled with shrieks and guffaws and even Roni managed to see the funny side of Sophie's outrageous behaviour for once.

Kath wiped away the tears with the bell-sleeve of her cream top. She left a stain of make-up on it. Never mind, it should come off.

"Are you sure we can't have a little peek, Roni?" Sophie coaxed. "We're all girls here."

If Roni could have ever swung for Sophie it was right then but she chose to ignore her childish antics.

"Okay but at least tell us what it was then," pressed Sophie. "Californian? Brazilian?"

"Oh that Brazilian is a killer, isn't it?" Kath spoke directly to Roni. "Just around the anus is where it hurt me the most – although it hurts less the more frequently you have it done. What about yourself, Roni? Which bit hurt the most for you?"

Roni realised in horror that Kath was deadly serious about her waxing exploits and she wondered how any woman could speak with such candor about an area which was so very personal. Apart from Peter – and the midwives when she had the girls – nobody else had set eyes on her southern region and they never would as far as she was concerned.

Roni's subconscious recalled her last encounter with Peter. It spilled out a flood of images, reminding her of how she could almost feel Darren's hands touching her. Perhaps in her imagination *he* had seen it because she had willed him to, but that was as far as it would ever get and what happened in her mind's eye stayed in her mind's eye.

Roni knew there was no way out of this situation until she had done the very thing she, quite simply, hadn't planned to. Tell the truth.

"Okay, I did it myself," she told them. "I bought a home waxing kit from the chemist, heated the stuff up and put it on." Roni couldn't look at anyone, not just yet. Not until the pain of exposing her faux pas had dissipated. "I didn't realise the wax was so hot though and I, erm . . . I burnt myself," she blurted out. "Really burnt myself."

Roni wanted to cry with embarrasment and she hated Sophie for bullying the truth out of her.

"Satisfied now, are we, Sophie?"

The earlier humour of the room died instantly and no-one knew whether to laugh at the ridiculousness of Veronica Smyth or be sorry for her.

"Did you put some cream on it, Roni?" Jude's tone was motherly and kind.

Roni just shook her head.

"Come with me, Veronica," said Sophie.

Sophie took Roni's hand and she squeezed it with rare compassion for this strange individual. Sophie had never met anyone like her before. Similarly, Roni had met few people like Sophie Kane before. Then again, Roni had been a recluse before the Curry Club, meeting only those who managed to bypass her tight security and actually make it to her front door.

She even shopped online to avoid mixing with people.

Roni followed Sophie into the largest of the two bedrooms and watched as Sophie slid back the mirrored wardrobe doors and set about retrieving tubs of creams, gels and lotions.

Sophie set them on the bed for Roni to make her choice.

"These three are the best for waxing pain, Roni. I've used them myself when I've been red raw and they definitely work. Take your pick."

Sophie walked to the door, leaving Roni with privacy and what little dignity she had left, but she couldn't resist one more question.

"Why didn't you just go into a salon to have it done, Roni? It would have been so much easier, you know . . . you could have saved yourself a hell of a lot of pain."

Roni sat at the end of Sophie's bed, clutching at the plastic pots of cream. A sadness masked her expensively made-up face and her eyes glazed over with a thin, moist film.

"I'm sorry, Roni. You don't need to answer that. It's none of my business." The woman had been through enough for one day.

Roni was remarkably touched at Sophie's unusual sensitivity. In fact it was a side to Sophie that she had never seen nor heard before. She waited for the sting to come. Sophie was never nice to her.

"It doesn't feel right to me, that's why. There are parts of the body which *I* feel are supposed to be private. You don't go getting it out for *anyone*, you know, Sophie," Roni said coolly.

Sophie felt a blow as Roni delivered her last sentence. She knew it was aimed at her and her loose morals. A below-the-belt dig – literally. But Sophie didn't fall for it. She was the one who was forever in control and she knew that Roni thought she was being clever, trying to outwit her – getting in a jibe before she herself could.

Only Sophie hadn't planned to hit out at Roni who had been through enough with her earlier humiliation.

But she changed her mind in a flash.

"You're right, Veronica." Sophie smiled sweetly at the rich woman who weighed down her bed courtesy of the world's finest jewellers and a few stone of excess weight. "You certainly don't go getting it out for *anyone*! There are names for people like that. *Those* are the type of girls who charge millionaire's husbands for providing them with the sex they don't usually get at home."

Sophie spoke to Roni as though they were discussing a third party, removing herself from the topic of discussion. She had cleverly chosen to agree with Veronica Smyth knowing full well Roni would have no recourse, no avenue to hit back at her.

Sophie had felt sorry for her, momentarily, but the truth was that she was a desperately hard woman to like.

"Here we go, ladies of the club . . . your curry is served!"

Sophie set down two large stainless-steel balti dishes while Jude followed close behind her and placed a revolving relish-server in the centre of the table. She moved the glass candlestick to the right a little to make sure her dish was exactly centered – its silver candle wobbled slightly and a tear of wax rolled down its pear-shaped body.

Jude hated it when things weren't perfect and most of what she had learned over the years was that presentation was everything. It was crucial.

Sophie was the same and Jude knew that she wouldn't mind her table being slightly rearranged.

Helena clutched her knife and fork, ready to feast

upon whatever it was that was making her mouth water. The aroma of the coriander, which was prettily scattered on top of each dish, floated in her direction. Its organic green colour screamed against the bloodshot shades of the thick red and brown curries. She couldn't wait to get stuck in and by God these women would have to be quick tonight because Helena was determined to eat to put on weight.

She smiled a secret smile to herself, knowing full well that Sophie's portion would, principally, be made up of boiled rice with a single spoonful of sauce put to the side of her plate. Jude would eat until she felt the food hit her stomach and then she would stop, but she ate ten times what Sophie would eat, and Kath would concentrate on drinking more than eating – as was historic. There was a familiar pattern amongst the curry-club diners. It was only Roni she would be competing with tonight – Roni could certainly do with losing a few pounds – although strangely enough Helena thought she suited the extra weight. She had never known her any other way.

Mentally slapping herself for thinking mean thoughts about her friend, Helena admitted as she dished a double helping of food onto her plate that Roni did have a tendency to bring most of her unfortunate situations upon herself. She was her own worst enemy in addition to being the enemy of others.

Sophie walked around the table dishing out the pilau rice – its pretty pink and yellow colours matched the small vase of pink peonies which sat at one end of the smoked-glass table.

Sophie stayed to the right of her diners, making sure she followed the proper serving etiquette – the way she liked to be served herself. She hated it when her side dish was put to the right or when her food was served from the left. It was these fine dining details which in her opinion singled out a service, taking it from adequate to superior, and it was upon fine skills such as these that she had built herself a rock-solid, lucrative business which was about to be added to.

"Oh my life . . . this food is amazing, Soph!" Helena spoke with her mouth full. "What are we eating by the way?"

Jude giggled at Helena devouring her food, cramming forkfuls into her mouth with gusto, still clueless as to what she was actually eating.

"The menu is in front of you, Hel," said Sophie.

"So it is."

Sophie picked up the typed menu which she had prepared earlier. It gave the order of the night with impressive formality. She handed it across to Helena who glanced down at it distractedly. She was too hungry to read.

"It's Lamb Madras," Sophie declared proudly. "I'm afraid the other one is utterly unexciting by comparison." She pointed to the red-coloured curry which was disappearing by the second. "Ladies, I give you the nation's favourite dish!"

"Fish, chips and mushy peas?" Kath teased, licking at a grain of rice which was stuck to her bottom lip.

Sophie rolled her eyes. "Chicken Tikka Masala. Apparently it's the nation's favourite Indian dish. Besides, if I had made fish and chips I wouldn't have had to bunk off so early this afternoon to slave away in the kitchen." She was deep in thought for a moment. "Leaving my right-hand man to hold the fort."

"How is Karl keeping, Sophie?" Jude was genuinely interested in him, regardless of his sexual preference. Correction, regardless of how Sophie described his sexual preference. To her, he was a gentleman through and through and she could clearly see how he looked out for his employer. Sophie had always maintained he was gay, but she could never see it.

"He's an old woman lately, Jude, that's what he is. He keeps giving out to me about my extra-curricular activities."

Roni's eyes flickered in Sophie's direction and Sophie was sure she saw the corners of her mouth curl.

"In what sense?" Jude probed.

Sophie picked up a forkful of boiled rice and chewed on it thoughtfully. "It's like he's getting jealous or something like that . . . I can't put my finger on it to be honest but sometimes he behaves really weird . . . like he thinks he's my mother . . . or my appointed keeper!" She swallowed the dry rice, helping herself to a little balti sauce, putting it on the side of her plate just as Helena had predicted. "I'm all for being looked out for . . . and I'd do it for him, for any of you. But the other day I woke up to see a load of texts and missed calls from him asking where I was. Psycho or what?" She frowned as she cast her mind back to her thumping head and aching loins which had greeted her that morning.

"It's called being a good friend," Roni grunted as she loaded her plate with copious amounts of food.

"What would you know about that?"

Jude felt herself tense at the bitchiness between Sophie and Roni. She hated it when they didn't get on.

"Maybe he cares about you, Sophie, that's all." Jude

tried to rescue them from the sudden change in atmosphere.

"Maybe he does, Jude, and I also care about him, a lot, but I'm big and ugly enough to look after myself. Besides, I've left home, thank you – couldn't get out of the place quick enough in fact so I don't want to feel under the thumb ever again, thank you very much. Being answerable to someone is not for me, I'm afraid, guys."

Sophie shuddered as she recalled the strict Catholic upbringing her mother had put her through. No wonder she was so promiscuous – she was barely allowed to look at the opposite sex never mind sleep with them. Sophie felt sad that she and her mother had never made up before she passed away but there was little she could do about it now.

"Where were you when you woke up, Soph?" Helena couldn't resist getting a dig at her best friend. She struck while the iron was hot.

"Ha ha, aren't you funny?" Sophie flicked a grain of rice in Helena's direction. "I was getting some actually, Hel, something you'd know nothing about!"

It was Helena's turn take it on the chin. "True."

Why was it that Sophie always had to have the last word?

Roni washed a mouthful of madras back with a large sip of red wine. She had never been in Sophie's salon and had never met this Karl athough she'd heard so much about him. Kane'n'Able was too cutting-edge for Veronica Smyth.

"You know, Sophie, true friends like him are hard to come by. It sounds like every girl should have a Karl," she preached blandly. "You're a lucky girl."

Sophie stopped and took in Roni's words and the truth rang in her ears. Deep down Sophie knew that she had a point.

"Oh, did Jude tell you her news?" Sophie changed the subject swiftly. Anything to stop a vicious retort. She looked across at Jude whose head was down. She barely raised it as Sophie waited for her to announce her new position.

"Come on, Jude."

Jude knew she had to say something, she just didn't know what. Announcements were not her thing – she preferred to be in the background.

"I'm working for Sophie now." She spoke the words without conviction but her eyes twinkled the truth of how she really felt about her new position. "I'm the new interior designer for her next project on Alderley Avenue."

There was a scurry of movement and hand-clasping around the table.

"Oh wow! Congratulations, Jude – you poor sod!" Kath chinked her glass against Jude's. "You kept that one quiet but then again so would I if I was working for that tyrant."

Sophie gave Kath an upper-arm dig.

Helena leapt from her seat and hugged Jude around the neck before kissing her on the cheek, leaving a stain of curry sauce which Jude wiped away tactfully when she knew Helena wasn't looking.

Helena was always one for positive news and soon it would be her turn, she had decided earlier shortly after her head was thrashed against the cab's interior. There was definitely something good in the air tonight.

The glasses were raised high above the ladies' heads, then touched each other harmoniously, clinking and chiming as they each hit a different key depending on the gravity behind each contact and the measure of their liquid contents.

"Speech, speech, speech!" the women cheered at Jude who had remained quiet and slightly abashed throughout. She wasn't used to being the focus of such revelry. That was not how *she* saw herself.

A watchful Sophie studied Jude's reserved body language. It was tense and uptight and certainly not that of someone who had been handed their lifelong dream on a plate.

She stood, picking up the empty square black plates, moving swiftly around the wooden floor, her stiletto heels clattering. She stacked the plates one on top of each other, noting through the balcony doors that rain had started again and the rainbow had long dispersed.

Jude excused herself to help Sophie. She grabbed the relish dish, smiling at the women who were still in congratulatory mode. She didn't know what to say to them. It was all very surreal.

The kitchen was immaculate with its recently oiled wooden work benches and its sparkling ceramic hob. It was a mass of white Shaker units surrounded by everything stainless steel bar the blackness of the hob.

Sophie turned to Jude. The gap in height was minimised by Sophie's four-inch heels and she wasn't too far away from coming face to face with her friend.

"He said no, didn't he, Jude!" The words were hurled from Sophie's mouth with a bitter tone before she could stop herself. "I knew it. I bloody well knew it. How could he do that to you? He's supposed to be your husband!" she whispered fiercely, keen that the others shouldn't hear her outburst. She slammed a jar into the integrated fridge. "It's alright for him with his new job, his big promotion – getting to do everything he wants to do in life without a thought for you –"

Jude touched Sophie's arm. "Stop. Please."

"I knew there was something up before, Jude! Your reaction definitely wasn't one of jubilation. What is going on?"

Sophie's eyes welled up and she wanted nothing more than to protect her friend from that chauvenistic pig who it seemed had her right where he wanted her. No wonder she was single – although she knew that was not the real reason she was single. She shoved it to the back of her mind where the secret had lived for many years now.

"He didn't say no." Jude was calm and controlled. "Sophie, I didn't tell him."

"What? What do you mean . . . why?"

"Because the timing wasn't right and because he'd been made partner and I didn't want to spoil his moment." She paused. "And because he needs me behind him right now, not working against him. Behind every successful man there is a woman," she mused.

Sophie closed the door of the dishwasher. "What about *your* needs, Jude? You *need* this opportunity and you *need* your life back. You know, the one you barely got a chance to live?"

"It was no-one else's fault that I fell pregnant, Sophie, and I wouldn't change what happened for the world. I was married, you know. It was hardly an accident."

Jude's eyes lit up as the love she felt for her children shone through. It burst out of her and Sophie could almost feel Jude's heart thumping with adulation.

"I have Tom and Anna, and regardless of what you think of Clive, a wonderful husband."

Sophie was wise enough to make no comment. She listened silently as her friend continued.

"I've simply realised lately that I just need to balance all of the above with the new job and that way everybody wins and Clive won't have a problem with it. I need to prove I can do it first . . . therein lies the problem."

"You mean everybody gets a piece of you while you struggle to cope and hit the deck?"

Jude held an assurance about her which Sophie couldn't fail to miss. Behind those eyes of hers was a boldness which she didn't recognise.

"I'm getting my life back, Sophie." Jude filled her empty wineglass with tap water and sipped at it. "I'll tell him when the time is right, I promise . . . but trust me on this one, that time is not *now*. Let him have his moment of glory because he deserves it."

"And so do you."

Jude turned to leave the state-of-the-art kitchen which sat above the split-level lounge. As she passed Sophie she grabbed her hand so tightly that Sophie was stunned. "I will never let you down, Sophie. I swear."

A calmness washed over Sophie. Jude's timing in allaying her anger was absolutely perfect. She had just been ready for a fight with Clive Westbury and it wouldn't be the first time.

13

Roni sat on the stained wooden bench in the pool chalet, agitated and nervous. Her feet dangled just inches from the mosaic beige-and-blue tiled floor and her legs swung to and fro. Her posture was stooped like a child on a naughty step waiting for someone to release her and tell her that everything would be okay providing she didn't misbehave again. As her swing deepened with fully extended legs, Roni winced as she scraped her big toe on the ridge of a tile. The blood-red colour from her nail-polish scratched across the pale blue tile with a rebellious streak and Roni looked at her toenail which remained unchipped. She was momentarily impressed. That was what happened when you paid a fortune for the best nail-polish available.

Up above, the skylight captured the sporadic bursts of rays which came and went as quickly as the ripples of water in front of her, and Roni stared up at its brightness until she was forced to look away when her vision became blurred.

At a loss as to what to do next to curb her

ambivalence, she walked slowly around the pool, passing by the dividing glass of the newly refurbished bar area and, for once, she could see how daytime drinking could be easy – especially when the heat was on. She nervously rearranged the dark-brown wicker furniture, pulling the table away from the glass walls and closer to the bar. Then she tided the terracotta cushions, plumping them up before replacing them tidily. Next she moved each chair so that they sat around the table with inviting allure – the distance between them was precise when she had finished.

Roni looked over at Darren's blue canvas holdall. That was all he had with him today – no cleaning equipment, no hoses, nothing but him with his teaching head on.

She froze, hearing a loud bang coming from a door beyond, and Darren walked in casually. He closed the door using the handle, leaving no memorial prints. He had learned his lesson and Roni felt bad for scolding him about the dirty smudges he left the first time he had visited The Tudors. She didn't know why she behaved that way, but just sometimes the simplest of things got her down and she wished so much that she could be like Jude with her chilled-out temprament and easy-going nature. But she was what she was. Still, she didn't like it, hadn't liked herself for a long time now and it didn't suprise her that others didn't like her either.

Darren's feet squelched along the floor as his flip-flops stuck to its dampness like suction cups, and Roni watched the muscles on his calfs protrude with the increased resistance from every step taken on the recently mopped floor.

He pulled his grey T-shirt over his head and she looked away fast, her head shooting in the opposite direction of its own accord and her chest thumping inside so loudly that she could hear nothing else, not even the classical music which played through the wall-mounted speakers. The girls had taken all the decent CD's with them and Peter had most of his collection scattered amongst his many cars – so her choice was minimal.

"All set then?" Darren stood at the opposite side of the pool to her in his knee-length cotton trunks. He kicked at the water with his foot, smiling with boyish pleasure. "It's like a bath," he laughed. "That temperature is fine for recreation, Mrs Smyth, but for intense exercise your muscles would burn out way too fast with the heat from that water."

Roni cast her eyes over his firm abdominals and up towards his chest. His pecs were tight and defined, scattered with a decoration of dark hairs which met in the centre and ran right the way down to his belly button.

She wished there was a security camera in the chalet.

Roni's brain suddenly registered the word *exercise* and she became aware that she was being spoken to.

"Exercise?"

"Don't look so shocked, I'm not talking right now!" he mocked her playfully. "It's so we can pick up the pace a little."

"What sort of exercise?"

"If you can get to the gym and work out to improve your cardiovascular fitness levels, you'll find our sessions less tiring on your body."

"We have a gym here," Roni acknowledged as she tightened the belt of her white full-length towelling robe. Her initials *RS* were hand-sewn and swirled decoratively across the lapel on the right-hand side, pretty in pink. Like most of her clothes this one still had the tag on it. She had grabbed it from the set of wall-pegs which sat behind the slatted wooden bench in the open-plan changing room. Three more remained there barely used – Peter's, Sarah's and Evie's. There was no need to guess whose was whose.

"I guessed as much," said Darren.

The girls were great swimmers and had had private lessons from the age of three while Roni had sat back and watched in amazement, swelling with pride at their lack of fear. She'd built it for them more than herself and rarely did she come into the chalet now that the girls had moved out. The silence was too unbearable. That was the downside of having them so young – they had left to go off to pastures new when she was no age at all, leaving her too young to be alone. But she couldn't blame them – their life was for the taking and they were indeed taking it, pleasures and all. She wasn't.

Darren glanced across at Roni when he felt it was safe to. He saw how she kept tightening the belt on her robe, as also she kept wrapping the lapels around each other so that not an inch of skin could be seen bar the pale flesh of her middle-aged feet. This was going to be the difficult bit, he thought, getting her to remove the robe and actually getting her into the water.

Darren sensed the tension as it floated above the water like a thick smog. He wanted to reel it in and bin it forever, keeping it trapped in its net. He also wanted to help this woman so much that it had become a revelation to him and he had thought of little else bar Veronica Smyth since that first meeting.

He had always been a decent kid and done his bit for the church, ran the odd race for charity and so on, but there was something he saw in Veronica Smyth that told him she needed saving and that her life was wasted. *Life is wasted on the living,* Darren's young, insightful mind repeated as he watched the nervous creature prepare to expose herself.

"Shall we get into the water now, Mrs Smyth?"

"It's Roni – call me Roni."

Darren pretended not to notice the quiver in her voice as he sat down, lowering his legs first before immersing his whole body into the warm liquid. "Just come in when you're ready, okay?"

With his face in the water, he kicked off from the side and swam with long manly strokes.

Roni grabbed the opportunity to drag the robe from her body before Darren could raise his head for further breath. She flung herself at the edge of the pool, sitting and leaning forward to throw herself in. Not that he would be able to see her in the ridiculous state of red thighs and a burnt bikini line. It wasn't right for anyone to see her so exposed, particularly in her current state, hence the bizarre wearing of shorts over her swimsuit.

Just as she was about to topple forward, Roni heard a bellow.

"Stop! No!"

Roni froze. The yell almost sent her in with fright. She shuffled her padded bottom right back to safety, using her arms to take the weight, wincing with the ongoing pain from her scalding incident. Still, the shorts over her new swimsuit hid the evidence nicely. It was the contorted facial expression that gave the game away.

Darren grabbed the concrete side of the pool gasping for breath, his hand only millimetres away from Roni's knee. He had swum in double time to get there.

Roni's heart thudded with his closeness and she hoped he couldn't see up the leg of her shorts where her burnt thighs were hiding.

"You were just about to jump into the deep end, Roni." Darren was mildly exerted as he spoke. "Now, I'm all for progress but perhaps we should take it slowly? Let's start at the shallow end, eh?"

Sophie chewed on her nails just as she did whenever there was something bothering her. She felt uneasy about coming between Jude and Clive and much as she didn't particularly like him, he was still her husband. She didn't *not* like him. She simply chose to reverse judgement for now – for years actually. It was her prerogative.

One thing Sophie wasn't good at was keeping things from people or pretending. She left that to people like Roni. Sophie's life was cut and dried, transparent for all the world to see. Almost.

In need of distraction, she grabbed her coat from the staff room and quickly checked the diary to ensure there was nothing booked in for her, even though she had already checked the moment she arrived at work. She knew there was nothing scheduled for today, that was her plan. Still, it was better to be safe than sorry.

Sophie's primary focus, these days, was the training academy which she had set up little over a year ago. The

Academy had been a huge success and it had afforded her an increase in revenue of almost thirty per cent since her brainwave turned into a lucrative venture. She took in the majority of the county's juniors, teaching them the theoretical material needed to do the job competently, and then training them in the practical side which they learned every Tuesday: student day. It had turned out to be a perfect plan. They benefited from a college-type education, achieving the necessary NVQ qualifications they needed to graduate, and at her own salon they became competent stylists by putting into practice what they had learned in theory. In no time at all Kane'n'Able had become one of the more favoured accredited providers of hairdressing schooling.

Sophie flung open the salon door and set off on foot back to her apartment. She had driven everywhere lately and was conscious that her body hadn't been treated to its usual blast of fresh air or cardio work-out. Though the exercise she *had* being doing certainly did count towards her calorific reduction – bedroom aerobics was as gruelling a workout as the gym – moreso in fact. What better incentive did a girl need to have?

Inside the apartment, the place was a mess and the only evident attempt that had been made to clear up was the removal of dishes which had now been washed and dried courtesy of the hidden appliances. The rest of the the table was almost as it had been after the guests left – just before midnight – rubber place mats, black napkins and a single bowl which held the four secrets – each one belonging to one of the women. One of them had been opened and read.

Sophie tipped the glass bowl upside down until the

papers fell onto the white curry-stained tablecloth. The smoked-glass table had been so expensive she had no choice but to protect it from cutlery scratches or slammed-down glasses.

Sophie unravelled each piece of paper, one at a time, smoothing them out until all four of them lay in a neat line, face up and flaunting their content. She grabbed the one she had read out, lying it down at the end of the neat row.

Sophie knew she could get thrown out of the club by doing what she had done, but no-one would find out.

As she glanced down at all five slips, each one of them relayed exactly the same message, typed by the same person: her. *"Why do women have to sacrifice their lives while the men have it all?"*

Sophie's stomach flipped as she reread all five pieces of paper. But she'd had to make Jude see that she had to move onwards and upwards and to do this she knew she needed the opinions of the other women. Yes, it was called cheating but there was a valid reason behind it.

Kath, always in favour of equality, had led the debate towards working parents, stating that both men and women had a right to have an identity other than being a *mother,* a *wife,* a *husband.*

Helena too was on Kath's wavelength but her slant came from an entirely different angle. Helena was tired of existing in a one-sided relationship and was in need of a little give and take. She would have loved for both her and Nathan to be working and earning and it would have taken immense pressure off her. She wondered if it was the same for the husbands? If so, she pitied them, the pressure on their singular shoulders; for she knew how it felt.

It was only Roni who spoke of women going to work as being subservient and degrading – a woman's place was in the home with her family where she belonged.

They expected little else from a millionaire's wife.

Jude said as little as she could get away with. She had listened to every word of advice and input from her friends and she had felt it significant that during their entire debate neither herself nor Sophie dared to meet each other's gaze. They both knew why.

As Sophie scrunched the papers together, she touched the bin lid, waiting patiently as it sprang towards her. She had tried to find a bin which opened with sensory perception, its lid popping up as she stood before it, but she couldn't. Set to discard the evidence of the five mirror-images, she stopped dead seeing the original questions staring up at her angrily from where she had thrown them after her guests had left – which of course she had sneakily replaced with her own interventions when no-one was looking. She certainly wasn't proud that she had broken the rules – nor had she planned to do it – but something inside her just flipped and she had to make her friend see that life was for living and if Jude could do this the right side of forty, or simply sooner than later, then all the better for her.

If it ever came to light and she was thrown out of the club, at least Sophie knew that she would have suffered in a worthy cause. Yes, she was a bitch, but this time she had behaved like a bitch for the good of someone who she knew deserved better. She had put her position as head of the club at risk and that was a testimony to the faith she had in her friend and to the life she so desperately wanted to see her rekindle.

Jude was like one of her own projects. She was like a listed building, solid and reliable on the outside, but dig deeper and it became clear that the foundations were starting to subside and that the cracks which had started to show a long time ago were now in hazardous need of repair. Sophie had seen the cracks widen over the years but it had taken her until now to be able to orchestrate a plan to fix them and she hoped more than anything that Clive did not stand in Jude's way. If he did, he would also be standing in *her* way and nothing stood in the way of Sophie Kane.

Roni flapped about in the water, hands extended as she gripped the poolside, clutching at its built-in ridge and kicking her legs out behind her. As each leg kicked out, an explosion of water sailed metres high with the velocity of each determined blow.

Darren made no attempts to suppress his delight at how hard Roni was working. He had imagined it might have been different, that she might have behaved like a child with its favourite toy removed, difficult and stubborn, but Roni so far had been a pleasure to teach.

He wasn't sure about the strange choice of clothing, but what did he know of women's fashion? Still, he knew enough to understand that shorts plus a swimsuit was slightly unusual. He grinned internally – everything about this woman was unusual.

"Roni, instead of kicking from your knee joints, can you try kicking from the hips like this?" He held both arms out in front of him, demonstrating smooth moves with long, straight arms. "Do the same as what I'm doing here but with your legs. It will create more buoyancy that way and you won't drown yourself – even if you are in the shallow end." Darren couldn't resist the dig. Of all the things he had expected, Roni plunging herself into the deep end on her first lesson wasn't one.

Roni smiled a half smile which quickly dispersed into a grimace as her muscles ached. It was all that she was capable of doing, letting the pain escape through expression as she concentrated hard on applying the correct techniques just as Darren had instructed.

She wobbled from side to side in the water, gripping the poolside ledge hard to stop herself going right over like a canoeist, and wondering what the hell had just happened. Water ran into her mouth which she spat out. She closed her mouth tight, once again throwing herself back into her lesson, kicking and splashing the water as her legs and feet pelted against it.

She was suprised at herself. She had never dared go past thigh level in the pool before and her hair had never been made wet of its own accord, but today as Roni pushed herself hard, the ends of her hair floating in the water like graceful seaweed which lapped around her mouth with rebellious buoyancy, it felt good. She was almost swimming – in her own mind – and it was one of the most invigorating experiences she had ever had.

And she had yet to leave the safety of the poolside.

"Are you breathing, Roni?" Darren, out of the pool, knelt down to take a closer look at his student. He saw her flushed, puffed-out cheeks and pursed lips. "Okay, that's enough, I think, Roni. Let's take a break so you can get your breath back before we move on to the next technique."

Darren sucked on the end of his water bottle, taking long slow pulls until his thirst was satisfied. It was hot in the chalet and the humidity from the water wasn't helping. He wiped the lid with his towel, offering it to Roni who looked in need of a little rehydration.

Oddly enough, she took it and wrapped her lips around it, supping in short bursts. She could barely believe it. There was a time not so long ago when she couldn't even entertain shaking his hand, and there she was wrapping *her* lips around something *his* lips had been on.

Roni groaned loudly. The lustful release echoed tantilisingly and she recognised the symptoms that she had experienced the other day with Peter rising to the surface. Now was certainly not the time.

"Sorry?" Darren asked as he withdrew the water bottle from her stubby fingers.

"Erm . . . nothing. I didn't say anything."

"Oh, okay. Right, we're going to try one more technique, Roni, before we call it a day."

Inside, Roni felt her heart sink. The joy of having life around the house was heavenly and she thought about the few people who had actually experienced the joys of The Tudors with its splendid architectural design and imposing characteristics. Suddenly, her home didn't feel lived in. It was lifeless just like she was – only today she felt full of the joys and remarkably relaxed with Darren, not at all imtimidated by his presence – after the initial shock of seeing him in his swimming trunks, that was. She was glad they were not speedos.

Darren slid into the water and took Roni's hand, leading her away from the confinements of the side. She hopped from one foot to the other beneath the water to keep up with him. Her breasts bounced unsupported, their soft flesh glistening with tiny drops of moisture.

Darren stopped in the centre of the pool, turning to face her.

"Turn around please, Roni."

"Turn around? But I'm facing you . . ."

"You need to turn away so you have your back to me," he explained patiently.

Darren manhandled Roni, physically directing her away from facing him to standing with her back to him. He placed his hands on her waist which had been sucked in by the tightness of the swimsuit and she flinched at his touch, freezing as his long fingers extended themselves around her torso, holding her firmly in place. Darren pulled her further back towards him and she could feel the heat exuding from his body penetrating her back.

"I'm going to hold your waist just like I am now, and I want you to slide down slowly until you're lying on your back with your head resting in the water. Okay?"

Roni nodded as she took in his assertive direction and he witnessed her nod of acknowledgment from behind. The fine hairs sitting just below her neckline had started to dry and frizz up and Darren noticed how its colour was different to the rest of her hair – blonde tips and dark roots.

Roni did as she was instructed, she had no choice. Peter had rarely been cross at her or dominant in any manner of speaking, but this was undeniably important to him and she was doing it more for the man she loved than the woman she was herself – whom she didn't love. And love him she did, she just needed to tell him more often.

"A little further, Roni, we've got to get you lying on your back in the water . . . drop back a bit more . . . I've got you. You need to be floating so you can look up at the ceiling."

As Roni slid further into the warm waters, Darren's hold on her waist loosened and his hands slid further north over her indulged ribcage. Roni ignored the tingling sensation she felt as she concentrated hard on following his instructions.

"A little more and you're there. I'm going to hold you under the small of your back in a minute, just to keep you afloat – I want you to experience the joys of being able to float in the water whenever you get tired, staring out into your very own sky." He laughed as he pointed to the circular velux with its plastic ivy hanging down.

Roni went for it with gusto, in a last attempt at bravery. She had never tried so hard in all her life. Her head banged against Darren's stomach as she flung herself back, butting it with some force, and she slid clumsily into the water with an accelerated pace that took him by suprise. Darren's hands slid upwards as he tried to retain his grip on the smooth material but his hands simply slid over the slippery wet lycra, stopping at the base of her breasts.

Roni let out a bloodcurdling yelp. "*Waahhh!*"

Using his position of strength, he lifted her from the water until she was standing, as before, safe on her two feet, before he casually released his clasp unperturbed.

Roni stayed with her back to him. She couldn't look at him, not just yet. Her nipples had hardened to his touch with the closeness of his hands to her breasts. She had wanted him to pull down her bra-cups and plunge right in. But she was disappointed with herself for the ungraceful climax when it had all been going so well.

Perhaps too well, but she'd overdone it at the end as she aimed for the big finale.

"Do you want to try that once more?" Darren touched Roni's shoulders and turned her around to face him.

She turned reluctantly.

"We didn't quite get it right, did we?" His laughter echoed throughout the chalet, bouncing back at them, stealing centre stage.

Roni's arms were folded high across her breasts. She couldn't risk Darren seeing her rock-hard bullets, couldn't have him knowing his touch had turned her on so. He was here in a professional capacity and here she was, a married woman who had made her marriage vows and meant every word of them. Adultery was for other people, not Veronica Smyth.

Roni recalled the day she had first met her group of friends at Jude's charity bash. Hazy as the night was, she still remembered Sophie reading out the first question of what was to become the first of many, only they didn't know it at the time. *'When does adultery become adultery?'* Roni stood in a daydream as she reminisced about that evening. She stiffened remembering her own response to the question raised. *'Just thinking about it . . .'*

She dropped her tightly folded arms and bobbed across the heated water, aiming for the tiled steps. She had practically committed adultery because she *was* thinking about it, had been since she met him in fact.

Roni had to call it a day to collect herself.

As Darren watched her abrupt departure, he knew something had happened which had disturbed her. He just didn't know what although he had his suspicions.

"Maybe next time then?"

14

"Mum!"

Anna sprinted across the schoolyard, eager to see her mother who she had missed more than she'd expected.

She flung herself into Jude's welcoming arms where she was held tightly and Jude kissed her forehead repeatedly, rubbing her back gladly. Her baby was home.

Tom beamed at his mother, lugging their wheeled cases behind him, struggling as the skis, flung over his shoulder, swayed dangerously, eager to wipe someone out.

"Go and help your brother before he kills someone, darling." Jude beamed at her beautiful daughter who was almost as tall as she was and as gangly.

Anna had been stopped when she was fourteen by a headhunter for Models NW but Jude had refused to see her daughter lose out on her childhood and had point-blank refused for Anna to pursue modelling as a career. *'If you're still interested after you've graduated from university, Anna, I will support you all the way, but education comes first.'* Jude had meant every word of it. For a moment it had felt like the same pattern emerging as she exchanged mother/daughter advice. Just as her mother had advised, intervening with prominent words when Jude announced she was going back to work as soon as the twins turned one. Her mother's words had gone down like a lead balloon, but Jude had elected to accept her advice because her mother knew best. She only ever had her best interests at heart.

Likewise, she was advising her daughter to study, head down. But of course Jude knew it was a little different. Anna was a child, a beautiful, academically gifted teenager who was dependent on her parents for both financial and parental support, whereas Jude had been married with two children and was financially sound from both the large inheritance her father had gifted his only child and from her husband who even in the inception of his career had all the promise of making partner and his salary reflected this promise. She had never doubted him nor the correctness of his decisions, but it was clear to see whenever she looked back that Clive and Hattie had been in cahoots of some description, unanimously deciding what was best for her and without, it seemed, the need to consult her.

At the time it never dawned on her to question them. Her mother had always been there for her, waiting patiently at the school gates come rain or shine, teaching her to bake, how to garden and how to enjoy all there was to enjoy about life. And Clive was the breadwinner, her partner, her lover and the father of her precious children. It never occured to Jude that children of working parents could grow up to be as harmoniously balanced as those whose parents were at their beck and call. Until now.

Anna's suitcase lay open on the white, voile-drapped,

four-poster bed and Jude began to unpack her belongings which had been flung together and dumped in carelessly. Not a single item was folded. Instead it seemed like Anna had punched the clothes in, leaving them broken and twisted, creased to smithereens. She stopped unpacking.

Anna lay on the bed next to her mother, her head resting on the pillow for support as she focused her attention on the pink Nintendo DS.

Jude saw the fresh altitude tan of her daughter. She smiled to see the white around her eyes from where the ski goggles had been. She was almost panda-like.

Anna had only to look at the sun and her skin changed colour. Tom was the only fair one in the family but he too carried the regal look which Anna had been gifted with. They were not identical twins, they couldn't be because they were of the opposite sex, but it was clear that they were brother and sister.

Jude remembered that she had a pile of tenders to sift through in order to select both the architect and the building firm. Sophie had told her clearly that it was part of her role now and she must just simply assert herself in making any necessary decisions. But sometimes Jude had to be reminded that she was now a working woman – undercover as it was – because she simply wasn't used to the discipline of it.

Her heart leapt with excitement as she thought about the finished salon. More so, how she wanted to delight Sophie as a way of repaying her. And delight her she would.

"Anna, come off that thing please, darling, and unpack your suitcase." Jude tapped her on the knee gently.

"Sorry?" Anna immediately closed the pink lid and gawped up at her mother. "Unpack?"

"Yes, please."

Jude stood to leave Anna's girly bedroom with its princess-like poster bed draped with soft pink voile. Her walls were covered with *High School Musical* posters with a large poster of *Troy* placed just above her pillow.

Anna set about pulling garments from the case, hurling them in various directions aimlessly and Jude had to forcibly stop herself from taking over. She wasn't sure that she had ever asked the kids to take control of their own belongings before. She had done everything for them. It was only when it came to money and education that Jude really put her foot down. Money was something which simply should never be talked about – that was all too crude – and education was as vital as taking in oxygen. The rest Jude was so relaxed about she was almost horizontal.

As she left the mayhem of Anna's bedroom, she headed downstairs giggling mutedly. She wasn't sure which had tickled her the most – the natural incapabilities of her daughter, soon to be sixteen, or the dawning realisation that she had absolutely mollycoddled her children since the day they were born and had never thought to question it.

There were lessons to be learned by all of them and Jude was suprised by how long it had taken her to see it.

Helena took the transaction slip from the elderly woman hunched in front of her. She glanced at it before dumping it in the bin beside her.

"I'm so sorry, Mrs Patterson, it's signed in the wrong place. Can I get you to sign another withdrawal slip, please?"

This time Helena marked a large X in red ink as clear as day and she watched the lady sign obligingly.

"Thank you, Mrs Patterson. It's easily done, isn't it?" Helena took the slip without making eye contact and tucked it away into a hole in the desk, where the slips would be collected after the bank had closed, and archived – somewhere.

She counted out the money from the cash float which was kept in a locked steel box in the top drawer of her desk – the keys were strapped to her at all times – clipped to her waistband.

Helena recounted it for the benefit of the customer who watched the proceedings with little interest. She handed the cash over. "Will that be all for you, Mrs Patterson, or can I help you with anything else today?"

The old lady stuffed the cash deep into the bottom of her bag, zipping it carefully and closing over the clasp. She was safety-conscious in this modern, crime-filled world. It wouldn't do to be careless.

"Yes, thank you, dear." She prised her overweight body from the grey covered chair using her two walking sticks, before hobbling out.

Helena did not see her out, she couldn't. The banking hall was too busy. Once more she scanned the long queues before leaping up and making a beeline for a single gentleman who didn't look a day under ninety. She took his arm gently.

"Follow me, sir."

Nathan followed her around the box-sized flat wearing a thunderous look. "You'll be back, you always are," he scoffed.

"Not this time, Nathan." Helena continued packing her stuff into the tatty suitcase she had used since she was a student. It didn't feel that long ago – probably because when she looked around she still lived like a student.

As she glanced around her, Helena bid a mental farewell to the place which had held her shackled on and off for the past six years.

"I've cancelled any direct debits that covered the bills to this place, Nathan, so you're on your own now. I did it for six years and you never contributed a penny so you'll have to learn the hard way."

Nathan was speechless. She had never gone this far.

"What the hell did you do that for?"

Helena picked up the ice-cream maker which Sophie had bought her last Christmas. It was her one indulgence, her favourite gadget and she used it regularly – as a meal replacement.

"I'm out of here, Nathan – for good. I keep telling you but you're not listening as usual. It's no longer you and me . . . it's you and *you*."

She stomped into the bedroom, wrapping her favourite gadget in a handful of clothes to protect it from damage, placing it in the only remaining gap of her suitcase. She pushed down on the dirty black squared canvas, zipping her wordly goods away. There was little else she had to take. The flat came fully furnished, so nothing bar the accessories belonged to either her or Nathan. All the electrical appliances belonged to the landlord, the same for the cheap, mismatched furniture, cushions too. The towels and bedding she would leave, they might remind her too much of Nathan. She took what was rightly hers and only hers. The rest was history. At least, it would be soon.

"This is the end. Sorry, Nathan."

Helena dragged the case off the bed, taking a last look around the room to make sure she had forgotten nothing. She didn't plan to be back. She had gone further this time than ever before and behind his cocky arrogant exterior, it was clear to see that Nathan was a terrified shade of ashen.

"You can keep whatever I haven't taken with me. I don't want anything that will remind me of you," Helena told him matter-of-factly, dragging the case down the narrow hallway. She opened the front door with a hurried twist of the scuffed Yale lock, then threw her single door key at Nathan who caught it with a surprisingly fast reflex for someone who was in a general state of lethargy.

He stared down at the key, gawping at it angrily, and Helena watched as his hand clasped itself tightly around it into a fist. She saw the colour of his knuckles change from red to white as his skin stretched. His face did the exact opposite and Helena knew it was time to leave.

"Goodbye, Nathan, and good luck with your board games."

As Helena closed the door behind her she heard the key being hurled against the inside of the apartment door. It pinged loudly and Helena could already see in her mind's eye the dent it would have put in the cheap material. She was glad to see the back of the place and while it wasn't ideal living with Sophie, she was only too pleased that she had somewhere to go. She had accepted Sophie's offer for the first time.

Helena allowed the case to drop clumsily from stair

to stair as she left the building. She chewed away on her bottom lip in distraction as she tried to erase those thoughts which – if allowed – would eat away at her ferociously. Yes, she had done it again today even though she'd promised herself that she would only do it on that one occasion. But this one wasn't planned. It had just happened. She needed to make a clean break from that loser and she needed the money that went with it. But she would definitely *never* do it again.

She meant it this time.

As the first hint of darkness fell across The Firs it sent Jude deeper into the soporific state she had been in for the past hour or so. She had completely lost track of time as she pored over complex tender documents, scoured catalogues crammed with retro-styled furniture and collected samples of paints and snippets of wallpapers from various outlets.

Jude was loving it, every single moment of it, and she felt alive and full of purpose. She rubbed her eyes, straining to see in the dimness which had closed in fast. The only light was coming from the outdoor lantern which was bright enough to land an aeroplane. Jude stared out of the living-room window at the yellowness which oozed from its diamond-shaped Victorian glass. As she continued to watch its static rays, Jude felt her heavy eyelids blinking rapidly as she tried to stay awake. She couldn't stop now, she was already behind on the project because it had taken her the guts of a week to firmly decide if she should pursue the task without the permission and support of Clive. But each time she had thought about turning Sophie down, her gut flipped over and her chest tightened and Jude knew that an opportunity like this one might never cross her path again. It was too good to be true. But it was true.

She didn't feel good about lying, it wasn't in her nature to lie, but she forced herself to accept the idea that she wasn't lying: she would tell Clive when the time was right. That time just hadn't arrived yet.

Jude heard the crunch of Clive's Jaguar pulling up outside the house. She could hear the upgraded sound system thumping through the car windows and through the double-glazed living-room windows into the house. Jude wondered how his ears could cope with the intense volume combined with the high-pitched belting sounds of heavy metal, his preferred genre.

She smiled to herself. Clive's taste in music had barely changed in the time she had known him. In fact, little had changed about Clive Westbury in those twenty years. He was still as toned and boyishly handsome as the first day they met on her first day at campus.

"Crikey!" Jude bounced up, snapping out of her nostalgic memories as the silence of the curbed Led Zeppelin disturbed her. It meant Clive had left the car and would be in the house within seconds. She gathered her papers, frantically piling one on top of the other before throwing them into the red-leather magazine rack. She strategically placed her *Interior Designer* magazines over the papers so they were well out of sight, but definitely not out of mind.

Jude raced to the kitchen, yanking open the fridge. In her quest to get ahead of the project, she had been so utterly engrossed in her work that the time had been stolen from beneath her and supper had been as far from her mind as an alien invasion.

"I'm home, Jude!" Clive shouted from the hallway and the door slammed behind him.

Jude quickly poured two glasses of red wine and walked casually to the kitchen door which opened out into the expansive hallway, alive with flowers and family portaits. They too told the life-story of her marriage to Clive shown through a montage of naturally captured images.

Her heart fluttered happily as she stared up at them.

Jude watched Clive remove his tie just like he did every night, throwing it over the antique pine bannisters. His jacket followed within seconds. Clive's routine was predictable and Jude liked that about him. His mood was unchangeably optimistic and that fierce determination he had engraved deep within him had never faltered. Clive Westbury got what he wanted.

He beamed at his wife, grateful for the reception and glad of the alcoholic offering.

Jude threw her thick blonde hair to one side as she leaned casually against the open doorway – it fell perfectly, wrapping itself around her shoulder and covering the top of her toned arm. Its length sat just above her breast, the ends of it twisted into silky locks.

Clive watched Jude. He knew she was deep in thought. He knew that because she always bit the skin inside her mouth when she was feeling pensive. He admired her perfect jawline which was made more prominent by the tilted angle at which she held her head. Her long neck was regal and flawless and her lips were covered in a natural gloss which enhanced their perfect shape.

"You look a bit tired, darling. Are you okay?" Clive kissed Jude on the lips as he took the wineglass. It was a perfect exchange.

"A little bit," Jude answered with honesty.

"What's for dinner?"

She looked around at her immaculate kitchen and stifled a snort. Even she couldn't cook and keep the place so tidy. It was pretty obvious that little culinary action had taken place in that kitchen recently.

"I thought we might get an Indian delivered?" She raised her eyebrows. "What do you think?"

Clive looked around at the showroom kitchen and shrugged his shoulders. "It's up to you, darling, I don't mind." He rubbed his eyes.

He was too tired to contest her suggestion and Jude felt rotten for not having dinner ready and waiting after his hard day at the office. After all, it was Clive who was keeping the roof over their heads, although it had been Jude's inheritance which had provided the sizeable down-payment for the four-thousand-square-foot dwelling set admist twelve acres of land heavily protected by tree-preservation orders.

"How was the kids' trip?"

Jude smirked as she recalled Anna's half-cocked attempt at unpacking her suitcase. "Brilliant! Tom was on the black runs the entire week," she boasted to her attentive husband. "And it seemed like Anna took the opportunity to sunbathe . . . with her goggles on . . . she looks like a panda."

They both laughed.

"Where are they?"

"They're at Mum's." Jude pulled open the hideaway drawer in the middle of the kitchen table, pulling out a wad of takeout menus carefully held together by a thick clamp. Everything had its rightful place in her house. She pushed the handles of the clamp together, allowing the menus to scatter on the table top. "They were desperate to see her. And she them."

Clive nodded his head, deep in thought. "Okay." He took a large gulp of wine. "Jude, are you sure you're alright?"

15

Sophie's phone bleeped to inform her that a text message was waiting to be opened.

She pulled the phone from the artillery-style jacket: R U free for lunch? Need to talk. Kath

Sophie looked up at Helena who it appeared was only now beginning to relax in the exclusive wine bar where they had met just ten minutes earlier.

"Hel, do you you mind if Kath joins us?"

Helena's eyes widened. "Why would I mind? The more the merrier."

Sophie replied to Kath: In Revolution James St. Not ordered yet. will w8 4u Soph x

Helena continually looked around her, taking in the type of place she never thought she would be in – not so soon after leaving Nathan anyway. The odd time they had been out together was in the student area of Manchester or to the local pub where the same age-old guys, barely breathing, continued to prop up the bar. This was a whole new experience for her and she had been rigidly tense when she walked through the door in her faded jeans and wearing Sophie's top.

"What are you doing for the rest of the day then?"

Helena chewed the end of her straw. She was enjoying her drink immensely and cocktails during the day had never tasted nor felt so good. Each sip forced her deep into relaxation. She was a free woman.

"Now that I've got no bills to pay, Sophie, I thought I might go and treat myself to some new clothes. It's been years since I've been able to do that."

Sophie watched her best friend, who just a short while ago had her shoulders so hunched with nerves that they were close to her ears. But now all she could see was a woman with a bright future ahead of her, as a singleton for now perhaps, but a happy one.

Sophie didn't know what her friend's future held but she could already start to see signs of the old Helena resurfacing.

"Go for it." She sipped on her sparkling water. She never drank on a working day. "You should get one of those tops, Hel, it really suits you." Sophie beamed, determined to compliment her friend in order to boost her deflated ego. There was no acting involved when she was around Helena though – the girl who knew her through and through – including all her worldly secrets.

"I might just do that. Thanks for lending it to me by the way."

Helena reached across the table and squeezed Sophie's hand. She went to speak but closed her mouth quickly. But Sophie knew. She knew exactly what her best friend was thinking and no words needed to be exchanged to see just how grateful Helena was with her escape route and evacuation plan.

"Do you think someone would be able to fit me in at the weekend for a re-style and maybe some hi-lights, Sophie?"

"I'll do it at home for nothing."

Helena looked embarassed for the first time. "Please let me pay for it. I told you I've got money, Soph, I kept hold of most of the last bonus I got, just never told that loser. Plus, apart from food and bus fares to work, I've got no other outgoings any more – thanks to you."

Her voice broke towards the end of the sentence and this made Sophie feel so good for her friendly deeds.

To the outside world it seemed that Ms Kane was self-absorbed, the centre of her own universe. But it wasn't true. It never had been. Sophie Kane was all about bravado when it came to suppressing her true emotions, but beneath the hard facade she had a heart that wished for a magic wand each time she saw someone in need. Sophie was the silent type who spent her money without discussing its tangible benefits with anyone. It was her business what she did with her impressive salary and Sophie had debit after debit going to some charity or another and whenever she heard people like Veronica Smyth say '*Charity begins at home*' she would squirm inside, desperate to stand on her pedestal and put the world to rights – or instruct Roni how *she* could help put the world to rights – but she didn't.

And she knew Roni wouldn't.

Kath came rushing through the door, eyes red and skin paled to the bone. Both Sophie and Helena exchanges urgent glances.

Kath was a constant picture of health with glowing skin and clear eyes, all offset with unruly red hair which went with her unruly dress sense and unruly but contagious personality.

She dived onto the seat next to Sophie, keeping her back to the other diners to avoid embarrassment, bursting into tears the moment her frame collided with the furniture.

Helena shuffled closer to Kath to protect her from any peering audience in need of a little lunchtime entertainment.

"What is it, Kath?" she asked her softly. "What's making you cry like this?"

Sophie handed her the white napkin, destroying its artistic folds and Kath dabbed her eyes with it, oblivious to the black streaks left both on her face and on the pristine linen.

"I don't know!" she cried. "I can't be sure – no, actually that's rubbish, I can be sure it's him."

The women looked at each other in confusion.

"What's him? Who's him?" Sophie asked.

Kath lifted her head. Her eyes were heavy and she could barely look at her friends as the alien words left her mouth. Kath had always been afraid that once she said them it would become real and true. Just like it was about to become now.

"Jason," she sighed. "It's our Jason that's been stealing the money. We caught him red-handed this time."

Sophie gasped at the news and Helena swallowed hard, not looking at either of the women. She sobered up immediately.

"What are you going to do about it, Kath?" she asked.

169

Fresh tears rolled down Kath's face. Her heart spilled drops of blood internally as it cracked painfully. She was unsure of what lay ahead as the tightly woven seams of bonded genetics frayed before her very eyes.

"I don't know what to do." Kath cried some more. She had given up putting on a brave face, she was too desolate for that. "What can I do? I mean, we suspected money had gone the other day – you know, the night we were in yours, Sophie, but as always we put the blame on ourselves when the money was short . . . but today we caught him – *I* caught him – hands in my purse pulling out what little I had in there to start with!"

"You could grass him up," Sophie stated bluntly and Helena flinched.

"No way! I'd never do that," Kath retaliated, taking staged breaths to calm herself. Her face contorted as she took in Sophie's callous words. "How could any mother grass up her own son?" She was momentarily stunned. "Although I'm not sure I can have him living under the same roof as us any longer . . . not after what he's done. It might seem like an overreaction to you both but it's been going on so long now that we're both at the end of our tether. It's so difficult living with someone who steals from you. My nerves are on edge."

"Could he stay with Neil until he sorts himself out?" Helena offered.

"Neil is fuming, Helena, wants to kill him in fact . . . but he will take him in to help us out. Jason's still only nineteen so we need to know where he is and that he's safe and if Neil doesn't take him in he won't be going anywhere. Let's face it, we've no other family to help out, have we?"

170

Sophie said nothing but her mind raced as she thought of solutions to help out her friend who was clearly in crisis. *Now* was one of those very moments she needed that magic wand.

"You know, Kath . . ." Sophie was apprehensive but she continued bravely. She knew better than to offend people when it came to their children – the killer instinct kicked in every time – and she was fully aware that might happen any minute now, after Kath heard what she had to say. "Perhaps a spell away from the home might be the making of him?" Sophie dared herself to be outspoken on this rare and highly sensitive subject matter. "Now I'm not saying it won't be the hardest decision of your life sending him away . . . but if all the other times when you've thought money was missing, Kath, *were* in fact down to Jason then it's not a one off, is it? It's something more serious and more sinister and who knows what he could go on to do. Crime has to start somewhere, doesn't it? It starts with petty theft but can go on to serious offences and that's what you need to think about." Sophie took one last breath, hoping truly that her friend would see that her words were as impartial as they could be and meant for all the right reasons. "It might just be the making of him, Kath . . . as might grassing him up."

Kath listened to Sophie like she always did. She didn't always agree with everything Sophie said, but most of the time she could see that Sophie meant well. Unless she was in *bitch* mode. She clearly wasn't now. "Sophie, if I put my own son in jail I might as well take the next cell to him because James would never forgive me, and do you know what else?" Kath's eyes narrowed with fierce conviction and her lips tightened in a way her friends had never seen before. "I will never, ever give that witch the satisfaction of knowing that we've failed as a family unit . . . *never* . . . not while there is breath in my body. It's just what she wants."

"Kath," Helena said calmly. "Jason wouldn't go to prison for petty theft. His offence wouldn't be serious enough for a jail sentence. This time I'm going to have to disagree with you, Sophie, by saying that doing that won't help him. It would only make matters worse."

Jude bent her head forward as the luminous hard hat was placed gently on it. She grinned as she stood back, catching her reflection in the window; she felt a part of things now.

She opened her black leather artist's folder and pulled out a series of pencilled sketches, handing them to the architect who had accompanied her to Alderley Avenue for a scheduled meeting.

He smirked at her apparent desire to do both his job and her own.

"What are you paying me for, Jude? You've practically done all the hard work."

"I'm not paying you, Sophie is," Jude corrected him.

Her insides swelled with pride and exhilaration. She had always been keen on architecture and never wanted to *just* design the interiors of already manufactured projects. For this one which meant so much to her, she wanted to be a part of it from the very start, watching it grow from a dilapidated broken structure to a completed magnificent one which stood out from the rest with attitudinal charm. Jude wanted to be one of those specialists who could map out a structural blueprint for the building's design, in addition to decorating, fixing and finishing it to perfection.

"They're only ideas now, John. I wanted to share them with you so you could get a feeling for what I think the finished place might look like – in my own head anyway." Jude was keen to clarify. She didn't want him to think she was getting ahead of herself. She pointed to the wall in front of them. "It's a pity really because that is a rock-solid wall and I'd hate to knock it down but I really feel that in order to maximise space we need to open up the downstairs – certainly at the front of the building anyway."

John stared at Jude's hand-drawn blueprints. Even the measurements were to scale and he was blown away by her level of detail.

"How come you know so much about architecture then?"

"Oh, I don't really. I just had an interest in it when I was at Uni and I've followed it since. I love Gaudi and Libeskind particularly, even though their work is completely contrasting." She laughed.

"What about your own house, what's that like?"

Jude was embarassed. She hated talking about herself. "Nothing special."

They took the wooden stairs to the upper floor of the building. Like the rest of the unit the stairs were solid and reliable, in need of little work bar a coat of paint. But as usual Jude had other ideas.

"I'd like this staircase to be completely removed, John." She hesitated, banging her hand against its solid wood. "I want to use the space here which is why it needs to go. It's not the sort of staircase I had in mind, it's way too old-fashioned. Ideally, I'd like a steel staircase fitted at the very back of the salon. It will cost a lot but I'd love it to start at the back of the building but, upstairs, come out at the front."

John frowned as he listened attentively.

"It needs to be built at a difficult angle so that when the clients take the stairs at the back, when they get upstairs they suddenly find themselves at the front of the building."

"Why?"

"Because the reception area for the beauty salon, which Sophie is going to charge rent for, is going to be upstairs and I want the clients who come up the stairs to be greeted with a light airy space which will be created by full-length windows giving amazing views of the street below." Jude was on a roll. "That's where the 'luxury' waiting area will be too – kitted out with leather sofas, a wall-mounted flat screen TV and the world's most expensive coffee-machine!" Jude threw her head back and laughed. "Boss's choice."

John shook his head as he watched the stunning vision in front of him. He had never come across Jude Westbury in his line of work although he had heard her name mentioned, usually relative to some charity event or other but none relative to this line of work. She was good.

"If the stairs simply go from back downstairs to back upstairs, they won't get the benefit of the natural daylight which will be exaggerated by the new floor-to-ceiling windows I've got my eye on."

As she smiled, her wide mouth shone with pearly whites and her flawless skin was plump with vitality, a cheating youthfulness. Jude didn't suffer from crow's feet – her smile spanned across her cheeks without the need to push up the delicate skin beneath her eyes, making her appear younger than she was.

"What is the world's most expensive coffee-maker then, Jude? I thought it was a kettle?"

"No! Although that's definitely a cheaper option." She was amused. "*Apparently* the Concordia Coffee Systems offer the world's most expensive coffee-machines . . . and what Sophie wants Sophie gets."

John took the opportunity to make a sexist joke. "Do you think the blondes will be able to work it? Those machines do require a little intelligence, you know."

He saw Jude's arm extend as a playful slap headed his way.

"Just kidding honestly!" he added as Jude retreated. "Although if they come in as blondes but go out as brunettes they'd have a better chance of success!"

Jude shot him a jovial but defensive glance in the name of all the blonde women she knew – Sophie Kane being at the top of her list. She knew really that he was just keeping her going and she liked the natural camaraderie they seemed to share. It helped, given they were to be working together for the coming months.

Jude was happy. More than happy. Today she felt like she was back in her twenties experiencing a day at the office like she'd never been away. Only she had.

Jude had told herself in the preceding weeks that she would have to apply what she had learned in the fifteen years as wife, mother and fundraiser to her new role. After all, only a foolish woman would believe that in a life of domesticity she had learned nothing. Jude had learned a great deal, even if the core of that education was the realisation that she needed to break free.

16

Helena flung the plethora of bags in the middle of the floor euphorically. She never remembered shopping being such fun but then again, with no money it was hardly fair to call it shopping.

She and Nathan had done a lot of window shopping. Some Saturdays they would wander into the town centre playing their favourite game of 'I spy', but it was 'I spy' with a twist. They would browse and pore over the clothes, shoes, toys, games, books and CD's they wanted and tell the other one '*I spy that when I win the lottery you can have . . .*' or '*I spy that when I'm rich and famous I will buy you that ring . . .* ' and Nathan would point to the biggest diamond he could see in the shop window.

Some days the game worked perfectly for Helena and she walked home linking Nathan in the comfort that one day, when he got his big break, she would be looked after just like Peter looked after Roni. On other days, she would simply stare at him, noting how engrossed he would become in his fabricated mind and this unnerved her. Life seemed to be one massive game to Nathan

Bream and it had taken Helena the guts of nine years –
six of them living together – to work it out.

She was losing her touch.

In the bedroom, the smaller of the two in Sophie's
apartment, Helena ripped off her old clothes, replacing
them with the new garments which lay carefully placed
on the bed, their tags hanging proudly.

She yanked on a pair of black skinny jeans which
made her look extremely skinny, and Helena decided she
would wear them when she was able to fill them out a
little more. She scoffed at the irony of others wanting to
look skinny, but there was skinny and there was bulimic-
looking and she wanted to be back to the size she had
been when life was normal and when her relationships
were normal. But Helena wasn't entirely sure what
normal was these days.

Quite often the Curry Club would make a statement
or a comment which made her question the stability and
mediocrity of the relationsips of her friends as they flagged
up issues in their marriage or proposed questions about
infidelity. Helena had taken to normalising her own
unusual affairs with Nathan because of this. But it was
only when she felt him squeezing her hand while
simultaneously scouring the contents of her mind that
she recognised she had narrowed the gap between trying
to put a positive slant on things and being completely
evasive of the cold hard facts. That night she had been
scared for the first time. Nathan had ranted and raved
before and she'd taken it on the chin – he was always
throwing his toys out of the pram and Helena knew this
was par for the course. But when he had grasped her

hand in his and penetrated her with that look, she knew he was trying to get inside her mind and transfer her thoughts into his. It had felt that way. His controlling streak had become more and more evident to Helena, yet strangely enough she had no real evidence to corroborate it.

After what she had done that day there was no way she would have permitted anyone to enter into her psyche. She had closed down her mind, emptying it of evidence. She knew she would never be proud of her actions – that she could be sure of – but one day when she could, Helena knew she would be able to put things right. It was all very short-term.

"That's the last of his stuff." Kath sniffed at James whose eyes had welled and dried repeatedly in the past half hour.

Kath had rewashed and ironed every item of Jason's and packed them with unusual precision in his holdall. She barely ironed her own clothes – didn't see the point – but if she was going to throw her son from his family home to teach him a lesson in tough love, temporary as she hoped it was, then she needed to make sure he knew it was done with care and that her actions were for the best. Not at all bitter.

There wasn't too much to pack in addition to his clothes and shoes which were mainly trainers. Just an iPod, DVD player, Wii and an eclectic mix of DVD's.

James lifted the bag into the boot of Neil's Ford Focus. He turned to his wife. "Is that definitely it, love?"

Kath could do little else but nod. She needed to keep it in for James' sake. She was the strong one of the two. Hadn't he been through enough?

James slammed down the hatchback, giving three loud thumps on the glass window using the palm of his hand and he watched as the car rolled down the narrow driveway.

It turned left towards Sentry Drive and Kath hoped that Norma would not be standing in the window as normal, watching the comings and goings of the street like she so often did.

Inside the house was quiet. It was always quiet in fairness but this time they felt it because they had made it that way.

Kath wondered how long it would be before Jason was back with them. She hoped it was temporary but she was enough of a realist to know that unless her youngest son grew into the man they hoped he would become, there was little hope of him moving back in. The stakes were too high. Their sanity was on the line.

Over the past year, Kath had noticed ten pounds here, twenty pounds there missing, and each time she had scolded her deluded self for miscounting or carelessly squandering her funds. But when she placed the money she was saving under the bottom right-hand corner of the mattress only to find that it had disintegrated like it was made from delicate tissue, she knew in her heart that her gut instinct had been right all along. Her son was a thief. The stolen money she could cope with, but he had stolen her heart too and stolen the comfort of their perfect family unit from under all of their feet.

The phone shrilled and Kath rushed into the hall.

"Hello?"

She slumped down on the bottom stair. It wasn't Jason. He'd only just left, she was being silly.

"Hi, Helena. We're okay thanks. Holding together well given the circumstances. How are you?"

Kath listened with interest as Helena spoke and her face lit up. "Okay, just a minute, I'll ask him."

She yelled to James who was watching the football.

"Jim, do you mind if I go out with Helena for a few drinks?"

The dense chant of football was muted and the silence kicked in. "No, love, you go for it!" he shouted back at her.

Kath needed a pick-me-up and right now Helena was so positive and vivacious that Kath hoped she might be infected with her new enthusiasm for life. Not that she wanted new, she wanted old. She wanted things to be just as they had been before her sticky-fingered son began helping himself to other people's cash. She quickly wondered when it had started. Had she neglected to provide him with sufficient material and immaterial things? Had she turned a blind eye to his basic needs, brushing them off as luxury items as she so often did? Kath pushed the negative post mortem out of her mind as she listened to an exuberant Helena desperate for a night out to catwalk her new fashion items.

"He's fine with it, Helena. Where shall I meet you?"

Her eyebrows rose to full height as she digested the instructions from her friend. "Do you know how expensive the drinks are there, Helena?" Kath gasped. "Have you won the lottery or something?"

Inside, the bar was the vanguard of fashion. Without a doubt it was the most modern, stylish bar Kath had ever stepped foot in and she felt immediately underdressed compared with Helena who towered above her in five-inch show-stopping heels. She looked like a runway model who had just stepped off a Parisian catwalk and Kath saw the heads turn to gawp at the new face about town.

In the centre of the bar was a feature fire place, built within a white granite surround which extended as far as the ceiling. Its fake logs crackled away imaginatively and the heat radiated throughout, warming the clientele in addition to the heat from the fermented alcohol they were readily consuming.

The drinks tables were high – round glass table-tops held up by beech-coloured leggy tripods. They appeared to be very stable for such a simplistic design as drinks were slammed down on them with alarming clumsiness.

The tall white-leather retro bar stools dotted around each of the tables oozed a bright, clean look – if not a little sterile – while the orange and red flames reflected against the white backdrop, adding light and warmth against their paleness.

Helena took Kath's hand and squeezed it. She was alive and kicking. She felt like she had shaken off the remnants of dirt and scrubbed away any remaining excess until all traces of the old Helena Wright had been washed away. She had stared down the plughole of Sophie's pristine white bath, watching as fragments of her old life disappeared. She didn't care if the underground sucked it away and took it on a dirty and perilous journey. She would never see it again.

"Those people are going, Kath." Helena pointed to a table close to the open fire. "You grab that and I'll get the drinks."

Kath headed to the table, standing back politely until the young fashionistas had gathered their belongings and left without feeling hurried.

"Thanks very much."

"Enjoy your night," the tanned dark-haired girl said kindly.

"I will, I'm not paying!"

The girls laughed as they headed towards the manned exit where the suited doorman bade them farewell.

Helena lifted the clasp of her new sequined clutch bag. The small decoration of sequins matched perfectly with the sequined design on the rear pocket of her black jeans. She had caved in and worn the skinny jeans. So what if she looked a little too thin? Wasn't it better than looking a little too fat? She felt the influence of Sophie Kane beneath her shallow thoughts.

Helena scoured the place for familiar faces. She was relieved to see that there were none. Nobody but senior bank management would be able to afford the prices of The Front Room anyway so she had no risk of bumping into anyone from work. Although she need not worry, she was on annual leave, it wasn't as though she was skiving off or anything. She hadn't taken her holidays last year because she was hoping to be paid for them, but the bank insisted that she take some and carry some over, so Helena had started off the year with six weeks leave and had taken only two days so far.

The fortnight off would do her the world of good.

She might even apply for a promotion when she returned to work.

"Champagne!" Kath clapped her hands with glee. "Oh wow! You certainly do know how to take my mind off things, Hel. Are we celebrating something that I should know about? You've taken over Jude's new job? Sophie's salon?"

Helena looked at Kath pointedly. "Life," she said lucidly. "I'm discovering the joie de vivre that I never thought I'd feel again, Kath, and it's all because I got whacked on the head in some taxi and had a bit of common sense knocked into me." She laughed at the stupidity of her own remarks but it really had felt like that. When she had rubbed her head, dazed and shaken, something had immediately felt different.

"Here's to you, love! You deserve a stroke of luck after the tough couple of years you've had."

Their glasses chinked together and they drank.

"So what's the latest with Jason then?" Helena groaned as the bubbles slid down her throat.

"He's out. Neil's taken him in." Kath lifted the glass to her mouth as a distraction.

Helena could see that she was hurting inside. She knew what it felt like to want someone but for them not to want you back.

"What are his plans, do you know?"

Kath shook her head. "He needs to get a job, Helena. Without one he won't have any money and he'll just find other ways of getting it." She clasped her unpainted fingers tightly around the glass. "I can only hope it's just James and me he's taken from and not anyone else. He really would be behind bars if that were the case."

Helena nodded slowly, her expression nonchalant. She listened well, it was part of her make-up, but she also knew Kath was in need of a little light entertainment and that the distraction would do her good.

"Hungry?"

"I'm always hungry . . . this body never stops!"

"La-la-la-la!" Helena put her fingers in her ears.

"I'm not talking about sex!"

They laughed like teenagers as Helena picked up the tapas menu and they 'ooed' and 'aahed' their way through it.

Kath giggled at her friend. She always knew that Helena was comical – when she wanted to be – but tonight, infused with fizzy pop, she had done a great job of making her laugh even if some of it was at her own expense.

"Okay, what about this, Kath? Olives. Humous and pitta bread, handcooked cracked-black-pepper kettle chips . . . washed down with another bottle of pop?"

Kath was amazed. "The other week, Hel, you couldn't even buy yourself a new pair of shoes. What the hell has happened to you because I'll have some of the same!"

"I've dumped that dickhead for starters, leaving him knee deep in a shitload of bills, all of which I stupidly paid for him for way too long, and I am now living in a luxury waterside apartment." She cleared her throat for effect. "Rent free, might I add, with my best friend. It's a simple as that." She added. "I do all the cleaning for Sophie and as much cooking as possible, although that's easy given she barely eats. All this as long as I save hard for a deposit for my own place. That's her only rule."

"She's a saviour." Kath digested the facts, marvelling at how the young woman had been transformed before her very eyes. "She's all bark and no bite, that girl."

"She is, Kath, but you know we've been best friends since we were tiny. We know all there is to know about each other."

"What's there to know about Sophie that isn't already transparent? That girl is as see-through as a piece of cellophane."

Helena looked away sharply. "I'll go order this stuff then, shall I?"

17

"What are we doing today then?" asked Karl as he took the clamp from Roni's tired hair. He handed it to her, desperate to remove it from his own stylish person. He didn't wait for an answer. "We're getting rid of that thing for starters!" He laughed. "It's not exactly the accessory I expected from such an elegant-looking woman."

Karl was deliberately sweet-talking Roni. He knew all there was to know about her from Sophie and, much as he tried to dislike her as a loyal offering to his friend, he simply couldn't. On the contrary, although they had only met ten minutes earlier, he found her shy, nervous and intriguing. There was something about her that was much deeper than her disjointed facade and he was looking forward to conversing with her over the next couple of hours.

"I don't know too much about hair." Roni looked at Karl through the huge circular mirror in front of her. "I'm happy for you to suggest something. It's been a long time since I've been in a hairdresser's to tell you the truth. I tend to do it myself . . ." Roni looked down. She fixed the black cape around her knees, covering her clothes protectively.

"I can see that," he teased her.

Roni was nervous about today but Sophie had been a dream when she had asked for her help. She offered her right-hand man with no hesitation and Roni knew the faith that Sophie had in his creative ability. She was extremely pleased, if not a little unnerved at how kind Sophie had been of late. She had helped Helena out, offered Jude the career lifeline she had been waiting for, and Roni had heard through the grapevine that she had lent a listening ear to Kath in her hour of need. Right now, it appeared that Sophie Kane was the glue holding the Curry Club together.

Perhaps though, thought Roni, it was *she herself* who was changing and not Sophie Kane? Maybe *she* was seeing things differently – for what they were – instead of finding fault and flaws. Life certainly did seem a little less tense and less bleak than it used to but she still needed a hell of a lot of work. The road was long.

"How precious are you about the blonde colour, Roni?" Karl placed his hands on Roni's shoulders as he leaned in to talk to her. He noticed how she shrank ever so slightly into her seat at his touch and he made a mental note to keep his usual tactile approach at bay. He wanted nothing more than for his new client to relax and enjoy the ceremony before she was duly crowned and suitably sent home as the new queen. He noticed that like many members of the Royal family, she too had slightly horsey features about her and she was also, like many of them in his opinion, both plain and yet strangely striking at the same time.

"I'd like to keep a few blonde streaks in if that's okay? I guess it makes me feel a bit younger." Roni blushed and looked down, avoiding eye contact with Karl.

"That's fine. You have to walk round with it, Roni, and you have to be happy and make choices which feel right at the time. If it's wrong we can always fix it later – but it won't be – I give you my word."

He lifted the brittle ends of Roni's hair which sat just above shoulder length when it was let loose. More often than not, Roni's hair was tied back in a scruffy bobble or twisted messily and stuffed into a cheap plastic clamp. Hair was the one area where she had tried not to neglect herself but it hadn't worked out that way and it was all down to her inability to sit in a chair with someone she didn't know and probably wouldn't like. The art of a two-way conversation seemed easy enough on paper, but for Veronica Smyth who spent much of her time alone roaming around her huge house, the skill of conversing was long gone. Roni had taken to buying off-the-shelf hair-dyes when she ventured out on the rare occasion, getting Peter or the kids to put them on when she could be bothered. She did as much behind closed doors as possible.

But she was getting better.

"The ends really do need to go, I'm afraid. They're completely dead, Roni, they're so brittle I'm suprised they haven't broken off. What I'd really like to do is add some copper colour to your hair mixed in with a few chunky blonde streaks just around the front." Karl took the colour chart and handed it to Roni, pointing out the two colours for her approval. She looked excited at the prospect of something new in her life.

"I'm thinking a short bob, arched into the back of your neck and longer at the front to retain the feminity of the style and of course the *bounce*." Karl laughed as he threw his head to one side dramatically. His black hair shifted position with his long fringe flicking from left to right. He swept it back into place, pushing it from his forehead, the styling wax keeping it thick and heightened.

Roni smirked at Karl as he preened in the mirror, redoing what he had just undone with the flick of his head. She could tell he was trying to put her at ease and it was working. He was so normal, so down to earth and so incredibly handsome with his silvery eyes and Mediterranean colouring. She had heard so much about this young man, yet had never met him. He didn't seem too camp to her – a little perhaps but not to the extreme Sophie had talked of.

"Okay," she said.

Karl set about his mammoth task. He was excited about it. He couldn't wait to spin her around when the job was done and show her just how good she looked. Karl could clearly see how well Roni was capable of looking. He had imagined her to be an oversized frump with a permament frown, but instead he saw a curvaceous middle-aged woman with perfect skin, decent dress sense – if not a little tacky – and a pleasant smile, contrived as it often seemed to be.

Roni's high cheekbones took away from the thinness of her lips and her blue eyes were crystal clear with naturally dark lashes. Her eyebrows had been overplucked and pencilled back in neatly. She certainly wasn't his type, she was way too old, but Sophie had given her an extremely poor reference as far as he was concerned. Then again, in fairness, compared to Sophie, she *was* plain and uninteresting. As were most women.

"Are you going away this summer, Roni?" Karl started the obligatory small talk as he mixed together two colours, squeezing the tubes into a small brown bowl until they were empty. He handed the tubes to his junior who needed no instructions to understand they were for the bin. He smiled at her gratefully.

"I think Peter wants to go away this year but I'm not sure where we'll be going." Roni set down the magazine she had been trying to read. "In fact, I'd also like to go away now that I'm . . ." Roni hesitated. Karl continued painting a layer of her hair from root to tip before wrapping it tightly in the aluminium foil which was being passed to him by his ever-so-attentive junior.

"You're what?"

"I'm erm . . . learning to swim," she whispered.

"Good for you, Roni, that's brilliant! You know, I still can't drive much, to the annoyance of Sophie, but I think you've just given me the kick up the bum I needed." Karl smiled at her in the mirror. He wanted to keep her relaxed and at ease in his company.

Roni was elated. It was impossible to hide the massive boost Karl had just given her. See, she wasn't the only one who *still* had much to learn. Perhaps she had been a little hard on herself?

"You've got your own pool, haven't you?"

Roni wondered how much he knew about her and she tensed immediately. There was absolutely no chance that Sophie would have been complimentary – she knew that was a dead cert.

Karl sensed the change.

"Yes, but we don't use it much," Roni answered. "In fact, we hadn't used it since the girls went off to university – until last week when I had my first swimming lesson. But apart from that, I can't remember the last time I got in it, to tell you the truth."

"What was it like then?"

Karl was like lightning. No sooner had he foil-wrapped one piece of hair, his comb was out grabbing another piece, thinning it out widthways with the thin handle of the multi-purpose comb.

Roni turned a shade of scarlet. She was sure her guilt was painted on her crimson face in bold lettering. She had enjoyed it so much.

"It was fine, thank you." Her tone was clipped.

Roni grabbed the magazine. She shoved her face deep into it to remove the iniquity which warmed her from the outside in and Karl couldn't help but notice how ever-changing her behaviour was. One minute she was nothing short of delightful, the next she was clipped, abrupt and defensive. There was definitely more to that woman than met the eye, more than he had realised early on in their encounter. She was the one to watch and all his money was placed on her.

Clive tapped his pen repeatedly on the desk. His heavy touch drowned out the sound of the rain lashing down outside the window of his new, grand office. The wet weather was typical Bank Holiday weather and Clive wished wholeheartedly that the liquid precipitation would clear the air so that it would be bright and sunny for May Day itself so that *The Trophy* could be filled

191

with family and friends as they took a recreational trip around the estuary. The leisurely sail had become an annual Bank Holiday event since they had bought the yacht and every year they went through disturbing amounts of champagne, each year beating the previous, hands down. Also, every year it had been gloriously sunny, adding to the comfort and ease of the day. Clive was keeping his fingers crossed that what was going on outside was freeing the clouds of oblate drops in prepration for a rerun of their unusual luck with the May Day weather. Clive looked forward to this day even more than race days. He got to spend time with Jude, Tom and Anna and all of their friends, giving him enough of a fill to last the remainder of the year. Not a word was mentioned about work on those days and what Clive loved about Jude's set of friends was that they didn't care what he did. None of them, bar Roni, was affected in any way when it came to what they had materially. If anything, he was the brash one. But on that singular day of the year, the Westburys entertained their friends for the love of it and to give them a day they could remember.

Clive had never said to Jude, but sometimes he felt like he missed out on so much because of the hours he put in. He felt like Jude was the lucky one with the power to do as she wished without any restrictions like the tight noose he felt wrapped around his neck. She got to take the kids to their hobbies and to collect them when they had finished, hearing all about their escapades on the homeward journey. Jude also got money in her bank account for doing very little as far as he was concerned. They had a cleaner, a gardener and a young girl who mucked out Polly, Anna's pony, in exchange for keeping her own horse in the purpose-built stables. There were times when Clive swore he would come back as a woman.

He stopped his habitual tapping and leaned forward over the paper-covered desk, pressing the black button on the intercom, which shrilled loudly.

"Yes, Clive?"

"Shirley-Ann, can you order four cases of Laurent-Perrier Rosé, please, and have it delivered to The Firs."

"Certainly."

"Thanks," Clive muttered, tapping his pen again with renewed vigour.

There was something bugging him today but he couldn't quite put his finger on it.

Last night Jude had been different – only marginally – but there was a definite change in her and he couldn't manage to pinpoint what it was, but it had consumed his thoughts all day. It couldn't be women's problems, could it? He tried to narrow it down in his mind but Jude had never suffered from PMS, PMT or any sort of hormonal mood-swings so he could write that off for starters. She had never suffered from anything which affected her mood and he knew how lucky he was not to have it in the neck from a nagging wife – *'her indoors'* – he had heard all the stories from the poor sods at work, some of whose wives had flown at them with knives during certain parts of the month. He shuddered at the prospect of living with a Mrs Bobbet.

It certainly couldn't be money problems, so generous was the monthly housekeeping he paid into her bank account. But something had been so different about his wife last night that it agitated him to the point of frustration. It had been the bane of his day so far and had set him back as he vexed about her levelled attitude and carelessly relaxed approach. Jude had been a paradox in terms of how she'd behaved.

When he had come in from work the house was in darkness with an unlit fire, and the whereabouts of her usual home cooking was anybody's guess. When Jude had suggested a take-out, Clive was astounded, but his tiredness repressed his disconcerted emotions.

It wasn't that he minded. He really didn't, it was that this was the first time in their entire married life that Jude did not have his dinner ready and waiting and it was this he couldn't get his head round. She was as consistent and as reliable as Big Ben.

He recalled mentioning his yachting magazine and Jude had sprung from her seat, delivering it straight to him. She was exuberant and full of energy in doing so yet she had little to say to him about her day when he had asked her what she had done.

Jude had never minded playing the domestic role, but even to her there was a clear difference between carrying out the day-to-day tasks of running a home and being subservient to someone. That was why when she had dived from her seat with the expectation that he couldn't even fetch his own reading material, Clive had become suspicious that Jude was hiding something.

She had waited on him hand and foot. Also, she had been different over the past number of weeks, distracted it almost seemed but with little to show for it. There were no major functions and no upcoming events in her diary. Not that he knew of anyway.

He had to talk to her.

Clive dialled and redialled Jude's number. No answer. Again.

He never left messages. They weren't allowed to at Staines & Greer for confidentiality reasons and the habit was a hard one to kick, even though she was his wife.

Instead Clive sent her a text: Want to meet for bite of lunch?

Clive knew she wouldn't say no. They had little enough time together as it was. His fault, not hers. She was a beautiful woman, anyone could see that, and for the first time in his life, Clive was nervous. His thickly coated arrogance had thinned out, leaving him feeling weak and questioning about the sudden change he had been witnessings.

Jude had still been Jude, but with a twist. She had bounced around the house with a spring in her step and she had a sparkle in her eye which he had not observed for a long time and Clive's gut wrenched as his mind raced to a conclusion which only nightmares were made of.

Surely not?

Karl removed the black gown from around Roni's neck, ripping at the velcro.

Mandy handed him a black plastic brush with long hairs and a knob for its handle and Karl dusted Roni's shoulders, shooing the debris of hair which had a proven ability to reach the strangest of places.

"Keep your eyes shut," he ordered her as he swung the chair around to face the mirror.

He got to work, finishing off his masterpiece.

As Karl sprayed the last of the hairspray, he set down

the can and stood back to admire his work of art. He and Mandy exchanged satisfied grins of artistic appreciation.

"On the count of three you can open your eyes, Roni . . . one – two – three!"

Karl was unusually nervous. He so wanted her to be happy because for some reason he had felt that this visit was about more than just a hairstyle. It was about the rediscovery of a person who was clearly dying to get out of there and show the world who she was. Only Karl felt that Roni was still learning who she was.

She was, it appeared, a late developer.

"I said one, two, three, Roni! You can open your eyes now!"

Roni kept her eyes shut. She was too scared to open them for fear that she looked like herself. True, she came in as herself, but she wanted to leave as someone entirely different to match the difference she had been feeling inside of late. She felt someone nudge her as her world remained in darkness.

"Come on, Roni, take a look at yourself!"

Roni opened her eyes, staring at the floor. She could do it. She only had to raise her head slightly to meet herself but she had always found looking herself in the eye hard to do. This was why she was so keen on her array of jewellery – it caused a distraction not just to her but to everyone who looked at her.

Roni gasped, her mouth flopped open, eyes widened in disbelief. She reacted exactly like those women she saw being made over on the television and *now* she knew that their responses were not fabricated in any way. She had reacted exactly the same as they did.

"Oohh!" She sucked in the air followed by a "Wow!".
That was all she could manage.

Karl and Mandy beamed at her. She looked incredible
and Mandy, young as she was, welled up upon seeing
how flabbergasted their client was at her new image.
Compared to how she looked when she walked in, the
transformation was extraordinary.

Roni's hair had been styled into a razor-sharp bob,
cut into her jawline and taken higher at the back, sitting
arched just above the nape of her neck. Just as Karl had
promised, the length at the front was a contrast of
womanly chic compared with the sharpness of the back
and sides, with copper-coloured shiny locks curled under
her chin and pillar blocks of blonde thickly coloured
around her fringe. The perfectly symmetrical shape framed
Roni's heart-shaped face, thinning it out cleverly. The
midlife jowl which was just beginning to show was
disguised, hidden from view as the silk, plumped-up
tresses curled in to it bluntly. Roni saw the slightly loose
skin below her jawline. It wasn't a permanent feature, a
little weight loss would soon bring her back into shape.
Already she could see how the restyle had distracted
from it and she only knew it was there because she
looked for it. She looked for her flaws before she looked
at anything else.

Her face lit up as she smiled at herself in the mirror
and right in the eyes too. They smiled back at her with
matching levels of intensity. But strangely enough she
didn't feel a bit emotional or weepy as she watched
Mandy dab her heavily made-up eyes with a tissue. She
felt at home, like she was back from wherever it was
she'd been – or not been as was the case. She felt like her

new look fitted her like a glove. It was as though someone had waved a magic wand and snapped her from the permanent state of hypnosis she had lived under for so long now. As she stared at the reflection of the striking woman in front of her Roni felt invincible.

Where the hell had she been? She was a millionaire's wife for Christ's sake, she could be out there doing the world of good for people who needed it – herself and her family firstly, of course. Instead she had been the centre of her own universe, inhabitants One, shutting herself away and shoving her purse deep into her bag like a metaphor for her life.

Roni's restyle had also restyled her life. It was there for the taking and she was damn well going to live it.

18

Jude saw the missed calls from Clive. She had had her phone on silence as she chatted over a relaxing coffee with John. The time had flown in while they covered all that was on their agenda, and more.

Jude found him easy to deal with and extremely professional and he had welcomed her ideas over the architectural structure which both pleased and flattered her immensely. She was off to a great start and she couldn't wait to show Sophie the proposed colour scheme and the professional ceramics she had discovered for the interior and fitting-out. It was a long way off and Jude knew she needed to be patient.

The latter she was finding difficult.

She excused herself politely, lifting her phone to return Clive's call, choosing the privacy of the outdoors. The café was too small, too intimate to speak with her husband.

She stayed back from the rain, leaning against the exterior window, protected by the brown-and-beige striped canopy above her head. She watched the rain fall from the end of the canvas splatting down onto the steel smokers' tables which were redundant and uninvitingly wet. It was ridiculous weather for the beginning of May and Jude knew how much her friends were looking forward to a leisurely float on the more shallow waters of the estuary as they immersed themselves in champagne and hand-made canapés. It was always a beautiful day and she hoped that the weekend would brighten up for them. It was, besides Christmas, her favourite day of the year.

Clive answered his mobile with clear agitation.

"Where have you been? I've been calling you all morning, Jude."

Jude was taken aback at his abruptness. "I'm at the Coffee Bean with Sophie. Why, is something wrong?"

Clive relaxed a little. He felt silly.

"No, nothing at all. I wanted to take you out for lunch, that's all. Where do you fancy?"

Jude cast her eyes at her watch and winced. She couldn't tell him what she was up to, not yet anyway. His partnership was still in its infancy and she didn't want it affected by her own indulgence. He would understand her motives at some point, just not right now.

"I was going to go to one of Kath's classes at the gym to be honest, Clive." Jude's insides turned over as she lied to the man who placed the platinum ring on her wedding finger. It was hardly one of the Seven Deadly Sins, but still she felt like a knife had been thrust deep into her and turned around with a full 360-degree twist.

"Oh." Clive hadn't ever been turned down before. He didn't know how to react. "Oh right, well erm, that's okay, Jude. You go to your class." He was hurt but he tried desperately not to show it. "Tell Kath and Jim I'm looking forward to catching up with them on Sunday."

"Thanks, Clive. I'll make us a special dinner later this evening to make up for it," Jude offered. "Love you."

"Love you too."

Clive set down the receiver and spun on his black-leather executive chair until it faced the window, turning his back on the pile of work which boasted fee incomes of tens of thousands of pounds. And more.

Jude did go to the gym but not religiously. She didn't need to. She was blessed with long slender limbs and a thin torso with 36-inch hips. A perfect catwalk model indeed but for the fact that she hated people looking at her and went out of her way to deflect attention. She and Sophie were the perfect antidote to each other.

Clive shrugged his shoulders as he stretched his feet out onto the newly painted white window-ledge. The room had been re-decorated before the firm allowed him to move in.

He could feel the draught against his ankles as the single-paned window rattled from the ever-increasing wind which had brought with it the terrible weather. He loved living in the north of the country, Clive considered, as the chill stretched up towards his knees, but there had to be something about living down south. The weather for starters. Still, he was in one of the most affluent areas of mainland England so it couldn't all be bad.

And with it came the most affluent and lucrative cases which needed his attention.

Clive mused about his intense workload and reluctantly spun around to be greeted by it. Damn! It was still there. Once more he felt a flash of envy towards Jude and her autonomous life. He would never have that freedom until mid to late fifties he reckoned, or sooner if his investment portfolio picked up from the massive falls it had suffered as a backlash from the worldwide recession.

As skilful an investor as he was, Clive knew he had to balance the financial loss he had suffered on his stock portfolio with the potential for inflated returns if he invested while the chips were down. Cleverly, he waited until the market hit rock bottom when he swiftly purchased an obscene volume of financial stocks knowing that the only way was up however long it took. He was in no real hurry. His timing had been perfect. It was not a 'false bottom' like many other analysts and experienced investors had predicted as they held out for the market to drop even further – which of course it didn't – it *had* hit rock bottom and when Clive's intuition had told him it would fall no further, he scooped up tens of thousands of banking shares, some for as low at 17p per share. The financial market rose and it rose quickly. Those who had waited for it to fall further desperately scrambled to buy before the offer prices shot through the roof. They had missed the boat while he was already on it, sunbathing.

Clive was lucky in life and lucky in love and he was already earning significant monthly dividend payments which Jude didn't know about. Nor did she need to. But he was still chained to Staines & Greer for the forseeable future. Jude was the lucky one of the two. Jetting off to the gym, getting her hair done – although not weekly, he admitted – having long leisurely lunches with her girlfriends. She was the girl who had it all. Not that he was backbiting – she deserved it all as far as he was concerned, and despite the telephone numbers of the many Cheshire Wags she had in her iPhone contacts, she was as far removed from being one of them as was the Pope from denying that abuse had taken place within the Catholic Church.

Jude was virtuous and kind to a fault and she peformed a multitude of charitable endeavours which continued to amaze him. Most of what she did was for others unlike his own calculated agenda. She chose to spend her free time well and by God, he adored her and he needed her more than she realised. She was the backbone of their marriage, the glue which held their perfect family together and she was the head-turner who had never failed to let him down. Jude Westbury was his trophy wife, in more ways than he could articulate.

Clive bounced up from his chair. He was hungry! That was what had been bugging him and giving him that empty feeling all day. If his wife couldn't join him for lunch he would take a well-earned break and dine alone. Any excuse to avoid the seven-hundred-page tax-evasion case he was working on with Noel Foreman QC. It wasn't easy on the stomach, never mind trying to digest it on an empty one.

Sophie excused herself to evacuate her bladder. It was close to her time of the month and as usual she did nothing but pee. She felt bloated, spotty and unattractive, yet her short trip to the bathroom turned every head in the room in her direction – fat as she felt, they didn't see it.

Sophie never stopped noticing the attention she

received. Some days she could take it or leave it, other days she needed it to survive and to feel that she was in her rightful place just where she belonged at the core of where it was all happening. She wasn't insecure, far from it, but Sophie held such regard for how she looked that her body was a temple to be worshipped, often by anyone who took *her* fancy, not *their* fancy.

Jude returned with two skinny lattes. The crockery wobbled dangerously as the missized saucers tried desperately to suction onto the base of the long glass-handled mugs, but without success.

John grabbed a glass mug, clutching it as it slid off its ill-equipped saucer, and a splash of hot froth scalded his hand.

"Shit!" He slammed it down to the side of him where Sophie had been sitting before she had left, then wiped his scalded hand on a napkin before cleaning the underneath of Sophie's mug. He didn't want it dripping on her expensive clothing. He was no expert but it was clear to see that she wasn't kitted out in Primark.

John had politely declined another beverage. He was coffee'd out and his body couldn't face another dose of caffeine.

"I'm so sorry, John." Jude looked concerned. "It looks a little red – are you hurt?"

"I'll survive." He grinned up at her. His hand was mildly pink compared with the other. "I didn't mean to slam it down. The glass was so hot I had to get rid of it, fast." He laughed at the silliness of his earlier reaction. "It was blisteringly hot!"

John abruptly leaned forward, grabbing Jude's wrist,

checking the time. His posture was a half-sitting, half-standing squat and she looked up at him, startled.

John smirked down at her, noting how naturally beautiful she was as she looked directly into his eyes with a surprised expression. Jude was oblivious of the fact that John's gaze lingered a little longer than it should have.

"Sorry, Jude, the battery is dead on my phone and I just needed the time." John sat down, shoving his hands into his navy woollen overcoat in search of his car keys. "I'd better go – I've another meeting to go to."

The rain had stopped and the sun was in desperate battle to conquer the remains of the day as it shone furious rays onto the streets below. It beamed through the glass window – the canvas canopy offered no sunscreen against its unusual blazing power and it illuminated Jude's face with an incandescent glow. Her olive-green eyes flickered as the light shadows tiptoed across them and when she blinked, her eyelids closed under a blanket weight of beauty before reopening with a Hollywood dazzle.

John knew that although he had to leave, he could have sat there all day just watching her. He had never before been in the company of such a woman who oozed such classic charm. One which he wanted to bottle up and sell.

Clive knew exactly what he wanted to eat. He had skipped breakast, something he didn't usually do and his body had felt robbed of energy as a result. He wanted a full-on fry with everything on it. The works. He was fighting fit with normal blood pressure and a perfect cholesterol level so just this once wouldn't hurt him.

He pulled out of the Staines & Greer car park, edging out carefully so as not to scrape the bumper as he reversed on to the street of the quiet cul-de-sac. It was a tight squeeze and the sheer width of the Jaguar didn't help him at all as he manoeuvered through the narrow gates, but he was a careful driver and, with only a centimetre to spare either side, the car pulled out unscathed.

It cruised past the busy shops of Appleby Square and Clive watched as suited office folks busied themselves with lunchtime errands, holding onto sopping wet umbrellas as they dodged the congested foot traffic. He continued on towards Alderley Avenue where all the best shops were, in his opinion anyway, and his eyes scoured both sides of the road for a free parking space. Anywhere would do fine.

He braked hard, holding up his hand to the car behind him offering an apology for the abruptness of his stop, and quickly flicked up the arm of the right indicator. He sat back with smug content as he waited for the red BMW to leave him with a free and ample-sized parking space. Perfect! He could have his fry without worrying about careless dents from other drivers whose own cars had seen better days.

Clive turned into the large space joining the other dozen cars who too had been blessed with impeccable timing. He pulled up the handbrake and removed his phone from its cradle, tempted to ring Jude once more given he was now in the area. He glanced behind him at the khaki-coloured mac which lay carefully over the cream-leather back seat before turning back to look up at the sky through the front tinted windscreen. The sun was out and the rain was off. He would leave his coat and risk it.

Clive sat at an empty table in the window of The Cove Kitchen. He adored the place, grotty as it was in its old-style nautical decor.

He and Will, and sometimes the rest of the crew, would meet there before a weekend race to fill up on '*the*' fry which had made a name for itself as being the best around town. He stared out of the window, people-watching. There were more people today than cars on the road, which explained why he was lucky enough to have bagged a parking space – although that would change once the lunchtime rush had passed and the cars were used once again to drive people home or back to their dreaded place of work.

Across the street there were many more coffee shops dotted amongst cards shops, a large double-fronted charity shop – which Clive knew sold mainly designer goods because Jude dontated much of her personal attire there – an upmarket award-winning butcher's shop and an estate agent's that had properties bought and sold on the same day. Such was the reputation of the area.

Clive slurped his strong hot tea, setting the mug down on the square pine table, avoiding the red-and-white gingham tablecloth which he didn't want to stain. His eyes gleamed as he saw Nancy, the elderly proprietor, walk towards him holding a huge white plate with a linen tea towel.

"It's hot, Mr Westbury," she warned him, setting the enormous platter before him. "Enjoy."

"Thanks, Nancy."

Clive wasted no time tucking in. His knive ploughed into a Lancashire herb-filled sausage which he dipped into a puddle of thick brown sauce and shoved into his mouth. He attacked a bacon rasher, pulling at it roughly and dunking it into the runny egg yolk before stabbing a fried mushroom on the end of his fork for good luck and somehow managing to fit the lot into his mouth though he had little room left to breathe. He couldn't feast on it fast enough, he was that deprived of vital energy. Energy which had been consumed by his own ridiculous thoughts of how his wife had seemed, well, different.

Clive sat back content and feeling more like his old self. He was proud of his empty plate, bacon rinds and all. It was something he wouldn't have dared to eat if Jude had been with him. Not that she had ever stopped him, but she was reasonably health-conscious which made Clive feel that he had to be the same though she put no pressure on him whatsoever.

Nancy would be pleased with him.

Clive stood up, pulling his wallet from the back pocket of his Hugo Boss suit. He withdrew ten pounds which would more than cover his bill. Nancy never failed to make him feel special and for that he tipped generously.

Her deceased father had been a client of Staines & Greer many moons ago when The Cove Kitchen took in an impressive amount of cash. It wasn't quite up to affording the legal services of his firm now – a firm which he was now a partner of.

Clive turned in the direction of the window to check he had all his belongings. He glanced out to see a tall, slender figure with long blonde hair on the opposite side of the road standing outside the door of The Coffee Bean. *Jude!*

His heart fluttered as he recognised his beautiful wife, and he grabbed his jacket from the back of the chair with a hurried glow. But Clive stopped dead when he saw a dark-haired man appear at her side, holding a hand towards her which she was closely inspecting. He watched her throw her head back with careless laughter – she looked so carefree and even from a safe distance away he could tell by the *leaning* body-language of the man, that he was interested. Interested in *his* wife.

Clive realised that he wasn't breathing. His head spun in a light whirl and he stepped back from the window after witnessing Jude kiss the unrecognisable man on the cheek. It was more than his eyes could bear to take in and he could watch no more.

The gym? Was that a euphemism for a workout of a different kind? An adulterous kind?

Clive knew now that his discerning intuition had been right all along. To think he had cursed himself for his feelings when all along he should have known that he was usually accurate when it came to sensing when things weren't quite right. He should have trusted himself and congratulated himself on his powers of perception because that's exactly how he felt when he met Jude – he just knew she was the one for him – a sixth sense he often called it.

Clive stood back behind the matching checked gingham curtains until he felt it was safe to leave. He didn't want to be spotted by either of them. What would he say? The man who usually had an answer for everything, a lawyer through and through, sharp-tongued and quick-witted.

Right now, he was speechless.

Back at his desk, Clive realised that he had no recollection of how he had got there.

He certainly had no recollection of just when it was that his marriage had gone so very wrong.

19

The scurry of activity at The Tudors was in full throttle and Roni was almost bouncing off the walls with delirious excitment. It was her turn to host the Curry Club.

So often she dreaded it, making the minimum of effort by purchasing ready-made Marks and Spencer's meals or Waitrose produce but today her efforts had surpassed themselves and she quite simply couldn't wait to show off her new look – show her friends just how much thought she had put into tonight's event. If they were happy, she was happy, and that was rare.

Of course, Veronica Smyth was not a cook in any sense of the word, never needed to be, but she had arranged for the best caterers around to prepare, to cook and to serve up dinner with some of the best vintage wines available.

Peter had picked them especially for her, plucked from the vast selection of his wine cellar which was a no-go area for her and the girls. He carried the key to his treasure chest with him at all times and his collection of wine was insured along with the rest of his material belongings.

Roni wasn't going to tell the women what was in store for them until closer to the time. It was to be her surprise and she was absolutely bursting with the anticipation of it all. She would text them and drip-feed their excitement, a little at a time.

She sent a text on her old Nokia 6210 mobile phone – she hadn't learned how to use her iPhone yet: 7pm at mine, pls dont b l8.Bring ur swimsuits!!! Roni

Helena heard the mobile phone in her handbag bleep just as she had turned the key to her locker, securing her bag and its remunerative contents safely inside. Security was a big thing for the bank and everything had to be under lock and key at all times, both the customers' money and the staff's belongings.

She stabbed the minature key into its lock once again, yanking open the door and dipping into her bag where she rummaged around, grabbing her phone to read the new message – whoever it was from.

She only had two minutes left before her coffee break ended.

Her eyes grew wide as she read the last sentence. Swimsuit? She'd never been near the pool in Roni's house. In fact, over the years she had never even set eyes on it let alone swum in it.

Helena thought that Roni must have received a bump on the head for she too had been that little bit different lately. Again, it was hard to pinpoint the changes, but Roni was being kind of *nice* and that wouldn't do. They girls simply weren't used to it. They could cope with her harsh ways and outspoken opinions – which usually served herself before others – and her predictability was somewhat reassuring, but the sporadic snippets of *niceness* they had seen were nothing short of disturbing.

Helena's feet dragged behind her, unwilling to return to the banking hall. Her body was half a foot ahead of the rest of her, with her lead-filled feet reluctant to follow suit without an absolute fight.

"Oh, Maggie!" Helena shouted as she saw her step out from the staff toilet. "Maggie!" she called again as she hurried to catch up with her. "Sorry to grab you so abruptly . . . but I wanted to ask you about the possiblity of promotion." Helena panted slightly, partly with exertion and partly with nerves. "I haven't really made the most of my qualifications – which is my own fault in truth – and I wondered what the chances were of getting on the Graduate Management Programme. Or am I too old now?"

Maggie nodded as she listened to Helena. She liked Helena and thought she was a real find, a hardworking girl who had such a way with the elderly folk that it touched her to watch.

"What's your degree in again, Helena?"

"Psychology."

"Useful!" Maggie laughed. "Pity it's not Business Studies or Economics."

"I know but isn't hindsight a wonderful thing?" Helena chortled.

"How old are you, if you don't mind me asking?" Maggie enquired.

"I'm thirty-one."

She and Maggie had a great relationship and Helena felt she could talk to her about anything.

213

"Well, what about Human Resources?" Helena said. "Surely Psychology would be useful there? Don't they do all that psychometric testing and those other behavioural-type interview things?" Helena was determined to make Maggie see how serious she was. "Maybe I could be trained up to work at head office doing job interviews and stuff?"

Maggie saw the sparkle in Helena's eye. She hadn't asked for anything over the years – in fact, Maggie was surprised at how little ambition she'd had for a young girl, but since she had returned from her annual leave Helena had been an entirely different person, and full of life. She looked better too. Her hair was styled and she took the time to apply make-up which she didn't usually bother with. Not that she needed it but it enhanced her delicate features and complemented her overall appearance.

"I could see you doing that actually, although I'm not sure what vacancies are coming up – particularly with the cuts in the training and development budget. There's an embargo on recruitment at the moment which isn't going to help your case . . . leave it with me though. Let me make a few calls to see what's coming up. You know I'd hate to lose you from the banking hall, don't you? The customers love you, particularly the older ones – you have such a way with them."

Helena said nothing. She didn't want the banking hall any more. She wanted out of there and as far removed from that place as was possible.

"I feel like I've outgrown it to be honest, Maggie." Helena flushed. "I've been doing the same job day in, day out for years now and I feel the need to move on. There have been some, erm, changes to my personal life and I would love to start doing things differently . . . now that I'm over thirty . . . and single."

"You don't look a day over twenty-one to me," Maggie squeezed Helena's hand. "I'm on the case, Helena. I promise I'll be in touch."

Helena stood back, watching Maggie walk away with brisk steps until she disappeared from sight and then her shoulders sank down with relief as the tension dissipated and her stomach churned with butterflies at the prospect of breaking free and making a new start.

She had put closure on Nathan – as much as he would let her with his endless texts – and now she needed to put closure on her job. Helena knew if she stayed there she would be asking for trouble. She was lucky there had been none already, more than lucky.

As Roni put the finishing touches to the room, she stood back taking it in, gulping at how between them they had transformed the traditional-style chalet hut into a contemporary open-plan party area.

The partition doors to the well-stocked bar were pulled back to allow the guests direct access to its counter and Roni had placed five chrome bar stools up against its black granite. The bar was to be manned all evening so that the ladies could take their pick of alcoholic delights. Everything was on the menu tonight at The Tudors and Roni was startled at how much she was looking forward to seeing the pleasure on their faces as she entertained them – with a little help.

A huge disco ball hung above the bar, spinning around as a natural breeze brushed past it, this way and that way. Its mirrored images dotted the walls and floor with a flicker of multi-coloured lights and Roni couldn't wait for the darkness to fall so that they could experience its full-on effect.

All around the walls, metre upon metre of luminous blue fairy lights were hung decoratively and tacked into place. Peter had done it last night – no questions asked – he was delighted at the changes he had noticed in his wife and right now he couldn't do enough for her or get enough *of* her.

Roni's catering team had re-invented the wicker furniture by draping the table with a black linen cloth, a perfect backdrop to the shocking pink napkins which she had requested they bring with them to match the fuschia-coloured wineglasses. Roni loved colour and while she also loved style, albeit her taste was a little tacky, tonight was about pleasure and enjoyment and fun, not about a perfect designer bash. She chose the black and the shocking pink to have fun with her girlfriends and fun they would have.

She had re-visited Karl to have her hair blown for the occasion – twice in a short space of time in fact – and Roni giggled as she recalled Karl telling her that she herself was '*now cutting edge*'." Veronica Smyth had only ever been *cutting*, a bit like someone else she knew. She laughed silently at the prospect of what she was becoming. While it was an amazing feeling to look in the mirror and be greeted by the face of a stranger, becoming less strange by the minute, she knew that she still needed to work on what was inside of her, and that could take a while. She was what she was and her fractious characteristics were congenital.

"Are you nearly ready, Soph?" Helena waited patiently by the front door.

"Yep, just getting dressed," Sophie shouted from behind the paper-thin bathroom door. "I can't believe Roni is opening up the pool for us, can you?" She didn't wait for an answer. "What's with that woman? Karl said she was in the salon *again* getting a blow-dry!"

"Maybe she's beginning to realise she's been in her own little world for too long, Sophie," Helena offered. "Been locked away like Rapunzel in the tower of her castle waiting for someone to rescue her . . . anyway, don't knock it, Soph, she's lining your pockets with every visit."

"Yeah, or maybe she's getting her end away with someone else and that's why she's so interested in how she looks all of a sudden?"

Sophie emerged from the closet-sized bathroom into the magnolia-painted hallway. It was such a confined space and so deprived of natural light that she could only paint it either that or white and she was too messy for white walls – at least her fake tan was anyway.

"You always think the worst of everybody, Sophie."

"No," she corrected. "I always think the worst of Veronica Smyth."

Sophie grabbed her Burberry canvas tote-bag from the floor and shoved her bathing suit into it along with a miniature washbag. "Anyway, what's with Rapunzel? She's barely got any hair! I know, she could thrown down her attitude . . . that would be long enough to extend from her roof space to the ground, wouldn't it?"

Helena tutted at her friend's silliness.

"I hope she's got showers we can use, Hel – my hair goes green if I don't wash the chlorine out of it."

"Then you'll look like Grotbags as well as acting like her!"

217

Helena opened the door and shoved her friend out into the plush hallway with its natural brickwork complementing the contemporary striped communal carpet.

"Cheeky!" Sophie pulled the door firmly shut behind her. "Wait! Have you got your swimsuit? I'm not getting in on my own, no way José."

Helena beamed and held up a small bag by its string handles. "I got a new one," she boasted.

"And a new body to go with it by the looks of things, Hel. Have you put weight on? You're getting a bit fat."

Helena swung her bag against Sophie's upper arm with force.

"You know, I could swing for you sometimes, Sophie Kane!" she snapped angrily. Okay, so she was *now* eating, of course she was going to put a little weight on but she was far from fat.

"You just did," Sophie replied rubbing her arm.

Roni stood before the door clutching at its handle. She'd waited until all the women arrived before allowing them into the room which had so transformed itself. After each one of her friends rapped on the ostentatious door-knocker, clutching at the brass jaw of the lion's head, she had ushered them into the kitchen as she usually did and now that she had them all together she was ready for them to make their grand entrance.

Roni opened the glass-panelled single door, pushing it right back to allow the women to enter. She stood back to let them past, watching their reactions.

"Wow!" Jude gasped. She had seen the pool chalet before but not looking like this.

"Do you like it?" Roni could barely contain her excitement.

"*Oh my God,* Roni! It's incredible. How could you have kept this little jewel from us for so long, you stingy cow?" Sophie winked at Roni. She didn't want her playful words to be taken out of context and nor did she want to be banned from swimming leisurely lengths, resting to sip on a Long Island Iced Tea to counteract the exertion.

"It wasn't always like this," Roni answered a little more shyly. She was aware that all four faces were staring at her and actually listening to what she had to say. "I'd never really used this room before apart from when the kids lived at home . . . until I started my swimming lessons, but I've come to absolutely love being in here."

She beamed with pride and her ample chest puffed out of her jersey cerise-pink top which she had kept since the eighties. This one didn't escape during her ruthless clearout, and it matched the colours of the night.

Helena squeezed past Roni first, rushing forward with excitement. She bent down on the immaculate tiles, dipping her hand into the water, rolling her eyes, immersed in its perfect temperature.

"The water is so hot, Roni, it's like a bath. Can I get in now?"

"It's not your birthday yet, is it, Hel?" Sophie teased her, which she ignored.

"Don't get in yet, Helena," said Roni. "We'll be eating soon."

"I don't think she *really* meant it, Veronica," Sophie pointed out.

"I've never felt water so hot," Helena went on. "It must cost you a fortune to run?"

"I do like it quite hot though."

"I'll bet you do!" Kath shrieked. "Some like it hot, eh, Roni?"

Kath was back on form, although every now and then she would go off into her own little train of thought and her eyes would be filled with a heavy sadness. Jude knew how close she was to her boys and she knew how much she would be hurting. It hurt her too knowing this but there was little she could do bar be there for her friend night and day.

"Darren says it's far too hot for swimming but –"

"Does he now!" Sophie was keen to hear more. "What else does Darren say about being *hot*, Mrs Smyth? You're looking pretty *hot* yourself these days if I may say so!"

Roni stood open-mouthed. Her cheeks shot to an impressive scarlet colour which clashed with her cerise top.

"Will you all stop interrupting me!" she snapped, turning quickly, heading towards the bar where she picked up a cocktail menu and sank her head into it. For some reason, Roni couldn't hear the name *Darren* without losing control. And she hated that.

"I think we've touched a raw nerve," Sophie whispered to Helena.

"What's he like then, this Darren? We haven't heard too much about him," Kath asked innocently.

"Well, if you'd like to all turn up at 10a.m. tomorrow I'm having another swimming lesson. You're more than welcome to come along as spectators." Roni spoke with a dry nonchalance as she handed out the drinks menus.

"Really?" Helena was amazed.

"No!" Roni sneered. "It's called sarcasm! Now will you please butt out of my personal life and choose a drink!" She thrust the cocktail menu at Kath who grabbed it excitedly.

Sophie belted out hoydenish laughter. "That's more like the Roni we know! *Will the real Veronica Smyth please stand up, please stand up!*" she sang, waving her hands around like a street rapper, her black leather skirt forced to ride up as she stood with her legs slightly apart and knees bent.

Even Roni struggled to suppress a smile. She was trying, but it was so hard to shake off the way she had been her entire adult life. She would try even harder, she decided. Outbursts like that were unacceptable.

"Soph?"

"What?"

"I can see your knickers from down here," Helena told her matter-of-factly.

"At least she's wearing some for a change!" Kath joined in.

Sophie turned to the women holding up a V sign with two fingers as a rude gesture to her friends.

"Sophie Kane. As charming as ever," said Jude.

As the darkness crept in, Roni flicked on the cosmetic lights which created an instant buzz of excitement. The blue fairy sort were draped like tinsel on a Christmas tree, dipped for decorative effect. The dark granite of the bar's surface was covered in table confetti, each tiny piece was shaped into a fun item. There were champagne bottles, butterlies and even miniature palm trees in shockingly bright, luminous colours.

On the main dinner table the black linen cloth was screaming with shocking-pink crystal sprinkles which had already caused one fuschia-cloured wineglass to break as the glass was set down on top of it, before wobbling to its death.

Jude sat with her pink napkin on her knee. Curry and white jeans didn't go well together and they were her favourite Calvin Kleins so she wanted to look after them. She set her knife and fork down, resting them carefully on the edge of her plate.

"Roni, this is really incredible, thank you so much. You have absolutely transformed this place. Maybe Sophie should have given you the contract and not me."

Roni looked away, unsure of how to react. She wasn't used to hearing words of admiration. Not from her friends anyway.

"Yeah, Roni, thanks a million for taking my turn." Helena was touched. "I really appreciate it."

For once, Roni was calm and content. Her back wasn't up and she wasn't waiting to be shot down by someone's snide remarks – deserved as most of them were.

"I'm not sure dinner in the communal hall of our shitty apartment block would have gone down too well with you guys." Helena shuddered. "Perhaps I should have asked Nathan if I could borrow the apartment for one night, given I'm the one who has paid the rent until the end of the month. Why didn't I bang my head two days earlier? Then I would have escaped payment!"

Roni had made huge efforts and they hadn't gone unnoticed but she still needed a little work on how to accept compliments. She nodded her head at Helena once more and the corners of her mouth turned up in a half smile. She knew she needed counselling to correct her people skills, but she had made such a turnaround in no time that patience was a virtue she needed to hold on to. She had been wearing an uptight, conservative facade for so long now that surely she could wait a while longer to metamorphose fully into someone different?

"Who did the caterering, Roni?" Jude enquired. "I could do with adding another firm to my list. The guys I use now are brilliant for finger-food but gourmet hot food like this is rather hard to come by."

"Stop saying *hot*. I'm getting horny." Sophie pushed her chair back from the table. She had eaten all she could. Her leather skirt covered little more than her underwear and her toned thighs were left for all to view.

"Anyone fancy a little girl-on-girl action since there are no blokes about?"

"*Hhhmm*."

The women turned around in the direction of the sound.

Rafi simply waved to them from the confinements of the bar and Sophie smiled back at him, dazzling and seductive. He was *hot* alright. Where the hell had that little jewel been hiding?

20

"Everybody has to be in the water before the question can be read," Roni ordered giddily. She had drunk one too many cocktails. But wasn't that what she was paying Rafi to do? Tend bar? It was his forte and he was damn good at it. He made Sophie's Long Island Iced Tea taste like it was from a packet, a blend of powder mixed with tap water.

"You'd better stay in the shallow end, Roni – you're pissed and you'll drown otherwise," Kath instructed pointedly, never one to mince her words. "In fact, you shouldn't really be in here. None of us should."

"Get off your soapbox, you fitness freak!" Helena scooped up water with both hands and hurled it at Kath. It landed on her head in one big splat and the noise echoed around the room followed by the shriek of drunken female laughter.

"Do you mind, it took me hours to achieve that frizzed look!"

One by one the women sank down into the tropical waters which lapped around them.

Sophie in her spotty La Blanca swimsuit, backless and with cutaway sides. Jude played it safe in a plain black high-legged costume showing off her eternal legs, and Kath was dressed in keeping with her feline streak in a fashionable leopard-print tankini. Every one of the women looked stylish and beautiful but it was Helena who stole the show. As she took the steps carefully, the women stared at her body beautiful. The thick black lycra pulled in Helena's barely there waist, nipping it into an hourglass shape, and thin as she was her full-sized C-cups were pushed together into an impressive cleavage, pinned with a massive diamante brooch. The spaghetti-thin straps draped over her shoulders and her stomach was a flat as any catwalk model's. She looked sensational.

"Oh my Gooodd! I sooo need to borrow that, Hel, please?" Sophie begged. "Pleeese!"

Helena raised an eyebrow at her best friend.

"I'm not sure . . . I'd be worried about you stretching it on me, Sophie."

"Ha ha, very funny. Okay, that's one-all now!"

Roni continued to have her back turned, still clad in her personalised robe as she commanded the staff who were scurrying around clearing away the remains of the spicy hot jalfrezi with military confidence.

The heat from the jalfrezi, which had been served with a mild dhansak, had burned Helena's mouth she had shovelled it in so fast. That was why, she explained, she had been drinking so quickly.

Roni untied the belt of her robe and let it drop to the floor – back in her leading-lady role – confident that her attire matched the glamour of her friends. Her attire, not her body. She knew she had lost a little weight because the swimsuit felt less compact around her midriff but she had a long way to go. What was helping her was not hiding her body any more. Exposing it made her feel more determined to work on it.

There was a gasp from the water and Roni looked instantly pleased. She hadn't expected them to have witnessed her weight loss. Not so soon.

Her delight was short-lived.

"That's *my* swimsuit!" Helena almost convulsed as the words spluttered out. "We're wearing the same swimsuit, Roni!"

Roni's face dropped instantly. Now it made sense, the gasp which she had naively taken as a compliment.

"I've sooo changed my mind about borrowing it now thanks, Hel." Sophie shot Helena a catty grin. "Two-one."

Roni looked down at her one-piece and back towards Helena who was clearly put out. It was identical – bar the size.

Helena chewed on the inside of her mouth where the skin had broken off, the backlash of her earlier ravenous greed where she had shoved the piping hot curry into her mouth without waiting for it to cool down.

"If I were you, Sophie, I'd start charging Helena here some rent." Roni spoke in a clipped tone.

"What do you mean?" Sophie asked suspiciously, ready to protect her friend.

"Well, if she can afford a three-hundred-pound swimsuit, she can afford her own place." Roni was truly put out.

The room turned to face Helena who froze under the gaze of so many.

"I am here, you know, guys – you're talking about me as if I'm not."

Jude looked uncomfortable.

"And actually," Helena said after a short delay as she took in the sea of mixed expressions, "I got it from that charity shop just past the Coffee Bean and for a fraction of that price, Roni."

Her retort satisfied the women.

Roni took the blue-and-beige tiled steps which descended into the pool, stopping halfway down so that the water was just past her knees. This was the exciting moment she had been waiting for. The Curry Club in her very own swimming pool. *Beat that, ladies!* She had already put to bed the Swimsuit Saga. Helena was younger and more attractive than her so she was bound to look better in it than she, but what Helena didn't have was obscene wealth. Roni won hands down.

"Okay," she called behind her.

A uniformed lady, mid-fifties, scurried over with a cocktail shaker which Roni took with great pleasure. She took it from the hands of her hired staff member without a word of thanks, shaking it vigorously, pulling off the smaller cap first and then the larger steel lid through which the liquid would ordinarily be sieved. She plunged in and grabbed a tiny piece of paper, handing back the steel jug to the waitress who was waiting patiently at the pool side. It was all very orderly.

"That will be all for now." Roni released the hired staff so she could read the contents of the slip in private. "You too, Rafi!" she called behind her as she unwrapped the tight creases with her manicured hands.

Roni cradled the paper like a baby after Sophie

splashed her, protecting it from the droplets of water which continued to rain down on her.

"Hurry up!" Sophie yelled impatiently. "My fingers are getting all wrinkly. My face will look twenty-one but my hands will end up like an ol' doll's."

"Don't splash me, Sophie, the ink will run."

"Yes, Miss."

Jude laughed out loud. Sophie was bold and funny and she didn't care what she said nor to whom.

"Okay, here goes. Listen up," Roni ordered Sophie who was whispering into Jude's ear.

"*Sieg Heil!*" Sophie held up her right arm and Helena forced it down.

"Don't even do that in jest, Sophie – that's not a bit funny."

"Children!" Kath chastised.

"Right," Roni proclaimed. She bent her eyes to the slip of paper and then read aloud in sheer amazement: "'*I'm doing something illicit but I don't know how to stop.*' Bloody hell! Illicit? Who'd have thought?"

As she glanced up, Roni saw the wide eyes of Jude and Sophie, and a gasp ecaped from Kath's mouth echoing through the chalet, bouncing off the walls.

"Read it again, Roni," Kath instructed.

"'*I'm doing something* illicit *but I don't know how to stop,*'" Roni read again, slowly and with emphasis on the 'illicit'. She needn't have gone looking for any further drama, it was right there in front of her

"What does 'illicit' mean?" Kath wondered loudly.

"Stop trying to cover up, Kath, you know that's not allowed. You always do that!" Roni piped up.

"I'm not covering up, Roni," Kath said earnestly. "I thought 'illicit' meant sexual or something of a sexual nature so I need to clarify the word's meaning before I can give any input. I can't talk about what I don't understand, now can I?"

Jude sank her shoulders into the water. She needed an injection of heat into her body, shivering as she was at the prospect of how dangerous the situation could be – whatever it was. Her blonde hair was twisted into a messy bun, yet she still managed to look effortlessly sexy.

"It means criminal or corrupt, Kath," Jude explained with only her head on display, the rest of her hidden below the surface. "Something that, naturally, shouldn't be happening and of course by the admission it seems as though that person has the sense to know they shouldn't be doing whatever it is they are doing." Jude continued to sink down into the jaccuzzi-like heat. She dipped low, the water lapping against her chin. She was a little tipsy which was unlike her but she had been working so hard lately that she had decided earlier in the day to take a few drinks. It would do her the world of good. "The only comment I have to make which is hardly rocket science is that – whatever you're doing, just *stop it*. I can say no more than that, I'm afraid. I would strongly advise you to quit it. *Now*."

"Me?" Kath was aghast.

Jude tittered at her reaction. Jude saw the funny side of practically everything.

Roni was still half in, half out of the pool, holding the slip of paper for dear life and clutching her chest, looking genuinely afffronted for Kath.

"*You* as in plural, sorry, Kath," said Jude. "I was speaking to the group, not to you directly."

"Oh. Okay. But you were looking at me."

"I have to look at someone!"

Jude pealed with laughter. She was so immersed in the liquid heat that she was dangerously close to swallowing some. She saw the reflection of a happy woman beaming back at her.

Roni finally entered the pool, holding the side for support and Kath edged closer to her holding out her hand to pull her further into the deep water where she was bobbing about merrily.

"What can the scandal be though? I mean, we've all got jobs. We haven't the time for anything else!" Sophie nodded towards Roni. "Except you, Roni, but the rest of us are busy working hard and playing hard. I just don't see how anyone's got time to be a crook on the side? And criminal at what?"

"Excuse me. I do have a *job*. I'm a wife and a mother and the lady of a huge house which is a full-time job in itself, thank you, Sophie."

"I meant a proper job, Roni, not being a domestic slave to two spoiled brats and an assuming husband!"

Roni's jaw dropped, then she remembered what she was trying to achieve so she said nothing.

Sophie waited for her retaliation but it didn't come.

"This is not about our Jason, in case any of you are wondering," Kath butted in. She could see just where that argument was headed and she didn't want her son being dragged into something which didn't concern him. He had enough to contend with. "But having lived with someone who has taken from me and James, I need to tell you to be considerate to those around you and to those you're hurting . . . because the pain is unbearable." She swallowed hard before continuing. "Try to stop and consider the consequences of your actions before you do what it is you're doing."

Kath hopped to the edge of the pool, leaving Roni chest-deep in water on her own. She gulped down her Cosmopolitan in one large medicinal gulp.

"I agree with Kath in that I don't believe that any crime can be committed without someone being hurt somewhere down the line," Sophie chipped in. "Keep that in your mind next time you're tempted to do your *illicit* activities."

"Were you talking to me just then?" Jude tried to keep a straight face.

"I have to look at someone, don't I?" Sophie punched the water and it splayed towards Jude, splashing the tanned skin of her chest. "Having said that, if it's drugs – unless you're dealing of course – then come clean because I'll buy them off you. There's nothing wrong with a bit of recreational drug-taking, I don't think." Sophie was treading water in the deep end. "Look how much I have to exercise to stay thin when I could just snort myself thin!"

Helena chuckled away. She and Sophie had taken all sorts of illegal substances over the years and loved every minute of it – although in fairness she was not sure they could remember every minute of doing it but what she could recall was quite an experience.

"What if the person doesn't know how to stop what they're doing?" Helena offered. "What if the habit has

231

become an addiction and the addiction has then become a habit?"

"That's what the note said, wasn't it? That the person didn't know how to stop," said Jude.

"I'm confused?" Roni panted as she fought against the water's resistance, trying to move towards the shallow end of the pool. She was breathless from alcohol and from the heat from the water.

"Anyway, so what, Hel?" said Sophie. "Who cares what the *label* is? Bloody well stop it or get some therapy if you can't stop it on your own – and obviously you can't, whoever you are."

"It's not as simple as that. A habit is something people do by repetition, whereas addiction is something where the person has lost control and become a hostage to the addiction." Helena spoke with technical confidence. "Addiction, in terms of behavioural change, is far more difficult to reverse than simply kicking a habit."

"So whoever it is needs to determine which of the above it is then?" Sophie asked.

"Quite," said Roni. "They've done the hard bit by understanding they have a problem. All they need to do now is decide whether they can stop what they're doing alone or, as I said earlier, if they perhaps feel they're past the point of no return and can't break from whatever – then get professional help."

Jude pushed herself out of the water and sat on the side, dangling her legs. Her face was flushed with the heat from the water and her thighs had turned a pretty shade of pink.

"Look," she said, looking in turn at each and every

woman, "whatever is or has been done, it seems that you've got away with it . . . so far, but that won't last forever." She was telling herself this as much as she was telling her friends. "Stop it now before you get caught. None of us are criminals here but we do all take wrong turns now and then or risks here and there and the odd white lie when we have to, but there's a fine line between a little white lie and knowingly breaking the law." Jude looked down at her colourful legs. "I think it's time to come clean," she told anyone who was listening, but moreso she told herself as she toyed with the secret she was keeping from Clive.

Sophie stopped treading water and swam to the side of the pool. She wondered if her friends were thinking of her as a prostitute-cum-call-girl. Did they suddenly wonder if she was paid for the sexual favours she dished out? Soliciting was highly illegal, she knew that. It had been mentioned before and her proclivity to treat men like they were cash machines didn't sit particularly well with the group – some of them anyway.

Kath swam slow lengths as she mused about Jason. That question might well have been composed by him. Of course it hadn't been. She had tried to put the women straight, but what if they hadn't believed her, thought she was using them to set her son on the straight and narrow?

As Roni braved the water, she tried hard to erase the adulterous images which had occupied her mind for too long now. Adultery was illegal. It was alright for Sophie to put herself about, she wasn't married. Roni was determined to use the underlying message of tonight's Curry Club and turn it into something positive. She was a happily married woman and she would stay that way . . . she was sure of it.

Helena floated on her back gazing up at the night sky. The water lapped around her face covering her ears and she could hear nothing but the silently voiced contentment of her new life.

21

Jude stared into the garden as she waited for the toast to pop up. She saw the daffodils in full bloom and watched as the Virginia bluebells swayed clumsily into the neighbouring crocuses. She loved the garden – it was her place of safety – and so often she sat at the bottom of it beneath the Japanese Maple tree she had planted shortly after her father's death, snuggling into the bench which she had dedicated to him.

Even though he was no longer with her, Jude knew that she would always be a daddy's girl. He had never told her what to do, gave her no advice whatsoever. *'You'll know if something is right for you, cupcake, in the same way you'll know when something is wrong for you. It's a feeling that will guide you – and only you will know.'* She believed him. Because he was right.

Jude decided last night that she would need to tell Clive about her double life, short-lived as it was. She was sure he would understand. She was hardly announcing that she was a mass murderer. It was *work*. But Jude knew how traditional he was, supported fully by *her* mother and it seemed she was the odd one out.

"Mum."

Jude looked around the kitchen, struck by how untidy it was, by her standards anyway.

"Mummy darling!" Tom scoffed.

"Yes, Tom?"

"The toast has popped up." Tom smiled broadly at her.

He reminded her of herself when she was his age. Tall and flat-chested.

"So it has. Silly me." Jude smiled fondly at her handsome boy.

She pulled the toast from the chrome toaster, buttering it with precision before cutting it into quartered triangles and delivering it to the table.

"Anna, come off the phone, darling. You'll be with your friends in less than an hour, you can catch up with them then."

Anna glanced up sulkily. She was a mass of teenage hormones. Jude simply ignored her daughter's haughty expression and set about tidying the kitchen. She began with emptying the dishwasher.

Her daughter would grow out of her childish ways, Jude thought as she lifted a pile of plates from their racks. They gleamed with a stark cleanliness, oozing lemon scent. In many ways Jude envied her daughter and the juvenile life she lived. Yes, she had exams to study for, but Anna was a bright and gifted child and the school already had her primed for one of the Oxbridge Universities. Anna had the best years of her life ahead of her whereas Jude's – until now – were firmly behind her.

"Mum, is Sophie coming out on Sunday?" Anna piped up.

"She said so, darling."

"Yeah! I can't wait. She lets me use her make-up *and* she braids my hair."

Tom stared at his twin sister. His gaze carried a look of absolute disinterest in her small talk.

"Who are you bringing, Tom?" Anna asked.

"I'm not sure yet, Anna." Tom looked at his mother. "I don't know how much room there is with all Mum and Dad's friends going. Anyway, I'll be too busy sailing the thing while you're sat on your derriere beautifying yourself." He teased his sister who frequently acted years younger than her age despite her natural intelligence.

"Oh, Tom, won't you just make somebody a wonderful husband one day!" Anna retorted with full-on sarcasm.

Jude stopped wiping the breadcrumbs which had fallen from the bottom of the toaster when she banged it against the shelf in haste.

Tom? A husband?

Jude rarely stopped to think of the children not being with them. She couldn't bear to think of another woman being the central female figure in her son's life, selfish as that was. She had been there for him every day during the past fifteen years, immersed in his life and very much at the core of it.

Jude understood in a flash why so many of her friends had returned to work after their children were born. Not only did they maintain their careers and their identities, they were left with a lifeline and a continuation of an existence that lived long after their kids had flown the nest. The justification for her return to work had just increased tenfold. If there had ever been a doubt in her mind it was truly erased now.

Anna was right, one day they would both be gone and she would be on her own, left with a filled past but a blank future. She needed a life in her own right – as herself. She would tell Clive over dinner tonight.

Roni's head was thumping and she found it difficult to concentrate. The movement from the water made her stomach churn and she hoped desperately that she would make a full recovery before tomorrow's cruise. Peter would be mad with her if she didn't go, it was his day too and he got on like a house on fire with Clive and James. Nathan he had never cared for much, they had nothing in common, but he was no longer on the scene.

"Ready then?" Darren stood at the side of the pool, peering down at her. She wasn't looking her best today.

"Mmh."

"Don't sound so enthusiastic," he chided.

"I'm concentrating."

"Good, that's what I like to hear."

"On not being sick, idiot!"

As Roni barked at him, once more he was reminded of the cold woman he had met on the first day, who reared her ugly head from time to time although with less frequency. He had noticed definite changes in her, but still, she regressed so quickly and easily into the hollow woman which he hoped she might have fled from.

"Do you really feel sick, Roni?"

Roni's face was a shade of ashen and her eyes had puffy bags beneath them.

"I really do. I'm sorry, Darren, but I don't think I can do this today."

Darren smiled at her. He felt sorry for how bad she felt, self-inflicted as it was.

"No worries." He offered his hands out to her, leaning down to reach the short limbs which she held up to him. He grabbed her petite hands and hoisted her clean from the pool in a single lift.

Roni stood, shivering as she continued to clutch his hands. She dared herself to look up at his flawless, boyish face, noticing how his skin had rid itself of the acne he wore when they first met.

"Sorry for calling you an idiot. That was mean of me."

"It's okay . . . hey, did you get your hair done?" Darren let go of Roni's hands as he felt her grip linger.

"Erm, yes."

"It really suits you," he spoke honestly. "I love the colour, it makes you look loads younger."

Roni was flattered and embarrased in equal doses.

"Thanks," was all she could manage.

As Darren bowed down for closer inspection, Roni tilted her face up until they were just inches apart, thinking he was set to kiss her. She moved in closer, aiming for his lips but as he pulled back unaware she kissed his chin.

Roni turned and fled. She was mortified. What was she thinking? Obviously something different to what *he* was thinking. He was checking out her *hair* not *her*. Stupid, stupid woman!

Roni knew she was too embarrased to look at Darren, but she also knew if she opted out of the swimming Peter would want to know why and she could hardly blame Darren for checking out her hi-lights. She knew she had to face the music. This was her first step as the *New Roni*, to tackle things like an adult.

She wrapped her robe around her hungover body and trudged back to the pool where Darren remained in exactly the same spot, unsure of what to do.

"I'm really sorry. I, erm, don't know what came over me," she whispered. "Please let's not allow it to get in the way of any further swimming lessons because Pe –"

Darren cupped Roni's face as though it were a fragile carving. He kissed her hard on the lips. He looked suprised by his own action as he paused to consider hers. "This is what came over you," he told her before stooping down to kiss her again, regardless.

'If you don't hand over the money I'll spill the beans on Sophie, you stingy bitch.'

Helena read the message again. And again. She had received a number of negative texts from Nathan but nothing like this.

'Get a job, you lazy bastard!' she replied with rage.

He wouldn't tell. Nathan was always spineless, he lacked gusto, conviction and his jelly legs wouldn't have the bottle to do it.

Let him get evicted. It wasn't her fault she had carried him for so long that he had forgotten what *responsibilities* were. He would learn the hard way like any other person. Failing that, he could always ask his mother, it was about time he got off his lard-arse to see her.

'You didnt spend al ur bonus I no it! Hand ovr o'wise I'm homeless & ul b friendless.'

Helena smirked at the prospect of Nathan aimlessly wandering the streets. He wouldn't last two minutes. *Friendless*? Was that even a word? What was wrong with her that she had stayed with him for so long?

'Enjoy al' fresco living, Nathan!' she giggled as she replied to him.

'Pls Helena? My Helena.x'

'Fuck off!'

Helena chose not to tell Sophie about the text messages. It would only worry her, and while Sophie was candid in her day-to-day affairs, she was a closed book as far as her past was concerned. She drip-fed information as and when it suited her and she was a good liar with an even better memory for it. She was brilliant in fact.

Sophie threw her keys on the timber worktop. She yawned and her eyes watered with tiredness. Today had been a busy day and she herself had undergone back-to-back appointments with cuts, colours and a six-hundred-pound hair-extension for one client – lucky with their new image but unlucky with the exorbitant bill – still, human hair didn't come cheap.

She headed into the open-plan living room like she did every night taking a few minutes to check out the views, see if any new yachts had moored and get a feel for the general comings and goings of the small but exclusive marina. It was not a working harbour but moreso a recreational mooring platform, and boats of various small-to-medium sizes moved in and out of there continually, but that was generally the height of it.

Sophie caught sight of a case of champagne in a

corner of the small balcony. She opened the balcony door, pulling it inwards and stepped outside.

"Helena!" she yelled. "Why have we got a case of Bolly on the balcony?"

Helena strutted into the living room in a red woollen shift dress, one that Sophie hadn't seen before. Her lips were painted scarlet and she looked as pretty as a picture. Her naturally brown hair fell down her back sleek and shining and the recent auburn tones added colour to her cheeks, lighting up her dainty face.

"It's for the cruise. I didn't think it was fair Jude buying the champers every year and since I've never been able to make a contribution, I thought I might make up for it. Last year Nathan and I must have drunk three bottles between us and now I feel so guilty for being such a sponge."

"That's very kind of you, Hel, but I'm sure Jude wouldn't see it like that, she's never one to count the favours she does for people . . . far from it. But Bollinger, Helena? There must be the guts of two hundred pounds' worth there," Sophie exclaimed, hoisting the heavy box into her slight arms. "You could have bought a decent case of Cava, saved yourself a small fortune." She carried it into the kitchen. "I'm not risking its disappearance," she puffed.

"But we're four floors up." Helena looked bewildered.

"I'd scale four floors to nick a case of this stuff, wouldn't you?"

Helena laughed, nodding. "I guess I would . . . but it would be a bit heavy to carry. Did you not think of that?"

"We should do that for a laugh one night, Hel, get a pair

of suction cups and see what's on people's balconies . . . nick a few things. It would be a blast."

Helena also wondered what else Sophie would do to get what she wanted. Although in fairness, she probably knew.

"Knowing my luck, Sophie, I'd end up with a haul of greying bras and odd socks!" Helena pealed with laughter. "Sophie Kane – the Wall-climbing Super Heroine." Helena imagined her friend in a skintight costume looking very much the sexy heroine. If anyone could pull it off, Sophie could.

"Thanks Hel, you say the sweetest things. I'm glad you see me as some sort of *heroine*. You're right, of course," she replied, tongue in cheek but straight-faced.

Helena rolled her eyes at Sophie's lack of humility, joking as she was. Humility? Sophie Kane didn't even know how to *spell* the word.

Clive drove home from work in cutting silence. The music he so often played on full blast had been rejected in place of his own thoughts which were more a dead march than a heavy-metal rant. He was beside himself and what was worse was that Jude hadn't seemed to notice.

Jude swept back her hair into a loose ponytail, twisting the bobble expertly as she waited for the kettle to boil. She watched its steam puff out furiously, its wetness coating the underside of the wall-mounted cupboard which held her best crystal glasses. She pulled the kettle away to allow its steam to evaporate into thin air, saving the cupboard from possible damp. As it clicked itself off, the steam dispersed back into the kettle and she lifted it from its cradle, pouring the boiling water over a pan of potatoes she had peeled earlier.

She was making Cottage Pie – not Shepherd's Pie, as Clive so often corrected her. *'Shepherd's Pie is made with lamb and Cottage Pie is made with beef.'* Clive liked to be accurate about what he was eating. There was no point calling something by the wrong name. To him it was as silly as cooking a turkey and calling it chicken.

Jude smiled as she tipped the steak mince into the pan of browning onions. She knew that Clive would be waiting for her to trip up as she dished up dinner. He did it everytime, although only in jest.

But tonight she would be accurate with her recipe, she would be error-free all evening and by the end of it she hoped the negative feelings from her covert operations would be vanquished, never to return. Her burden would be lifted.

She hadn't planned what she was going to say to Clive, but she had planned for her mother to collect the children from school and to keep them for the evening, returning them at bedtime which should give them sufficient time to celebrate – in whatever form it took – but that was as far as she had gone in terms of forward planning.

Deliberately too, for she didn't want the evening to appear contrived, nor word-perfect. She wanted simply to tell it as it was, nothing too rehearsed – and the timing would be right now that Clive had eased himself into his new role.

Jude heard the key force itself into the front door. The lock was a bit stiff and fixing it was on Clive's list of jobs among a dozen or so other jobs – not big jobs – just picky, annoying tasks which when fixed would make life easier for all of them. Jude had given up waiting for many of them to be done. She had her deadlines, six months, and then she would get someone in. She was glad she was so laid back.

"I'm in the kichen, Clive."

Jude poured two glasses of a Chilean Cabernet Sauvignon and walked to the doorway ready to hand one of them to her overworked husband who had been looking a little tired during the past few days. It had become a routine over the years. Her propped against the kitchen door watching him remove the same garments he removed every night and in the same order, waiting patiently to extend him an alcoholic offering combined with a tender welcoming kiss. Sometimes when the children were there, they too would rush to the door to greet their father and Jude had the pleasure of watching the three of them, her perfect family, and she was sure her heart would literally burst one day.

Clive had already removed his tie and was undoing the top button of his starched white shirt when he noticed Jude leaning against the oak door frame. Once again he was struck by her effortless beauty. He would never get tired of looking at her.

"You look wrecked, darling," Jude told him as she leaned in to kiss him on the lips. Clive's return peck barely touched hers – instead he took the wineglass, kissing it full on with an open mouth, allowing its contents to roll down his throat at hurried speed.

They moved into the kitchen.

"What are you making for dinner?"

"Cottage Pie," she laughed. "*Not* Shepherd's Pie."

If Clive got the joke, he certainly didn't appear amused by it.

"Are you okay, Clive? You look a little off-colour, darling?"

Clive was not a man to mince his words. He was a lawyer through and through, direct and ruthless.

"Who was that man you were with at the coffee shop the other day?"

"What?"

"The dark-haired guy who was so obviously smitten by you." He polished off the remnants of wine and refilled his own glass thoughtlessly. "And *you* didn't look particularly uncomfortable with *him* either," he added nastily.

Jude's open mouth could find no words to say.

"I've seen changes in you, Jude, too many to go unnoticed – is it because of him?"

Jude began to shiver as her husband's words hit her.

"What? What on earth are you saying, Clive?"

"I'm saying that you're different. You've always been so predictable, Jude, but now you're behaving erratically. I can cope with the truth . . . just be honest with me . . . if it's because of him, please tell me and put me out of my misery."

Clive could feel his emotions fighting to reach the surface but he knew he had to curb them. It was more upsetting than he had imagined.

"Are you having an affair with him?"

Jude gasped. Was this what she had achieved by lying to her husband? Her protective feelings towards him were proving to be her own antagonist.

"God no!" Her eyes welled with tears for what she had unwittingly put him through. Or at least, what *he thought* he was going through. "Oh Clive, my darling! I love you so much." She took his glass from him, casting it aside so she could embrace him. "You are all the man I could ever . . . have ever wanted. You and you alone. I would *never* do that to you . . . to us, our family, and you of all people should know that."

Jude knew the moment had arrived to admit to Clive what she had been doing – her explanation for the changes in behaviour he had been witnessing.

"I've been working, Clive," she announced, matter of fact and with some relief. It seemed so trivial now. "Sophie offered me the job of Interior Designer for her new salon on Alderley Avenue and John is the architect we're using to redesign the structural interiors. It was purely business, Clive, I swear. I know I should have told you earlier. I'm so sorry."

Clive's shoulders dropped as he too relaxed. The poison he had been prepared to dish out evaporated from his train of thought. It dispersed into a strange calmness which was quickly replaced by confusion.

"But you don't work . . . what are you talking about?"

"I do now. I was going to tell you, darling, but it was the same day you got your promotion and I didn't want to steal your thunder, so I was waiting for the right time to tell y –"

"Oh and that time is now?" Clive snapped. "Don't you think I've got a right to know if my own wife is working? What else are you up to that I don't know about, Jude?"

"Now you're just being silly!"

Jude was cross and he could see it.

So what? He was more than cross. He had been ready for the fight of his life when he stepped across the threshold, ready to put her straight that if she didn't want him, then he didn't want to be there. But he was too hurt and too angry to admit that he was ready for the fight of his life to fight for *her*, his beautiful wife, not against her. She was his rock.

"Oh, my wife takes on a whole new life and doesn't even think to tell me? Don't tell me I'm the silly one, Jude. Speak for yourself. *Stupid* in fact!" he barked, pacing the kitchen floor like a barrister delivering his summation.

"I told you, Clive, I didn't want to steal your thunder or put you under any more pressure, not at such an important time in your career. I was trying to be considerate in holding back the news until it seemed appropriate. Why can't you see this for what it is?"

"And you don't think me wondering why you had been acting differently wasn't putting me under pressure? Me seeing you with another man *after* you had turned me down for the *gym*. You're the one who has the easy life, Jude . . . why the hell you would want to change it is beyond me. You're spoiled rotten. You have everything you want handed on a plate . . . you always have . . . and yet you still want more. Look around you, Jude. Do I not give you enough?"

By now Jude was crying. She was hurting beyond belief.

"I only wanted to achieve a little something for myself," she sobbed. "You have your work, your partnership, your own identity . . ."

"Identity? You call being a *staff number* an identity?

I'm a blank cheque book, that's what I am. A dogsbody who works to pay the bills and to provide you all with this affluent lifestyle. I made partner because I work so damn hard that I bring in most of the fee income in that place and this is how I'm repaid by my wife!"

"I can give something back now, Clive. I can pay for some . . ."

Clive snatched the bottle from the centre island and stormed towards the kitchen door.

"It's not about the money, Jude, it's about the lying and the secret life you seemed so comfortable living." Clive's tone of fury had lessened, much to her relief.

"What can I do to put it right?" Jude sniffed. Her red eyes filled with tears still to fall.

"You can tell Sophie where she can stick her job, Jude. That's what you can do."

22

The phone shrilled at full volume, vibrating the cheap chest of drawers upon which it sat.

Kath rolled over, nudging James. He was out for the count so she leaned across over him, grabbing the phone before it rang off. Who the hell would be calling in the middle of the night?

"Hello?" Her voice was hoarse and a thirst for water came over her.

"Is this Mrs Hamilton?" a stern voice spoke out.

"Yes. Who is this? It's two in the morning." Kath was angry at being woken. She was more angry that James was still comatose. She kicked at him roughly and he stirred.

"This is PC Tisdale calling from Cottley Police station. I'm sorry to call you at this hour."

Kath sat upright. She threw back the duvet and bolted from the comfort of her bed to stand.

"What's happened? Is it Jason? Is he hurt?"

James rubbed his eyes and gawped up at his wife. He mouthed to her: *Put it on speaker.*

"Your son Jason Hamilton has been arrested for breaking and entering. He has asked if you would consider guaranteeing surety in order to release him. Are you able to come up to the station so that we can let him go tonight?"

They stared at each other, stunned by the blow.

James nodded at his wife and began to dress, grabbing garments from here and there. He was panicking and Kath could see his mortification as clear as day. It carried a huge sign saying '*It must be our fault . . . we've let you down . . .*'

But it wasn't their fault and Kath knew this. She came from a long line of bad blood – so she knew that volatility and deviousness was in his blood too. He had been brought up with the love and tender care of his elder brother and yet one of them was a devoted son, kind and considerate, and the other was a walking time-bomb who it appeared was prepared to wipe himself out along with everybody else.

"We're on our way."

Kath replaced the handset and yanked at her pyjama top. She swiped her jeans from the floor, pulling them over her underwear without bothering to change them. As they dressed, the silence between them was drowned out by their own private thoughts. Each of them knew what the other would be thinking – struggling to come to terms with how rapidly their son had declined – since he left school it seemed.

"How much is bail money, James?" Kath whispered. She thought if she couldn't hear the words it would be like she had never said them.

He stopped tying his laces and looked up. "I've no idea, love. I've never had to bail anyone out before." He

251

continued the intricate job of tying a double knot in his black fine-grain leather shoes which he normally kept for best. But he wanted to make a good impression at the station. Show them that as parents they were responsible and devoted to the best interests of their son. He wasn't from a socially deprived or broken home. He came from a loving enviroment where all four of them mattered in equal measures.

"I never thought I'd be bailing one of my own kids out, Kath." His voice broke and Kath clutched his shoulder.

"It's maybe just a phase, Jim," she told him unconvincingly. "He'll grow out of it."

The taxi pulled up outside Cottley Police station. The driver asked no questions. He could see by the ghostly transparency of his passengers that things weren't good.

He pulled away into the darkness.

Kath stood at the foot of the steps which led to the entrance of the station. Her reluctance to climb them grew stronger by the minute. She was mortified. How had it come to this?

"Come on, love. I want to get him home."

"Me too." She sniffed. "But at the same time I want to kill him."

"Me too."

Kath took the first step, followed by the second until she was at the top. Her usually strong, muscular legs were floppy and weak.

"Only he can't come *home,* Jim, he doesn't live with us any more. Remember?"

James saw the pain in her eyes. He wanted to protect her so much from this but he couldn't. He also wanted to shake his son for what he was putting his mother through.

"It's a short-term solution, love. He'll be back on the straight and narrow before we know it and home with us, where he belongs."

Inside, the station was remarkably busy. A number of drunk and disorderly cases had just been brought in. Some were singing in jovial chant, others turned the air electric blue with their foul mouths and abusive language aimed directly at the officers.

"*Oi, Pig, I need a drink*!" barked an unsightly male character with trousers stained at the crotch and what looked to be dried-in vomit on the chest of his dirty fleece.

He stared at the new arrivals, spitting at the floor and a wad of phlegm landed inches from Kath.

James grabbed his wife's hand tightly. He headed towards the reception desk, waiting impatiently for the uniformed officer to complete his paperwork and lift his head.

"Can I help you?" he asked eventually, pushing his paperwork to one side, evidently stressed.

James cleared his throat. He didn't know what he was supposed to say.

"Our son, he was brought here." His face was flushed with disgrace. "We got a call from –"

"Name?"

"Jason Hamilton."

"Take a seat, please."

James spun around. The black plastic seats were taken up by the overflow of recent arrivals. One empty seat remained, covered in a liquid which he imagined to be urine.

"We'll stand, thanks."

They huddled together in a far corner of the room. They didn't belong here – their son didn't either.

"This place is horrible," Kath whispered in his ear, her hand still clutching his. "Imagine what it's like in prison, Jim."

Horror bled through James' veins. Prison was where his youngest son would end up if he didn't turn his life around and fast, but it would be over his dead body, he swore. No son of his would ever be behind bars.

Kath wondered at the *illicit* statement which was read out by Roni so matter-of-factly. She was still convinced the women might think it was she who was seeking advice through the persona of her son. But it wasn't her and she was so intrigued as to which of them it could be. None of them was a criminal. Then again, her son wasn't either.

Helena went to speak to Sophie, but hesitated. Again. She had done this all morning and she couldn't quite bring herself to confess the scurrilous texts she was receiving and with increased frequency from Nathan. The first batch she had ignored – been downright rude and dismissive in response to them – but the last couple of messages had carried a threatening undertone. Worse, a violent undertone, and Helena cursed the day she ever confided in him about Sophie.

At the time it seemed perfectly normal to share her burden, they were going to be together forever, start a family. It just hadn't worked out that way – a metaphor for her own life.

Sophie strutted into the living room to be greeted by the May sun whose rays had appeared only in the past five minutes. She squinted as she looked out of the open French doors at the activities down below.

"The sun always shines on the righteous," she told Helena smugly. "Didn't I tell you it would be a perfect day for it?"

Helena shook her head at her best friend's cockiness. "What are you all of a sudden? The Met Office?"

"A woman of many talents is what I am. A superhero who can also forecast the weather. Michael Fish combined with Linda Carter," Sophie giggled. "Yep, that's what I am . . . couldn't have put it better myself!"

"Hhm. Do your many talents cover *illicit* subjects, might I ask?" Helena was jesting with her but Sophie didn't see the humour.

"No. You may not ask. That's not fair, Hel. Rules are rules. Obey them or you're out."

Sophie stepped outside, plonking herself down on a chrome patio chair. She strapped her shoes around her slender, permanently hair-free ankles.

"I was only joking, Soph. Lighten up."

"You know what I'm like over that constitution. It's there because we're governed by it and we've all signed it, honouring our committment to the club. Anyway, that's my life's work, that document, and I'm still proud of it." She laughed at her own admission. "I never even wrote an essay at school which was as good as that constitution! I'm damn well proud of it."

"Quite right. Sorry, Soph. My lips are sealed . . . but my thoughts aren't!" Helena chortled.

Sophie slid her other foot into the shoe's excessively high instep. She froze as she recalled the time – not so long ago – where she herself had broken the rules so blatently, noting how quickly she had forgiven herself for it. But it wasn't for her own sake – she offered herself a get-out clause – it was for a friend in need and Sophie had to make her friend see that *her* life was for the taking and not just for giving and she could not regret her actions, contradictory as they were to everything she believed the club should be about. She had never seen Jude so happy.

"What's up?"

Sophie continued to dress her foot, snapping quickly from her guilty regression.

"Nothing. Just thinking about Jude and how different she is since she started work. She doesn't say much but you can see it in her eyes. '*Your eyes are the window to your soul,*' my gran used to say and she's right. I can see right through Jude if I look into her eyes for long enough. They tell the truth and nothing but."

Helena turned away. Her eyes blinked rapidly. She had never thought of Sophie being the kind of person who set about *noticing* things like that. Deep things. Sophie had always appeared to take life in her stride and only really notice what was in front of her – when it came to people that was. When it came to work she could notice a spec of dust from three hundred yards away and smell a rat in a different continent.

"Ready?" Sophie called out.

"Yes, ready . . . Sophie?"

"What?"

Helena looked sheepish.

"You're not really going out in that skirt, are you? Don't you think it's a little short?"

Sophie roared with laughter.

"I expect those comments from frigid Roni, not from you. What's got into you?"

"It's just that all the husbands will be staring at you the whole day – it might make the wives feel uncomfortable."

Sophie's grin turned to stone in a flash.

"Well, isn't that just their problem and not mine. I'm not hiding my legs just because there happen to be a load of men on board who think with nothing but their dicks, Hel. I am what I am and they can fuck off if they don't like it."

Helena picked up her bag, muttering under her breath. "Oh, they'll like it alright."

But she already knew that Sophie would know that and it was that which made her angry.

'*One of your husbands is shagging someone around this table.*'

I wonder who that could be, she thought with an unusual bitchiness which reared itself after her unfair scolding.

Sophie couldn't keep herself covered up even for the sake of her friends. She had to *dress to impress* as always even if the occasion didn't suit. Helena wondered if her aggravation was because she rarely got a look in when it came to attention – when she was with Sophie at least – but at the moment Helena knew she was receiving more than her fair share of male attention delivered through speedy glances or the turn of a head. This was the only time that Helena had ever got cross with her best friend. What was the harm in dressing in a pair of jeans or long trousers once a year? Especially on a boat. Everybody had to conform sometimes.

But then Helena remembered what she had done – on

more than one occasion now – which was far worse than the flash of a leg or the exposed flesh of a firm cleavage. Her actions were something she would have to live with forever. But if she played her cards right and her numbers came in, she would be able to put it right. It would all be fine.

The Trophy bobbed merrily, basking in glorious splendour.

Clive and Tom were on deck, wiping down the white-leather seats and making sure the yacht was shipshape before it was opened to their nearest and dearest.

Dozens of bottles of champagne filled the fridge in the eight-berth cabin below and the overflow was placed upright in an electric cool-box which Clive had running off the generator. The caterers would be coming shortly with the finger buffet and home-made canapés which would be served for lunch and throughout the day and Clive knew they – as a family – would impress their friends once again.

Fond as he was of material belongings, his big house, expensive car and gadgets of every description, Clive loved opening up his home and the yacht to share his wealth in a bid for the ultimate enjoyment. His own enjoyment firstly. He'd wondered many a time why Pete didn't share his views. The Tudors was a work of art, quite magnificent, but it wasn't lived in. Probably his wife's influence, he had surmised long ago.

Clive's stomach sank as he recalled his argument with Jude. For the first night in many he had slept as peacefully as a baby because he now knew that Jude wasn't having an affair but he was still angry that she had lied to him and because of it he wasn't giving in easily. She created the mess she was in and she would have to be big and ugly enough to fix it. Sometimes, he felt, Jude could be naive. So naive that she didn't see the alluring way in which John was looking at her when he could see it clear as day from across the street. She was better off away from work and from the letches who might cross her path. Jude had made Clive feel nervous for the first time in their married life.

Kath and James were dressed and ready to leave for the big day but they couldn't go without trying to understand what had gone on the night before. They were exhausted but there were things that had to be said.

In the taxi home Jason had said nothing. Kath had sent him straight to his old bedroom to sleep on it. They would say all that needed to be said in the morning. As much as they were relieved to have their son home, they had treated him like he was a petty criminal, behaving aloof and standoffish towards him. He wasn't going to get an easy ride this time.

"Why did you do it, Jason?" Kath was furious with her son but she refused to let go of his hand. Her grip carried a mixture of love, animosity and anguish and she couldn't quite work out which one was which.

"I was only keeping a lookout, Mum, I swear to God!" he implored. "The guys told me to keep dixie . . . said they were breaking in to steal the cricket bats for a bit of fun . . . they said they were going to hide them under the tree next to the clubhouse."

It was clear that he felt stupid and used.

"I didn't know they were gonna rob the place, Mum, honestly . . . I swear."

James paced the newly fitted carpet. His feet

squashed down on the flower-heads and twisted-leave patterns and even with his short legs he managed only seven steps before he reached the other side of the room. Kath said it was small, he had always found it cosy but today it closed in on him.

"The other blokes didn't tell the same story as you though, Jason . . . and they're supposed to be your friends? They said it was your idea to rob the place . . . so who's telling the truth?" James scoffed. "If it's you, son, and you are telling the truth then it's gonna be your own stupidity that'll take you down. You weren't brought up to be a criminal, Jason!"

Jason kept his head down through the entire episode. He knew he had let his parents down big-time. Yes, he had taken from them but it was a bit of money here and there. That aside, he wasn't a criminal. He just didn't quite know who he was. What he was.

"There won't be a next time."

Their heads shot in Kath's direction. She dried her eyes and dropped her grip on Jason's hand. '*Perhaps a spell inside might be the making of him.*' Kath recalled how Sophie dared herself to be outspoken, the sign of a true friend. '*I'm not saying it won't be the hardest decision of your life.*' But what did Sophie know about losing someone you loved with all your heart? A piece of her would die if Jason ever went inside. Kath knew that something had to be done to frighten her son into taking the straight and narrow. '*It might just be the making of him,*' Sophie had told her earnestly.

Once again Sophie was right. She was impartial to the situation and her words were harsh but carried the hallmarks of selfless wisdom.

Kath's tone was chilled and both Jason and James froze as her coldness filled the air with arctic temperatures. "Next time, Jason, you're on your own and there will be no bail out. You'll be left inside to suffer until you've served your time and learned your lesson. Do you understand?"

She wasn't Elizabeth, disowning her son for no apparent reason than his choice of female companion. She was a loving, devoted mother who was learning that she had to be cruel to be kind. She would never be cruel for cruelty's sake but it was time for the cruel love to kick in.

23

"*Ships ahoy*!" they yelled at Tom as he unravelled the bowline, having already freed the stern-line seconds earlier.

Clive reversed the yacht from its berth, pushing back slowly until he had sufficient room to turn and motor forwards.

The first of many pops exploded.

Tom held on to the mast rig as *The Trophy* slowly drifted out, away from its home where it had been static for many months. It creaked with joy as it broke free from confinement.

Anna clapped her hands gleefully. This was her favourite day of the year and if Sophie Kane was there she would be a happy girl for the rest of it. Sophie reminded Anna of her Barbie dolls, only Sophie Kane was a real-life Barbie doll and Anna could think of nothing but playing with her all day.

"*Bon voyage*!" she yelled out.

"We're hardly emigrating, Anna." Tom smirked at his sister.

Clive steered *The Trophy* around a smaller yacht which was homeward bound. Giving it a wide berth, he veered to starboard, heading towards a rocky opening that was marked by two huge stone boulders which penetrated deep into the bed of the sea. Once he passed this point the rules would be different, the speed could pick up and they could officially start the party without disturbing those relaxing in the port, choosing instead the safety of the harbour.

They wouldn't be in the open sea – he didn't plan to go that far – but they would be far from the exclusive clubhouse where they could make as much noise as they wished and take the speed up to six knots before shutting off the engine, simply drifting until either the time dictated or until the weather assigned otherwise.

Another loud pop exploded, firing a cork high above. It elevated like a blasting rocket, reaching high on the mast.

Will looked up, tracking its movement. He stepped back in an attempt to catch it as it landed, trying to gauge its course and guarding his own step at the same time to avoid an accident. There were too many handbags on board today for his liking, although he liked the owner of one of them particularly. Well, two of them to be precise but he had always preferred blondes. So his ex-wives would say.

The cork plopped as it hit the water and Will raced towards the longest bench on board the yacht and dropped to his knees.

"Excuse me," he spoke quickly, pretending not to have seen up Sophie's miniscule skirt. Black underwear. His favourite. He grabbed a large netted pole which was carefully hooked beneath the custom-made white-leather seats and, racing to starboard, hung over slightly scooping up the cork and swinging the net back on board. His first catch of the day. He hoped it would not be his last.

"Aah!"

Roni let out a squeal as water from the net splashed over her, but Will didn't care. There were fines for littering and he left those undesirable marine behaviours for other people. Much as the Yacht Club was filled with wealthy, affluent types, there were many too who had inherited money and with that money came no class. Those people had no etiquette, no idea how to handle themselves in the swanky world of yachtsmanship. Will could suss them a mile off. He had witnessed beer cans floating in the water, drunken men urinating overboard and one couple having sex on the deck in broad daylight while families with children passed by. He had heard later they were high on cocaine.

Those people were no longer members of the prestigious marina and Will was glad. He hated the lack of respect some people had for their sport. Sailing was an elegant, sophisticated sport and its pleasure was there for the taking and for the giving.

Will loved the feel of the wind belting against his face as he raced for pole position. The thrill of danger as the boat heaved to the side with such velocity that were he not strapped on he would be a man overboard. Those moves, although dangerous, were also necessary if they were to turn and dip with great speed. But most importantly, Will loved the teamwork it took to man the yacht – which was unhierarchical. No man was better than the next when you raced, the same thread ran through each of them binding them together as tightly as the sail held onto its mast.

Sophie couldn't wait to get the party started although she sensed something was wrong with Kath but she knew that a greedy dose of the good stuff might cheer her up – or open her up – perhaps allowing her to talk about what it was which was so clearly bothering her.

Jude too didn't seem her usual self. That light which had burned with an intense flame now flickered low. Sophie sensed that it must be a personal issue because Clive was full of the joys of spring – literally – as he steered his prize posession into the calm open waters before shutting down the engine of *The Trophy*.

"What's up, Kath?" Sophie asked.

The women had separated from the men. It wasn't a planned meeting but they'd each been drawn to their own sex like a gender-magnet had pulled them apart, avoiding the temptation which came from the close proximity of two sexes confined in a small space.

"Yeah, you don't seem yourself today." Helena stroked her hand.

Kath bit her lip and forced herself to hold it together.

"We had a bit of trouble with our Jason . . . last night . . . down at the station," she told them. She was embarassed but she knew she needed to talk about it.

She glanced at James laughing away, a can in one hand and a canapé in the other. She wished she could shake the sadness off so quickly but being a mother was different to being a father. She had a nine-month advantage over him.

"He got roped into keeping a lookout for what he thought was a prank at the cricket clubhouse but the little sods burgled the place and the police don't believe Jason's side of the story."

"What's going to happen to him then, Kath?" Sophie was keen to know.

"I don't know, Soph. It's up to the clubhouse to decide if they want to press charges." She polished off the pink champagne. "They got the money back so they might drop them."

A sigh of relief came from Helena's direction and Kath was grateful for her empathy.

"Where was the money found?" Sophie asked.

"Apparently one of them dropped it when they heard sirens but the lads are saying it was Jason who dropped it . . . not them. It's their word against his but the clubhouse has the last say and we're just waiting to hear." Kath twisted her empty glass in her hands, watching as it spun around and around. "Do you mind if we talk about something else? I really want to use today to take my mind off things . . . although just telling you guys has lightened the load. Thanks for listening."

"That's what we're here for," said Jude. She filled Kath's glass dangerously high, grinning as she did so. "All it will take is a little undercurrent, Kath, and you might spill that when the boat rocks. You'd better drink it up fast."

Kath grinned at Jude. She knew that Jude was trying to cheer her up by getting her drunk on her favourite pink fizz and it was working. She could feel it working like a non-prescription relaxant.

"The boat has already rocked, Jude. It's capsized in fact."

Jude laughed heartily. "You know what I love about you, Kath?"

"Everything?"

"The fact that even when you're rock bottom you still manage to hold on to your sense of humour."

Jude slapped her hard on the back. The full-on affection thudded against Kath's ribs and she jolted forward, her champagne glass wobbling in her hands as she clutched at its stem.

"Sorry!" Jude shrieked as she raced to fetch the mop. Spillages meant falls and falls meant insurance claims. Clive had her well trained.

"Where is it?"

Kath looked at Jude blankly. "Where is what?"

"The spilled drink?"

Kath chortled away as she watched Jude's eyes scour the floor for the pink fizzy liquid. "I'd already knocked it back, Jude. I thought I saw a huge wave in the distance so I played it safe," she told her nonchalantly. "By the time you'd hit me it was gone!"

Jude was amazed. Kath's body on the outside was impeccable, a glowing picture of health, but she dreaded to think what state her liver was in. Kath might as well throw her donor card overboard. It was going to be as useless as her wet signature.

"Ladies." Will approached them with a chilled bottle of Laurent-Perrier Rosé wrapped in a white linen napkin. "We gentleman were wondering if we could join in your game?"

"Which game is that, Will?" Jude was puzzled.

"Strip poker?" Sophie asked innocently.

"The Curry something?" Will chose to ignore Sophie's flirtatious comment. He didn't know how to handle her yet but he was up for it if she was.

Roni looked unsure until she caught Peter's eye. He smiled at her like it was their first encounter and her heart fluttered with joy before sinking to the pits as she remembered the passionate embrace with Darren.

"It's called the Curry Club . . . but we only play it during the week, Will," Sophie announced. "We've nothing planned and it has to be organised for it to work anonymously. Perhaps we had better stick to strip poker."

Will took in the words which left the red bee-stung lips. He kept his eyes away from her breasts which he had already glanced at once or twice – when he thought it was safe.

"Suits me, but I'm not sure those prudes would be up for it!" Will laughed. "We've all heard so much about the Curry Club that we'd love to play it if you would allow us? Perhaps another time then?"

"I suppose we could play it again – but not for real – just for a bit of fun?" Helena offered as she looked at her friends one by one.

"Okay."

"Fine by me.

"Great."

Sophie linked her arm in his and led him to the eight-berth cabin below, clutching at the handrail to stop herself wobbling from side to side. The wind had picked up a little and *The Trophy* rocked gently, swept along with the incline of the breeze.

Will wished he had fled down the steps before her. The view would have been to die for.

"I'll explain the rules to you and you can explain it to the others. Okay?"

"Yes, boss."

He grinned at her with his wide mouth. The deep-rooted wrinkles under his eyes scrunched together as his mouth pushed them up. His tanned face had been exposed to much outdoor weather and it showed.

"Don't call me 'boss'," Sophie groaned. "I feel like I'm back at work."

She sat down on one of the two fabric benches which also doubled as beds and Will squeezed in beside her, eager to hear more.

"What do you do, Sophie, if you don't mind me asking?"

"Not at all. I'm a hairdresser," she told him proudly. "I own Kane'n'Able on the High Street and am just about to open another salon in Alderley Avenue."

Will's forehead contorted. A few seconds later his eyes were wide with realisation.

"Two-year lease, option to buy at the end?"

Sophie frowned at him, nodding at the same time.

"That's right," she answered in amazement.

"I think that might be my property you're leasing." Will was shocked. "How weird is that? I knew it was a hair salon that had taken over from the previous tenants but how incredible it would be if it's you! It must have been meant to be."

He looked delighted at the prospect of having an excuse to see her again. He might keep the property-management company away from this agreement, take care of it himself.

"Funny, Clive didn't mention it was one of Jude's friends when I told him about letting it out to a hair salon. He'd already advised me to sell it, you see, but I'm not sure the timing is right . . . hence the two-year lease decision. Does he know it's you, Sophie? He probably didn't put the two together. Let's face it, it could be any salon really, couldn't it?"

"No offense, Will, but not *any* salon could afford the rent and rates of Alderley Avenue," Sophie replied. "But Clive knows it's me, he drafted the contracts up a few months back."

"Weird. It must have slipped his mind."

Will rarely met his tenants, had no need to. They dealt directly with his letting agent who looked after everything to do with the leasing arrangements and all aspects of property management. All he knew was that he received his income, less a hefty deduction for their services at the end of each month.

"Small world," Sophie said slowly as she processed just who it was she was dealing with. You never knew when you needed to call in a favour. "So where else do you have properties, Will?"

Sophie was keen to expand her enterprise, and acquistion of the best premises in all the key locations was vital to her success.

She edged a little closer to him.

He smelt her recognisable perfume – Vera Wang – he had bought it for his PA at Christmas time. He looked at Sophie, taking in her petite frame, perfectly tanned and perfectly toned. She was so hot she was almost on fire and he could think of nothing else but diving into the cold waters to put his own flames out. If he had to take her down with him, then so be it.

Roni was glad when she saw Sophie's head pop up from the lower deck. She was in need of distraction and it seemed the more she drank, the more guilty she felt. At that moment, she would have preferred the harsh words from Sophie's mouth compared with the gut-wrenching stabs which penetrated her insides.

Will followed Sophie up the narrow wooden steps, pretending to be a gentlemen and avert his gaze, but he looked alright – stared in fact. He saw the white creases under her pert bottom where the sun had failed to tan. He saw the thin line of black string which *tried* to cover her private area and he watched the muscles on her inner thighs tense with every step taken as her slight weight was placed on each step.

Will wasn't sure how long he could cope with the closeness of Jude's friend. It wasn't fair her being on board, not just to him but to all the men there.

"Jude!" Sophie yelled. "Here a sec!"

Jude left Tom and headed starboard towards Sophie who was perched next to Roni on a slatted wooden bench.

"Did you know Will owns my shop on Alderley Avenue?"

Jude was gobsmacked. "No way! How strange is that?"

Roni's head turned from side to side as she watched the exchange of excitement. "Don't you mean *his* shop?" she corrected.

271

"Surely Clive must have known that Will owned it when he did the contracts for me?" Sophie said thoughtfully. "Maybe he felt it better not to say that he knew the property owner, I guess? Conflict of interest and all that." Sophie chewed the inside of her mouth. "Really, he should have given the contracts to someone else to do if he knew us both . . . I'm not sure that was a good move of his actually."

Jude sat down opposite, perching herself on a hard plastic storage-box where Clive kept his fishing gear.

"Clive did the contracts for you . . . for Alderley Avenue?"

"Yes, although when I decided I was going to ask you to be the designer, I took yours to another solicitor to avoid any domestic issues." Sophie wriggled with discomfort. The seat had no cushion and it was rock hard against her unpadded bottom.

"But he did all the others?"

Roni paled and her hand flew up to her mouth.

"Oh, God," she whispered. "Was this early March time, erm, by chance?"

Sophie nodded.

"Were you two in The Archers together?"

"Yes." Sophie wondered where on earth Roni was going with this conversation but Roni's extreme uneasiness had demanded her attention.

Roni's neck went red and blotchy as she spoke.

"I am so sorry . . . so very very sorry . . . to both of you." Roni couldn't look at them. "It – it was me who put in the question about 'shagging' someone's husband . . ." She whispered as she said the words, biting her bottom lip. "I saw the two of you together, you were leaning into him looking so relaxed, Sophie, and I assumed that –"

Sophie bolted from the bench, standing tall over Roni. A raging anger burned inside her but she knew the time was not right to let it out.

"You assumed that I can't be with a man without *shagging* him, Roni?" she whispered back in a choleric tone. "What the frigging hell do you take me for? Okay, so I've done some things . . . more things than I should have, but Jude is my *friend*, one of my best friends."

Sophie spun around to face the waters. Her eyes welled with the injustice of it all and she fought with all her might to repress her emotions. Sophie Kane didn't cry. Yes, she was a loose woman and, yes, she enjoyed a little sexual activity, a lot maybe, but for Roni to think she would do that to her own friend was a shock to her system. Is this what people thought of her? A slut? A husband-grabber? A girl who charged for sexual favours?

Roni and Jude flew to her side, each of them linking their arms in hers. One she wanted, the other she didn't.

"I'm sorry, Sophie. I truly am, please forgive me?" Roni's face was scarlet and the red blotches had worsened, spreading down towards her plumped-up chest. "You've always said that if something is bothering us then it needs to be discussed through the Curry Club." She had adopted a fake jovial tone. "Well, that was disturbing me for ages and I didn't want to say anything to Jude so I thought that raising it would scare you into stopping something you might regret."

Jude looked uncomfortable hearing Roni admit that she wouldn't tell her if Clive was having an affair.

"Let's look on the bright side of this, Sophie. I guess we should be pleased that we finally got to the bottom of that one." Jude spoke candidly but her undertone was one of uneasiness. "I know it won't help the way you feel right now . . . but at least Roni has owned up to it. That must have taken a lot of guts."

Yes, and those were the guts that Sophie wanted to punch at that very moment, she thought, clenching her fists.

Roni smiled a half smile at Jude, but she was too embarrassed to look at her for long. True, it had taken some strength but when she was wrong, she was wrong and there was no point hiding it.

"I wonder why Clive didn't tell me about the contracts?" Jude changed the subject.

Sophie wiped her eyes, cursing at the sight of black mascara on her hand. She hadn't let the tears fall but they had leaked onto her bottom lashes and she would need to fix herself quickly. She was more furious at herself for getting upset than she was at Roni for her admission or at Jude for not laughing at the hilarity of the situation. She had waited for her friend to rush to her defence, throw her head back and laugh at Roni's insane imagination, but she hadn't.

How the hell Roni thought her capable of sleeping with her friend's husband was beyond her.

Sophie Kane was risking the design of her new salon by using someone who had been out of the game for a decade and a half. She had put her position in the Curry Club at risk in order to make her friend see that life was there for the taking. She would have walked on water for Jude if she had to.

"I told him not to tell you," Sophie spoke in a hushed tone. "I told him I was going to offer you the job so he had to keep it quiet until I'd had the pleasure of asking you officially. I thought that if he mentioned anything to you then there'd be a chance he'd slip up. You know what men are like!"

It was Jude's turn to pale. She removed her arm from Sophie's and swung around to look where Clive was sitting, laughing and joking without a care in the world. He looked more like his old self today.

"You mean he *knew* the job was mine?" Jude's hands flew to her hips. "Did you not think to say it to me, Sophie? All along I'd been keeping it from him until the timing was right and yet *you* knew that *he* already knew. You could have put me out of my misery long ago . . . and stopped me from lying to my husband." Jude was upset. She felt betrayed by Sophie.

Roni ducked from between them and headed towards Kath and Helena who seemed to be holding a more jovial conversation. It was getting awkward and she had done enough damage for one day.

Sophie shook her head at her friend coldly.

"Clive told me that there was no way in a million years you'd take the job, Jude. He told me to offer it to someone else." Sophie had never seen Jude look so disappointed in her. But it wasn't her fault. She'd done everything by the book. "He said that you didn't want to work and that you liked the easy life you'd had since the twins were born. He said something like '*Don't hold your breath*' – then something else about having life handed to you on a 24-carat plate . . . Or similar words amounting to the same thing."

"Oh. Did he now?" Jude's facade changed from forlorn to fierce. "Easy? With twins?" she snorted.

Jude took hold of Sophie's hand, standing upright. Her posture oozed confidence and control.

"I will never let you down, Sophie, I've told you that before and regardless of what my husband's opinion is of me working, I will see this project through to the very end even if it kills me." Jude almost spat the words out and Sophie realised then that Jude had told Clive. She guessed it hadn't gone down particularly well but she needed to know for definite.

"I take it you told Clive?"

Jude nodded.

"But you know what, Sophie," her eyes narrowed with steel grit, "that will be the last thing I tell him in a long time. Here's me thinking I'd betrayed *his* trust when all along it was he who had betrayed *mine* by trying to keep me exactly where he wants me! Anywhere between the kitchen and the bedroom! He's going to have to work damn hard before my faith in him is restored. The equilibrium of that house needs to change. And fast."

Kath trotted over carrying a tray of canapés. She didn't notice the closed body language of the women – she had come in at the end of the conversation, just catching the last words.

"The *equi*– what? Will you guys bloody well learn to speak *English!*"

24

Under the endless blue skies *The Trophy* cruised along at continued speeds of six knots. It was fast enough to enjoy the thrill but slow enough to enjoy the view of the north-west Pennines which flowed into the heart of the Irish Sea. Not that they would be travelling the seventy-mile distance needed to officially reach the Irish Sea from where they were positioned. Clive had planned to stay within, or as close to the estuary as possible. If anything, if he reconsidered his route, he might divert towards the River Dee – the view of North Wales would be great on a clear day like this.

Anna sat on the deck, her skinny legs crossed one over the other like she was sitting in a school assembly. She still looked like a child, tall as she was. Her shoulders leaned back against Sophie's knees and she held up her DSI, squinting from the sun as her hair was pulled and twisted free of charge.

"Don't squint, Anna, you'll get crow's feet."

"But I'm only fifteen. Aren't I a bit young for wrinkles, Sophie?"

Sophie held Anna's hair with one hand while she reached into her handbag, grabbing a packet of hair grips with the other. She slid the grips in, keeping the barrel curls in place, ignoring Anna as she winced, her young eyes watering.

"Beauty is pain," Sophie told her. "And no, you can never be too young to start looking after your skin."

Anna wiped the tears from her eyes. The fine blonde hairs across her hairline were scraped back tightly, sending her tear ducts into overdrive.

"Nearly there, honey."

Anna closed the lid of her DSI. She couldn't do two things at once like most other girls she knew. She was a one-task woman and it suited her perfectly. She had watched her mother fetch and carry after them and her father for so many years that she swore she would go out to work and hire a nanny to look after her children. She would never live a life of domestic subservience. She had started her campaign from a young age.

Sophie squeezed out from behind Anna's bony torso and hoisted the lanky teenager to her feet. Anna was like Jude, tall, shapeless and with barely enough breast development to fit into a bra. Okay, Jude was larger in that area than her daughter was, but her breasts had only really developed after the children were born – much to Clive's delight.

"How do I look, Daddy?" Anna yelled to Clive even though he was only a matter of feet away.

Clive took in the view of his baby girl. She was so like her mother that it brought a lump to his throat. No boy or man would ever get their hands on his daugher, not until she was at least thirty.

He shuffled towards her, merry from drink and high on the success of the day. Everyone was having a blast. He was oblivious to the tension that had occurred just moments earlier, unaware that he was at the heart of it.

Clive took hold of her slight face which tanned even from the mildest of rays and he kissed her button nose.

"Beautiful, Anna. Just like your mother."

Sophie's stomach flipped with the tenderness of his words. She had always known what Clive thought of Jude, just sometimes she felt that he misunderstood her. Looks could be deceiving and her calmness had been deceiving him for years.

"Thanks, Sophie." Anna bent forward and kissed her on the lips. She towered above Sophie whose ankle-band heels had now been removed – for her own safety. "And now I have your lipstick too!" she giggled, skipping off to torment her brother.

Sophie grinned at her and Clive watched as his daughter ruffled her brother's gelled hair. He ducked away, as passive as ever.

"I hate to say this, Clive, but she definitely takes after you. What Anna wants Anna gets," Sophie declared. "She even managed to swipe the lipstick from my very own lips!"

"Lucky girl," Will piped up.

Clive cogitated as he looked from Anna to Sophie. The shade of lip colour looked entirely different on each of them with their different colouring – Anna, with her tawny dark skin compared with Sophie's peach-coloured complexion which Clive knew was entirely fake.

"She is like me, I admit," said Clive, still watching her. "Tom has Jude's gentle and laid-back nature but he has my fairer complexion, and my unfortunate daughter seems to have inherited my impatience."

"They're gorgeous kids, Clive." Sophie meant every word of this. "If I had kids I'd want them to be exactly like Tom and Anna."

Clive thought he heard a flicker of emotion in Sophie's voice.

"You have to get married first," Clive told her. "We need to find you a man, Soph."

"I'm right here," Will butted in. Tact was not his forte.

Sophie shuddered as she stared out into the dark-blue waters, watching the reflection of the yellow sun as it shone against the endless blue backdrop.

"Firstly, don't be so old-fashioned . . . you don't need to get married to have kids, you just need a sperm bank . . . and secondly, thanks but no thanks, Clive," she quivered. "Never again."

"Again?"

"What do you mean 'again'?" Sophie asked.

"You said 'never again'." Clive was an avid listener. He missed nothing.

"Did I? I don't know what I'm talking about today, Clive. Too much of the good stuff, I guess . . . talking of which . . ."

Sophie turned to make a beeline for the downstairs fridge. On her way she brushed past Roni, who she still hadn't forgiven. She tapped her on the shoulder, cupping her gel-nailed hands around Roni's ears as she whispered into them. "The only person I've been *shagging* lately is Rafi."

Roni gasped. She spun around, open-mouthed. "How could you? He's my barman."

Sophie's nostrils flared. The cheek of it. Her and her double standards. "What? Would you prefer I shag other people's husbands, Veronica . . . instead of a single guy?"

Roni knew she deserved it. She should have realised that Sophie would have been considering her revenge. They were on equal footing now.

Roni wondered why her life couldn't be simple like Jude's or Helena's. Why was she always knee-deep in trouble or consequence? She was trying so damn hard to be nice but, in truth, she found it much easier being a bitch. Perhaps she and Sophie had more in common than they realised?

As *The Trophy* drifted through the marina, Clive manoeuvered it slowly and carefully as he aimed for the berth. It was time to put his baby to bed. He paid greater attention to the task than usual because of the amount he had drunk – they had all drunk.

Will rushed from port to starboard, yelling out spatial measurements and generally easing Clive back to their rightful pitch: number thirteen. It certainly hadn't been unlucky for them.

"Just let the wake carry it forward now, mate," Will slurred a little. "It's in the bag."

Jude clutched a black plastic bag which clunked when she moved. The empty bottles banged against each other clumsily as she dragged it along the floor of the boat, feeling the strain of its increased weight. It was sickening to think they had consumed so much alcohol between so few people.

Tom rushed over to help his mother, prising the bag from her hands.

"I'll collect the rubbish, Mum," he ordered fondly. "You go and chat to your friends."

Jude stroked his cheek. She was a little drunk and the day had been filled with as many ups and downs as the water on which they were sailing and Jude – in true nautical style – had thrown caution to the wind. She didn't want to be the odd one out.

"Thank you, darling," she said, slurring slightly.

Kath rummaged into her frayed gypsy bag. The mustard-coloured tassels whipped against each other as the wind picked up. She lifted her mobile phone, switching it on. She was eager to see how Jason was, but of course there had been no signal from where the boat had bobbed about for the afternoon so she had turned her phone off, preserving its energy.

James enjoyed the view from where he was sitting. He had his wife perched on his knee, his arms wrapped tightly around her just beneath her breasts, her soft but toned bottom sunk into his thighs and he felt like he could have stayed in that position for a long time.

Today had been a super day for them both, a true distraction which had been delivered with impeccable timing.

The gang were a great craic.

"Five missed calls, Jim."

Kath bolted from his lap and the contents of her handbag flew across the damp plastic floor.

"They're from Neil . . . it must be our Jason again," she panicked. "What the hell has he done now!"

Helena was first to the rescue, as calm as ever. She stood next to Kath, saying nothing but offering her a calm reassurance by being at her side.

Sophie frantically opened the last bottle of bubbly and poured her friend a glass of it while Jude crouched on the sticky floor in front of her ready to do whatever it was that needed to be done.

"Take deep breaths, Kath," Helena ordered in dulcet tones. "You're holding your breath. Consider that he may have been calling to see if you were enjoying yourselves. Don't fear the worst until you are presented with the worst."

"Do you have a signal yet?" James spoke hurriedly and Kath nodded, exchanging a look of dismay. "Do you want me to ring?"

"No, it's okay – I'll do it."

Kath rang her eldest son, breath held as she waited for him to answer.

"*Breathe,*" Helena whispered.

Kath said nothing as the phone was pressed to her ear. She had no words to say. She continued to listen until she had heard all she needed to hear.

"Thanks, Neil. I love you, son," she told him with motherly fortitude.

Kath looked at the sea of concerned faces staring at her, aware that she had given nothing away. There was nothing to give away, not according to *her* emotions anyway.

"I'm sorry, Jim."

Kath stood up, calm and controlled, pulling James away from the stare of compassionate faces. She took hold of his hand, leading him to the far side of the boat which was free from earshot – as free from earshot as they were going to get within the spatial limitations.

"It's your mother, Jim . . . I'm so sorry, love . . . but she died this morning . . ."

The witch is dead! Kath cheered in silence. She had longed for this day ever since the hospital visit where Elizabath had offered her cash in exchange for her newborn child. But Kath knew that she must keep her emotions empathetic in favour of her husband whose heart would be breaking over what he had lost. In truth though, he had lost her long before she died and they both knew that.

James' head spun with dizziness and he sobered immediately. The news hit him hard and this itself took him by surprise as his chest tightened and his heart pumped furiously. But why did the news hit him so hard? He had no mother, he hadn't for a long time not in the *motherly* sense, so why did he feel like someone had dealt him a blow to the stomach? One which made him feel like doubling over to stop the pain.

"I need to get out of here," he told her quietly.

Helena lay sprawled on the sofa watching the television screen. At the same time she was completely unaware of what it was she was – not exactly *watching* – but more staring at with her eyes because her mind was very much elsewhere.

Nathan had sent her another text.

'Times up. 500 quid & I'll be silncd 4evr.U got 2 wks or I'll do it.'

Do what? Helena had no idea what Nathan would do. Was it to her, to himself? If not, then who? Helena knew that Nathan was volatile, but what worried her was the extent to which he would go to get back at her. She was unsure as to what he was truly capable of but she did know that he was deperate and *almost* homeless and desperate people took desperate measures usually without a care for the consequences. She didn't need a psychology degree to work that one out.

"What are you watching, you lazy cow?"

Sophie's slippers flipped against her heels as she snatched the remote from Helena's flimsy hand. Its weakness was a match to her soporific state.

"It's your turn to cook," Sophie ordered. "I'm starving so get a move on."

Helena grinned at Sophie. She could always rely on her friend to be unchanging no matter what crap life threw at everyone around her.

'*If the crap doesn't stick, you're laughing,*' Sophie would say, '*and if it does stick, brush it off and get the fuck on with it!*'

Sophie was consistent in everything she did. Her immaculately presented exterior, her frame of mind, her short-tempered nature. She was a little piece of normality in Helena's wild imagination which had been creating pictures of havoc since Nathan's texts had begun.

"One grain or two?" Helena prised herself from the sofa, shoving her feet into her flip-flops as she made her way to the open-plan kitchen.

"Very funny. What are you watching by the way?" Sophie's hair was wet. It dripped onto her pink towelling robe which matched her pink *Hello Kitty* slippers.

"I wasn't really watching anything, Sophie, to be honest. I was daydreaming."

Sophie flicked through the television channels. She was in the mood for a good meal and a night of relaxation. She was still tired and a little worse for wear after yesterday.

"Yeah! *America's Next Top Model*!" she shrieked. "I love this programme . . . ooh, and it's a brand-new series, Hel. Come on, let's snuggle."

Helena yanked open the cupboard doors, pulling out various carbohydrate-based foods. She opened the fridge to be greeted with little produce – nothing that wasn't out of date anyway.

"Loser! Anyway, I can't snuggle, it's been so long since I had sex I might not be able to resist you."

"You're only human," Sophie scoffed without taking her eyes off the television. "And excuse me . . . *loser*? I'm watching this programme in the name of research. I need to understand what hairstyles are in fashion . . . the cutting-edge trends of my neighbouring countries." Sophie craned her neck to make eye contact with Helena who was behind her, still banging and clattering but with little to show for it. "Perhaps I should see if there is a *banking* programme on for you?"

Helena ignored Sophie's comments. She was still consumed by how she could get hold of five hundred pounds over the coming week. If only she knew what Nathan would do if she chose not to hand it over. Surely he was all talk? He certainly hadn't been much of an Action Man. Any wonder she was gagging for it.

"Did you hear from Kath by the way? She hasn't returned any of my calls." Sophie filed her nails with a pink animal-print emery board as she talked to the empty room. Only the television talked back.

Helena stopped what she was doing and threw a packet of dried pasta onto the work surface. "Oh sorry, Sophie, I meant to tell you."

She sat down next to Sophie on the white Italian-leather sofa. It was warm from where she had been lying minutes earlier.

"James' mother died."

Sophie didn't move a muscle. She continued watching one of her favourite programmes, glued to the models who were being hoisted into the air for an elevated photo shot.

"Good. She was a hateful bitch anyway."

Helena snatched the remote from Sophie, pausing the television – something they were still getting used to – pausing and rewinding a programme as and when took their fancy. Sky Plus was brilliant.

"Sophie! The woman is dead. Never speak ill of the dead. Have some respect, will you?" Helena was outraged by her friend's lack of compassion but Sophie pushed herself upright reclaiming the TV remote, rudely grabbing it whist simultaneously launching a dagger in the direction of her friend.

"Helena, she was a horrible little cow when she was alive. I'm not one for hypocrisy, you know that. I speak my mind and that's my opinion." Sophie stretched out her legs. She didn't want varicose veins. "She tried to take Neil away from his mother. She offered Kath *money*, Helena, in exchange for her own flesh and blood. The woman was evil if you ask me and at least now they can put proper closure on her once the funeral is out of the way."

Helena took in Sophie's frank retort. She had a point but still, in her opinion, speaking ill of the dead was simply profane. It shouldn't be done.

"Will you go to the funeral?" Helena wanted to know.

"I will if Kath wants me there – but I'll tell you this, I certainly won't have any respects to pay to her and I can't for the life of me understand how James can have any respect for his mother given what she did to him, let alone bother to go to the funeral for her."

Helena stood up aghast.

"He'll go because she was his *mother*, Sophie!

"*Exactly!*" Sophie exclaimed. "That's my point – *Mother!*"

25

Roni huffed and puffed as she battled with the cross-trainer in the gym she hadn't seen for years.

Peter used it and the girls did when they came home, not that they needed to, but the gym was a part of the house she rarely ventured into. Then again, the same could be said for the swimming-hut until of late.

Roni managed a smile, grimacing with exertion, as she thought of the last Curry Club and how different it had been to all the others which had gone before. The heated water, the mouth-watering cocktails and a team of staff on hand to fetch the women anything they wanted – including *sex* as it had recently transpired. It had been perfect and she knew that the benchmark had been raised. Hers was officially the one to beat.

Her cheeks wobbled with each energetic jolt and her breasts were hoisted up and down with each step as she lunged down and up in laborious repetitions until she could cope no longer. The sweat rolled from her forehead, trickling down her temples and Roni wiped it away with a starched white towel leaving traces of foundation smeared against it.

She stepped down from the high-tech piece of equipment to be met with wall-to-wall mirrors which spanned the entire circumference of the room. She hadn't noticed them during her workout, the large built-in monitor was as much as she could see in front of her and it suited her perfectly. She loved watching Jeremy Kyle and today's story had her hooked as three teenagers sat waiting for the DNA results to come through in order to determine which one of them was the father to baby Rhianna.

The sprung, grey floor was decked with an impressive collection of hand-weights which rested against thick wooden skirting boards and a huge red gym ball stood next to them. A line of padded floormats separated the cardio equipment from the muscle-toning aids and hand-weights and Roni stepped across them, entering into a whole new world of exercising. One that she much preferred – lying down.

As her feeble body crashed on to the mat, Roni dared herself to look in the direction of the mirror. She couldn't look too bad – she was lying down sucking her abdominals in hard, a move which Kath taught her called the *vacuum*. The first thing she saw was her double chin. She flinched and turned away fast. Roni dared herself to take a second glance, her eyes creeping down towards her thick waist – if you could call it a waist – her midriff was expansive and lacked definition. She stopped at her generous thighs which almost looked swollen from the knees up. She felt repulsed.

Roni pushed herself to her feet and stood sideways.

Perhaps she preferred her figure this way, she was certainly more narrow side on than she was head on, but still she felt as though she was six months pregnant. Was it any wonder that they gawped at Helena in her swimsuit yet gasped after she herself removed her robe. Of course, she knew that they were gasping at the identical clothing herself and Helena wore, but Roni suddenly imagined that her body had also made them feel ill, so soon after eating. It made her feel ill just looking at herself.

She ran through the gym into the massive hallway which led to all the major rooms downstairs. She practically launched herself at the Sheraton sideboard, grabbing the telephone desperately.

"Come on!" she shrieked as yet another mirror captured her reflection, throwing back her identical twin and one that was no thinner than she.

"Answer!"

The hall was awash with flowers from friends and neighbours and the scent of freesias floated in the air.

Kath paused before answering the phone. It might be from *his side* and she hadn't seen nor spoken to them since Neil was born. They had cast her aside like vermin and yet now the phone had been ringing as though nothing had happened as they delivered up-to-date news.

She picked up the handset slowly.

"Hello?"

"Kath," Roni barked, "have you seen the state of me? I mean, you're a personal trainer – how the hell could you have let me get into this state? I look like I'm about to give birth . . . why didn't you tell me I looked as bad as this?"

Kath was stunned. Whatever she had been expecting, it certainly hadn't been an irate Roni. "What are you talking about, Roni? Calm down a little, love."

"My figure – if you could call it that – my body – it's a mess, Kath. Only because the gym is bloody-well covered with mirrors did I manage to get a good old look at myself, a three-hundred-and-sixty degree look at myself . . . and I look . . . I look . . . hideous!"

Kath suppressed her amusement as she re-arranged a vase of long-stemmed lillies, careful not to get too close to the pollen. Hard as she'd tried, she couldn't remove the make-up stain from her bell-sleeved top and she knew she had to try harder to look after her clothes, because replacing them before they practically decayed was just sacrilege. Also, it was rare for Kath to pay full price for any clothing but this purchase was definitely not on the reduced rail.

"Roni, firstly, stop being so hysterical. Secondly, you don't look hideous."

Kath stopped what she was doing to think. She could lie to Roni or she could tell her the truth. It really was that easy.

"You could do with a *little* work, Roni, I won't lie to you, but it's nothing that can't be put right with a bit of effort."

Kath wandered into the living room, plonking herself down on the brown sofa. A wad of multicoloured cushions supported her back and she allowed them to take her weight.

"You're not particularly big, Roni, a fourteen isn't big but because you don't have height in your favour it means you can't carry it off as well as others can. I'm afraid that five-feet-two gives you nowhere to hide."

"You mean I am a fat poison dwarf!" Roni blurted out.

Kath's eyes blinked with tiredness as she observed the sympathy cards on the slate hearth. Her friends had been rallying around both of them and she was touched by their individual acts of generosity. She could choose her friends but she couldn't choose her family. And she had chosen her friends well – even Roni.

"Roni, we are about to bury a *poison dwarf*." Kath swallowed hard. "Trust me, you are not one of them. Listen to me now, Roni . . ." She spoke from the heart. "Your kids love you, Pete adores you and we all think the world of you –"

"Except Sophie," Roni scoffed bitterly.

"In fairness, Ron, Sophie doesn't like many people."

"True."

Unbeknownst to Roni, Kath's eyes had welled with tears, but they were tears of frustration. Twenty years of pent-up emotion was ready to spill out, bile and all. But Kath would be damned if she would shed a tear for that old cow. She believed in life after death and if Elizabeth was watching her now she would never give her the satisfaction.

"And anyway, Sophie does like you but she also likes to wind you up, but that's beside the point, Roni. I'm trying to tell you to put your life into perspective."

Kath stood up and left the room. She couldn't bear the hypocrisy which came with the messages of sympathy – they were everywhere she turned – and the *witch* was dead. Soon she would be buried.

"It's a bit of excess weight, Roni, you're not lying dead in a box waiting to be buried nor are you dying with a terminal illness. We can fix it between us but, please, trust me when I say that the more relaxed you are over it the easier it will be to shift the weight."

Roni took in the words from her friend. They were spoken with uncharacteristic tenseness. Kath was usually in a constant state of relaxation and Roni felt bad for lashing out at her. No-one forced her to indulge in rich foods and fine wines, did they?

"You're right, Kath," Roni answered curtly. "I'll pay you double. When can you start?"

"Let me get this funeral out of the way first. Okay?"

Helena recognised the face as the old lady hobbled towards her, sticks first and body last. She panted heavily as each stick was lifted in turn and planted down again in a bid to shuffle forward at a snail's pace. Her distorted legs bore the brunt of too much weight and her face twisted with pain.

Helena rushed forward, holding out her arm.

"Here, let me help you," she offered kindly. The sympathy tone wasn't there but that was because Helena knew the elderly didn't want *sympathy*. They simply wanted to be treated the same as everybody else.

The lady took in Helena's slight frame and chortled.

"I'm not sure you could take the weight, my love."

"I could always sit you on my chair and wheel you in." Helena giggled at the prospect of it. The elderly rebelling in a banking hall the size of a football pitch, whizzing past at breakneck speed. "I could play skittles with you on the chair," she teased. "See how many people you could knock down."

"Sounds good to me. I'd certainly like to take down some of those high falutin' banking people . . . you know, them ones at the top."

Helena knew it would be wrong to involve herself in that conversation. She tried to keep her face as impassive as possible. "No comment." The corners of her mouth twitched when she spoke the words which were counter to her real opinions on '*them*' types.

As they chatted, the area between the main entrance and Helena's desk was covered in no time and Helena had parked the lady comfortably, resting her walking sticks on the desk to the side of her.

The old lady untied the knot beneath her chin, removing the transparent rainhood. Her hair was wrapped tightly around a set of blue rollers, gripped into place by long steel pins.

Helena watched smiling as the rainhood was placed over the handle of one of her walking sticks.

"What can I do for you, Mrs . . ." Helena paused vacantly. Her mind had gone blank.

"Patterson."

"That's right. I'm so sorry, Mrs Patterson. I knew I recognised you but your hair is different from the last time I saw you."

"It shouldn't be . . . it . . ." Her hand shot to her head and she shrieked with embarassment. "I forgot to take my rollers out!"

She grabbed the rainhood, thrusting her head back into it, wincing with pain as her heavy-handedness caused the sharpness of the rollers to impale her scalp further.

"Oouch!"

"It's hard work being a woman, isn't it?" Helena observed. "Beauty is pain, or so my friend tells me. She's a hairdresser."

"You're right, love, you've got the beauty and I'm in pain!"

They laughed harmoniously.

Helena had such a way with the more mature customers of the bank, but it seemed she had yet to serve a client under the age of sixty. Not that it bothered her; she loved the stories they told, their brazen out-spokenness which she guessed came with age, and the joie de vivre which many of them had in abundance.

"What can I do you for today then, Mrs Patterson?"

Helena waited as the lady delved deep into her oversized tatty bag smeared with stains. She littered the desk with hairbrushes, coin bags and photographs of young children – presumably her grandchildren – until she eventually found what she was looking for.

"It's this, my love." She opened a red passbook, holding it out for Helena to see. "The last time I came in I got some cash out but it seems the money has been taken out twice."

Helena took the book from her hands, scanning it.

"That shouldn't have happened."

She saw the two lines identically printed across both pages of the passbook: 15/4/2011: £500.00.00 . . . Balance £69,753.98. The line below was an exact replica bar the remaining balance of £69,253.98.

Helena pushed back her chair, holding onto the red book.

"Give me a minute, Mrs Patterson, and I'll check out withdrawal slips, see what you signed for."

"Thank you, love."

"No worries."

Roni realised she hadn't even bothered to send her friends a card to acknowledge their bereavement. But she knew that Kath hated her mother-in-law with a vengeance and that it was thanks to her Tai Chi and Yoga that she had managed to meditate her way through life in peaceful accord. Still, she would need to do something.

Showered and dressed, she took the time to apply her make-up, starting with foundation. Next she applied a two-tone soft pink to her eyelids starting with the lighter colour which she dusted into the corner of her eyes before using the darker shade on the outer lids, sweeping it out for a smoky effect, just as she had been taught at the Estée Lauder counter. Roni was also a fan of Benefit make-up but she forced her daughters to buy this for her, convinced she was too old to be seen at the high-fashion concession desk.

After her conversation with Kath, Roni had taken her advice and put towels over all the mirrors. Not in the gym, however – that would be an impossible task. Roni had recognised that her impatience would be detrimental to her efforts if she didn't find a way to alleviate how she felt about herself physically. Mentally, she was still work in progress. The answer had been easy.

'*Don't look at yourself,*' Kath had advised her. '*Not until you start to feel better about yourself will you look better . . . through your own eyes, Roni . . . it's what you see that counts.*'

Roni had already *seen* something she liked through her own eyes – the unveiling of her new self, Karl proudly standing behind her, beaming at his work of art. Roni's heart beat in double time as she imagined how good she would feel when *all* of her was new. It would be like looking at a total stranger. Aesthetically, she could get there through Kath's help and with regular visits to Karl but inwardly she still had a lot of work to do.

She looked around her, wondering what Peter would say on his return from work. The place did look rather odd. Her en-suite mirror was draped with a lemon-coloured, bath-sized towel and the antique white cheval mirror in her bedroom had been especially selected to receive first-class attention with its pale-blue shade matching the coolness of her duck-egg-blue bedroom. She felt better already but there was something she needed to do before she forgot. The rest of the towels would need to be hung later.

"You're sacked."

"Who is this?"

"This is Veronica Smyth of The Tudors."

Roni didn't take any messing and she certainly didn't expect her staff – part-time as they were – to mess around between the sheets with her friend.

"I said you are *fired*, Rafi. I hired you as a bartender not as a male prostitute," she snarled. "I'll post any monies owed along with your cocktail book."

"Prostitute? Hang on a minute, Mrs Smyth," he begged. "*She* was the one who accosted me. I barely stood a chance . . . it wasn't my fault!"

"Not my problem any more, Rafi."

"But . . ."

Roni hung up. She could cope with a little flirting,

isn't that what bartenders did? It was part of their job to be charming, but on this occasion it seemed he had literally charmed the pants off Sophie Kane. Or she him. Roni didn't care who had instigated it but she knew that if he could sleep with one of her friends, he could not be trusted. Sophie she'd never trusted anyway, yet she still referred to her as a friend.

Roni stopped dead as a thought passed through her mind. Who was it that she was cross at? A young man full of testosterone or a middle-aged married woman who had initiated a kiss with a man far younger in years than Rafi? Roni felt vile about her double standards.

She had cancelled this week's lesson, replacing it with an excuse which Darren had the sense not to question, but come next week she would have no choice but to be back in that pool beside him.

The holiday brochures had been pored over by Peter and her side of the deal was that she should be able to swim, even just a little, to take the weight off his concerns. '*I can't relax when we go away, babe – it's like when the girls were little again. I feel like I have to watch you constantly and I work so hard, love, that I want to relax when I'm away from work. Shut down.*'

Roni was feeling the pressure from every direction. Peter was not letting up, Sophie would be furious with her when she discovered Rafi had been fired, no doubting hitting back with spiteful revenge, and Darren, well, he was on her mind far more than she cared to admit. Each time she thought of him she drooled with bloodythirsty lust.

Helena sank back into her seat.

"Sorry to have kept you waiting, Mrs Patterson."

She handed two slips of paper to her.

"Is that your signature?" Helena asked her.

The elderly lady looked down at the crisp white pieces of paper filled with pre-printed red boxes and her messy signature scrawled identically on both sheets.

She nodded, frowing intensely.

"It is indeed mine . . . and it's not easily forged as you can see." She managed a grin. "I can't imagine why I took it out twice though and I certainly don't remember spending it." She scratched the front of her hairline, flinching as she accidentally tugged on a roller. "Well, I guess if I can come out with rollers on my head, I'm going to have to admit to losing my faculties." She continued staring at the bank slips until Helena withdrew them, shuffling them neatly, stapling them together for filing a second time.

"It happens to the best of us, Mrs Patterson." Helena stood to assist her to the exit. "Now go home and take those rollers out before your head explodes with pain."

26

Sophie slipped her hand beneath the duvet while he was still sleeping. She could think of no better way for him to wake up than with a massive hard-on with her skilled hands wrapped around it. He had been an extremely giving lover and it was rare for Sophie to invite anyone back to her apartment, but Rafi *was* one of Roni's employees, now an ex-employee, and if the Symths had trusted him in their home then so would she trust him.

Sophie gritted her teeth as she considered how to get back at Roni for firing Rafi. She would make her pay for it.

Rafi stirred from his sleep, groaning with pleasure as Sophie's hand slid up and down his more than average-sized erection. He flung back the bedclothes, grabbing her, forcing her on top of him so he could enjoy the view thus intensifying his orgasm when it came.

Sophie rocked back and forth, whimpering as his fingers flicked expertly against her clitoris and she came quickly with an explosive burst which sent her into a frenzied howl. She knew it would wake Helena but she couldn't help it. Her body had succumbed to his touch and she had become lost in the moment.

Rafi continued to rock her, holding back to extend his pleasure until Sophie's phone shrilled from somewhere around the clothes-littered bedroom.

"Don't answer it," he panted. "I'm nearly there."

Jude stood staring at the shutters of the new salon. She couldn't move a muscle. Her feet were glued to the floor and her mouth had dried up like nothing she had known before.

It was only 7.30a.m. and thankfully few people were about but Jude knew that in half an hour or so the street would be busy with hurried workers and passing cars and yet she had absolutely no idea what to do.

She read the graffiti again and again with disbelief. Who had done this? Why had they done it and why Sophie Kane? Somewhere, deep down, it made sense to Jude. A part of her believed what she read. It explained a lot about the behavioural deficits she had witnessed over the years – if it were true of course – only something told her it was.

Karl sprinted down the concrete steps of his bedsit, racing past the ongoing flickering of the lampost which had become the bane of his life. He headed in the direction of Alderley Avenue taking every short cut possible.

Jude had woken him this morning in a panic, muttering something about vandalism to the exterior of Sophie's new shop. He had dressed without showering or cleaning his teeth. His initial thoughts were to race to the crime scene, hoping that Jude was overreacting in some way, only Karl knew that Jude was as calm as they came and for her to react with such a sense of urgency something very wrong must have happened.

Karl dialled Sophie's mobile as he sped through Congleton Parade onto Priory Way, dodging a litter bin which he nearly ran head-on into.

He wasn't suprised she was unhappy about being disturbed, but when he mentioned vandalism the line went dead and Karl knew that meant she was on her way. He was sure too he had heard a man's voice in the background but Karl hoped he was imagining it. His mind told him one thing but his heart *felt* another.

"I was on the verge of coming. What did you do that for?" Rafi groaned with sexual frustration.

"There's a problem at the shop . . . I need to see what the hell's going on. Why Karl can't sort it by himself is beyond me."

Rafi jumped from the bed before a naked Sophie, who was about to step into the shower.

"Not so fast, young lady . . . we have unfinished business."

Sophie slapped his hand as he closed in on her and he deftly caught it, placing it on him and gliding her hand up and down until she had satisfied him in just a few strokes.

"There," she expressed blankly. "Now can I get in the shower or are there any more paid sexual favours I can do for you?"

Rafi grabbed a handful of tissues from the mosaic-mirrored tissue box.

"Now that you mention it . . ."

"How does *fuck off* grab you?"

As he reached the top end of Alderley Avenue he spotted Jude standing there facing the shop, not moving, and he curbed his pace, recovering from his anaerobic bolt. He was all for exercise, but sleep to sprint was a little unrehearsed and too spontaneous for his liking.

He wiped a bead of sweat from his forehead, pushing his hair back from his face, aware that he hadn't gelled it. Ordinarily he wouldn't leave the house until he was the epitomy of high fashion with his razor-sharp image and sleek, jet-black hair, but when Jude had mentioned the words *Sophie* and *trouble* in the same sentence, Karl had lost it completely and the only thing on his mind was to protect his friend.

As he continued on towards number seventy-six he saw the whitness of Jude's face, her wide eyes scared and questioning and he knew the news was bad. She beckoned him with urgency, waving her hands for him to come quickly and Karl picked up his pace once more. He was by her side in a matter of seconds.

"What the . . . ?" He too paled to the bone as he stood before the steel shutter ruined with slander.

"What the hell is that all about?"

"I don't know," Jude whispered. "What shall we do?"

Karl immediately regretted ringing Sophie. There would be no hiding it now. If the accusation were true then something told Karl this was a secret Sophie would never, *ever*, have exposed of her own accord. He had assumed there was an attempted break-in or some type of criminal damage. It had never occured to him that someone might be up for incriminating his friend.

Sophie drove a little faster than usual. She had a few minutes of time to make up as a result of her distractions with Rafi. He was so totally hot, Sophie thought, but she also recognised the signs that she'd had enough of him already. They had been together on a number of occasions now and he was getting too close and too comfortable with her and that wouldn't do. It was almost like he felt she owed him something because he'd lost his job. "Life's a bitch," Sophie muttered. It wasn't her problem. Neither was he. She made the choices and she pulled the punches. Not him. Not any man. Never.

She cruised along in fifth gear wondering what sort of vandalism had struck her shop. Nothing ever happened in Alderley Avenue, it was one of the richest streets in the country and she had never known of any such event happening there before.

Her heart flipped as she imagined the worst possible situation. A cast-aside lover? A rejected admirer? A spiteful stalker? They were all possibilities, but Sophie had been cunning, clever enough to charm her way back into the hearts of scorned lovers even as she dumped them and they held on to the hope that she had been nice to them . . . didn't that mean she might come back?

She laughed arrogantly, turning Charlotte Church up to its maximum volume as she belted out '*I love it when you call my name . . . I love it when you call my name . . .*'

As she swayed from side to side, watching herself in the rear-view mirror to see how sexy she was while the provocative words fell from her tongue, she frowned at

Karl and at his camp manerisms. He exaggerated everything. Sophie stopped singing suddenly, choosing to tut instead as she recalled the panic in his voice. He was ever the drama queen and she hated that about him. She liked men to be real men, not the overreacting, effeminate types. Still, everything else about him was perfect.

As she absorbed the oversized graffiti which was sprayed in blood red, Sophie's knees gave way and Karl caught her as she collapsed, scooping her up in his arms. He held her close to his chest, not knowing what to do. His reflexes had kicked in at the optimum moment but as he held his boss – his friend – in his arms, Karl knew he needed to plan the next move. He had two women relying on him and he couldn't let either of them down.

Sophie's reaction had told him all he needed to know. She had confessed to its truth via her physical actions and Karl could feel the burden of Sophie's load leave her body, pushing down on his as the weight increased in his arms. He was determined to absorb the impact of her shock.

"Open the shutter quickly," he ordered Jude, feeling the strain of the dead weight, naturally light as Sophie was. "The keys are in her bag."

Jude sank to the ground, scouring Sophie's oversized bag for the keys. She cast aside tampons, make-up and a red leather purse bulging with cash and overhanging receipts.

"There are loads of keys in here, Karl!" she panicked.

Karl hoisted Sophie higher into his arms. She was easier to hold that way. She was so out for the count she couldn't even cling on to him and his biceps trembled with exertion. He had lifted Sophie hundreds of times before, pulling her from the floor on drunken nights out, piggy-backing her when her shoes became too painful to walk in and she was light as a feather. But today, she was a heavy load which sagged in his arms.

"That's them . . . with the big red key-ring. Hurry up, Jude."

Jude's hands shook as she forced the key into the bottom of the shutter. Its grey steel sat low to the floor just millimetres from the pavement. She slid her hands under it, yanking up the sheet, using all her strength, desperate to erase the scurrilous allegations which had been so cruelly painted with poison – thrusting them out of sight with relief.

Jude stood back watching as the shutter curled itself into oblivion, wincing with pain. She had scraped the skin from her fingers in haste as she slid them under the steel ledge and she watched as blood rose to the surface covered in a mass of grit which she wiped away, dusting it onto the floor. If only Sophie's problems could be wiped away so easily, she thought sadly.

Karl kissed Sophie's forehead as she lay lifeless in his arms. He fought back the tears, seeing the colour continue to drain from her beautiful face, and he wanted nothing more than to hold her forever, keeping her away from the prying eyes and perverse touch of all men bar him.

Inside, Jude scoured the room, grabbing a hard-backed plastic chair. "Here, use this." She dragged it towards him and he sat heavily, almost falling into it, Sophie resting in his arms. He tried gently to push her upright but Sophie's energy had dissolved and her listless body flopped forward.

"She won't stay up, Jude."

"That's okay, Karl, better in fact . . . put her head between her legs. She'll come around quicker . . . here, let me."

Jude stepped in, tilting Sophie forward, pushing down lightly on her narrow shoulders, holding her head just above her knees. She exchanged empty glances with Karl as he held her, stopping her from toppling forward. Neither of them knew what to do or what to say. They watched like concerned parents as she slowly came around, pushing up weakly against Jude's resistance.

"Sophie," Jude dropped to her knees before her, "are you alright, darling?"

Something was different about Sophie. She was afraid and exposed, unable to look them in the eye.

"It's okay, Sophie . . . nobody saw it but us. We'll scrub it away and it will be gone forever." Jude swallowed hard.

Sophie looked like a sick child, pale and malnourished, and Jude wanted to hold her close until she was better and strong, back as the Sophie they all knew and loved. Most of them.

"Hey, you." Karl forced a beaming smile at his boss. "I'm going to have every last trace of those stupid words gone before you know it, so come on and pick yourself up, dust yourself down and get on with it like you always do." He spoke in false tones. "We'll leave the shutter up for today and when it's dark tonight I'll remove every last trace of that ridiculous slander, boss."

"I'll help you too, Karl," said Jude.

Sophie looked up at him. The luminous attitudinal

blaze she was renowned for had gone and what was left was a faded shadow of her former self. She went to speak but she could find no words to say. She never thought she would see this day. She imagined her secret would go to the grave with her. She certainly hoped it would.

"Is it true?" Jude whispered.

For once, Jude knew there was no point skirting around the issue. She also knew the answer to her own question – Sophie's reaction had told her that – but she needed to hear it from her friend in order for her friend to get over it. She needed to talk about it. Confess.

Sophie nodded slowly, biting her bottom lip to stop it quivering with shame, but the tears flowed and she broke into a hysterical bawl. One which came straight from her heart, taking her breath away.

"It's tr–ue," she sobbed convulsively. "I w–was so ashamed . . . I nev–er told anyone."

Karl and Jude exchanged wide-eyed glances, their mouths open at the admission which she had already silently confessed. But hearing the words audibly tinged with heartbroken grief hit them harder than the inaudible version which they had earlier accepted.

"*Soph–ie Kane ma–rried a fag-got!*"

"Take deep breaths, Sophie." Jude held her hand, stroking it as Karl patted her back with tenderness.

"Don't speak for a minute until you feel a little more composed."

Jude wasn't used to giving out the orders but she had to take control of the situation and if it meant being a little more outspoken than usual then so be it.

Sophie did as she was told. A rarity indeed. She inhaled

and exhaled as instructed, faltering with uncertainty. She had been able to deal with the past because it was locked away in a tiny part of her brain where she had chosen the most complex of combinations, thus removing the capability for speedy access.

Making gallant attempts to compose herself, Sophie forced herself up in the chair. Her shoulders slumped back. The eye contact was still a struggle for her, but she knew she needed to offer her friends an explanation for the words they had the misfortune of reading.

"I got – married when I was eighteen," she hiccupped, breathing deeply before continuing her proclamation. "To a guy na–med Ricky. We worked togeth–er. It was my first job and we hit it off stra–ight away. He asked me to ma–rry him within three months of us dating and I said y–es. I loved him," she confessed sadly but appearing calmer by the second. "I woke up on the last day of our honeymoon . . . and he was gone." The tears flowed once more but the energy to drive them had absconded. Sophie was weak and feeble. The memories had drained her. "He left me a note to say . . . to say he was gay . . . and being with me but being the only man *not* to fancy me had made him realise it." Sophie stared into the open space, talking to her invisible counsellor. "His message said that it wasn't fair to himself . . . living a lie . . . and I've never seen him since," she sobbed again, clearly heartbroken. "He w–as the love o–f my l–ife."

Jude followed suit with tears flowing. How could any man have done that to her? Walked away from his bride after only a matter of days?

"Oh Sophie, I am so sorry, darling." Jude clutched her friend, grabbing her roughly as the desire to protect her from further pain took over. She leaned into Sophie's body, still on her knees, their shoulders pressed up against each other, cheeks touching.

Jude held her until she felt the lifting movement of her chest normalise. She was breathing less erratically now and it was safe to let her go. She needed to look at her.

"What about you though, Sophie?" Jude talked softly. "You've allowed yourself to live a lie too by holding on to the past . . . letting it shape you. It's unimaginable what happened, but at least he accepted what he was . . . is." She hesitated. "You haven't . . . it seems." Jude was aware of the alien words she spoke. She had never given her true opinion in her adult life but Sophie was desperately low and it was her turn to resurrect her friend. "It's time to let go, Sophie, come clean. You have done nothing wrong, Sophie Kane," Jude declared.

"I fell in love, Jude, that's what I did wrong." Sophie's tone was filled with anger and betrayal. "But I'll never do it again. Never."

Karl cast his mind back to a time where Sophie's tongue had been cruel and vicious when he had remarked on one of her many sexual encounters. '*What? Would you prefer I took it up the bum like you, Karl?*' she had barked at him.

Sophie had clearly protected herself by assuming his mildly effeminate ways were a clear sign of his homosexuality hence her brusque defense mechanisms. She had chosen to make assumptions that every male hairdresser was gay. Yet she could not have been further from the truth.

Karl's teeth ground together as an indomitable force rippled through him. He would have to prove her wrong.

27

James fell to his knees in the box-sized hall, dropping the phone which bounced once before lying still face up. He ignored the voice which called out to him repeatedly.

"James . . . James . . . are you there? Talk to me, Jim, please. I'm only reading what I've been asked to read. I'm so sorry . . . so, so sorry."

He gasped for breath, struggling to come to terms with what he had just heard. Struggling moreso with the cruel blow he had been dealt. A blow which was planned, premeditated and executed to the nth degree, exactly how she would have wanted it. She had got her way in the end.

'I don't know how to tell you this, James,' his sister had announced with trepidation, *'but we've just discovered that Mum left a will . . . instructing that you are . . . erm . . . banned from her funeral.'*

Banned? From his own mother's funeral? For what reason? What had he done which was so wrong that his own mother had kept the fire of wrath burning for twenty-five years? Was love a crime?

Tears streamed down his face and the walls closed in around him and his vision blurred with shock. He was going to pay his respects, say goodbye and finally put closure on the wound which had lain open and exposed for so long but one which he had managed to keep bandaged and covered with his wife as his nurse. But even on her death-bed it was obvious that the blazing bitterness carried a strong abrasive flame which would burn for infinity and her death almost seemed irrelevant as his wound ached with the salt which was rubbed into it with a heavy hand. The incision became deeper as his sister's words echoed in his ear. He was torn apart.

Kath tried to push open the front door with one hand, using the other to close the porch door behind her. The porch was a tiny space, like the rest of the house but it served its purpose fully. It kept out the draught and gave a home to wet shoes and dirty boots which were not allowed on the lightly coloured carpets.

Struggling to open it, she peered through the frosted glass, eyeing the guilty figure who was clearly blocking her entrance.

"Jim!" she called through the inch-sized gap which she had just about managed to open with brute force. "I know I'm thin, love, but I'm not bloody emaciated. Get out of the way, I can't get the door open."

James shuffled forward on his knees. He was too weak to stand. His eyes stung with the double dose of salt which stained his ageing cheeks as they rolled down the creases of his permanent laughter lines.

Kath popped her cheery head around the door, catching sight of his tormented face.

"What's wrong?" she cried with alarm, joining him on the recently hoovered carpet, inhaling the scent of air-freshener which she hoped was CFC friendly. It would be if he had used the one which she'd bought, but sometimes James popped to the shops alone bringing products back crammed with chemicals and tested on animals. He would never learn. "Jim?" Kath was shocked at the transformation. He was fine when she had left for work earlier that morning. What could have happened since then that was worse than the death of his own mother? "Talk to me, please. Why are you crying, love?" She stroked his face noticing how the bags beneath his eyes had sagged with lack of sleep. Even she was suprised at how badly he had taken the news especially as he had got through life with such fortitude. His tribulations had been invisible to all who met him and he was a strong, stable, family man who, to outsiders, carried no insecurities from his past. Between them, they had managed to play a good game.

Kath lifted the handset from the carpet, pressing a key to see who had called last. She redialled the unrecognisable number of the last caller.

"James?"

Kath knew the voice. It sounded just like Elizabeth and she wanted nothing more than to slam the telephone down. But she knew she couldn't.

"It's Kath actually."

"Kath, it's Sandra . . . I'm so glad you called back. I've been worried sick about our James. How is he?"

Kath watched as James forced himself up. He shuffled to the kitchen like an old man. She heard the flick of the kettle as it was switched on. It chugged immediately, hissing angrily in the background.

"How is he *now* or how has he been for the past *twenty-odd years*?"

"It's been a long time . . . I know that."

"What's going on, Sandra?"

"I'm sorry, Kath, I really am so very very sorry . . . but . . . it appears . . . erm, Mum has banned James from her funeral. I'm so sorry, Kath, it's as much a suprise to us as it is to you. . . but he still wants to go . . . only we have to abide by her wishes." She hesitated. "Do you understand?"

The same rage which devoured her twenty-five years ago erupted, spilling deadly lava through her veins.

"*Understand?*" Kath could neither see nor hear anything. "That *bitch* that you call a *mother* has banned her own son from her funeral and you want me to understand? I'll tell you what I understand . . . I understand that she gave up her only son on account of me, sacrificing seeing *our* beautiful sons . . . her grandchildren . . . stopping you and Rebecca from seeing your own brother." Kath failed to see Jason's reflection through the porch glass. He was listening to every word. "Our kids have grown up with no cousins, wondering what the bloody hell they have done wrong and why they're different from their other friends. They had a grand-mother who never saw them . . . we've had no family to support us for twenty-five years and that poor man who is . . ." her voice broke, "who is practically . . . an angel from heaven . . . has now been banned from paying his final respects and putting closure on that evil witch. The

315

only thing I understand, Sandra, is that I want to *dance on her fucking grave!*"

Jason felt it was safer to remain at the other side of the door but he knew that his parents needed him. As he left the confinements of the porch, he watched his father walk from the kitchen where he stopped, shoulder to shoulder with him, both of them watching as Kath slammed down the phone so hard that it smashed, sending pieces of grey plastic flying through the air.

James' face had hardened and Kath knew she had said too much but she'd held it in for so long that she'd taken the final blow and what was done was done. She couldn't take it back.

"I'm sorry," she whispered, the realisation of her venom stinging the air. "I didn't mean to say those things, Jim . . . I was . . . am so angry. I still cannot for the life of me understand how you can go and pay your respects to someone you didn't respect when she was alive."

Kath was furious and, much as she tried to hold back her views, right now it was impossible. She was fuelled and ready for a fight. Just not with her husband. She was fighting *for* him, for his acceptance by the rest of his family and for him to see that he should not go where he clearly was not wanted. She loved him too much to stand back and watch him make a fool out of himself.

"That's my mother, Kath. You shouldn't talk about her like that – it's not fair."

"How can you be so bloody sentimental, Jim? Stop and look at what she's done to you . . ." Kath laughed a hard, bitter laugh. "You know what, Jim? She's *dead* and she's still doing it to you. Let it go. It's over now!"

She brushed past him, taking the stairs two by two. Kath had never known herself to be so insensitive, certainly not concerning such a delicate subject. But she failed to see his point. The woman was dead and yet she still had that hold on him. That noose wrapped tightly around his neck. It was time for them all to let go.

Downstairs Jason flung his arms around his father, squeezing him tightly. He had never felt such a need to hold him until the moment he heard the breaking news spill from his mother's lips through the frosted-glass panes.

Jason released his embrace.

"They're dropping the charges, Dad. I thought you and Mum might like to know."

James could do nothing but nod. He could find no pleasure, no hope and not an iota of mirth in any part of his body.

Jason saw as clear as day the emptiness which had excavated his father as his spirit died before his young eyes.

He turned to go, planting a jovial thump on James' back. There was no reaction.

As Jason took long strides into the outside world where life for everyone else continued as normal, he muttered to himself, "She'll pay for this."

"What the fuck did you tell him for, Helena? The guy was a loser from the start and yet you tell him the biggest secret of my life!"

Helena started to cry. When Nathan threatened her with texts warning of his potential outburst, it had never crossed her mind that he would actually carry them out. Nathan was spineless. He lacked courage and the conviction to be bold or daring. He certainly didn't fit the bill of graffiti artist and all round slanderer. But it had to be him. He had practically confessed before he'd even done it.

"I only told *him*, Soph, I swear. But I never told him anything else . . . ever . . . I swear on my life, Sophie. We were drunk one night and I let slip about your wedding. I tried to tell him I'd made a mistake but he was having none of it. He badgered me for weeks afterwards until I came clean about it. It wasn't my fault. He bullied it out of me like only he could."

Sophie switched sofas and parked herself next to Helena. Yes, she'd had the shock of her life and she had felt herself and her pride stripped to its core until the physical effects took hold and she felt numb, but it wasn't really Helena's fault and she had to accept this. It was *his* fault. Ricky's. Not Nathan's.

"Okay, okay." Sophie rubbed her back as she continued to cry.

"I've ruined everything for you, haven't I?" said Helena.

Sophie handed her a tissue. "No, you haven't. Don't think that. Thankfully only three of us have seen it, I think. Oh and that wanker of an ex-boyfriend of yours but I think we might have got away with it." Sophie stared out of the glass doors into the clear blue skies dotted with a splattering of white cloud. "But I need to come clean to the girls. Don't you think? Here's me preaching to everyone about sharing our innermost secrets with the club and yet I've been keeping the biggest secret of my life for heaven only knows how long."

Sophie leaned against Helena, hugging her tightly.

"Well, no more, Hel. It's time to face the music and it

may well be a good thing that's happened. It's forced me into dealing with it."

Helena nodded. She had confessed to Sophie, shown her the threatening texts from Nathan and yet somehow she was fast becoming the hero in this unusual set of events. Sophie was a true friend forgiving her so soon.

Karl took the stairs two at a time, keeping his hands away from the filthy, greasy handrail which was nothing short of contaminated. The once-white communal walls were scuffed with careless scores and the paint had flaked off where the damp, high walls joined the ceiling. The ancient carpet stank of urine and Karl lifted the rolled neck of his John Smedley jumper above his nose and mouth to keep out the germs.

He knocked on the door.

As the door was pulled back Karl let rip with a right hook which smashed against Nathan's nose. A crunch echoed and blood splurted from each nostril.

Nathan shrieked, clutching his nose as the blood leaked through his clenched fists. But he could not retaliate, the pain was too immense.

Karl grabbed the collars of Nathan's unironed shirt, ignoring the blood which dripped on his own immaculate hands.

"Try it again and I swear I will kill you." He released his grip, wiping the blood with a tissue pulled from the pocket of his faded jeans. "Understand?"

Nathan nodded. His eyes spoke fear of the man who stood before him. "I think you broke my nose," he said, muffled.

Karl smiled a warm, charming smile. "And next time

it will be both of your legs I break if you pull a stunt like that again."

As he sped down the grotty stairwell, Karl grinned to himself.

Nathan would never tell. He was too spineless. Plus there were no witnesses so it was Nathan's word against his. Karl had never struck a man in his life and he didn't intend to again, but this needed to be done. From what he had heard about Nathan, he was a man on whom subtleties were wasted, useless with his self-absorbed nature.

Nathan Breem needed a man to sort him out. He had bullied women his whole life, it appeared, and Karl had waited for Nathan to strike him back – only he didn't – but he guessed if he were a girl things might well have been different.

Sophie had been right about him all along. He was a loser and Karl could not for the life of him see how Helena, bright and intelligent, had stayed with him, shared a bed with him for so long.

A lot had changed over the past month, Karl considered. Helena now had her own money, sharing a luxury flat with her best friend. Jude had a job which had seemingly revived her. Roni's make-over had transformed not just her but her zest for life and Kath, well, her life was there for the taking. She wasn't the bitter twisted woman lying rotting in a box.

28

Roni dared to take a sideways glance at her reflection, willing a vision of hour-glass beauty to reflect back, but all she saw was an ageing woman. A *once was,* not an *is* in terms of her current physical state involving both face and body.

How could it be then that Darren had kissed her? A young, athletic man who could undoubtedly take his pick of younger women with perfect bodies and pert breasts. Roni was sure he had returned her kiss out of sympathy in a brave attempt to remove the stupidity she had painted all over her face when she kissed his chin. But the fact of the matter remained. He *had* kissed her back. A long, hard kiss smack bang on her lips and in between them and she had kissed him right back too. Her lips, which had spilled many a cruel word to many a person, were quiet for no more than a few moments, but it was long enough to leave Roni wanting more.

She had prepared herself for this week's lesson. She had also learned a lesson and that was to arrange it *before* and not *after* the Curry Club event which was the highlight of her week – that was until Darren Ford came into her life – *he* had fast become her highlight. The perfect distraction for a woman on the verge of hormonal imbalance.

Sophie arrived at work earlier than normal. She couldn't sleep and, although she was exhausted, the noise in her head wouldn't stop so she chose to extricate herself from the duvet, heading into work for the perfect distraction.

Yesterday had been one of the worst days of her life. Her stomach had twisted and turned until she was physically ill and the back of her throat continued to burn each time she swallowed. She had not felt so bad since that day she lazily stretched out her hand to be met with a cold, empty pillow, followed by the touch of crisp paper carrying words which Sophie knew would change her life forever.

Not only had she not forgiven him, she had not forgiven herself for the blinding love she carried for him and the blinkered stupidity at failing to notice the signs. Looking back, it all made sense. They fought over the hair-straighteners. He borrowed her clear mascara, and Sophie struggled to get a look-in when it came to the pokey bathroom they shared. Ricky was a clotheshorse. He was immaculately tailored, perfect in every way with manicured nails, bleached white teeth, blonde-tinted hair and a permanent out-of-a-bottle tan. In hindsight, they must have looked more like brother and sister than husband and wife – short-lived as it was.

Sophie locked the salon door, leaving the keys in the inside lock, flinging her handbag on the steel counter of the reception desk.

The salon was impeccable and Sophie knew that Karl must have stayed behind for hours last night bleaching the sinks, cleaning the brushes and polishing the glass mirrors until they shone so furiously they could have landed a fleet of jets. Her heart thawed a little as she thought of his concerned face and his warm hand stroking her back. She knew she was lucky to have him. More importantly, Sophie knew that he could be trusted not to leak her past failures into the present day.

In the kitchen, she grabbed a cafetiere from the single white unit below the stainless-steel sink and scooped richly scented ground coffee into it. She added an extra scoop for good measure, in urgent need of a caffeine fix. As she rolled down the foil packaging, taping it down to keep in the freshness, she heard a loud bang.

Sophie walked casually and unhurried to the front of the shop. She couldn't rush today. Her body carried no fuel and her mind carried nothing other than what was in front of her that very second.

Karl mouthed through the glass to her: "Your keys are in the door. I can't get in, you eejit!"

His muffled tones amused her and Sophie managed a smile as he continued to force his keys against hers in battle. It didn't work. She'd tried it once before when Karl had left his keys stuck in the lock. Only that day, as she stood in the frozen temperatures banging away at the door and ringing the salon telephone, Karl was oblivious to all but Keane as his MP3 player belted in his ears. Sophie had not been a happy boss until lunch time.

She turned the key, pulling back the door to let him in, feeling weak with the exertion but strong enough to force a smile upon the flawlessly pale skin of her right-hand man. His jet-black hair made it seem even paler.

"What are you doing here, Karl?"

Karl pulled his beanie further onto his head as he shivered. His dark-angled fringe was swept to one side just above his eye-line and razored ends stuck out from the bottom of the hat.

"I work here."

The corners of Sophie's mouth turned up.

"I know that. I mean what are you doing here so early?"

Karl winked at her, his grey eyes filled with smoky humour. "Well, I was woken up at some ungodly hour yesterday and it seems my body clock is firmly stuck in middle of the night mode. I'm no longer running in Greenwich Mean Time."

"Half past seven is hardly ungodly!"

He whipped off the khaki army jacket which he had bought at the charity shop, fixing his black cardigan, pulling it over his black jeans. Black clothing was compulsory and Sophie had no issues concerning what her staff wore – within reason – as long as the colours were in sync, so black it was.

As Karl altered his appearance in the round mirror of his own styling unit, he saw Sophie watching him. Her face carried a look of repulsion and he could read her thoughts through the repugnance of her disturbed expression. He absorbed her train of thought and Karl knew it was time to put her straight.

He turned to her as she leaned against the reception counter like it was propping her up.

It was.

"Sophie. You know *I'm* not gay, don't you?"

Sophie snapped. "I don't really care, Karl. It's your business."

"But you do care, Sophie, because you've made so many references to my campness over the years, haven't you? Not to mention digs concerning what *you* think are *my* sexual preferences . . . and it's time I set the record straight."

Sophie jolted forward to leave. She didn't want to listen but Karl paced forward, standing right in front of her, blocking the way to all roads but him. He took hold of her hand, capturing her mesmerising sea-blue eyes in his. Tired as she was, Sophie Kane was a vision of absolute beauty even without sleep and without make-up and Karl was one of the few who knew the virtues she kept hidden from sight. Inside she was kind to a fault, considerate and generous, yet she chose to mask her best attributes with attitudinal bravado.

"Sophie, it all makes sense to me now. All those off-the-cuff remarks, the sly digs . . . your incessant one-night stands and your bizarre choice to use men at *your* sexual disposal," he told her quietly, noticing how she flinched at the emphasis of the word *sexual*. "Everything I have heard you say or do over the years has been nothing more than you trying to regain control because of what happened. It's been you, Sophie Kane, versus the males of this world, fighting your very own anti-bloke crusade. Punishing them all for what happened to you."

Sophie pushed against Karl. She didn't want to hear this, but he forced her to listen.

"Stay, please. Hear me out." He held her shoulders firmly. "It wasn't your fault, Sophie. Of course it's horrendous what happened, but you were both young and it was a long time ago. You need to write off the experience once and for all because all you're doing is punishing yourself by not letting anyone else get close to you."

"Like you, you mean?" Sophie replied bitterly.

Karl knew she would bite back and he expected it. "No, not like me, Sophie, like anyone. What happened to you must have been heartbreaking, but . . . but not every male hairdresser is *gay*." Karl laughed at the absurdity of her logic, even though it made sense to him now that he knew of her past. "Okay, some of my friends are and I am happy to hang out the odd time and do the gay scene with them, but that's because I'm their friend and I am in no position to judge them. Plus they do the straight scene with me, Soph." He pulled her towards him, holding her tightly and she sank into his chest. "It's give and take just like any other friendship . . . any other relationship . . . but *I'm* not gay . . . and I should know!" He laughed with frustration.

Karl felt her feeble attempts to laugh back as her warm breath exhaled against his freshly shaved jawline. She would come around fast. He knew it. She was making amazing progress already. Sophie Kane always bounced back no matter what shit was thrown at her.

"How come you haven't had a girlfriend since I've known you then?"

Karl hesitated, then said, "I guess I'm waiting for Ms Right to come along and sweep me off my feet."

Sophie allowed herself to sag against Karl. He was warm and safe and scented with familiarity.

"Me too," she admitted softly.

"Really!" Karl teased her as he brushed a lock of blonde hair from her eyes. "You too are waiting for Ms Right? Interesting. I'm definitely watching that one."

Sophie punched his stomach gently.

"Aagh!"

"You know what I meant."

Karl wrapped his arms tightly around her. One around her waist and the other wrapped around her shoulders. He held her tightly, enjoying the closeness, and Sophie gave in to it, melting with the security of his fixed but tender grip.

"Hey, I'll tell you something that will cheer you up, Soph."

Sophie lifted her head. Her eyes were glazed as she looked up at him.

"What?"

"I think I broke Nathan's nose!"

"What? How? When?" She broke into her hallmark grin.

"I paid him a little visit yesterday and put him straight on a few things, let's just say. Oh and I left him with a wee reminder of what I will do to him if he ever steps out of line again!"

Her eyes were wide with disbelief. Karl, the gentle, considerate employee she had kept by her side for years. The Karl whom she thought she could read like a book was not a man who was capable of breaking someone's nose.

"I am starting to cheer up already. That definitely deserves a high-five, Karl."

They slapped hands high in the air.

"Wait until I tell Helena! It's been a long time coming."

Helena sat in the staff vending area on the stained red-canvas-backed chairs. They were low to the ground and she felt like lining them up and laying her head down to catch forty winks. She had barely slept since Sophie told her the news. News which had herself, Karl and Jude elbow-deep in solvent solution which had taken the top layer of skin from her pen-pushing hands as she scrubbed for hours until she had cleansed herself as well as the sterile shutter. Still, the planned invective had fast become a piece of history saved by the quick reactions of those first at the scene and protected from further outflow by a small circle of friends.

She watched the LED board add a minute to its red luminous clock before prising herself from the chair reluctantly.

"Helena."

Helena turned in the direction of the voice she both recognised and liked.

"Oh, hi, Maggie. How are you?"

The suit-clad figure of authority beckoned to her. "Have you got a minute?"

Helena glanced at the wall-mounted clock. "I'm due back from my break, like, now."

"Just tell them I kept you late," Maggie instructed.

She held open the staff-room door which led to a long corridor on the first floor of the building which they shared with a second-floor stockbroker and a third-floor high-net-worth insurance broker.

The toilets, kitchen and managers' private offices led off the hardwearing tiled carpet and tubes of flourescent strip-lighting pointed to the stairs which led to the ground-floor banking hall. The area was dark and drab and in need of a lift into the twenty-first century. It was stuck firmly in post-war era with its large trellis which peeled as it gripped the walls, its cracked exterior struggling under the weight of the ceiling.

Helena jumped up and followed Maggie, keeping pace with her long legs as she strode purposefully towards her office.

"Take a seat, Helena," Maggie offered as she smiled at the young woman who she had become so fond of over the years.

"Thank you."

Maggie sat on the worn tan-leather chair, grimacing as she tried to stop it from swivelling.

"You know this chair makes me feel sea-sick every time I sit on it but whenever I ask Head Office for a replacement they tell me we have to stop spending until the recession is over."

Helena laughed as Maggie gripped the desk, steadying herself.

"And the joke is that it's the bloody board of executives – you know, those who set the targets, budgets etc, who are responsible for the recession in the first place but their pompous arrogance prevents them from seeing it." She spoke directly to Helena, never losing eye contact and Helena could see that, if pushed, she would be a force to be reckoned with. "Still, I'd like to keep my job so I'll say nothing. I'll just take a travel-sickness pill before I come to work every morning!"

"I suppose we're lucky to have jobs with the state of the economy," Helena offered jovially although she was a little nervous about why Maggie had beckoned her.

"Indeed. Now where were we?"

Helena shrugged her narrow shoulders.

"Yes, of course. I spoke to Head Office and they have a whole load of university graduates starting on the Graduate Management Programme. Basically clever kids on cheap labour which is perfect for us given the current climate."

"Am I getting on the programme?" Helena leaned forward with excitement. "A few years too late but better late than never!"

"No, no. Far better than that, Helena. You are going to *write* the programme for new starts. Put together an induction programme starting with the basics of banking, including covering all the necessary regulations. I want you to compile a brief synopsis of all the internal roles right from the bottom up to board level so they have an understanding of their potential career opps . . . plus if you could create a timetable for them which has a balance of both classroom training combined with the shadowing of *carefully* selected people in all of the roles I brief you in . . . that too would be super. I only want them to learn from the best."

Helena was speechless. She could say nothing.

"It won't be possible for them to shadow anyone at board level of course but we may be able to arrange for some of the more promising ones to pair up with heads of departments." Maggie spoke without emotion like she was delivering the lunch-time news.

Helena was ready to burst.

"The real challenge for you though, Helena, is the

psychological observations you will need to undertake. Head Office wants a full report on each of the students giving their learning style percentages, you know, Acti –"

"Activist, reflector, pragmatist and theorist," Helena burst out with excitement. "I remember it like it was yesterday."

Maggie broke into a smile at her sheer enthusiasm. There was no-one more equipped to do the job as far as she was concerned, but Helena would be missed in the banking hall.

"We'll talk more over the coming days but how does 1st July suit you for a start date with an annual salary of twenty-four thousand?"

Helena gasped. That was almost an eight-thousand-pound jump from what she earned now. The possibilities were endless. She could save fast for a deposit and buy her own place. *Casa Helena*. She would host the Curry Club, welcoming her friends into her own abode with pride instead of shame. She need never borrow anybody's home ever again.

Helena was on the road to recovery. She had a new wardrobe of clothes, a promising career, a boss she adored and a best friend who had forgiven her lapsed stupidity on the strength of a single word. Oh, and an ex-boyfriend with a broken nose as per Sophie's latest text. But more importantly, she would be out of that banking hall, away from it for good where she could make a fresh start as the professional that she was.

"Where do I sign!"

29

Kath kicked off her rubber-soled pumps, using her feet instead of her hands which were tied up, wrapped around her mobile phone.

"James says I can do the Curry Club on the day of the funeral, Jude – he says it would be a good distraction and it is my turn to host but I'm not too sure. What do you think?"

Jude held the receiver, putting down the salon equipment brochures which she had pored over for hours, tapping away on her calculator, multiplying every item by eight and coming up with a figure which exceeded her seventy-five-thousand-pound budget every time.

Sophie had insisted on eight work stations after deciding that she would opt for the *rent a chair* strategy for Alderley Avenue. She had elected to charge each of the top stylists she was all set to interview two hundred pounds per week inclusive of all overheads and products – including colours – which was where they could easily net two hundred pounds per day for themselves. It was the colours that brought in most of the income, she had told Jude. That way she could gross sixteen-hundred pounds per week and could have the bank loan cleared in no time at all, saving thousands of pounds' worth of interest.

"I don't think James would have suggested it if he hadn't meant it, Kath. Do you?"

Kath sat in her white cotton Sloggi underwear with matching sports bra. She had finished teaching her daily Yoga class and was heading for a dip in the pool followed by a long spell in the steam room where she hoped the intense wet heat would draw out her impurities. She needed to feel cleansed and revived. That was the Catholic in her.

"No, no, you're right, he wouldn't. I was thinking of inviting partners this time actually, Jude. It will be a bit squashed and all that – oh and you might have to eat off your knee . . . but would that be okay?"

Kath waved to one of The Hamptons' members as they too headed for the exclusive solarium. She didn't care what state of dress they saw her in. To Kath, a body was a body. You came in naked and you went out naked.

"Can't we eat off plates?"

"Huh?"

"You said we have to eat off our knees but I'd much prefer a plate please." Jude giggled at the stupidity of her sense of humour. She would never be a comedienne and she preferred laughing at other people's jokes, but lately she was at her happiest because she was working, her life held a clear purpose for her and despite the fracas she'd had with Clive, she would continue to work until the project was complete and then she would set the record straight with him. Perhaps she simply needed to get it out of her system.

"Jude Westbury. Are you starting to get a bit funny in your old age?" Kath teased, taking a cleansing wipe, removing her light make-up. She didn't want it clogging her pores. The dirt needed to come out of them not be sucked into them as her pores opened with the steam she was soon to be a part of.

"Hey, less of the *old*. I'm still the *right* side of forty. . . unlike some."

Kath paused. "Hang on a minute . . . only just, *young lady* . . . I'm saying that while I can," she quipped affably. "Anyway, let's see if you look as good as me when you're my age." Kath snorted whole-heartedly. She knew she looked good with her flawless pale skin complementing her fiery red hair. Her cheeks were consistently dusted with a natural red tint making her look crisp and fresh as a summer's day. But she held not an ounce of vanity. Everything Kath said was in jest or tongue in cheek. To her, beauty was on the inside and she had no need for the sparkling bling which Roni wore like a suit of armour.

"You do look amazing, Kath. James is a lucky man. What's your secret?" Jude paused for a second. "Alcohol preservation?"

Kath held the phone, gobsmacked. Her friend had transformed herself since she had begun to work for Sophie. She was usually so quiet, saying very little, but now she was a spirited lively woman with a dry sense of humour that had been hidden away.

"Actually," Kath cleared her throat, "yes!"

She tittered away with childish glee. Laughter was the best medicine for Kath and anything which made her heart happy made her happy.

"You wait until Wednesday, Jude. I'm going to get my revenge."

"Don't worry, Kath. Your cooking will be the perfect revenge."

Roni scribbled on the dry-wipe board which was hung in the laundry-cum-utility-room. She had to write everything down, else she would forget it. 'Keep Wed free. Curry Club couples night. Kath's.'

Roni was pleased that it was couples night. Peter had heard so much about her nights out with the girls, yet he had not had the pleasure of experiencing one of them with her. The annual yachting event, yes, but he hadn't experienced being a part of the closed circle and perhaps he would now understand what it was which attracted her so to the Curry Club and its strange proceedings. She would be proud to see him witnessing her fit in with the group as they played their favourite game.

She was becoming one of them more easily as the days passed.

The doorbell chimed through the house as loud as a church bell and Roni froze. It rang again. This time she forced the top back on the wipe-board pen, dropping it onto the narrow tray which sat at the bottom of the board before racing through the kitchen and into the ballroom-sized hall.

Roni could see Darren's outline through the glass panes which sucked panels of light into the house. She had cancelled last week but she knew better than to do it again. She was on a mission to learn to swim. A choiceless mission.

"Coming!" she yelled, rushing to the mirror to fix her hair before she would open the door to the man whose lips had embraced hers. "Shit." Roni grabbed the towel from the mirror, throwing it on the side dresser, quickly licking her fingers and thrusting them through her sleek hair which she was still getting used to.

Darren was unusually early and she wasn't ready yet.

Roni opened the front door with a pounding heart. "Hi there."

Darren beamed down at her. "Good morning. Is the lady of the house in?"

Roni threw back her head with laughter. She liked his boyish charm, his occasional cheekiness. But more than anything, she adored his insightfulness even though at times it unnerved her.

"*I am* the lady of the house," she snapped, trying to suppress the humour behind her tone.

Darren released his grip on his holdall, letting it drop to the floor.

"You certainly are, madam."

He edged closer to her, staring down the gap of her soft pink jersey shaping its expensive fabric around her vital statistics, peering at her ample breasts which were large and sagging.

Roni saw the look on his face and her head felt light. Her stomach danced with regret as she pulled him in, slamming the front door behind them.

Darren pushed her backwards until she was pressed against the heavy silk wallpaper, yanking at the bottom of her sweater, pulling it over her head and dropping it at his feet, stopping to take in her breasts which spilled out of her matching pink bra. A roll of fat sat beneath the bones of the bra, with another more bulky roll pushed over the waistband of her beige tailored trousers. But Darren didn't care. He had slept with too many women, girls to be precise, with pert 'C' cups and ironing-board stomachs and thighs he could wrap his hands around. But in front of him was a woman who had experienced life and her body reflected this. He wanted nothing more than to make Veronica Smyth see that she was as perfect as they were – more so in fact – and for her to embrace the beautiful woman she was.

Roni's chest rose and fell as her breathing became louder and more erratic when Darren's soft hands slid up her arms, stopping at her shoulders. He gently pushed down her bra-straps, pulling back the protective lace of her ample cups and watching with lust as her pale breasts and saucer-like pink nipples fell into a natural southerly position. He had never seen a more beautiful sight in his life.

Darren knelt down to kiss the stretch marks beneath her breasts before taking in one of her large nipples which filled his mouth.

His trousers were bursting with the intense load he had carried for this strange woman since the day he'd met her and Darren knew that if he could make her see that she was inviting and sexy without the ostentatious jewellery she so relied on, her bling of armour, he would be a happy man. He would exit her life as quickly as he had come into it.

She was almost there.

Roni arched her back. Her lustful groan filled the hall with a pornographic symphony as she felt her trousers and then knickers pulled roughly past her knees. She was glad she had waxed and that her body was in better shape. Her redness had fully healed and she had shaved her legs too in advance of today's lesson. Roni was swimming alright – in a sea of lustful waves.

"Lie down," Darren whispered as he freed the trousers from her one foot at a time.

As Roni lay down obediently, Darren unbuckled his washed-out ripped jeans, stepping out of them. His impressive erection waited impatiently.

Roni gasped when she saw the size of it.

"I'll be gentle, Veronica," he assured her as he dropped to the floor, resting on his biceps which took the weight of his six-foot-four frame. "Guide me in."

Roni took hold of his thick penis, rubbing it against her clitoris in small circular moves before guiding it to its rightful place where it disappeared, lost amongst the crude cries of eroticism. As they thrust against each other, the longing each of them had held for very different reasons peaked to a climax and Roni's body shuddered as waved contractions washed her away to a place she had never been before – taking the guilt momentarily with it.

Jude picked up the sample pots of paint, a mixture of purples, carrying them to the checkout. Sophie had asked for nothing but for her to remain within budget. She had made no demands on colours, furnishings or even the layout of the place and Jude, surprisingly, found her the easiest person to work for.

She smiled as she admired the shades of colour stuck firmly to the front of the miniature tins. She had opted for a combination of deep purple combined with a complementary mauve which would brighten the effects of such a bold statement. Jude planned to have the thick skirting boards sprayed in silver and covered in a coat of clear, hardwearing varnish which would stop them from scuffing easily and more importantly create a chrome effect to match the overall aesthetic look she was so determined to capture. Deep, earthy colours offset with a contemporary steel finish. She couldn't wait.

As she handed over the cash, she glanced down at her driving licence which she kept in the plastic-coated section of her purse in case she needed it at short notice, although it would hardly be because she was stopped by the police for speeding. Random checks perhaps. It was more for large credit-card transactions like when she purchased her BMW X5 which Clive had suggested she buy on her platinum card so they benefit from the extra Air Miles. Clive Westbury saw the value in every penny he spent and it came back to him two-fold.

Jude flinched as she read her date of birth with its eight numbers seperated by forward slashes. It only seemed like yesterday since she was at university, getting lost in the endless corridors, walking for miles to reach the library and falling in love with the man of her dreams. Now here she was on the verge of turning forty and life had passed her by so quickly that it was scary. More than scary, damn outrageous, and it was only of late that Jude began to feel like she was living again – alive in more ways than simply breathing in oxygen and exhaling its toxic pollutants – she was living the stuff that her dreams were made of. She was living her *dreams* and yet she had never felt more awake.

Jude pulled out from the car park, manoeuvring slowly as she passed the Parent and Child spaces. Anna had once run out in front of a car when she was a toddler. Jude had her back turned for a single second as she unclipped Tom's safety clasp, lifting him from his car seat when she heard the screech of slamming brakes followed by the piercing cries of her beautiful daughter. The car hadn't touched her. She was one of the lucky ones. Jude felt as much for the driver of the car as she did for herself and Anna that day.

Even as young kids, Tom and Anna were head-turners. Both of them. They had inherited the best qualities of herself and Clive and life came to them so easily that it brought a lump to her throat as she cruised along, heading back to Sophie's shop to test the sample paints now that the plastering had dried out. It would take double the coats than if the walls had simply been left in their original condition, which they could easily have been – but Jude felt that the refined smoothness would add to the artistic perfection she was hoping for.

Both Tom and Anna were in the top sets at school, excelling too in tennis, polo, dressage for Anna and golf for Tom. The children had had life handed to them on a plate since the day they were born and Jude had been there to dish out more as soon as their hungry mouths were open and willing to take it.

She too had led a priveleged life and it was second nature to her to allow her children to benefit from the same upbringing, organic and uncontrived. It was Clive, however, who wanted the *opposite* of the life he had where his parents struggled to make ends meet and it was his past which drove his future. It had shaped him well and truly, moulding him into a cast-iron, non-malleable figure and Jude knew that he was not easily persuaded and it was this that worried her.

30

Jason stood behind the protective trunk of a tree which had no doubt witnessed every burial since the existence of the graveyard. Its roots spanned the width of a car jutting out above ground level, with complex shapes and a twisted infrastructure holding its seventy-foot-high torso firmly in place.

He watched as the Volkswagen hearse rolled to a perfectly controlled stop and the pallbearers shuffled towards it, clearly dreading lifting the weight of someone who was a central figure in their lives. A mother figure. Someone who would soon be rotting away, experiencing the dreaded lividity of greying skin and the stiffened muscles of rigor mortis.

Jason recognised some of the mourners. They were his aunts, uncles and cousins. He should have been there, so should his father, and he wanted nothing more than to perform a demonstration of disrespect to the decomposing body who had torn him away from a whole side of family that he never got the opportunity to know. He was a child for Christ's sake. What did it have to do with him? Yet he and his brother had suffered at the hands of an adult spat and he had felt like the odd one out for as long as he could remember.

He laughed scornfully at the wonderment of his parents as they struggled to understand his provocative behaviour. How blinkered where they? Consumed in their own plight. He had been brought up knowing his grandparents existed and yet he couldn't see them. He had heard stories from friend of friends who knew the family, hearing how they spoiled his cousins while he and Neil got nothing and he had eavesdropped on his parents when the contention between them climaxed, hearing the bitterness in their voices. Jason knew that his life was not the same as the life which his friends had lived. He was robbed. Robbed of relationships which should have come as par for the course and he was still hurting from the insecurities he was left with.

"Let's do it one more time," Darren ordered as Roni panted hard.

"I can't. You've worn me out," she puffed.

"Stop being a wimp."

Darren jumped into the water taking the yellow float from her. He lay on his stomach stretched out, kicking his legs just below the water's surface. He made no splash as he demonstrated the technique to his trainee.

Roni watched carefully, determined to imitate it to perfection.

"You're doing this, Roni." Darren kicked his legs above the water soaking Roni in the process.

"Oi!"

He handed the float back to her. Their fingers touched

as they exchanged the piece of floating rubber and Roni felt a bolt of electricity pass through her.

"Lie flat on your stomach and remember to kick from your hips not your knees," he ordered. "All you're doing, Roni, is using too much energy splashing about and that's why you're glued to the same spot not moving anywhere and yet tiring yourself out unecessarily. Don't stop until you've reached the other side . . . I don't care how tired you are. We're nearly done."

Roni lifted her chin, squirting out a mouthful of bleached water as she tried hard to mimic the actions of a seamless Olympic swimmer. She felt her body dipping as it struggled to stay afloat. Her legs simply refused to stay close to the surface. They wanted to walk on the floor to get to the other side instead of swimming and it was that which Roni's mindset had to forcibly change.

Darren mused as he watched his protégée tackle the challenge of the entire width of the pool. He would be sad when he had to say goodbye to her.

Roni was kind, endearing and enigmatic, but most of all she was – had been – a lost soul searching for her very core and she was within a cat's whisker of finding it. Darren knew that his work with Veronica Smyth was nearly done. She would soon be able to swim. Okay, she'd never be a natural, that was evident, but she would soon be able to manage a few strokes without the float aid which was about to be taken from her for good. She was a strong, determined woman who could tackle anything she desired once her mind was put to it but it was the *way* in which she tackled things that had caught Darren's attention within moments of setting eyes on her. It was her worst enemy. *She* was her own worst enemy.

Darren swam across to the other side of the pool where an exhausted Roni puffed away as she clutched the safety of the side.

"I did it! I did it!" she roared. "I didn't put my feet down once . . . did you see me . . . did you?"

Darren lifted her into his arms.

"I did indeed."

She was featherlight as the buoyancy absorbed most of her body weight.

Roni wrapped her legs around his waist. Her arms clasped around his broad shoulders and an oral battle recommenced as the fiery passion which they had tried to suppress reared its lustful head once more. Darren ripped at the bathing suit, baring her breasts, lying her back in the water as he teased them with his tongue and Roni's groan echoed through the chalet as she was set free.

She was becoming unrecognisable to herself.

Kath added green cardamon pods to the mortar followed by whole black peppercorns and three sticks of cinnamon. She ground them down by pressing hard, whistling away as she enjoyed the roughness of her actions. It was cathartic and it took her mind off the funeral which was taking place not too far from where they lived.

"Do you want some help, love?" James popped his head around the kitchen door. He was desperately trying to be brave and Kath applauded him for agreeing to the Curry Club on what would inevitably be one of the most difficult days in his life. The men would be great company for him tonight and Kath hoped the question they pulled out would make for light discussion.

Helena had called earlier with plans for how she thought the night might go but all she had instructed was for Kath to think of a sexist joke. Kath was still in the dark about what form the night would take.

She trusted Helena.

"That would be great, Jim, thanks."

Kath pulled a net of onions from beside her and thrust them at him. "Here, that'll give you something to cry about," she laughed.

James smiled weakly. He recognised that all his wife was trying to do was distract him, add a little humour to this difficult day and he appreciated it. They had made up from the earlier spat. Kath had every right to be angry. Why wouldn't she be? She'd stood back and watched her kids lose out on birthday presents, Christmas presents, and attention more importantly.

"How come I always get the rubbish jobs?"

Kath added two teaspoons of ground cumin, coriander and turmeric, watching as the colours changed into autumnal reds, a contrast to the bright, fine day which radiated from outside the small kitchen window that looked out onto a flagged garden filled with herbs and potted plants.

"Can you cook?"

James shook his head.

"Well then."

He pulled a knife from its stand, using it to break a hole in the net, ripping at the rest of the bag it until half a dozen onions escaped, rolling beserkly around the cluttered work surface. One dropped onto the floor and he bent down to pick it up as another one fell landing right on his head.

Kath squealed with laughter.

"Give them here," she laughed. "Go and watch the television or something."

James looked hurt. He was easily wounded the past few weeks.

"I can do it, Miss Bossy Boots. Seriously now, pass them over, Kath, I'm okay. I need the distraction. . . plus I can tell the guys later that I cooked too!"

"They might believe it but the girls will know better!"

Kath glanced at his hand, pointing to it with the clay pestle.

"Jim, you can't chop onions with a bread knife, you eejit. Here," Kath grabbed a sharp chopping knife from the pine block, "use this."

"Thanks." James chopped the stalks from each end of the onion and Kath counted to ten silently as she watched him waste a good inch either side. She would need double the onions by the time he had finished using only the middle of them.

"Where's Jason today? I spoke to Neil and he said he'd gone out but he didn't know where."

James wiped his eyes with his hands rubbing at them hard. "Aah!"

"You don't wipe your eyes with the same hand that's been holding the flesh of the onion." Kath was fast becoming exasperated. It was reminiscent of the boys when they were little and keen to help her as she took one step forwards and two steps backwards. But they had to learn, it was educational. James on the other hand was too long in the tooth to take on a culinary role. Kath had given up long ago and she dreaded being ill because she knew the only decent meal she would get was a fried egg on toast. But the irregular shifts he had always worked meant he had little time to learn any culinary skills.

James splashed his face with water, drying it with a clean tea towel which he grabbed from the top drawer next to the sink.

"I think I'll go for a walk, love."

Kath was relieved that he would be out from under her feet. As usual, he had done half a job, leaving her to peel and chop the rest of the onions. The kitchen was the only place he ever let her down. Not that she really cared. On a scale of life, it had mattered little to her.

"You do that. Maybe you could stop at the off-licence on the way back and stock up on some beer for the guys tonight? I've plenty of wine for the girls."

"Will do, love."

He kissed her forehead, avoiding the smear of orange powder on her left cheek.

"Love you."

"Love you too."

Jason waited until the funeral procession had left the graveside after the short service. It was more than she deserved in his opinion. Maybe she'd been a good mother to the others, he'd never know. She certainly hadn't been a good mother – any mother in fact – to his father, nor a good grandmother either. She didn't deserve the salty tears nor the biblical words the wind carried in his direction. She could go to hell for all he cared. She had ruined the family life he wanted, but never had.

He trudged slowly towards the open grave when the coast was clear, peering down into it. The scattered earth he had seen fall from shaking hands lay on the beech surface of the coffin beneath long-stemmed white roses which were – ironically – his mother's favourite flower. That was their only similarity. That and James.

As he stood glaring down at the wooden box with narrowed eyes, Jason realised that he had no plan of action. No idea of what he was to do in order to serve up the revenge he so wanted to impart. She was dead. Wasn't that revenge enough?

He picked up a mound of freshly dug earth, hurling it violently against the coffin, followed by another and another until his arm ached heavily. Yet still his heart felt no lighter. He wanted to do something for his father. A manly son-to-father gesture to show just how much he loved him. Let him know he was sharing the burden of his pain. But as the tears flowed down Jason's face, it suddenly became clear. His father wanted nothing more than him – his son. He'd lost his mother and he didn't want to lose anyone else, certainly not to a set of prison bars.

Jason was crippled with guilt over what he had put his parents through over the past number of years. One day it would be him standing over the graveside of his parents. A day which he hoped would never come but he knew it was inevitable. He wanted to make them proud, just like they were proud of his brother, Neil, and he wanted to be back in the family home where the four of them had shared precious memories, filled it to the brim with love and laughter.

Jason kicked clods of soil into the open pit thoughtfully, his white trainers soiled. He needed to get his act together, get a job and earn the trust of his parents because he was not prepared to rip apart another generation. Never.

"How did you get on, love?"

James' flushed cheeks had transformed themselves into a perky smile as he set down two carrier bags filled with beer cans, leaving them on the floor at the entrance to the kitchen.

"Fine thanks . . . do you know this . . . I can't believe how much better I feel already, Kath. That walk has really cleared my head. I feel great. But it's colder than it looks." He rubbed his cold hands across Kath's warm face noticing that the orange stain had spread to her other cheek.

"Get off! You're freezing."

"And you're *hot*."

Kath pulled away, concentrating on her battle with the age-old can-opener which refused to pierce the can of tomatoes she needed to finish her rogan josh.

"Put your energy into something more useful." She winked at him, pushing the can away from her, surrendering to its stubbonness. "And why do you keep using those bags, Jim. It takes thirty years . . . or something like that . . . for one of them to biodegrade. Use the bag for life under the kitchen sink next time. I keep telling you."

James grinned at his wife. She wasn't bossy by nature but when she was forced to concentrate in order to deliver on time, she turned into a Sergeant Major type, bellowing instructions followed by threats if those instructions weren't carried out. Only there was no malice in Kath's voice. Its volume was raised but that was the height of it. She was mildly stressed.

"Sorry, ma'am." James saluted her. "Might I suggest a punishment of forty spanks with the hairbrush?"

Kath washed her hands using her favourite organic seaweed handwash. She lifted them to her nose inhaling its blend of essential oils, marvelling at the lather it built up in a matter of seconds.

"This stuff is brilliant . . . even the bottle is bio-degradable," she was talking away to herself, "this stuff is full of vitamins, minerals and free ra –"

James had crept up behind her, snuggling into the side of her warm neck. He kissed it with an open mouth, covering much of her exposed skin.

"I love it when you talk dirty," he groaned, spinning her around to face him. "Now get upstairs into that shower . . . I think you need a good rub down after chopping all those onions." He winked at her. "Serves you right. You should have let me do it," he chided wagging his finger at her.

"Hhm. We would probably be sitting in the A&E department, Jim, if I had let you loose on those onions! Honest to goodness, it was like having the boys under my feet again."

Kath laughed as he picked her up, throwing her over his shoulder like a rag doll. She was glad he was feeling better. He had lost his libido of late which was hardly suprising given the torturous time he had been faced with, but Kath knew that he was slowly coming to terms with what had happened. Recognising that he was not to blame in any way for the decisions *she* had chosen to make. *She* was. But she was gone now. Six feet under.

31

Kath opened the mahogany dividing doors which separated the living room from the dining room, the latter being the larger of the two rooms.

James had been saying for years that they should switch the rooms, using the larger back room as the living area and transferring the rarely used dining room to the front of the house. He hated the relentless noise of the thud which came from the heavy leather football of his neighbours' kids as they bounced it for hours on end until it drove him crazy. More than crazy in fact, for a man who was generally so easygoing. He wanted nothing more than to grab it and puncture the living daylights out of it and every other football on the street. But Kath liked to see what was happening in the world, and much as she liked her neatly paved garden with its colourful array of greenery, she didn't want to look at it all day. It didn't do anything to keep her attention. There were only so many one-way conversations a woman could hold.

"Come through, Pete." James shook his hand and kissed Roni on the cheek. She smelled of the perfume

Poison which he had once bought Kath before she marched him back to the shop, its wrapping still intact.

'*Please don't buy me anything that's called Poison. Feng Shui is about creating harmony and I'm not sure I'll feel particularly harmonious by wearing something with a name like Poison,*' she told him bluntly. Kath was a stickler for positivity. She ate, slept and breathed it but she wasn't prepared to breathe in *that* stuff.

"So, what's your poison?" James chirped in the living room, looking at Roni to see if she understood his comical gag. He had well and truly dusted the cobwebs off with his long walk earlier and his bedroom antics had cheered him up no end. He was surprised at how much better he felt.

"White wine, please, James. Do you have Sauvignon Blanc?"

James grinned as he took the bottle of Dom Perignon from Peter. He only drank beer so the exorbitantly expensive bottle was wasted on him but something told him his ever-knowledgable wife might know what it was he had just been handed.

"Roni, my love, the only thing I know about wine is that it comes in a bottle . . . let me ask my better half."

Roni smiled kindly. She adored James, always had. What was there not to adore about his easygoing nature and the constant smile his eyes carried, even through the tough times.

Roni was conscious that this was a delicate day for all the family – him particularly – and she didn't want to appear too fussy. She was tired of creating those demands and she felt lightened and happier by being just that little bit nicer to people.

353

"Don't worry. Just give me what you have," she offered kindly and Pete squeezed her hand as he watched her lovingly.

"That was sweet of you, Ron," he whispered when James left for the kitchen. He was surprised that she hadn't turned her nose up at his ignorance, made some condescending retort to his honesty. "I'm so proud of you, Roni my love. You've been so different lately . . . much less, well, angry with the world I suppose I should say, even though it doesn't sound too complimentary . . . although it is a compliment, I assure you. I'm not sure how else to put it really, princess."

Roni looked away. The guilt was killing her but she was desperate for more of Darren. He had whetted her appetite and left her feeling ravenous 24/7. Perhaps that was why she was being nicer to all who came into contact with her, it lightened the load a little – washed away some of the tarnish which made her feel dirty yet rejuvenated.

"What's changed you then? Is it Darren?"

"Pardon?"

Pete noticed her flinch and he pulled her to him.

"Look, I know I've really pushed you this time but it was for your own good . . . that guy has been an absolute lifesaver, Ron, don't you think? I've never seen you so confident since you started doing something for yourself. I had to be cruel to be kind, don't you see?"

Roni nodded, snatching the drink from James' hand as he whistled his way back into the living room. She took long gulps, relaxing as Pete turned his back on her as the first of many football conversations kicked off. She knocked it back in full when she was sure no eyes were on her. The other day would have to be a one-off. Lying was no way to live her life. She was trying to make life more simple, more enjoyable. Not add to its complications.

"How do you get a man to stop biting his nails?" Kath read from the handwritten slip she had pulled out a minute earlier. The paper was folded so tightly that it had taken her the guts of a minute to unravel it. The alcohol wasn't helping her usually spot-on coordination.

"Chop his fingers off?" Sophie suggested.

Karl prodded her waist, whispering in her ear.

"You're such a cow."

"No, that's not right, Sophie . . . although James nearly chopped his fingers off today trying to cut onions with a bread knife! Dope."

"Typical man!" Pete teased camply.

Sophie shifted upon hearing the effeminate tones. Some things were too close to home. She hadn't told them yet but she would, as soon as the game was finished.

"Excuse me, Pete. You barely know where the kitchen is," Roni laughed. "I'm not sure you've ever chopped an onion in our entire married life!"

Pete pulled a comical face as he thought back over the years. "Actually, love, I think you're right . . . but I thought onions came chopped-up, you know, in those little clear bags?"

Now it was Roni's turn to blush.

"Or from some outside catering company!" he teased.

Helena snorted, grabbing a napkin to cover her mouth before the red wine dribbled down her chin onto her new white broderie anglaise smock. She had expected Roni to retort but she did nothing but break into a grin.

"I'm not a natural cook, Pete, so if you want to eat anything decent I have to outsource it."

"Now, now, children," Kath chided. "Back to the joke . . . You stop a man from biting his nails by *making him wear shoes*!"

The room roared with the laughter of friends who had come together to create a distraction for their grieving friend. The Curry Club had become The Comedy Club for *one night only* and it had gone down like a storm. It was Helena's idea. She was the brainstorm behind the psychology of laughter mending broken hearts and it seemed to be working. The constitutional formalities of the event had been cast aside to make room for light-hearted entertainment to be enjoyed by all.

"My turn now."

Clive took the bowl as it was passed around the round six-seater table. It was a squash with nine of them packed like sardines around its circumference but at the same time it was cosy and intimate.

Clive unfolded the paper swiftly, already laughing before he read the joke out loud. He was loving throwing harmless digs at the women who didn't seem to be finding them as funny as his male friends. There was a categorical gender separation going on tonight.

"You're going to love this, Jim . . . although I bet it was you who put it in! Here goes, fellas . . . '*Why is the space between a woman's breasts and hips called a waist?*'"

Clive scanned the table to see if there were any takers.

"*Because you could easily fit another pair of tits in there.*"

Jude gasped as the boys fell about with wild laughter, snorting childishly.

"You know me and my boob fetish," James piped up. "I can see how you'd think I put that in there."

"You said the T-word, Clive." Jude's eyes were as wide as saucers.

Normally, Clive was so gentlemanly and swearing was something he never did. Jude had never seen him behave like this, not when he was entertaining his clients, nor when he was socialising at work. She suddenly got an insight as to what her husband would be like on a night out with the boys, letting his guard down and being himself. Clive rarely allowed his council-house roots to shine through, he was polished and contrived in his behaviour – in everything he did – and Jude could only surmise that it was a testimony to their friends that he was allowing himself to be stripped back to the Clive she had married who was penniless, naive and untouched by the hold of the Cheshire Set.

"Sorry, darling. I was only reading what was on the slip." He winked at James the moment Jude looked away.

"Pink bowl, please," Sophie ordered. "This is brilliant, Hel. I haven't laughed so much in ages . . . and it's all at the expense of men!"

Karl stiffened and she felt his posture harden beside her.

"I didn't mean it like that," she whispered into his ear. His chair was pressed up against hers and Kath could see that he was enjoying the close proximity.

Karl smiled at her lovingly. Sophie had been a different woman, a far cry from the anti-male slanderous bitch she had been for most of her adult life. Certainly since he had known her anyway. She was healing inside, Karl could see that, and more importantly he loved what was unfolding before his eyes. He was still nervous of what she would come out with but it would take time for her to fully get over what she had experienced at such a young age. He was a patient man and time was something that Karl could give her. She had everything else.

"Girls, girls, you're gonna love this," Sophie continued. '*Why does it take one hundred million sperm to fertilise one egg?*'

Roni shrugged her shoulders to distract herself from the clear link between the joke and Darren's penis which had penetrated her repeatedly.

"I don't know, why does it take one hundred million sperm to fertilise one egg?" Helena and Jude sang, giggling away at their perfect timing.

"*Because not one will stop and ask for directions!*"

Kath clapped her hands loudly while Jude snorted at Clive who was mimicking the *loser* position as he placed his finger and thumb in an *L* shape on his forehead.

"Ha ha, very funny."

"Pass the white bowl please, mate."

The male jokes were in the white bowl and the female jokes in the pink bowl. Helena had decided this earlier. Actually, it was supposed to be a blue bowl for the men and a pink bowl for the women, only Kath didn't posses a blue bowl so the white had to do instead. That way, Helena suggested, each gender got to ridicule the opposite sex by ensuring they only pulled out *their own* set of jokes which for some reason lacked tact, political correctness and any sense of decency – that was not a part of the brief – but they had split their sides as all hell broke loose and Kath felt sorry for her neighbours listening to nine pairs of lungs at their loudest.

"Last one now," Kath instructed. "We need to clear the table for dessert."

Pete rummaged in the ceramic bowl. He raised his eyebrows to increase the tension.

"Gentlemen. '*How many men does it take to open a bottle of beer*?'"

"Oh! Sorry. That's in the wrong bowl, Pete. Take another," Helena apologised. "I must have got muddled up somewhere along the line."

Peter grinned at Helena. She didn't know what was about to come.

"No, it's not, Helena, listen. '*How many men does it take to open a bottle of beer?*'" he repeated, grinning slyly, bursting to declare the punchline. "None! It should have been opened by the time she brings it to the couch!"

"Bloody brilliant!"

Karl and Pete high-fived each other with a manly pound.

"Are you listening, wench? That man's got the right idea!" Karl teased Sophie who simply laughed.

For once, she didn't feel the need to come back with feminist revenge. Earlier, she had meant for her comment to be nothing more than a tongue-in-cheek quip. There was no premeditation nor malice behind the words and that was rare indeed. Sophie felt lighter than she had done for as long as she could remember. Certainly, in her adult life anyway.

"Erm, hang on a minute? How come I get a dig for my earlier *innocent* comment and you get to call me a wench? Where's the justice in that?"

Karl wrapped his arm around her toned bronzed shoulder, pulling her closer to him until the physical distance between them had disappeared and their bodies became one. Sophie let her head flop against his chest. She felt safe there and Karl felt her relax against his body as it took the full weight of her.

"Because, Ms Kane, I have worked for you since the salon opened so I guess that means I've got, erm, seven years before we're even!"

Sophie punched his stomach lightly without moving from the warmth of his body. She saw Jude smile at her from across the table. It was a warm, endorsing smile which needed no words. Even Roni seemed taken aback at the ease with which they were folded into each other.

"You two look really nice together," Roni spoke out frankly. "A handsome couple indeed. You could be the new Posh and Becks."

Sophie bolted upright regaining her composure.

"What? We work together. He's my right-hand man, Roni, not my boyfriend . . . besides, Karl's got black hair, Becks has got blonde hair."

"For the moment," Jude quipped. "He changes it as often as he changes his Calvin Kleins!"

Sophie thought about Rafi for a moment. She had called it a day with him which didn't go down particularly well. She was still angry at Roni for firing him. She'd no need to take her anger out on him, it was a pointless and futile attack which was meant for her.

"That Rafi's a great cocktail-maker, Pete . . . what a pity you had to let him go," she said slyly.

Peter looked at his wife and then back to Roni who avoided his gaze.

"Did we let him go, Ron? I hope not because he's the best we've had to date."

Roni shook her head. She knew her disingenuous actions had been found out.

"No, no. He's been away but he'll be back with us soon," she lied.

Sophie smiled at her. She would be forced to give him his job back now, what with Peter's expectations of seeing him behind his bar at some point. She'd achieved what she set out to do – getting him his job back – and she felt better for it. She didn't want to leave him dateless and jobless.

"Oh, Roni," Kath jumped in, trying to rescue the situation, "I can't believe you brought a bottle of Dom Perignon, that's way too expensive. You'll have to take it home."

Roni looked at Pete who shrugged, pointing at Helena.

"I should have said it wasn't from me, Jim, sorry. I didn't think. I was holding it for Helena while she went to the loo . . . distracted by the football I was! It's from you, Helena, isn't it, pet?"

Helena blushed with embarrasment as all eyes feasted upon her warm glow.

"It's just a little offering for all you've been going through." Helena looked down shyly, ignoring the raised eyebrows across the table. Helena shoved the one-hundred-pound bill to the back of her mind. It was a 2002 vintage. That stuff didn't come cheap. But they'd been through so much with Jason and the burial that Helena wanted to treat them. Kath and Jim's budget would never cover that stuff. Then again, neither did hers.

A dog barked incessantly as Sophie stood at the back door to Kath's immaculate yard chatting to Clive. She wafted away the smoke from his cigar as it danced towards her like a Chinese dragon, sinuous and threatening.

"Sorry, Sophie." Clive switched the fat cigar into his other hand, holding it as far from her as possible. Clive hoped Jude wouldn't smell it on him although that was highly unlikely. The next street could probably smell it, it was that potent.

"So what do you think then, Clive?"

Clive used his free hand to push his hair back from his face. Sophie noticed he did this continually and she was desperate to pull out her scissors and fix his fringe once and for all. The style was all wrong for his shape face anyway but it didn't detract from his handsomeness.

Clive cogitated about what Sophie had just said to him – in the strictest of confidence. It made sense, he had to give her that much, but he wasn't used to conceding. He carried his father's stubbornness.

"Okay, Sophie. I'll give it some thought. That much I can promise you. But I can't promise anything else."

Sophie stuck out her hand, waiting for Clive to extend his.

"I'm sure you'll make the right decision," she told him, squeezing his hand a fraction too tightly.

Clive released himself from her firm grip. He liked Sophie, she was a resilient woman, a contender, just like himself but it wouldn't suit him to be married to a girl like her. He preferred Jude with her laid-back nature and her uncomplicated way of living. He loved that she was the core of their family, the keeper of his home and the trophy on his arm. But Clive knew that Jude had changed over the past months and, much as he was hoping she would change back, something told him that her change was as permanent at the lines on his forehead. He had a lot to think about.

"Sophie, I was considering buying Jude a piece of Cartier jewellery for her 40th birthday. What do you think?"

Sophie stared at the man she had been talking to so candidly for the last ten minutes. His arrogance infuriated her.

"Clive, have you not listened to a word I've said!"

32

Jude stood impatiently as she waited for the colour to take on the smooth plastered walls. It would take a base coat plus two further coats to finish the walls to the high standard they needed to be and, although the plastering had dried out, there was likely to be a little remaining dampness which would suck some colour out of the walls – which is why she had opted for a deeper purple than had been her original choice.

The REM reception had recently been delivered. It sat on the left downstairs, still wrapped in its thick plastic, and Jude couldn't wait for the painting to be complete – which according to her schedule should be ticked off before the end of the week – so that the floor could be tiled in high-shine black granite tiles and so that Jude could dress the place with contemporary accessories and cutting-edge gadgets.

Jude touched the paint lightly, it had dried in – all two coats of it – and in her mind's eye she saw the backdrop of the deep purple walls finished with the sprayed silver skirting boards reflecting off the high-gloss floor tiles. The curved reception desk made with its laminated Alu Brosse front panel would be lit by an LED illuminated strip and textured glass shelves would create the workspace available for their computerised booking system – a touch-screen facility which would be available for self-arranged bookings.

Jude pulled the phone from her pocket in haste.

"Hi, Sophie, it's only me. I was wondering if you had given any more thought to the beauty salon yet? I've done as much as I can do down here . . . for now at least. Can I make a start on the upstairs yet?"

Sophie sat in her pillar-box-red TT which was parked outside the cash-and-carry wholesalers.

"You know what, Jude, I'm not sure if that girl is definitely going ahead with upstairs but I am going to rent it out . . . I want the income from it, to be honest . . . so go ahead and do it exactly as you would for yourself – that way I could let it to anyone without too much alteration."

Jude punched the air. "Cheers, Soph. Will do."

While Sophie had given her a blank canvas for the colour scheme and design of the salon, Jude had felt restricted by the endless list of necessary features required for the salon kit-out which had reduced her own choices tenfold. She never realised there were so many considerations involved. But now she was in a position to make every solitary decision there was to make by herself. She would do it just like it were her own. Only Jude knew that her working time was almost at an end even though she was creating a new beginning for another lucky soul.

"Does this phone never stop!" Sophie groaned as she stood in the reception area waiting to hand over her trade card before she could access the warehouse and its competitive pricing. She didn't recognise the number.

"Sophie Kane speaking."

Jason had bobbed about nervously as he waited for the phone to ring. He had never felt so scared in his entire life.

"Hi, Sophie. It's erm, Jason Hamilton here."

Her eyes widened. "Hi, Jason. I didn't expect to hear from you. What can I do you for?"

"I, erm . . . didn't expect to be calling you, Sophie . . . so, erm, please don't tell my mum, erm, Kath . . . will you?"

Sophie grinned as the quake in his voice broke through. He was very nervous, she could tell. He'd also had a tough time of it lately and Sophie hoped he wasn't in any further trouble.

"I won't, Jason . . . unless it's something sinister that they need to know about of course. Or if you've won the lottery and you aren't planning on sharing it with them . . . you know . . . simple stuff like that!" she laughed.

Jason was pacing back and forth outside the Kane'n'Able salon looking oddly suspicious, as though he was about to tear through the doors and hold the place up.

"I wondered if you had, erm, any vacancies? Mum mentioned the new salon and I . . . I thought perhaps you might need a general dog's body . . ."

Sophie roared with laughter, ignoring the attention she received from the customers queueing to enter the store.

"I didn't see that coming," she told him, wiping a tear from her eye. "I expected you to ask me for bail money or something like that, Jason, but not a job!"

Jason had not expected Sophie to laugh. He was serious. He would have to do better than this.

"Look, Sophie. I have no, erm, experience what-soever . . . but I'm willing to work for free until you trust me enough . . . and I thought that, hhmm," he cleared his throat, "I might go on to college, you know, learn how to be a proper hairdresser. I've always been interested in it . . . actually."

Sophie's body pricked with goosebumps which made her shudder like someone had walked over her grave. Her spine shivered at the revelation she had heard loud and clear. The inflection in his voice was so familiar that she felt a blow to her stomach as the memories came flooding back.

"Jason, are you trying to tell me something?"

Jason felt the tension of the past years melt away and the emotion he had carried around with him for so long – confused isolation – set itself free through his tearducts.

"Yes," he sobbed.

Sophie raced back to the carpark, shoving her trade card into her pocket.

"Where are you, sweetheart?"

Jason's shoulders convulsed. "Ou–tside yo–ur sa–alon."

"Stay there. I'm coming to get you."

As Sophie drove through the streets ignoring the speed limits, it all made sense. His confusion, his inability to decide what to do in life, how to be. No girlfriends or any other serious relationships. No real male friends. No real friends, in fact. Her self-absorbed thoughts had got in the way of her seeing straight. Jason was gay. He was coming out of the closet after years of repression, lashing out in anger that no-one understood him because he didn't understand himself. Of all the conversations the women had shared over Jason, their bewilderment about his difficult behaviour, his strange volatility, it had never occured to them that he might be in need of help of a different kind other than a good measure of discipline.

But Jason had a confession to make and it had taken witnessing the burial of his grandmother to make him see that the time he had with his own father mattered so much to him. The relationship they had was far too important to be ruined, thrown away through his rebellious actions as he tried to cover up his true identity. Jason had guarded the secret out of love for his father and out of a fear that if his father couldn't cope with his son turning out to be gay, then he – single-handedly – would be responsible for the break-up of yet another generation. And that wouldn't do.

Helena sat at her desk scribbling on a piece of paper. She had doodled away the past half hour as the sunny weather kept the customers at bay, basking in the glorious rays. The banking hall was rarely this quiet but it gave her a chance to clear out her desk and make a start on the plans for her new role. She couldn't wait. It was the opportunity of a lifetime and it had taken her until her early thirties to achieve something she should have done in her twenties. Nathan Bream had held her back, only she hadn't realised it at the time.

Helena saw a client she knew – Mr Peters – approach Maggie directly. You couldn't fail to notice that she was staff with her oversized name tag hanging loosely from the black lanyard, her name in bold with the words *Branch Manager* typed out below in matching font. Helena watched, trying to gauge the conversation. It was clear to see that Mr Peters was not a happy man, but Maggie as ever was calm and influencing. They headed towards her and Helena swallowed hard at his agitated expression.

"Helena, Mr Peters has a problem about a withdrawal. Can I leave you to sort it out, please?"

Helena smiled sweetly. "Of course. Take a seat, Mr Peters."

He sat down, armed and rigid.

"How is your grandson? I remember you taking out money for his birthday present . . . house deposit, wasn't it?"

Maggie smiled at Helena's memory, watching as her natural interpersonal skills disarmed the angry gentleman. She walked away, content that all would end well. She had yet to receive a single complaint about Helena.

"That's right. You've got a good memory." He sat back in his chair, upright and a little stiff and Helena could see that she had her work cut out.

"How is the new house coming along then?"

"He's not actually in it yet but he should be by the end of the month." His shoulders relaxed a little. "Thanks for asking though. I'm impressed with your memory."

"I never forget a friendly face."

Helena leaned forward on the desk, hoping he would copy her body language and relax before she embarked on unravelling his complaint.

"Now, what seems to be the problem, Mr Peters?"

Maggie watched Helena from behind the counter – its bulletproof glass muffled her words but she could see already how the gentleman had collected himself in no time at all. Helena Wright would be sorely missed from that desk. The place wouldn't be the same without her but Maggie knew that if she didn't promote Helena, she would lose her. She was too good for that place anyway. Always had been.

Sophie, Jason and Karl sat in the white Shaker-style kitchen at the back of the Kane'n'Able salon. Jason's eyes were red raw and puffy and Sophie held onto his hand, stroking it tenderly as though he were her own son. She felt his pain even though her own pain was caused by someone like him. But Sophie knew that if he came out, admitted to all who he was and what he was, then the propensity of him breaking someone else's heart would be abated. Between them, they could stop someone else going through what she had gone through and Jason too could live his life freely.

She would never know how Ricky ended up, but somehow she imagined that he wouldn't have suffered like she had. He was a taker, self-centered to the end, but at the time her youthful immaturity had blinded her.

"I'm scared that they'll never take me back in if they know I'm . . ." He couldn't bring himself to say the words.

"Gay?" Karl risked saying it but what was the point in denial? He had come this far.

Jason nodded.

"Look, Jason, I've rung your mum and dad and they're

on their way over here now," Sophie told him earnestly. "I had to do it. I can't even say I'm sorry. I absolutely believe it was the right thing to do . . . for *you*."

Jason dived from his seat, sending the chair crashing to the foor.

"What . . . why . . . I'm not ready."

She stood, facing him head on, reaching up and grabbing his shoulders roughly. "You've had long enough to be ready, Jason . . . let it out . . . now's the time. You've nothing to be scared of. Okay?"

Jason chewed on his nails. He looked like an overgrown child who had lost his way.

"Mum told me about you and Ricky . . . I'm so sorry about that . . . that's erm, that's the other reason why I need to do something about . . . well . . . *it*."

Karl eyed Sophie to see how she reacted. She barely moved a muscle and his heart somersaulted with pride in her stoic backbone.

"It was hard, Jason, I'm not going to lie. In a way what happened shaped me for the worse even though I was in denial over it . . . but if he'd had the strength, like you, to come clean and be to honest with himself . . . he could have saved me a lot of bother . . . and an awful lot of heartache."

Karl saw the pain and depression sweep over her face.

"But the sex was good, wasn't it!" he teased. He didn't want Sophie to change entirely, become a frumpy, celebate mother figure. There was so much about her that was endearing and far more of her traits he wanted to keep than to change. "You have to take something positive out of it, don't you, Soph?"

371

"It was good actually." She grinned. "But you know what, guys? I'm tired of it now. Been there. Done that. Got the T-shirt."

"You're lucky that's all you got."

Sophie slapped Karl across the arm deservedly and Jason managed a smile. He had noticed the relaxed exchange between the two of them, the easy banter, but moreso the way they looked at each other, his face filled with admiration and her gaze filled with adoration for her staunch companion.

Helena waved to Mr Peters who shuffled away, lifting his hat to bid her farewell. That was one of the things she loved so much about dealing with the elderley – their respect towards people – the traditions they kept hold of such as walking on the outside of the pavement to protect their women, ready to draw their sword at the first sight of danger. Young folk had a lot to learn from them.

Helena's telephone shrilled loudly. When the hall was busy with children screaming and people chatting it seemed quiet, but now with the scarity of foot traffic the phone seemed to shrill loud enough to wake the dead.

Helena shuddered as she thought of Elizabath rotting away. Where was her head when she had considered that a vintage bottle of Dom Perignon might ease the pain?

"Helena Wright."

"Maggie here. Two things, Helena. I have your contract here for signing so you may like to check it over. Secondly, I need to take a look at the complaint form, please. It needs investigating. I'm not having an error like that again and I need to get to the bottom of it, so be as thorough as possible with your details please and I'll pass it to the complaints team to look into. Whoever did that needs to be reprimanded."

Helena stared into the blank room. When one door closes, another opens, she told herself. Only Helena wondered this time which door was going to close first.

33

Hattie stood in the centre of Jude's kitchen, shaking her head.

"Darling, are you ill?"

Jude chortled at the sight of her mother stuck for words for once.

"No, Mum. Why?"

Hattie pointed to the breakfast dishes in the sink, the endless pairs of shoes by the back door and the stacks of paperwork sprawled across the black-granite centre island.

"It's just that I've never seen a thing out of place, darling, but lately everywhere seems to be so . . . untidy."

Jude flicked on the kettle and made a start on the dishes. She grabbed the chrome swivel spout of the tap, pulling it down, aimimg it at the dirty crockery where it power-blasted the dried-in cereal which was proving itself difficult to remove.

"I did ask the kids to wash their own dishes this morning, Mum, but it seems they haven't."

Hattie blinked repeatedly. She must be hearing things.

"Jude, darling, why would you ask the children to wash their own dishes when you've got all the time in the world?"

Jude continued to scrub at the square white bowls with the soapy scourer.

"I've been working," she declared boldly. "Sophie asked me to be the interior designer for her second salon, Mum, and I said yes . . ." Then she added before her mother could pass further comment, "And I've loved every minute of it."

"But you don't work! You certainly never told me about it."

Jude grimaced. She had heard those words before. *But you don't work!*

"I'm finishing off this project and then I'll stop. I just need to get it out of my system . . . it's been too long, Mum. I've spent the guts of fifteen years wondering what I *could* have achieved from life and now, short-term as it is, I'm living out those dreams. Is that so wrong?"

Jude could not recall a time where she had spoken so candidly to her mother.

Hattie took two spotty Kath Kidston cups from the cupboard above her.

"Dreaming is for other people, darling. Wouldn't you prefer to keep yourself in the real world, focusing on the important things in life. Like your family?"

Jude rinsed the dishcloth, throwing it in the middle bowl of the Villeroy and Boch cream ceramic sink. She dried her hands on the tea towel before folding it perfectly, replacing it over the steel bar of the oven.

"I am in the real world, Mum. The *working* world, doing something for myself and remembering that I have all these capabilities other than using them for making beds, cooking dinner, chauffeuring the kids around, entertaining Clive's clients . . ."

Hattie shook her head at Jude in dismay.

"What does Clive have to say about it? I can't imagine he's particularly happy, darling."

Jude took over from her mother. She spooned the coffee into each cup, pouring boiling water over it. It sizzled as it came into contact with the dried granules.

"He doesn't know," she answered truthfully. Jude could never lie to her mother.

Hattie fetched the milk, pouring it into a matching spotty milk jug. She stood back admiring its pretty design before her daughter's words sank in.

"I don't know what is going on here, Jude, but I do know that lying to your husband simply won't do. Imagine what your father would think?"

Hattie's tone grabbed Jude's attention. Her mother had been cross with her only a handful of times in her entire life. But Jude stood tall as she felt a waft of cold air hit the back of her neck.

"Dad is right behind me on this one, I know it." Her chin wobbled as she felt the coldness travel down her spine. "He'd say '*You go for it, girl!*' . . . that's what he'd say."

She hurried from the kitchen before the tears flowed. Her father would have pioneered her like he always did and Jude needed someone on her side. She wasn't strong enough to take on Clive and her mother with their archaic values and 1950's approach to life. She had tried it and enjoyed it for the most part until she felt the void inside her swell until it reached bursting point and

Sophie Kane had stepped in to save her before its toxic spread. Her timing was perfect.

Jude felt isolated and hurt at their short-sightedness and her stomach sank as she counted down the weeks before this wonderful chapter in her life would be closed, for good. She felt a little spark of the light which had shone so brightly fade away.

Darren sat opposite Roni in the juice bar of The Hamptons where she had suggested they meet. She rarely went near the place and knew very few people, so bumping into anyone – bar Kath – was highly unlikely.

She sat back in her chair as far from him as possible, willing him to do the same. But Darren leaned forward across the table, his long arms covering the width of it, within touching distance of her hands. She could feel the warmth exude from them – his soft but skilful, boyish hands.

Roni went to speak but hesitated. Her face was flushed and her neck red and patchy and Darren wanted nothing more than to hold her, tell her that from this point on, everything would be alright. He knew it.

"It's okay," he spoke in a low voice. "I know why you've asked me here, Roni . . . and it's okay."

Roni bit her lip. It had started off as an innocent crush. The new arrival in her home had stirred something in her, awoken her sexual desires, but Roni in her wildest dreams never imagined that it would turn into anything else. She never imagined that anyone would want her, like her even. Few did.

"It has to stop. I can't do it anymore, can't risk it," she whispered, playing nervously with her symbollic wedding rings. "I can't cope with the guilt . . . it's killing me."

Darren noticed that Roni had no other jewellery on apart from her rings. She was usually weighed down by the stuff, it was a statement of her financial assests visible for all to see, but today she was free from her decorative trinkets and she looked all the more beautiful without their restraint.

"I never meant for it to happen, Roni." Darren took hold of her hand as it left the safety of her other hand reluctantly. "I could tell there was something unique, something different about you when I met you . . . but over the time we've spent together I've seen exactly what it is."

"What?"

Darren longed to reach out and kiss her but he couldn't. Never again.

"What is it about me, Darren? Because I don't see it. I see a horrible cow who has taken pleasure in being mean to people. A woman who has kept herself shut off from the rest of the world and a woman whose purse-strings could have done so much good for others . . . but haven't. That's exactly what I see."

Darren's gaze penetrated her tired bloodshot eyes.

"Ditto, Roni. I see exactly what you see, but I also see the woman who will be reborn out of acceptance of *who* you are and *what* you are. You've just mapped out your own life, Veronica. You have just shown yourself by your own admission the person you want to be."

Roni blinked and giant tears fell onto her soft pink cheeks. No-one had ever seen the promise in her like Darren. He had brought to light her failings without ever saying the words but he had left her to route her own course in life without any intervention. He was making her do the work.

"Why did you sleep with me if you saw the bad stuff?"

"Because I saw the good stuff too – trying desperately to escape – and believe it or not I didn't plan to sleep with you, Roni, but I did want to make you feel wanted, womanly and beautiful . . . just like you are. I'll never regret it."

Roni considered his words. There was something mystical about him, too insightful for a man of his young years. It was like Darren had been here before, in a past life. How else could he know so much when he had barely begun to live his own?

"It worked," Roni sniffed. "I do feel good actually. Better than I've felt in years. I feel oddly revived but strange at the same time . . . I look in the mirror and I see *me* but I don't *feel* like me."

"What do you feel like?"

"I feel *better* than me."

Darren took long gulps of carrot juice, setting down the empty glass.

"And it shows . . . you know, I think my work here is done. I can do nothing more for you than you can do yourself. Keep practising what I've taught you and keep reminding yourself what you have learned for yourself, Roni. *You* did all the work here, not me. Remember that."

Roni nodded. She was afraid to speak for fear she might cry.

"Life is wasted on the living, Roni. Don't let your epitaph be that."

Darren stood to go. His face was taut as he stared down at the complicated woman below him.

"You'll always be the lady of the house in my eyes, Veronica Smyth."

The corners of her mouth twitched as she tried to force a smile upon her face, fighting back the tears. No man had ever made her feel so alive, so accepted like he had. Because she had never allowed them to.

"And you'll always be the man who saved my life."

Kath raced through the salon followed by James. It had been a while since the telephone rang, spilling troubled news and her gut flipped as she prophesised her youngest son's latest scrape. Sophie had been through enough lately and Kath only hoped nothing had been done to her. She hoped his sticky fingers had not been near the tills.

Jason kept his head down upon hearing the scurry of feet, the familiar squeak of his mother's trainers across the tiled floor. Karl stood to go on hearing their arrival but not before he extended his hand which Jason grabbed, his face pleading with him to stay.

"Good luck, mate . . . not that you'll need it."

Karl stood back as Kath and James brushed past him, stopping dead at the sorry sight of their son whose eyes were glued to the floor. He had no place here now. Jason was with his family and they needed privacy.

"What's going on, Jason?" Kath was angry. She was in the middle of teaching her weekly Yoga class when Sophie had rang Marina – The Hamptons' manager – advising her of a family emergency and Kath had sped home in a taxi, picking up James before heading on to Sophie's salon. He was still on compassionate leave.

Sophie pulled out chairs for them to sit on. One either side of Jason.

"It was me who called you here, not Jason, and he's done nothing wrong. Not that I know of anyway." Sophie winked at Jason as he dared to make eye contact. "Right, I'll leave you to it. Give me a shout if you need anything."

James sat with his arms folded, his mouth tight and his forehead contorted with a deep frown.

"I buried my mother last week, son. This had better be good."

Suddenly, Jason felt closed in. Trapped and in need of air. He stood up, moving away from the leaking emotions of his parents into a part of the kitchen which was free from contamination.

"I'm not in any trouble, Mum and Dad. I promise you," he told them, staring at his starched white trainers. "I know I've taken money from you and I swear I'll pay you back every penny . . . *every* penny. I . . . just I couldn't do the jobs you wanted me to do, they weren't me so I, erm . . . I pretended to go to work every day but I had no money and I didn't think you'd miss a few bob here and there. It was more a cover-up than anything else."

Kath uncrossed her legs, sipping on the glass of water Sophie had left before she made a sharp exit.

"It was more than a few bob. Now will you please tell us what is going on, Jason?"

He swallowed hard, ignoring his racing heart that made his head dizzy and his legs light. The room closed in on him and he felt like he could pass out any minute but he had to do this. It was now or never.

"Mum, Dad . . . I'm . . . I'm . . . gay," he muttered, focusing once more on the floor, not daring to witness the expressions of the parents he was about to truly let down.

Kath looked from her son to James and from James back to her son before breaking into a soft smile.

"Is that it, love?"

She flung her arms into the air as the relief washed over her.

"Wh . . . what do you mean '*Is that it*'? I'm telling you I'm gay . . . coming out of the closet." Jason shook his head. Perhaps they didn't understand what he was telling them.

James leapt up and embraced his son with both arms. He held him tightly, squeezing him with all the love only a father could give his son.

"We know what 'gay' is, Jason. We're not that backwards." He stood back, taking in his son with his fierce bravery. He took after his mother, there was no disputing that. "But what you are in that respect is of no consequence to us, no consequence whatsoever, son. Criminal behaviour, stealing, all that stuff is unforgiveable . . . you turning out to be gay isn't." James paused. "I'm not going to lie to you . . . I'd prefer it if you weren't, I really would, and in many ways I think life would be much easier for you lot . . ."

Kath cast him a sharp dagger.

"Sorry, not '*you lot*' – I meant *you*. But you are what you are and there's not a damn thing that anyone can do about it." James shook his shoulders a little too ferociously as he completed his declaration. "But we love you. Do you hear me? *We love you* and that's all that matters. You're my son now and you will be my son until the day I die and I want nothing more than for you to be by my side where you belong."

Kath stood back, watching the two generations sink into one another without any awkwardness.

Her family was made from the best of blood, its thickness glued them together, bonding them unlike any other family unit because of what had happened to them. As a mother, Kath's compulsive approach was all down to the actions of a bitter, twisted woman, but as she watched the men effortlessly embrace she knew she had the last laugh.

"Can I get in there, please. He's *our* son, Jim. I should know, I was sick for the whole nine months I carried him."

James rolled his eyes, winking at Jason.

"Don't I know it. I'll never hear the last of it!"

Kath squeezed in between them, joining the family hug until Jason lifted his head from her shoulder where it had been resting. It had been a long time since he felt able to embrace his parents – or anyone else. Avoidance had become a part of his life for many years now and with it came the inability to be touched by either man or woman. He felt like a little boy again safe in the arms of his adoring mother.

"The burglary, Jason. Did you do it? It's confession time today."

Jason made the Sign of the Cross.

"I swear on my life that I didn't do either of them. I was in the wrong place at the wrong time . . . that's all I'm guilty of, honest, Mum."

Kath let out a huge breath of relief. The difficulties of late were turning themselves around.

"I've got some other news, Mum and Dad!"

"I think I need a drink, Jim. There's only so much news a person can take in one day!"

Jason threw back his head and laughed. His eyes

danced with relief and he felt light and free. Understood. Moreso, he understood himself. He didn't fancy women, never had, but when he looked at a man – even the boys from his school days – his thoughts carried impurities that Jason had considered evil – downright wrong. In a way it still was, he thought, but there was a name for it now and the taboo of homosexuality was dispersing fast. To some, it was almost a fashion statement. Not to him though.

"I've got a job."

James thumped him on the back.

"Congratulations, son. Where?"

Jason gathered up the glasses and began filling the sink.

"Here," he declared proudly. "Sophie is giving me a job. I'm on probation for three months and if it works she's going to put me through The Academy until I'm a fully trained stylist."

Kath burst into tears. Overnight her son had turned from a confused, rebellious boy whose life carried nothing but a contentious future, into a confident man whose prospective was looking up by the moment. She didn't care about his sexual preference, not one bit. She never would.

34

Helena stared at the contract Maggie had given her. The annual salary screamed out to her and Helena knew it could put her on the property ladder where she could start again with financial independence. But she couldn't sign it. She didn't deserve to because there were things she had to put right. Things she had done which were very wrong that needed correcting.

Helena dialled Sophie's number as tears of shame rolled down her face. How could she have done it to them? Innocent people who had worked hard and saved hard their whole lives?

"What's up, Hel?" Sophie answered in bright, cheery tones. She was happy that the Hamiltons' situation had ended well and the world was a brighter place because of it.

Helena sobbed uncontrollably. She couldn't talk.

"Helena – what's wrong – talk to me. What on earth has happened that's got you like this?"

Helena pulled a tissue from her navy work trousers which fitted her better as the weeks had gone by. The waistline no longer hung down past her emaciated hips.

"I'm a crim – inal!" she cried. "I ne–ed help ple–ease!"

"What have you done, Helena?" Sophie's voice was calm but authoritative.

Helena held the phone to her ear as she sat in the corner of the rundown coffee shop, facing the wall. Her untouched coffee was stone cold. She didn't know where else to turn, to go to, so she chose a rundown cafe where she wouldn't risk seeing anybody she knew. And then she broke down.

"I – I've been lau–dering mo–ney from the old pe–ople in the ba–aank," she blurted in as hushed a tone as was possible given her lack of vocal control. She was lucky, the place was empty, completely empty hence her reason for choosing it. "I ne–ed to pay it ba–ack . . . I thi–nk I've been fo–und out."

"It was you, wasn't it? Something *illicit?*"

Helena nodded and Sophie took the silence to be an admission.

"I had my suspicions about you, Hel – you threw so much money around that I often wondered where you were getting it from . . . now I know . . . you stupid cow."

Helena blew her nose on the already soaked-through tissue, ignoring the concerned look from the waitress who smiled at her kindly from the far side of the grotty joint.

"I ne–ever meant to do it . . . it was Na–than who sta–arted it. He ma–ade me do i–it," she hiccuped, grabbing a clean napkin from the red plastic container. "It's all his fault."

Sophie grabbed her keys, shoving them into the pocket

of her biker jacket. Her sandwich would have to wait until later for the second time today.

"Look, that doesn't matter now – just meet me at the flat right away, do you understand?"

"Okay."

"Stupid, stupid, girl," Sophie muttered to herself as the enormity of Helena's confession sank in.

She ran to the front of the shop towards Karl where she whispered in his ear. His jaw dropped as he took in the news, the kind which generally appears in the newspapers or on the television. It wasn't a piece of news that belonged to him and his set of friends. Least, it shouldn't have.

Sophie opened the till and lifted the coin tray, pulled out a cheque book from underneath it and began scribbling on the *Payee* line before adding her messy signature to the bottom of it.

"I'm going to sign the cheque, Karl, but I'll leave the amount blank. Head over to the bank as quick as you can and I'll text you with the details of how much I need you to withdraw." Sophie spoke in hushed tones, tearing the cheque from its book. She handed it to Karl.

"Consider it done."

"If it's more than five grand you'll need your ID."

Karl pulled his wallet from the back pocket of his low-hung combats, pulling his V-necked black T-shirt back down to cover the top of his waisband. He flashed his driving licence at Sophie who grabbed his arm, kissing him on the cheek.

Karl held Sophie close to him for a minute, inhaling a concoction of smells from hair conditioner to body cream and once again something in him stirred for this blonde bombshell whose life, it seemed, was being taken over by the mistakes of others. She had barely laid her own ghosts to rest.

"I can't believe the day, can you?" he whispered.

Sophie shook her head, smiling weakly, but behind her Caribbean-sea eyes Karl could see she was vexed about the state of her best friend.

"I picked a bad bunch, didn't I?"

"You wouldn't have them any other way, surely?" Karl coaxed her as he folded the cheque neatly, shoving it deep into his pocket.

Sophie said nothing as she headed towards the salon door.

"Sophie."

She turned impatiently. She had things to do, lives to fix.

"I wouldn't have *you* any other way. You know that, don't you?"

Sophie's knees trembled at the dulcet tone which carried words of such sincerity from the lips of the man who had been her trusted friend, her ally. She stared deep into his smoky-grey eyes, marvelling at the stark blackness of his eyelashes and thick but neatly groomed eyebrows.

"You too," Sophie exhaled as the words left her. She swallowed hard as she looked at Karl in a way she had never thought to look at him before. Handsome he was, truly, but at that moment as she took him in from head to toe Sophie felt winded and unable to breathe. She needed fresh air.

"Hi, Mum."

Anna jumped up from the kitchen table, leaving her homework to embrace her mother.

"Hello, darling."

Jude clung to Anna stroking her hair, just as her mother had done to her when she was a child – still did. Jude kissed her forehead without the need to stoop down.

"Where's Tom?"

Anna released her grip and returned to her homework. She would fly through it which would give her more time to spend with Polly, her beloved pony, with whom to date she had shared all her worldly secrets.

"He and Dad went out to see a man about a dog."

Jude chuckled to hear her daughter using such euphemisms. It was easy to forget that Anna was coming up sixteen and was almost an adult.

"Anna Westbury, you do make me laugh. Where is he really?"

Anna grinned knowingly. "He and Dad have gone out to do stuff for your birthday but that's as much as I am prepared to divulge without killing you. Okay?"

"Okay," Jude nodded with a straight face before breaking into a watery smile. Admist the chaos of trying to balance her work, temporary as it was, with the endless domestic chores Jude had almost forgotten about her birthday. "I'm sure forty sounds so old to you, doesn't it, darling?"

Anna spun around to face Jude.

"Not really, Mum. Lots of my friends' mums are already forty – Lottie's mum is *fifty* . . . and that *is* old. It's good that you had us young actually because you look so slim and pretty and I know you'll never let me down at school." She chewed the end of her pen thoughtfully. "There aren't too many fat mums at the school actually . . . but you're definitely the fittest and all the boys in my class fancy you."

Jude pulled open the fridge, removing a fillet of pork from the chiller cabinet.

"Do they now?"

She was always amazed at how childlike Anna was in general conversation given her academic achievements. Anna was top of the top in all subjects. She excelled at everything with minimum effort yet her unaffected charm kept her from arrogant gloating. Anna just got on with life, did what she had to do and never complained. At least she hadn't until Jude had presented her with a weekly list of jobs. Tom took his list willingly, anything to help his mother, but Anna needed a little more coercion as she set about dusting her bedroom, huffing loudly. She was a princess and princesses didn't clean. She was certainly daddy's little princess.

"Did Grandma call?"

"No."

Jude ripped at the plastic removing the pork loin which she placed on a small granite chopping board which blended with the matching worktops. She grabbed a Sabatier knife, slicing the meat expertly into two-inch-thick medallions.

She was still upset about the exchange she had with her mother. Times had changed and Jude felt that her mother wanted time to stand still and for her to behave as a carbon copy of her. But she was more like her father, receptive to change, eager to learn and willing to grab an opportunity before it raced past her. And she had. But it would soon be let go and Jude knew that a piece of her would go with it.

"What do you want for your birthday, Mum?" Anna called out with her back to Jude, scribbling away furiously. "I've been saving for ages to get you something really great."

Jude didn't answer. What she wanted was a career. She'd had it for a couple of years before she fell pregnant and she had showed promise – even she could see that.

"I've got everything I need, darling," she lied.

Anna did not reply. She knew her mother well enough to hear the artificial tone. Anyone else would have missed it. She also knew what her mother wanted for her birthday, she just wanted to hear it for herself.

Helena sat on the steel chairs of the balcony sipping a neat whisky. The ice rattled each time the tumbler was picked up and she inhaled its alcoholic potency in a continued bid to calm herself, although she knew it would take more than a fiery shot of liquid to nullify her actions.

Sophie sat opposite her. She was angry at her friend. More than angry, and she wasn't giving her an easy time.

"Tell me again, Helena. I want every detail before I give you a fucking penny."

She leaned back with her arms folded and legs crossed. The sun shone directly at her and she squinted, shifting her chair to an angle where she would not be blinded nor induce premature ageing.

"It started with Nathan. He kept putting pressure on me, telling me I could buy him time . . . but we could barely afford to eat let alone buy him anything –"

"The lazy bastard," Sophie butted in.

Helena knocked back the remaining contents of the glass.

"I kept thinking of a way – any way – to make money and then one day a customer, an old lady signed her withdrawal slip in the wrong place so I got her to sign another," she said, barely able to look Sophie in the eye. "And then it came to me . . . that if I could get some of the others to think they too had made a mistake, asking them to sign another withdrawal slip, it would allow me to withdraw cash from their accounts too . . . only with a clear audit trail. My tracks were covered. They had all signed the slips so it was their word against mine." Helena wiped a tear from her face as it rolled down. Her fingers trembled as another rolled down her other cheek. "It was only supposed to happen once or twice, I swear, and the plan was to pay it back before anyone noticed. . ." Helena took in Sophie's look of disgust. "I'm not a criminal, you know I'm not, Sophie . . . it was a desperate move to get us out of a ho–"

"The problem was that you couldn't stop it, could you? You loved having the cash to throw around – the new clothes, the champers, the social life . . . etcetera, etcetera."

Helena nodded. "But I only borrowed from the people who had shedloads of money, not the poorer ones . . . I didn't think they'd miss it."

Sophie jumped from her seat. She had heard enough.

"Oh, well, that makes it alright, doesn't it!" she snapped angrily. "Karl is at the bank now, Helena, cashing a cheque for you and do you know what you're going to do with it?"

"Yes," she whispered shamefully. "Pay it all back into their accounts."

"Indeed. You are going to find a way to pay every

penny back before you get caught and end up behind bars which is exactly where you belong."

Sophie stormed from the balcony into the living room. She screwed the cap back on the whisky and slammed the bottle into the cupboard against the other spirits. Grabbing her phone, she typed a message with nimble fingers and impressive speed: 'Get 5k. Don't know full damage but not good. X'

As Sophie picked up her bag she shouted to Helena.

"Don't come home until you can prove to me that you've paid back every last dime. And then we'll sort out how you are going to pay *me* back."

Sophie left, slamming the door behind her. This had to be the longest day of her life.

"I thought *my* life was fucked up!" she snarled, racing down the communal steps of the luxury apartment block. Everything she had achieved in life had been done with integrity and hard-earned cash. It wouldn't do to cheat or take something belonging to someone else and Sophie's candid approach had worked wonderfully. No-one else could ever take the credit for her achievements bar her. She was one of life's survivors, a woman of action and she could sleep at night while those around her lay awake, crippled by contrition.

As she fled to her car, Sophie cast her mind back to that night in Jude's garden where she had coaxed the women to join the Curry Club, to forge their friendships by a unique approach which hadn't been done before. As she opened the low-hung door of the TT and sank into its leather seat, slamming the door to a close, she whispered: "Be careful what you wish for next time."

Sophie hadn't bargained for the darker side of

people's lives. She thought it would be fun, interesting, with a measure of sex thrown in here and there. She hadn't bargained for confessions of a criminal nature, nor an adulterous nature – although that one had been put to bed – nor had she reckoned that she herself would cheat in order to help out a friend blinkered by coercion from a mother and a husband who should have been pursuing her dreams with her.

Sophie thought about the secret she too had lived with for so long. A secret which she had the willpower *not* to share with the club, but a secret which had come out regardless. Strangely enough, she woke each morning feeling light and happy. The noose which had hung loosely around her neck had freed itself, falling down, and unknowingly she had stepped out of it leaving it like debris to be swept up amongst the garbage.

Roni splashed about in the pool, alone but for her thoughts. Just a week ago she was making love in the lustful waters to a man who was not her husband. She, the woman who thought that just *thinking* about adultery made someone guilty, and yet she had gone against her own standards casting them aside for a young man who came into her life and left it in a flash. But Darren Ford had left her with a legacy. He had given her the oomph in life to get up and go, to start living before it was too late and while Roni was still struggling with the guilt of what she had done to Peter, she knew that she would be a better person because of it. She had been saved in many more ways than she thought possible and Peter had already noticed her new approach to life, her change of image, improved energy levels and calmer disposition. His wife had been reborn.

Roni ripped at the piece of paper she had carried in her purse since the last Curry Club event. She was relieved when she found out it was a couples' night – 'The Comedy Club' – which meant she wouldn't have to put in her own question that had a one-in-nine chance of being pulled out.

'Can having an affair save your marriage?'

35

Helena pulled out the list of account numbers which she kept in the zip compartment of her handbag. Next to them were the amounts and dates of all the withdrawals she had made – taken illegally. In her other hand she clutched five thousand pounds worth of fifty-pound notes which Karl had slipped her as he waited on Sloane Street for her to return to work. The money would soon be gone, rehoused where it belonged and her mind would be an easier one to live with from that point onwards.

But there was something else she had to do first.

Helena knocked on the door, willing her knees to stop trembling.

"Come in."

She pushed open the door to be greeted with a welcoming smile.

Inside, Maggie bounced around on the unstable chair as she moved papers from one place to the next in an attempt to clear the over-kill of paperwork which seemed to be going nowhere.

"Just the girl, Helena. Sit down, won't you?"

Maggie pulled out a blue folder from the bottom drawer of her desk. The drawer creaked as she tried to slam it shut.

"Bloody drawer's stuck. Does nothing work in this place?"

Helena managed a smile. She had to be brave, pretend that nothing was wrong as she broke the news to the woman who had been one of her closest allies throughout her journey with Northern Direct. This place had been the making and then the failing of her.

"I found out what happened to Mr Peters' account," Helena looked Maggie in the eye. It was killing her but she had to be conniving if she didn't want to end up behind bars. "My float was carrying an extra £500 that I'd clean forgotten about. I reported it to the Audit Team the other week but the discrepancy wasn't picked up . . . but it's all sorted now and the money has been recredited to Mr Peter's account along with a manual application of interest and a twenty-five pounds ex-gratia payment by way of an apology." Helena handed Maggie the complaints form. "It's all documented in here."

Maggie smiled as she took the paperwork from her to counter-sign.

She scribbled her name next to Helena's without bothering to read it, handing it straight back to her. She trusted her.

"Good girl. I'll leave you to post that to Head Office if you would?" Maggie suggested, pulling a batch of CV's from the blue folder and plonking them on the desk in front of Helena.

"These are the new graduates, Helena. I need you to

go through their CV's and interview test results before putting together a formalised plan of ac –"

Helena interrupted. "Wait . . . there's something I need to tell you first."

Clive wrote the last of the invitations to Jude's party, blowing the gold ink dry before slipping the thick cream card into its envelope.

His secretary had offered to both write and deliver them for him but Jude was worth far more than to cast off the importance of her birthday and Clive insisted on doing as much as he could by himself. The children were helping too, Anna by distracting her mother with trivial conversations about what she might like for her birthday and Tom by designing the invitations at school as part of his GSCE Graphic Design coursework. He had gone for comedic effect by designing a caricature of Jude with a ball and chain shackled to her feet. On the rear the design was of a different nature and Tom couldn't wait for his mother to see it. He had printed two A3 size posters, one of the front and one of the rear and was planning on decorating the party room with them. He was sure his mother would see the funny side – once she understood what was happening to her, of course.

The party was very much a family effort and Clive couldn't wait to see Jude's face as she entered the room to see her nearest and dearest there to celebrate the past forty years of her life. It was a last-minute affair though. He hadn't expected that Jude would like a party – she hated being the centre of attention – but what Clive had planned was about more than a party and everyone but Jude knew of it already. The invitations were late, he was hopeless, but the event had been put in people's diaries the minute the idea came to him, with a little help from Sophie, so they were more of a formality really, a keepsake.

He smiled fondly as he picked up a framed photograph from the dust-free window ledge. It was a photo of their wedding day eighteen years ago and his wife hadn't changed a bit – she was as stunning now as she was back then and Clive bit his lip as he recalled this young, determined woman intent on setting the world of interior design alight. It had been shortlived.

He pressed the intercom, scoring a line through *Invitations* on his indecipherable To-Do List.

"Shirley-Ann, would you mind contacting Veronica Smyth and reminding her to check the catering company are still on for tomorrow night, please?"

"It's already been confirmed, Clive. You asked me to do it yesterday."

Clive tapped his pen nervously. Beneath the table his foot tapped with agitation.

"I know . . . but would you do it anyway, please, and check that the hired glasses are *definitely* crystal. Jude doesn't like drinking from thick-lipped flutes."

"No problem," her tinny voice rang out. "Will that be all?"

"Erm . . . did you fetch her dress from the dry-cleaner's?"

"Yes, it's hanging on the inside of your door."

Clive looked up to see the green silk Karen Millen shift dress hiding behind a thin coating of plastic.

"Sorry, Shirley-Ann . . . I'm just a bit stressed. That's all from me . . . and thanks for everything . . . appreciate it."

Clive stared down at his watch.

"I'm off out to collect Jude's present."

Kath sat on the usual bottom stair as she opened the handwritten envelope. That stair could account for so much in her life. She had made love on it, taught the children to tie their shoelaces on it and cried on it when the going got tough. And tough it had been.

Kath unfolded the sheets of paper as she raced through line after line, keen to get to the end to evidence details of the sender because she didn't recognise the handwriting. But Kath need not have read past the first couple of lines to see who the letter was from. It was the content which threw her. She fled through the rest of it, wide-eyed and incredulous at the speed at which the news had come. And good news it was. She just hoped James would see the news as good too.

She blinked repeatedly as she folded the letter carefully back into its envelope, leaving it on the hall unit for James to pick up on his return from work. Their world had been a paradox lately. A wayward son who was on the verge of becoming a criminal and all because he couldn't find a way to deal with who he was. It had taken the burial of his estranged grandmother and the alienation of him from the rest of his family to give him the wake-up call that his life was for living and for accepting. Now they had something else to deal with. When did it ever end, Kath wondered as she sat alone in the sanctuary of her favourite place in the house. It didn't, she answered her own question . . . it was called *life*.

"Happy birthday to you, Happy birthday to you, Happy

birthday dear Mummy, Happy birthday to you!" Tom and Anna yelled raucously at Jude who was delighted at the fuss.

Clive walked into the kitchen holding an enormous topiary of calla lillies with tropical leaves folded artistically among them. It was clear to see the weight was killing him.

"Happy birthday . . . again . . . darling."

Jude opened her arms wide enough to secure the bouquet, breathing in its familiar scent. Her green eyes welled to a glaze and Clive cleared his throat with manly effect in an attempt to steer off the emotions he was battling with at the sight of his beautiful wife in her silky green dress.

"You look amazing, Jude," he whispered in quivering tones.

Jude stared down at the bouquet before setting it at the kitchen table which was decorated with a plastic purple tablecloth with the number *40* printed repeatedly in bold red. She shook her arms out with relief, freeing herself from the weight of what appeared to be half a florist's. However many flowers were there, they weighed a ton.

"My wedding flowers . . . you remembered."

Clive pushed his fringe back from his face. He was finding it harder than he thought and Anna laughed at her parents' mushy exchange.

"Pass me a bucket, Tom!" She mimicked being sick, ignoring Tom who lighltly tapped her upper arm.

"Behave. It's called being romantic."

"Of course I remembered." Clive ignored his tittering children who were very much acting kindergarten age as the excitement took over them. "I stare at that picture every day, Jude, pinching myself . . . I'm the luckiest man alive . . ." He turned abruptly, scanning the kitchen for his keys. Anything to distract him from his unusually volatile emotions. "We'd better go now."

Jude stood in the kitchen, the hub of her family home, surrounded by flowers, birthday banners and an array of pink and purple balloons. She giggled away counting the number of times she could see the number 40.

It was the thought which touched her the most. The effort they had gone to and she had been so busy finishing off the upper floor of Sophie's new venture that she hadn't had the time to notice anything suspicious going on.

"You still haven't said where we're going to."

Clive stood back from the kitchen door, bowing as she passed him. He pinched her bottom playfully.

"I saw that!" Anna squealed.

Tom called out as he rushed outside to open the passenger door of the recently valeted Jaguar. "Your chariot awaits, my lady."

Anna tied the blindfold across Jude's eyes. She doubled it and then trebled it, anything to make sure her mother had absolutely no idea where she was going and Jude suffered the entire journey in a cloud of blackness.

"We're here!" she cried with teenage excitement. "Don't move a muscle, Mum."

Jude felt a light breeze and heightened noise as the car door was opened and a hand grabbed hers, squeezing it tightly.

"Watch your head, darling," Clive told her, placing a protective hand over it.

As Jude bent forward to exit, he caught a glimpse of her pert breast in the Victoria's Secret lingerie he'd had shipped in from the USA and he felt himself twitching down below. Jude preferred the American stock to the British stock and he was glad he remembered that. His wife was a vision of extraordinary beauty, compelling talent and wearing underwear which he would have preferred to see on the floor.

"Keep hold of my hand, Jude. You're not allowed to touch anything other than me. Okay? I mean it . . . not a thing."

Jude felt a little nervous. She had assumed she would be taken to L'Escargo for dinner perhaps with pre-dinner cocktails at the trendy new cocktail bar, Shakers. Obviously not. She was clueless as to where she was headed and the drive had been longer than normal so she doubted she was anywhere local.

Clive dished out silent orders to Tom and Anna, pointing to the door which was opened and ready for her to cross by the time they reached it. He put his finger to his lips, non-verbally sending Anna to tell everyone to remain absolutely silent as they approached. Anna removed her shoes, taking her muted role seriously. She didn't want her mother to hear the route she was taking.

Tom stepped in close to his mother, taking her other hand. It was crucial she touched nothing and guessed nothing and kidnapping her temporarily was for her own good.

"One . . . two . . . three!"

"*Waahh!*" Jude shrieked as she was lifted into the air by the two men in her life. "What are you doing?"

Clive and Tom snorted as they hoisted her up the

stairs, setting her down when they were safely at the top and through the frameless glass door which Anna had pulled back and was leaning against to keep it open.

Anna nodded at the room, counting on her fingers, 'One, Two, Three,' she mouthed.

"Surprise!"

36

Jude's ears almost burst as the voices penetrated. A single word echoed harmoniously making her jaw drop as she took in the sound of familar voices. She heard her mother call out her name. She heard Kath's raucous laughter and recognised Sophie's loud shriek which amplified above the other sounds of people cheering and yelling congratulations.

Clive kept Jude facing forward as he ordered the room to absolute silence and Hattie wiped a tear from her face as she looked at Clive who lovingly held the hand of her daughter.

"You're not allowed to look just yet, hence the blindfold, sorry, darling. But let me tell you for now . . . there are lots of lovely people who have turned out to celebrate your birthday."

He grinned at Sophie who already had her tissues out. Sophie was such a wuss lately. Karl's arm was draped around her. He pulled her closer, kissing the top of her head.

"Ladies and Gentleman, thank you for coming out to

celebrate the birthday of a wonderful wife, mother, daughter and friend."

The room went into an uproar led by Kath who wolf-whistled at a blushing Jude. Her cheeks flamed from beneath the black bandana which Anna used as a headband.

"What do you get for the woman who has it all?" he teased, offering her a perfectly wrapped small square box. He lifted her hand, dropping the package into it and Jude gasped as she touched it.

"A divorce!" Kath heckled.

"Trust you!" Clive winked at her, grinning. "Go on, Jude, open it!"

"But I can't see what it is." Jude had no idea what was happening to her. It felt weird and she was a little unsure how to react.

Laughter filled the room as she began to pull at the thick paper, her world in darkness. Everyone there knew the exact reason for the blindfold and it was adding to the fun of the event. A thick smog of frenzy was simply waiting to burst out.

"Just open it as best you can, Jude, and then we might let you in on the secret . . . What'd you think, guys?"

"Ye-a-h!" they yelled back and Clive's eyes danced with excitement, his smile reaching from ear to ear as he nodded eagerly, willing Jude to lift the lid of the red-and-gold Cartier box, its luxury wrapping now discarded on the floor. Jude felt the smooth box – it was like satin beneath her touch. She felt a ridge brush against the palm of her hand, her fingers advancing past it until she was sure she could feel what could only be a lid. She pulled at it until it opened. She couldn't hear it but she could sense its upward motion and the breakout of clapping corroborated her accurate train of thought. The audience gasped. The lid of the box was piped elegantly with a gold endorsement and sitting in it was a hand-made platinum J-shaped keyring encrusted with diamonds. A genuine, bespoke gift from Cartier, Paris.

Clive knew it was time to let his wife in on the secret. She would only look down at the gift for the next few seconds. Her curiosity would get the better of her in the short term, he was sure of it.

Standing behind her, Clive gently untied the double knot Anna had secured so well and the black cloth slid down past Jude's face. He grabbed the material, whipping it away, passing it to Anna who was standing beside him.

Jude looked down immediately, caught in the suspense of the gift above everything else, which was unlike Jude, but she knew she must be holding onto something very special for Clive to behave in the covert manner he was definitely behaving that evening.

"Oh, oh, my goodness, Clive, it's incredible!" She lifted the keyring delicately from the box, amazed at its weight. The diamonds sparkled, joyous at their escape and flickers of small, brilliant light dotted across Jude's gasping face. "Thank you so, so much."

"Don't look up yet!" said Clive, standing close in front of her. He held her head gently, keeping it tilted forward and downward. He needed to make sure her vision was blinkered as he talked to her. Any moment now she would understand why.

He was nervous now. Extremely nervous.

"That's only part of your present, my darling, darling

wife. You can look up now, Jude . . . turn around," he whispered in her ear, ignoring his welling eyes and allowing the light grip of his hands to slip from holding her head.

Jude turned around slowly, the bright lights sending her eyes into kaleidoscopic overdrive.

"*Dah nah!*" Anna shrieked, pointing to the wall behind her.

It was only then Jude recognised where she was.

"What?" She stared at the unrecognisable steel words above the recognisable reception desk and then back at Clive, shaking her head in utter bewilderment. "I don't understand what's going on . . ."

Clive grabbed a set of keys from his pocket, lifting her hand and placing them in the centre of it.

"The rent and rates are paid for the first year, Jude. The rest is up to you, darling. Don't forget to attach your keys to the keyring – I thought it might stop you losing them, what with an expensive keyring weighing them down." Clive closed her hand over the keys, squeezing it a little too hard and Jude winced, bringing her out of the state of disbelief she was in.

"I still don't get it, Clive. I – I –"

Clive kissed his wife on the lips. He didn't care who was watching. "Happy birthday, Jude." He stroked her flawless face. "Welcome to Westbury Interior Design, everyone!"

"Thank you," she replied softly as the penny dropped. She had never been so slow at understanding anything in her life but this, this had all come as such a shock that she could barely believe it. Still. "Thank you."

She watched the actions of those around her –

anything to understand what the hell had just happened and Jude shook her head as the children scrunched up the sheets of paper which had been covering the sign to the place she had been working on for some weeks now. The sign must have only gone up that day because she didn't leave Alderley Avenue until early evening the day before.

She had been designing the upstairs of Sophie's salon for someone else – in her own mind at least. Sophie had told her, '*Go ahead and do it exactly as you would for yourself, Jude*' but at the time Jude had thought nothing of it. Nothing at all, until now.

Hattie could wait no longer. She flung herself at her only child, clutching at her with maternal pride. She had watched her daughter's reaction as the papered veil was unfolded and she saw the disbelief on her face. Hattie knew her daughter needed her right now.

"Westbury Interior Design, Jude! Who'd have thought it?"

Jude didn't answer Hattie. She could do nothing but continue to stare at the illuminated chrome lettering which was displayed behind the curved reception area with its steel counter and glass front, but not at all sterile against the bright fuschia walls and floor-to-ceiling glass windows which sucked in the light just the way she imagined it would.

Jude took her mother's hands. Her faced contorted with ongoing confusion.

"But . . . the other day, Mum . . . you made it clear what you thought about me working . . . you said –"

Hattie chuckled affably. "I know what I said, sweetheart. It was mostly a cover-up." Her chest puffed out as she demonstrated her important role in the family operation. "I'm not going to lie to you, Jude, my traditional values haven't changed . . . some of what I said was true, but I saw something different about you . . . a newness that I hadn't seen since you were a kid. Something that neither I nor Clive want to be taken away from you. Ever."

A single tear rolled down Jude's face as she held her mother tightly. "Thank you, Mum. Thank you, thank you, thank you."

Hattie beckoned to her friends to come over.

"Thank young Sophie here, not me."

Jude embraced each of her friends one by one as they lined up to offer multiple congratulations. She stopped at Sophie Kane who was chatting away to Karl who now appeared to be a permanent fixture at her side.

"You," Jude drew in a deep breath, "you had it planned all along, didn't you?"

Sophie gave an appreciative nod, sinking deeper into Karl's loving hold. "Actually, not all along. I did originally plan to lease it to the beautician girl but she messed me around so much that I knew I wouldn't be able to stand the sight of her let alone share a building with her."

Helena prodded Sophie. "As patient as ever, I see."

"I have my moments . . . Helena."

Helena had been duly silenced and Jude, Kath and Roni swapped inquisitive glances.

"Go on," Jude urged, smoothing down her silk dress over her perfectly toned stomach. Her blonde tousled hair fell loosely down her back.

"I put my idea to Clive . . . who was reluctant at first . . ."

"Aren't they all!" piped Roni and the women laughed. "You have to let them think they're the ones behind all the big decisions. I've been doing it to Peter for years now."

"Roni, get you!" Kath was amazed. Manipulating anything or anyone was not in her nature. That gene had escaped her.

"You'd know all about that, Helena . . . with all your psychology training, I suppose."

Helena glanced across at Sophie and then back to Roni.

"I suppose I should do, Roni, but I've decided that the subject doesn't hold much interest for me anymore." Helena curled her straight lanky hair around her slender fingers. She was nervous. She hadn't even told Sophie what her future plans were. "I handed in my notice at the bank today . . . I've had enough. I'm going travelling around the world for a year," she laughed meekly, "to find myself, as they say. I spent too long with Nathan and too long without anything else and all I know right now is what I *don't* want out of life . . . but I haven't a clue what I *do* want."

A black-and-white-clad waitress headed towards the ladies, carrying a tray of champagne and Roni recognised her immediately. It was the supervisor who worked for her from the catering company. Roni beamed at her, a full-on smile with affectionate eyes and pearly white teeth and she smiled back sheepishly. It was clear to see that she'd expected to be ignored. She was a servant to people like Veronica Smyth, that was all.

"Thanks so much," Roni whispered to her as she grabbed two glasses of champagne. "Good to see you, Nancy," she added, glancing down at her name badge.

The woman smiled at her, pleased, and Roni smiled back, then turned to Helena.

"Dearest Helena," she said with confidence as she handed one of the glasses to her, "here's to you finding whatever it is you're looking for!"

Sophie and Jude smirked at each other as they took in the stranger who stood in front of them, thinner by the day and a transformation of the edgy, volatile woman they had first met.

"Cheers, ladies!"

Clive watched as the five woman raised their glasses high, chinking them against each other.

"Oh my God! I forgot to tell you this." Kath downed her glass in one, grabbing another from a different, passing waitress who was manning the room attentively. "James' family sent a letter – a proper handwritten letter saying they want to re-unite – as a family." She almost choked on her words, she spoke them so quickly in between greedy gulps. "She's only been dead two minutes and they want him back."

Jude sensed her exhilaration and her nerves and she glanced over at James who was at ease, laughing without a care in the world. He looked years younger.

"What are you going to do about it, Kath?"

Kath watched the honest, hard-working man she had loved her entire married life. He was her first love and would be her last love. Her soul mate. "We're going to meet up next month for lunch, take it from there I guess. The boys are sceptical about getting hurt again but they want a family so they're willing to give it a shot. They've a lot of ground to cover with their cousins . . . they don't even know them."

Helena held her glass high. "All's well that ends well."

"Here, here!" Sophie saluted and once more the slender flutes were raised high. Some higher than others as had been the metaphor for the lives of the women – yet they touched each other, chinked together without spilling a drop just like the tightness of the bond the club had sewn around them.

Sophie turned to Karl, kissing him unexpectedly on the lips. She lingered for as long as was socially acceptable given the size of the crowd. He swept her blonde hair from her eyes, cupping her face as he kissed her back.

Sophie knew that she was over the pain which had held on to her for so long. It didn't hurt her anymore when she thought about it. The Curry Club had been one of the strangest thing she had experienced bar her short-lived marriage to Ricky. She had used the ladies for her own judiciousness to begin with – to benefit her as she watched and learned from them and by them – but in the end it was *her* they turned to for help when they needed it and it was *she* who had served what she had learned from them right back with a generous helping. She had resurrected Jude, rescued Jason and repaid Helena's debts, and her deep-rooted altruism had compensated her with a dependable, stoic man who helped her lay her ghosts to rest. She could love again and she could trust again.

Roni pulled Kath to one side. Her floaty skirt swished as she moved closer to Roni, puzzled at why her friend needed to speak with her in private.

"What's up, Ron?"

"I wanted to do something for you, Kath, you

413

know . . . with all that you've been through and stuff."
Roni's eyes were alive with kindness. It was bursting
through. "I found this the other day when the gym was
being cleared out. I thought I'd lost it but it had fallen
behind one of the machines."

Roni took hold of Kath's arm and secured the watch
around her wrist, pushing down on the security clasp.

Kath gasped as she held her wrist close to her face.
"Roni, this is a *Cartier* watch . . . I can't take it . . . it –"

Roni stood at full height, a look of assertion across
her face. "You can and you will, Kath. You do so much
for others and yet you have so little for yourself . . . when
was the last time you even had a holiday?"

Kath shrugged her shoulders. She could find no
words to say as she stared at the most expensive piece of
'*anything*' she'd ever possessed.

"There you go then . . . sell it for all I care, Kath. I
won't be offended, I swear. Do with it what you wish as
long as *you* and your lovely family get the benefit of it.
You *all* need a break."

Kath launched herself at Roni, gripping her tightly.
What had happened to her? She was a new woman, a
woman of substance and a woman of rare compassion.
Kath had always considered her a friend, but right now
she was considered more than a friend. Kath could see
that her kind mercies were meant to be an offering with
no hidden agenda and no rebound.

"Thank you, Roni, love. Thank you so much for this
beautiful gift . . . I'll take it because you want me to."

"I do."

As they joined the rest of the group, Tom called to his
mother.

414

"Mum, look at this." He pointed to the poster he had so carefully designed, identical to the party invitations upon which he had created a caricature of his mother shackled to a ball and chain in the kitchen. Jude laughed as his boyish humour.

"Now look at this!"

He flipped the poster around, smiling proudly at his father.

"Do you like it, Mum? The design of it?"

"Tom, it's exactly what I would have designed for myself," she told him proudly, taking in the luminous pink and grey swirls on the rear of the A3 sheet. There was a bright boldness to the pink shades which combined with grounded earthy grey tones worked perfectly. It was both traditional and contemporary at the same time and the damask-style printed weaving added character and chic.

"Good. I'm glad you like it because that's the design of your business cards!" he chuckled, throwing a small square parcel in her direction. "Only these ones have actually got the company name on. Sorry, Mum, *your* company name."

Jude caught the parcel, ripping at the paper, letting it drop the floor as the excitement took over her. Twice now she had unwrapped gifts and she couldn't think straight.

"*Westbury Interior Design – Director – Jude Westbury*," she read aloud, oblivious to the claps and cheers of her friends as they celebrated her new venture.

"I wanted to check you liked the prototype first, Mum. If you hadn't I'd have been stuck. I wouldn't have been able to give you a birthday present!" Tom laughed, advancing towards his mother.

"Thank you, darling – you're such a clever boy, Tom. You know, you're showing real skill already – I mean that – this design is amazing work for someone so young."

Tom, holding a glass of Coke in his hand, chinked it against his mother's thin-lipped champagne flute.

"I had a good teacher," he told her. "The best around."

Sophie snatched the batch of cards from Jude abruptly, thrusting her glass at Karl.

"What are you doing, Sophie?" Jude frowned as she watched her friend manhandling the small squares of card on which her life's ambition was imprinted.

Sophie turned to face her, the corners of her mouth curled up slightly before she broke into a massive smile. "You've got a business to run. I'm giving your cards out while there's so many people here." She wagged her finger at Jude. "Never *ever* waste a PR oportunity, Jude!"

Sophie disappeared among the reams of people and Karl stood alone, holding two glasses.

"Some people never change," he grinned.

"Well, I for one wouldn't want her any other way," said Roni.

"Veronica Smyth! What has happened to you?" Helena watched in amazement as Roni smoothed down her sleek bob. Her arms were free from precious metals and her hands carried only her wedding rings.

"I'm learning and I'm living, Helena, that's what I'm doing . . . because on some people, life is wasted, wasted on the living and I won't be one of those," she declared boldly. "And part of learning means you have to take people as what they are. You guys accepted me for what I am – was – and I now need to do the same for everyone who crosses my path."

"I guess we're singing from the same hymn sheet there, Roni. There's definitely something in the air." Helena bit her lip as she looked from friend to friend, saving her best smile for Sophie who had rejoined the group empty-handed but for a few remaining business cards. "I'll tell you what I'm going to miss though . . ."

"What?"

"The Curry Club. I'm really gonna miss it." Helena looked momentarily dejected.

"And it will miss you too, Helena, but you'll be back in a year and we won't be going anywhere, will we, ladies?" Kath declared proudly.

A fierce nodding of heads followed.

"No way!"

"I propose a toast!" Sophie swiped a full bottle of champagne from Nancy as she walked past. She refilled the glasses to the brim, slurping at hers as it spilled over the top, the bubbles tickling her nose. "Here's to the Curry Club!" she saluted.

All five glasses shot in the air, resting against each other, close and dependable, just like they were.

"To the Curry Club!" they cheered.

"Some like it hot, eh, Soph?" Karl teased, closing in on Sophie. She looked irresistible in the black dress she wore, designed simply at the front, but scooped dangerously low at the back, stopping at the dimples just above her bottom.

"Mhm. The question is, though, Karl, just how *hot* do you want it?" Sophie muttered in his ear.

"As *hot* as it comes, Ms Kane. As hot as it comes."

If you enjoyed
Some Like it Hot by Amanda Brobyn
why not try
Crystal Balls also published by Poolbeg?
Here's a sneak preview of Chapter One

Crystal Balls

Amanda
BROBYN

POOLBEG

Prologue

Slumped over the battered suitcase, she flings up her hood, protecting herself from the violent grey rain as it hurls down from the murky London skies. Each drop whispers words of failure, basking in its power to pelt her harder and harder. Gloating like a playground bully. Her torso is already numb but no amount of physical affliction can come between her and the gruesome mental punishment which holds her trapped in anguish and despair.

Unable to hold back, a tear escapes from her tightly closed eyes, followed by another and another, and she begins to sob uncontrollably, not caring about the weird looks from passers-by. None of whom are bothering to ask if she's okay. But hey, this is London.

"This isn't how my life is supposed to be!" she screeches hysterically, her voice breaking under the exertion. "I'm talented," she whispers, sobbing, "and I don't – know – what – else I can do – if I can't do – *this*."

She breaks down once more and her shoulders convulse with each sporadic heave of breath as she cries wildly. Red eyes squint from beneath the oversized hood and her face glimmers with an iridescent wetness as she continues to weep in desolation. She is now oblivious to the awkward glances from the foot traffic around her. Her best monologue yet, wasted on their closed ears and selective eyes. Wiping her runny nose on the arm of her sleeve, she hangs her head in remorse, immersed in a fog of blankness.

How can she tell her mother she's failed? Failed her.

Her mother had spent her own early years wanting to make it as an actress, under the constant repression of an unambitious family telling her to wise up and live in the real world. So from the moment her own daughter could walk and talk, she was pushed incessantly by a woman who was clearly living her dream through her offspring. Every ounce of energy her body possessed was injected into allowing her child to have the opportunity to become that very thing she never was.

"And I have failed her," the girl repeats again and again. "I have failed her."

The dream is no longer.

She stands, slowly and painfully, cold from being static for so long and stiff from putting her body through excessive auditions day and night, year upon year.

Dragging the heavy case behind her, she trudges heavily through the sopping streets of Soho, looking for a home and silently praying for someone to take her away.

Chantelle clambers up the stairs, thumping loudly on each one, with all the grace of a baby elephant. How is it that weighing in at only eight stone such a little thing is capable of creating a mini-tremor?

Breathlessly she knocks at the office door.

"Tina, are you in there?"

"No, I'm not here!" I answer with playful sarcasm. "I'm the boss and I've given myself the afternoon off!"

Chantelle enters, panting heavily, and plonks herself at the opposite side of the desk. An immediate emission of stale cigarettes fills the air.

"Chantelle! You told me you'd given up!" I exclaim with the disgust only an ex-smoker is capable of.

"Well, I've kind of given up so I wasn't lying," she explains, straight-faced and earnest. "I've actually cut back which in reality means I've given up what I *used* to smoke." She stares at me, looking smug and clever at her response.

I can't even contradict her – there's logic in there somewhere.

I trained Chantelle as a saleswoman, a better one than even myself, but the downside is that she has an answer for everything and at breakneck speed.

I'm feeling mellow today after a joyous meeting with my accountant and it's a day for celebrations. Let her kill herself with lung disease if she wants to, providing she abides by the rules of no smoking on the premises or in front of the building or during any type of hospitality event. I guess I can't ask for much more, apart from asking her not to *really* kill herself of course. She's my right-hand woman and I'm not sure I could survive without her, but as much as I tell her, I'm not quite sure she believes it.

"Chantelle, don't you know how unattractive it makes you look?" I preach. "You're drop-dead gorgeous but you ruin it all by having a fag hanging out of the side of your mouth." I laugh off the frustration. "Very ladylike! And why do you keep knocking, you daft sod? If the door isn't shut tight, just come on in. Open-door policy, remember?"

Chantelle nods approvingly. "You know what, Tina, I got so used to being treated like a skivvy and a nothing in my old job, it still seems, well, kind of weird that you're the boss but you're so nice at the same time."

Her honesty and respect are admirable qualities although I can't help but feel that, at twenty-seven, she ought to be showing signs of greater maturity and aiming to work as more of an equal rather than being happy as a subservient. And this is why I made her the office manager twelve months ago, a recognition well deserved and well overdue in terms of her entire career span.

Needless to say, I headhunted her from Goldsmith

426

Kings which was easy given she hated it – well, hated the owner really, and for all the same reasons I had done. Her reputation promised her to be worthy of recruitment and, once the word on the street was out – that the chauvinistic pig's success was practically off the back of Chantelle – I made her an offer I knew she couldn't refuse and, after her obligatory notice was served, she was all mine. And I certainly didn't intend to lose her. I love her, the punters love her, the wives and girlfriends are taken in by her natural charm and flattery, and Chantelle graces her way through each day with the ease and simplicity of a woman who works purely for the passion of it, never asking for anything but always giving. She has been and still is indispensable.

"Earth calling Tina!" she teases.

"Sorry, Chantelle, I'm in a world of my own." I roll my eyes at her. I don't want to keep telling her how valued she is, knowing how uncomfortable it makes her.

"Penny for them?" She smiles at me affectionately. "Oh my goodness, talk about food for thought!" Bright-eyed, Chantelle suddenly jumps up, digging her hand deep into her jacket pocket and pulling out a newspaper cutting. Leaning over the desk, she quickly unfolds it, holds it in front of me, positioning it far too close to read. She dances around impatiently, hopping from one leg to the next.

"Please say you'll come, Tina, please!" she blurts out, looking down at me with big dark-brown eyes set firmly in you-cannot-say-no mode. Although, to see those eyes, you have to look past her ample chest first.

"Will you give me a chance to read it, for heaven's sake? I don't even know what it is!"

I scan my eyes quickly over the article while Chantelle childishly bounces around, twitching like she has heavily overdosed on speed.

She is clearly desperate to speak again and, seeing my eyes lower towards the remaining lines, she bursts out uncontrollably: "Will you come with me, please, Tina? I've always wanted to see one of those guys but I'd be too afraid to go on my own. Honestly, Tina, this means so much to me I can't tell you. Please come with me!" She takes in my reluctant face. "Pretty, please?"

"Chantelle, breathe," I tell her. "Just take deep breaths." I stare at her like she is a woman possessed. "I've never seen you like this before – you're usually so collected."

I flick through the article once more. My gut reaction is a no, but her excitement and near-desperation have stirred something in me. She opens her mouth to speak again but I silence her with my finger to my lips like a kindergarten teacher. It works beautifully. Why have I never tried it before?

"Hang on a minute. Just let me read it again. And will you keep still? You're making me feel sea-sick."

I digest the article for the third time, reading it slowly and mulling it over in my head, but I begin to feel quite uncomfortable at the prospect of it. It's fine for Chantelle but not for me. I'm not the lost little girl who needs to find herself. That was in the past where it will firmly remain and this is the here and now and, from where I'm sitting, it's looking pretty damn good. I know exactly who I am and where I'm heading and I simply don't see the point of paying thirty quid for some deranged spoof to impart a pack of lies. I can understand Chantelle's interest, however, and in her shoes I might well share her sentiment.

The article, a full-page spread, is promoting Liverpool's first Psychic Fayre where it aims to demonstrate communication and contact with the spirit world, through mediumship and clairvoyance. Fine if you're into that sort of thing, I guess, but the idea of it all fills me with ambivalence. I really don't like it. What if they ask you questions? Personal questions? What if the next thing you know is that some crook has stolen your identity, cleared out your bank account and eradicated you from your own existence? You are not really you any more. Someone else is you.

Shaking my head, I quickly attempt to figure a get-out clause.

"You know what, Chantelle, I really don't feel comfortable going if I'm honest. It's a complete waste of money and probably run by a group of phoneys." I hate doing this to her but in a way I'm also trying to protect her. "I mean, think about it logically, it can't be authentic, honest gov."

Chantelle leans across the desk, practically lying on it face down. "Please, Tina, oh please!" she begs. "I really need someone with me and you're just the person to keep me grounded. I can't go with Colin because he doesn't believe in that stuff and my nan would kill me if she knew what I was up to." She laughs. "My nan says it's the devil's work, not that I believe that but . . ." her black-olive eyes widen with innocence, "but I can be a little naïve sometimes." The corners of her mouth turn upwards and her thick lashes flutter prettily. "I get so taken in by it all. I really do need to have someone there with me."

What a performance, Chantelle! Move over, Hollywood.

"Look, I'm not really the right person to go with you," I point out adamantly. "I'm a cynic who is in control of her life because she made it happen. I am where I am because of sheer hard work and this time around I ain't gonna fail!" My voice breaks a little as I recall that very phone call to Mother asking to be rescued. "It's up to you, Chantelle. You have to create your own destiny and make your own luck in this life." I feel a sudden stab of pain. The fight to turn my life around came at a price but, still, I live to tell the tale and what doesn't kill you makes you stronger. Or so they say.

I watch her despondent face and mellow slightly. I step down from my invisible soapbox. "It's about action and about doing, Chantelle." I look around me. "Blood, sweat and tears has been injected into this business. At one point I only had the clothes on my back." I shake my head at her, conscious that I may have been a bit heavy. "A crystal ball can't map your life out, Chantelle. All it will do is make your pocket lighter." I take in her obvious disappointment. She's as transparent as they come, and wears her heart on her sleeve. I find her simplistic approach rather endearing. I try to make light of the situation by grabbing her hand. With my index finger I trace the contour of her palm, holding the hand firmly as she tries to wriggle it away. My manicured nail trails slowly along her jagged lifeline, deliberately tickling it to torment her.

"You have a long life in front of you, my dear," I begin in jest, my voice quaking for dramatic effect. "You will live way into your nineties but your faculties will have left you long before." I stifle a giggle. "Your chest will go south and your pelvic floor will join it after having nine children . . ."

"Ouch!" Chantelle's eyes begin to water at the prospect.

"You will come into money, a lot of it, but you will always remain faithful to your employer!"

She snorts at me wickedly.

"Oh, and all nine of your children will have different fathers!" I put her hand down. "That will be fifty pounds, please!"

We both laugh as Chantelle examines her chest, thankful of its northerly position. Her face screws up and she pants heavily. "I'm about to drop another one!" She stoops down, holding the small of her back. "Get the towels, quick!"

I grab the cutting, crushing it into a ball, and hurl it towards her. "You're sick, Chantelle! And close your legs, will you? I can nearly see your kidneys!"

"Hang on a minute?" She regains her perfect posture. "*I'm* sick? Pot and kettle come to mind." She chortles. "I'm not the one who slept with a fifty-year-old!"

Bitch! "He said he was forty!" I retort. "My God, don't remind me of that, you big horror! I was only twenty-three at the time!"

"Which makes it even worse!" She tuts. "Slapper!"

My shoulders shudder with nausea. We were in the throes of foreplay when he asked me if I was ready? I replied yes but what was the question? After he noisily climaxed, alone, the cheeky bugger turned and said, "I thought you were ready? You've got a lot to learn, sweetheart." He got out of bed, still semi-erect, leaving me there naked and humiliated and not knowing whether to slap him or try again. I told Chantelle that story after a few too many!

Chantelle retrieves the crumpled cutting from the floor and throws it in the bin across the other side of the room. It lands perfectly. She smirks, turning back to face me. An impish devilry decorates her exquisite face – she truly has no idea how beautiful she is.

Every piece of displayed flesh shines with a dark-gold hue. Her thick black eyelashes protect eyes so dark a shade of brown they can be mistaken for black from a distance. Her dainty nose, a Hungerford inheritance, portrays an air of aristocratic exquisiteness and dark red lips in a permanent yet unaffected pout add the penultimate finish to perfection. The finale, however, is a heart so pure and full of virtue that humility would serve her well if it bowed down. As is expected, Chantelle is unaware of the degree of influence and control she possesses and, what she uses, she uses in jest. With her charm, ravishing appearance and a bit of Machiavellian practice, she could actually be quite dangerous.

"It ain't worked, Ms Harding!" She shakes her finger at me. "Stick to what you know about, girl, cos palm-reading and comedy just ain't your thing." She struts about the room in gangster fashion. Terrible American accent – piercing to the ears in fact. At least my gypsy voice was believable even if the content wasn't! "Seriously though, Tina, how about I just get a reading done and you can wait outside? At least then you're not wasting money and I get someone to go with?"

When you put it like that! I suppose I could consider it. Conceding, I mean. What harm can it do really? It can't be that bad if they're using the Royal Fort. People use that hotel for weddings and conferences. In fact, it's a pretty good endorsement for their business, using such a prestigious location. Perhaps that's part of the master plan? I'm not interested in having a reading but I guess there are no reasons why I can't support my own staff in doing so and it's very rare for Chantelle to ask for anything.

"Okay, okay, I'll go with you," I give in reluctantly. "But only book yourself in, Chantelle, seriously, and don't try to convince me otherwise. Anything to get you out of my office. Some of us have got work to do."

A jubilant Chantelle runs around the desk, bending forward to hug me. She's practically sitting on my knee!

"Thanks, Tina!" she grins. "You're the best. I can't wait!"

Skipping heavily to the door, she turns serious for a moment. "Oh yeah, Tina, Brian Steen's PA rang earlier to remind you about the meeting." Her eyes twinkle. "Don't worry – I told her you've been looking forward to it all week." With a cheeky smirk, she closes the door behind her and seconds later the floor vibrates with the thud of her descent.

What is it with that girl and how, once again, have I managed to succumb to her charm?

I thought I was the boss around here?

If you enjoyed this chapter from
Crystal Balls by Amanda Brobyn,
why not order the full book online
@ www.poolbeg.com

POOLBEG WISHES TO

THANK YOU

for buying a Poolbeg book.

If you enjoyed this why not
visit our website:

www.poolbeg.com

and get another book delivered straight
to your home or to a friend's home!

All books despatched within 24 hours.

POOLBEG

WHY NOT JOIN OUR MAILING LIST
@ www.poolbeg.com and get some
fantastic offers on Poolbeg books